Dangerous
Defiance

*Willow Heights Preparatory
Academy: The Endgame*

Book One

selena

SELENA

DANGEROUS DEFIANCE

For anyone who's ever been afraid that letting someone see your

damaged parts will make them run.

You are seen. You are worthy.

SELENA

one

Note on Content:
This book is not intended for readers with triggers.

Eliza Pomponio

"Do you know who he is?" Bianca asks excitedly over brunch.

"No," I admit, misery weighing down every word I speak. "Just a name. I'm supposed to meet him this afternoon. I've never even heard of him."

That's not surprising. I don't know anyone in the Valenti family because they're all self-serving assholes who don't do anything without evil motives. I know all I need to know—stay away.

And now I know that one of them is about to become my husband because my father decided to sacrifice me as a peace offering with the most ruthless Italian crime family in New York.

"Maybe it won't be so bad," Bianca says with a sly smile. "Maybe he'll be cute. I mean, I'd fuck Al Valenti."

"Well, it's not Al. Who, let me remind you, is three times our age."

"And hot as fuck," she says decisively. "He's got that Al Pacino thing going on, y'know? Not to mention he'd know what he was doing. We're virgins, E. I don't need no high school boy who's only out to get his. I need a man with some experience who knows how to keep his wife happy, spoil her right."

"I don't need a man at all," I say, draining my mimosa and tipping the glass toward our live-in cook, who also serves the meals when it's just family or a few friends. "Why do we have to get married so young, anyway? I like my life how it is. I don't need a change."

"Because they're afraid you'll let some guy *float the love canal* before tying the knot. We're lucky they wait until we're eighteen now. In the old days…" Bianca wiggles her eyebrows.

I push my plate away and slump back. "At least I wasn't engaged from birth. That shit still happens, even if they wait until we're eighteen to marry us off."

"You knew this day was coming," Bianca points out, munching away on a piece of cantaloupe with a glimmer of smugness in her eyes. Fucking frenemies. She's probably laughing on the inside, hoping I'm miserable for the rest of my life.

"It's coming for you, too," I remind her, accepting my third mimosa of the morning with a nod of gratitude. "You're seventeen."

"I just pray I don't get some creepy old dude who can't get it up," she says, wrinkling her pretty nose. "There's a sweet spot in the middle between too young and too old."

"Dear god, I'd pay to get some creepy old dude who can't get it up."

"You're crazy," Bianca says with a wild laugh. "Don't you want to have sex? Besides, they only give you to someone like that if you're done for, and they want you out of the way."

"Fine by me," I say. "Out of sight, out of mind. I could live my own life, and he'd die in a few years, and I'd have the rest of my life to do whatever I want."

"Not me," Bianca says. "I want to be right in the middle of things, not shipped off to some old guy's mansion in Montauk where nothing ever happens. I'd die of boredom."

"Want to trade places?" I ask. "You can have my engagement."

"No way," she squeals. For all her big talk, she wouldn't trade with me even if she could. Men may have brainwashed women into thinking marriage is something they want for the past few centuries, but *our* eyes are open. Marriage is the end for women. Not the end goal, but the end of any other goals.

*

"Are you ready?" Sylvia asks, peeking her head into my room.

"What, am I supposed to put on a ballgown and descend the stairs in slow motion so my future owner can get a look at the goods he's getting in this transaction?" I ask, rolling my eyes.

Sylvia tuts and comes into the room, tugging at the hem of my sundress. It's the same one I wore to church and then brunch. I'm not about to change even an outfit for this guy. It's bad enough that I have to marry him. I don't have to change who I am for him.

"Never hurts to make a first impression," she says, standing back and looking me over.

"I'll make a first impression either way," I say. "I'm not looking to make a good one."

She shakes her head and sighs. When Mom left, Dad tried hiring a nanny to watch out for me while he was gone, which was always. Too bad he couldn't keep his hands off her—or any of the ones that followed. I spent more than half my life watching a parade of young women full of promise come into our home to teach and guide me, only to leave it a few months later with tear-stained faces and broken hearts.

SELENA

After all that? I'd still rather be one of them than a wife. They left him cradling their wounded egos, with stories to tell their friends. Mom fled like a refugee in the night with stories of her former life she could never tell a soul.

"Look at you, all grown up and ready to start your new life," Sylvia says, looking like she might actually cry. She's toughed it out a lot longer than most of the others, lasting a few years now. She tries to be both my sister and my mother, which makes me a little sad for her. It also ensures I don't confide in her like a sister or respect her like a mother, though I do like her. Dad stopped paying her when I turned eighteen, but she sticks around for the other benefits—the posh lifestyle and, I assume, the dick.

Yes, I know more about my dad's sex life than the average girl wants to, but he's never hidden things from me, which I appreciate. I grew up sitting on his knee while he played poker, for fuck's sake. I know way more about the Life and all it entails than I probably should, including the mistresses. Bianca's always grossed out at the thought of her parents getting busy, but it's so obvious in my house that there's no squeamishness around it. It's an unspoken but well-known fact that Anthony Pomponio gets all the pussy he wants.

"Can we just get this over with?" I ask, sighing as Sylvia rummages in my handbag. She produces a tiny bottle of breath spray and brandishes it at me.

"How much did you have to drink at lunch?" she asks in a scolding tone.

"Not nearly enough," I mutter, but I open my mouth and let her make my breath minty-fresh nonetheless. She leads me out of the room and down the hall. And even though I got a good buzz going so I wouldn't be nervous, I can suddenly hear every beat of my heart echoing like the thud of a drum leading soldiers into a doomed battle where they're outnumbered three to one.

"Wait," I say, grabbing Sylvia's hand. My mind is skittering over the possibilities. Who did Al Valenti pick for me? Probably someone hideous inside and out, someone who will punish me for all the lives my family has taken. Suddenly, my mind flashes to the tattooed giant they call *Il Diavolo*, someone so brutal the devil himself would be terrified, and my knees go weak. "Did you meet him?"

Sylvia gives me a conspiratorial smile. "He's a looker," she whispers, squeezing my hand.

"Who is he?"

"I don't know. Some new guy."

"A *soldier*?" I ask incredulously. They picked a nobody for the daughter of a legendary mafia don?

I'm too offended to come up with a response. It's not Sylvia's fault. I know she thinks it's an honor to get to be anyone's wife, but a *soldier?*

Before I can ask more, I hear my father's voice from the study below. I can't make out what he's saying, but I focus on trying while I wobble down the steps. I drank too much to cope with this situation, but oh god, it really wasn't enough. The desire to stop by the wet bar grips me, and before I know what I'm doing, I'm heading in to grab a shot or ten before I have to meet this asshole. I need something to calm the urge to tell the loser he'll never marry the likes of me.

"Just to settle my nerves," I assure Sylvia as I snag a bottle of Patron and pour myself a shot.

Ten minutes later, my father arrives in the doorway, a scowl on his face. "What are you doing in here?" he demands, his bushy brows lowered in a glower.

"Isn't he supposed to come sweeping in here to court me?" I ask, throwing my arms wide. I stumble a bit, bumping into the leather sofa and collapsing back onto it.

"Get her some coffee," he snaps at Sylvia. "I'll bring him in here. But you're not getting out of this, Liza. It's already been decided. Nothing you do now will change that. And I won't have you making a fool of our family."

"Yes, Daddy," I say sweetly.

A minute later, he's back, a tall figure towering behind him like a shadow stretched out on pavement in the late afternoon, larger than life. But the man who steps in behind him isn't boisterous like someone you'd use that term to describe. Instead, he's stiff and formal, a frown knitting his fine brow. His sculpted jaw is clenched, and his angular features are set in angry lines. The moment my eyes meet his dark, cold gaze, everything in my body reacts. I must have had too much to drink because suddenly my belly does a little flip like I might be sick, and my heart starts racing, and my blood seems to tremble in my veins.

One look in his bitter chocolate eyes, and I can tell I've made a terrible mistake. I should not have taken those tequila shots. I should not have expected Al's ugly-ass uncle to come to collect. No, this guy is so much worse. He's not some old guy who can be manipulated into doing my bidding with insincere flattery about how hot and young he still is. This guy *is* still hot and young. Too fucking hot, and way too fucking young. He's not going to be dying of too much alfredo sauce anytime in the next fifty years.

Suddenly, I can't breathe. My marriage won't be over before I'm twenty-five. It will never be over. This isn't a sacrifice for the family. It's a life sentence. I can feel the shackles around my ribs tightening with each breath I try to draw as he holds me pinned with his gaze, the venomous cruelty in his expression boring into me as if he already hates me more than I hate him.

He's a Valenti, after all. My family has killed as many of them as they have us. And now I'm at his mercy. He's probably already thinking up what sadistic tortures he'll inflict upon me for the rest of my life.

My knees go week. Oh god. I'm doomed.

He strides to the sofa and stands over me, looking down at me expectantly, like he's lording his height over me. When I don't jump up to bow at his feet and tell him how happy I am that I'm being sold off like a head of cattle to an absolute no one, he frowns even harder. Then, the dude sticks out his hand like we're in a fucking business meeting.

"I'm King Dolce," he says. "You must be Eliza."

Damn it. Even his voice is sexy, rich and smooth like melting chocolate.

But despite his looks and his voice, he's too uptight to be sexy. I mean, the guy is seriously trying to shake my hand like some stuffy old guy from a Jane Austen novel.

Yeah, fuck this. I'm not doomed. I'm not going to give in that easily. I don't lie down and roll over for anyone, even my future husband. In fact, it's even more important that I show him I won't be controlled. If he were old, maybe I could stand it for a few years. But if I'm going to spend the rest of my life with this prick, I'm going to have to lay down the law real quick. Starting with the fact that I don't respect anyone who hasn't earned it.

Ignoring his hand, I cock an eyebrow and meet his gaze with a challenge in my eyes. "You're supposed to be able to handle me?" I ask. "You can't be any older than I am."

He takes his hand back, looking momentarily speechless, like he doesn't know what to say.

"Eliza," Dad barks. "Stand up and meet your fiancé."

"Oh, right," I say, struggling to rise from the overly soft couch. "Sorry, Daddy. I'll be on my best behavior. Nobody wants a diamond with flaws."

King offers a hand again, this time to help me up, but I ignore it again. I heave myself up and find myself staring straight at his chest. Damn, this guy is tall, easily six foot four and clad in an Armani suit. I thought he was just some grunt like my ex, Tommy. He must be important to afford that kind of wardrobe—or at least rich.

For a second, I check out the way he fills out that suit from his broad shoulders to the sculpted muscles I can see hinted at beneath his white shirt. He checks me out at the same time, looking me over like he's making sure his purchase is up to his standards. When at last I raise my eyes to his, he's scowling even more fiercely.

He can't possibly find fault with my appearance. Can he?

"Let's give these two a moment to get acquainted," Sylvia says, edging toward the door. "I'll have sandwiches sent up."

"Good idea," Dad says. "I'll be right here."

I almost laugh. No way is Daddy leaving his little girl alone with a Valenti. Maybe there's still hope for me yet. I may have cried and begged when he told me about the engagement, but there are other ways to get what I want. I have no power here, so I have to rely on the power of manipulation. But hey, a girl has to work with what she's got.

King is still glaring daggers at me, not stepping back. He's so close I could reach out and touch him if I wanted, see if those muscles are as hard as they look.

"Are you drunk?" he asks, an edge of incredulousness in his voice.

"Are you judging me?" I shoot back.

He just stares at me a long moment, the muscle in his jaw working like he's holding back from saying what he wants. Good. He should be intimidated. If not by me, then by my father, one of the heads of the five Italian families in the city. I have to hand it to the guy, he's got balls, coming in here alone while our families have been at war for a decade. It could have been a trap. Still, he's smart enough not to insult Daddy's little girl in front of him.

"It's nice meeting you," he says flatly. "Let me know if you'd like to get together again before the wedding to discuss specifics. Otherwise, I trust that you're more than capable of making the arrangements."

Now I'm the one left speechless. I gape at him, caught between indignation and anger. He seems as uninterested in me as I am in him. Much to my annoyance, I find myself feeling resentful, even insulted, by his indifference.

"Haven't you come to woo me?" I ask, a mocking edge to my voice.

"I don't think that will be necessary," he says. "If you need my approval on any wedding decisions, you can email me, and I'll sign off on it."

"Email you?" I repeat incredulously. "*Approval?*"

"Unless you'd like to meet again before that," he says, leveling me with a look my father can't see from his position behind him. King is challenging me.

Well, two can play that game.

"No need," I say, lifting my chin. "We've got an event coordinator."

"Then it's settled," King says. "I'll see you at the altar."

Without another word, he turns and strides over to shake my father's hand. "Your daughter is as lovely as I'd heard," he says. "I'm honored to have the opportunity to bring our families together with this union."

I want to scream and hurl the bottle of tequila at his head, but my father already looks like a pressure cooker about to blow its gasket, so I settle for sloshing more alcohol into the two shot glasses I retrieved earlier. As soon as King is gone, Dad strides over to the bar and rips the shot glass from my hand.

"You will not disrespect our family like that again, do you understand me?" he roars, his face twisted in rage. The legendary Pomponio temper is nothing to mess with. Dad doesn't have a short fuse, but when that fuse is lit…

I scurry off the chair and around the bar, putting the solid oak between us.

"I'm sorry," I wail. "It's just that he's so horrible, Daddy! He's going to kill me. He's going to make me pay for the war between our families. I can't marry him, Daddy! I just can't. I'll die!"

My father's nostrils flare, and he heaves a series of heavy breaths as he stares at me, his face returning to something closer to its normal color. He used to always fall for my tantrums, but I think he's catching on. Maybe he's right. Maybe it is time I moved on to a new family, a new man who doesn't know my tricks quite so well.

"The wedding is happening," he says. "And that's final. Do you understand me?"

I nod, swallowing down the lump in my throat. I might have been faking the hysterics, but that man really was horrid, and I really do fear what the future holds, what punishments he'll consider fitting to pay for the crimes of my family. As much as I hate it, though, there's no escaping fate.

I've always known this is my duty to the family, the price of being a Pomponio. I'm proud of my name and proud of where I come from. Part of that heritage means marrying for political reasons. I'll just have to make the best of it. Maybe King has a more dangerous job, one that will make me a widow before I'm twenty-five, despite his age. If not, I'll just have to put my foot down from the start, show him I'm not some subservient little house slave. I've always been a rebellious daughter. Now I'll be a rebellious wife instead. I'm going from being my father's property to my husband's, after all. Does it really matter which man is trying to control me?

Dad takes my silence for obedience and lets out a heavy breath. "Sylvia can help you plan. I'd also like you to involve the daughters of the other Families. One from each Family as a bridesmaid along with some of our girls. With all five families together, we look stronger than ever against the Russian and Irish organizations."

I don't have to ask why we're showing unity to the Bratva. There are lots of other crime families besides the Italian ones. Dad will want to show the whole city that we're peaceful with the Valentis. It protects us from their allies and makes us look stronger than ever.

"Do I have to invite Lizzie Salvatore?" I ask, dreading the thought of the trashy little New Jersey princess being one of my bridesmaids. She's fun to party with because she's been doing it since she was thirteen and she knows all the party spots. But she'll probably cut her dress to right below her ass, get falling-down drunk, and conveniently forget to wear underwear. I might not care for my groom much, but that doesn't mean I don't want a nice wedding. Every girl deserves that, even if she has to marry a heartless stranger.

"All the families," Dad repeats. "You got six weeks. You'll use the place in the Hamptons for the reception. And I expect you to call your future husband and make an apology. A man doesn't want to marry a drunk."

With that, Dad takes his leave. I slump down on the couch, laying my head back and taking a deep breath. Despite the day's events, I'm not a drunk. I wish I were. Then I could just numb out the whole thing. Swim through the soup of life in a disoriented fog.

Even I know I wouldn't be happy with that, though. Yes, I like to party and get stupid on occasion, and lately I've been doing it more than I should. But alcohol is a rebellion, an assertion of my independence. It's not something I use to cope with life's traumas. I can deal with those just fine on my own. I don't need help. I've fought too hard for my little freedoms to walk into a cage of my own making.

two

King Dolce

"How's things?" I ask, watching my brother carefully as we stand in front of the mirrors, a tailor at our feet. Guilt twists inside me, like it does every time I look into his haunted eyes. He's going to have to learn to hide that look if he's going to survive in this world. The mafia's not the only place that will destroy a man if he doesn't put on a coat of armor too thick for pain to penetrate.

"Fine," Royal says, holding out his arms and adjusting the sleeves of his coat, shrugging to make sure it settles onto his shoulders right. I can tell he's been hitting the weights hard. He's as big as I am now, though he's only sixteen.

Beyond him, the twins are getting their trousers pinned, too.

"Don't give me that shit," I say to Royal, lowering my voice. "I'm your brother. I know you're not fucking fine."

It's been eight months since the kidnapping that was supposed to be staged but turned way too fucking real. Six months since his twin disappeared into a dark river and never returned. I stopped expecting him to go back to normal a long time ago. But I don't want him to hate me for this, to think I walked away and washed my hands clean of them. If I could have traded places with him in that basement, I would have. If I could have traded places with Crystal in that water, I would have.

I should have saved him. I should have saved her.

I've failed them all so many times, in such catastrophic, irreparable ways.

"I can't believe our big bro is getting married," Duke says, throwing an arm around his twin's shoulder and grinning at me. "It's like you're a grown up or something."

I manage a half smile. "*Or something* sounds about right."

"Yeah," Royal says. "We should be asking *you* how things are."

They've been here a few days, and I've already told them how things are. But it's hard to talk with our parents around. Ma needs a lot of attention, and Dad's always lurking, looking for an angle to work to his advantage.

"I don't even know the girl," I say with a shrug, holding my arms for the tailor to pin my sleeves. "She didn't want to get to know me before the wedding. It's weird, right? Even if she didn't choose this, you'd think she'd want to get familiar with the person she's spending the rest of her life with."

"Guess she has the rest of her life to get to know you," Royal says.

"Hey, you're lucky, alright?" Duke says. "You'd never get a girl that hot to marry you if she did know you."

He and Baron crack up, and I slug his shoulder because that's what I'm supposed to do, but it already feels different, like when I walked into Ma's the night before I became a made guy. Like this is a memory, a life I'm no longer a part of. It's only been a couple months since I left, and over the past few days we've caught up on anything we've missed. They'll always be my brothers, my first family. But they've also always been closer with each other. I was the protector, almost their dad. I looked out for them and tried to keep them safe. And now I don't.

"Think about it this way," Baron says. "You get the goods, and you don't have to work for it. You don't have to get her to like you or worry if she's going to say yes. You don't have to do anything, and you get one of the hottest girls in New York."

"Yeah," I say, remembering the bratty girl I met at her father's house. Pretty sure I'll be doing plenty of work in our marriage, even if love's not part of the equation. Love plays no part in the Life, and it will play no part in mine.

That's for the best.

SELENA

"Don't even worry about us," Royal says, throwing an arm around the twins' shoulders. The three of them look like a wedding photo, all the happy groomsmen getting their tuxes altered for the big day. Looking at them, you'd never know how toxic our family is. From the outside, we look like the perfect Italian family, living the fucking American dream.

"Yeah, man," Duke says. "It's your wedding. You're supposed to be the happiest man alive, right?"

"I think Dad's the happiest man alive," Royal says bitterly. "He thought you'd be a grunt in Uncle Al's army, and here you are marrying the daughter of a don."

It's true. I never expected to marry, let alone be important enough for the Valentis to arrange a marriage for me. And not just to anyone. They chose me for a mafia princess, the daughter of a mob boss. They're counting on me to bring unity between warring families. My marriage is a symbol of peace, but it's more than that, too. It's a lifelong assignment, which means Uncle Al plans to keep me around. He may even be testing me with this, seeing if I'm a suitable candidate to be groomed as an heir to his empire.

"Dad's going to piss himself when he meets Pomponio tomorrow," Baron says, interrupting my thoughts.

"Get ready to see our esteemed father groveling like a teenage girl trying to get backstage at a *Just 5 Guys* concert," Royal says in disgust.

"Speaking of teenage girls groveling... I found a pair of identical twin strippers for your bachelor party tonight," Duke announces. "Blondes. Same age as you. It's going to be epic."

"Strippers?" I ask, cocking a brow.

"*Blonde, identical twin* strippers," Baron says, like he's correcting me. "Damn, I've missed New York. You can find anything here."

"And hey, if you're not up for the task, me and Baron can entertain them after the show," Duke says with that grin that's just a little too much, like he's just a little unhinged.

"Thanks," I say, distracted by Royal's quiet, tense posture. I watch him in the mirror as the tailor perfects the cuffs of his steel grey suit, the same color we're all wearing. I know he doesn't want to talk about what happened, and I don't blame him. I just need to know he's okay. Leaving my brothers was the hardest thing I've ever done, and even though I didn't have a choice, part of me wonders if they're ready to handle life on their own. I don't want them to think I'm turning my back on them the way Crystal did before she died.

Even in death, she chose someone else.

Our enemy. Love. And maybe herself.

Royal will never forgive that.

But I can't take care of him forever, just like I couldn't take care of her. I can't take care of our little brothers, either. This job forces me to take care of myself and my new family, whether I like it or not.

While Duke and Baron get hyped for the party, I turn to Royal. "They good?"

From the way they act, you'd never know they lost a sister six months ago. I know we all feel it though, that loss. We've all changed. Those six months were hard on all of us, and I'm glad to see the twins acting like kids again, falling over themselves with excitement about strippers. I couldn't care less about a party, but it's tradition, and it makes them happy. And if I can make them happy for a night, or even a moment, it's worth it.

"Shit, you sound like a mom," Royal says. "Chill the fuck out."

He didn't say *our mom*. He said *a mom*. Ma isn't the type to worry about anyone but herself, so it always fell to me. It's hard to let that habit go.

"You're right," I say. "I have a wedding to worry about, and after that, making sure the bride's father doesn't send you my head in a box."

The corner of Royal's mouth lifts, and he throws an arm around my neck and rubs my head with his knuckles like we're kids again. "This ugly old thing?" he asks. "I'd take one look at it and send it back."

The twins jump on us, and we wrestle around a minute before breaking apart and making sure we haven't ripped our tuxes. We've always been affectionate with each other, physical. It makes me happy that Royal can still have moments of normalcy, that he didn't lose that with everything else.

We finish up at the tailor's and leave, the twins bounding ahead like puppies, frolicking in the sweltering New York heat. I get that sense of being out of place again, like I'm just playing a part. The mafia hasn't changed me that much in the six weeks since I was sworn in, has it? I'm still a Dolce, even if I'm a Valenti, too.

Maybe I never quite fit into their carefree lives, though. I was always standing a step away, watching for snakes in the grass while they raced around like they were fucking invincible. Now that I know how just how fragile life is, how easily lost, how precious, it's even harder to understand that freedom.

I turn to Royal again. "I know I'm not there to help out anymore, but don't cut me out. It's my family, too."

"Is it, though?" he asks, cocking his head and squinting against the late afternoon sun. "You're getting married. You have a new family. You and your wife."

I hadn't thought of it that way. The Valentis are my family. The Dolces, too. But he's right. Eliza and I will have our own little family, just the two of us.

Somehow, I don't think it'll be as cozy as it sounds.

"I'll still always have your back," I say to Royal. "If you need me, shoot me a text. I may not be anything special here, but I've got connections. If anyone fucks with you…"

"I'll take care of it," he says. "I got this, okay? You don't have to be the hero all the time, King."

"You know I'm no hero," I say bitterly.

We don't speak of Crystal. Not directly. No one in our family does. She's the ghost that haunts each of us, but we pretend she's not here, as if acknowledging it might make what happened real.

"You can have our backs, but you gotta move on," Royal says. "You got enough to deal with here. You got a life here. You can't be worrying about shit halfway across the country when you can't do shit about it. This is your future. New York, the Life. Not Arkansas."

"True," I say, but it still sits funny inside me, knowing that I can't look out for them anymore. They're on their own, with each other to look out for. I have to let them go, to trust they'll make it on their own. They're not my past, but they're my childhood, my roots. Once I get married, my new family comes first. Whether or not I love her, or even like her, Eliza becomes top priority. Taking care of her is my most important job, and that means making sure I don't fuck up and get myself killed. I can't be worrying about my brothers and what they're doing. I've got to watch my own back now.

"You're getting married in two days," Duke crows, turning to walk backwards until we catch up with them. "You ready for the last hurrah?"

"Yeah," I say as we reach my car. I open the door and slide in behind the wheel of the Evija. I should probably get a bigger car, something safer, but I've held onto this for so long it's like a part of me now. The one thing that never changed when I went from Manhattan to small-town Arkansas and back.

Royal slides into the passenger seat while the twins jump in the back, jostling for space.

"Strippers, here we come!"

"Show me the pussy," Duke yells, like he's repeating the "show me the money" line from *Jerry Maguire*.

I turn to Royal and squeeze his shoulder. "Take care of them, okay?"

He nods. "Take care of yourself."

"What's the holdup?" Baron asks. "I've got titties to see."

I grin and shake my head, shifting into gear. Royal's right, as usual. I need to focus on staying alive—for their sake, too. They don't need to lose another sibling. And I love these idiots way too fucking much to live in the same state. If they were around here, I'd never stop worrying about them getting themselves killed, not by the mafia but by their own dumb decisions. In turn, that preoccupation could get me killed. I wouldn't be sharp, and my life depends on staying sharp. They'll always be my family, but it's time to stop worrying about their future and look to my own.

three

Eliza Pomponio

"Girl, I can't believe you didn't invite me to your dress fitting," Lizzie Salvatore says, swatting my arm to get my attention. I'm happy for the distraction as we linger on the beach behind my father's Hamptons house, sipping champagne and chatting about my impending nuptials with our nearest and dearest. The rehearsal dinner was a giant snore, including my fiancé. I've never met a man more indifferent and unfeeling. If only he'll be indifferent to me, not give a fuck what I do. I hope he's gay, and he has no interest in women whatsoever.

"Bianca came with me," I tell my occasional partying companion. She's dressed in a red satin number that would be better suited for a street corner, and with the newly bleached blonde hair and the accent that comes out even stronger when she drinks, she screams Jersey Shore trash loud and clear. When I'm drunk, too, I don't care. But at an event that's supposed to be classy, she makes me cringe.

"Bianca?" she asks incredulously. "You know she told you to get the one that made you look like a tank, right? She can't stand for anyone to look hotter than her."

"Don't worry," I say. "I had a second opinion."

Since I'm too classy to tell her what I really think, I hold back from saying that while it's true that Bianca advised me to get the most unflattering choices available, Lizzie would have made me look like a prostitute.

These are my friends. The closest thing I have, anyway.

Not that I'm crying about it. I cultivated these friendships. If I'd tried, I might have been able to find more genuine ones. But I wanted to live big, not have quiet sob sessions on my bedroom floor every time I broke up with a boy. When things go wrong, you move on. Dwelling in the past is a recipe for disaster. I live in today. Not yesterday, and not tomorrow.

Tomorrow.

Oh, god. I have to swallow past the throb of nerves in my throat. Tomorrow is the wedding day. The first day of the rest of my life or whatever.

Maybe I do wish I had a friend, at least one real friend, who I could share these fears with.

I think of my mother, somewhere just across town, in the same city. I wonder what she'd do if I showed up on her doorstep asking for advice, for opinions about my dress.

I push the thought away, shoving it down deep into a box and slamming the lid. My mother isn't here. We had an announcement in the papers, and if she wanted to read it, she could have. She could have come. She could have called.

But she lives her own life now, free from the ties that bind the rest of us, society and tradition and all that shit.

Which means I have Bianca, who would do anything to make me look bad, and Lizzie, who has slipped away. I spot her standing in front of my future husband, her bear claw nails lightly raking his forearm as she smiles up at him. He's taken off his jacket now that the rehearsal is over, his sleeves rolled up to his elbows against the heat. His arms look tan and strong in the shadows of the evening as we stand around the back patio under twinkling strings of lights. Everyone is mingling and chatting while the workers remove the tables we had set up for an elegant dinner behind the house.

Lizzie lays a hand on King's chest, pushing him backwards a step, into the shadows of the porch. Anger roils inside me. Not because I'm jealous. I don't care about him or who he sticks his dick in.

I'm pissed because this is the kind of friend I have, one who tries to shove *my* fiancé behind *my* house and probably hike up her skirt and let him fuck her against the wall while I'm not a dozen steps away.

This is who I have to turn to, to confide my deepest fears, ones that go well beyond cold feet. I want to pretend I don't care, but my throat tightens. I look around for someone to rage to, at least, but all I see are acquaintances, no one who would care what Lizzie is doing.

I spot King's mother, giggling and flirting with his dad like they're still a couple in love.

Of course his mother is here. Everyone's mother is here.

There's Bianca's pretty, perfect mafia mother, the one who carries a Glock in her purse right next to her red lipstick. There's Lizzie's stepmother, the one she grew up with since she was little. Her mother was killed around the same time that mine left. Maybe in some other world, that could have made us close. But not this one. Lizzie was the poor tragic girl with a dead mom. I was the one whose mom scandalously ran off to live her own life, the one whose father should have hunted her down; he must be weak to let a woman walk away and leave him like that, tut-tut.

At last, my eyes find Bianca and Sylvia standing together, their heads tilted toward each other, their eyes sparkling and their wine-stained lips hiding dreamy smiles as Al Valenti throws them a bone and says a word or two to them in passing. If I didn't know the man was evil, that he was responsible for Jonathan's death along with hundreds of others, I might think he was hot. But I know the cold hard truth about mafia men, and I want none of it.

"You seen King around?"

I turn to find one of his brothers. Now there are some guys I can't deny are attractive, all muscle and dark chocolate eyes with lashes that would make any girl weak in the knees. Just like my fiancé.

"He's over there with my lovely bridesmaid," I say, tipping my champagne glass toward where they disappeared. "If I was a betting woman, I'd say she's asking for help with an undergarment situation."

He frowns, glancing from the shadows and back to me. "You don't care?"

"Why would I care?" I ask. "I don't know the guy from any of you." It's true. I can't remember which one this is. They all have ridiculous names that belong to a family desperate for recognition.

"King's a good guy," he says, as if I have some reason to believe him.

"Okay," I say, sipping my champagne.

"Come on," he says, nodding toward the edge of the porch. He takes off, and I want to turn away, to prove how little I care, but I find my feet following him. Maybe I want to prove to myself that I can have a real friend. That Lizzie's just telling him that if he hurts me, she'll kick his ass, which is even more ridiculous than when regular girls say it, since my father can do that for me. Still, it would mean something to me, even if it was an empty threat.

When we step around the corner of the house, King is standing with his back to the wall, a glass of champagne in one hand, his other hand in his pocket, his pose all casual disinterest like it has been all night. At least he's no more excited about her than anything else.

Lizzie, meanwhile, is standing way too close to another woman's fiancé, not pressed up against him, but just letting her tits brush him when she throws her head back and laughs like she's not doing it intentionally, trying to drive him crazy with her body. I always marvel at the way she does that, how she controls her whole world with her body, like it's a magic wand.

"King," his brother says. "What are you doing?"

King shrugs, not even having the decency to look chagrinned. "Talking to Eliza's friend."

He meets my eyes over her head, and I see that look from our first meeting—a challenge. Is he trying to make me jealous?

That's so hilarious that it's actually sad.

Lizzie grins at us, reaching up to run a nail down King's cheek. I can hear the quiet rasp of it over his stubble, and I wonder what it feels like. Then I curse myself for wondering.

"I was just telling this cutie here that he's not married yet," she says with a saucy grin. "He's still single for one more night."

She's watching me, too, with a smug sort of challenge in her eyes. King's brother looks at me. They're all waiting for me to blow up.

Like it's that easy to make me lose my shit.

"You're right," I say, shrugging one shoulder. I take a sip of champagne. If I'm honest, Lizzie is hot, and her dye job isn't as bad as I pretend. If King wanted to fuck her, I wouldn't blame him. Just because I have no interest in him doesn't mean I don't understand that he's a man who has certain needs. And hell, I can admit it—he's sexy as sin. Any girl would want him. I can't exactly blame Lizzie for trying to get a little taste of him before he's off the market, even if she is my friend.

Like I said, we're not the kind of friends who have each other's backs and look out for each other.

We're not like King and his brothers, all of them looking exactly alike, so there's no question of where they belong and who they belong to. They sat together at dinner and goofed off, and even though King seemed to think he was above all that, that doesn't mean he wasn't part of it in some way an outsider couldn't see. If his part is to look on like an indulgent ass, he's still a cog in the big moving puzzle of his family. I heard his dad left his mom, but at least she showed up for him—not just for the big day, either, but for the rehearsal. And there I was, just me and my dad on our side of the table. No seat for my mother, none for my brother.

Because King's family killed him, and my mother left, and I'm happy for her. I am. So fucking happy. She has her own life. I'd make the same sacrifices to have my own.

"Eliza," King says, after the longest silence of all time. He puts his hands on Lizzie's shoulders and pushes her back a step so he can slide away from her, toward me.

I hold up a hand. "It's fine," I say. "I don't mind. Do what you want. You're a free man."

I turn and walk away before he can say anything else. I have nothing to say to him. I may be forced to marry a Valenti, but I'll never love one.

My throat aches as I hurry away from the lights, the people. I cross the sand toward the water, relieved to leave the voices and laughter behind. I've always known this day would come. I'm prepared. Up until now, I've done everything alone. This is no different. I don't need a friend or my mother. I just need to gather myself, to remember who I am and what I have to do. I know I'm strong enough.

I will bring peace to my family, so no one else loses a brother to a Valenti. That's what this is about. Not love. Not romance.

Just business.

I close my eyes and dig my toes into the sand. Tomorrow is supposed to be the happiest day of my life. So why do I feel so fucking sad?

four

King Dolce

The music starts, and all eyes go to the entrance. The audience stands. I've been standing, but suddenly, I need to sit down. This is real. I'm getting fucking married to a girl I've met exactly three times—once for an introduction, once for engagement pictures, and once for the rehearsal dinner last night.

At the photo shoot, Eliza apologized for being drunk during the first meeting, but I told her I understood. She probably thought it was some kind of platitude, and I wasn't going to go into the details about my sordid family, so we left it at that, the words sounding hollow and insincere. I may not have been happy to see her that way for our first meeting, but I do understand. After all, it wasn't my father who taught me how to survive the Life,

43

how to go numb and feel nothing. Ma taught by example, showing me firsthand the one rule you need to make it in the mafia.

Feeling anything is weakness.

My bride steps into the aisle, and a tight little ache starts in my stomach, right below my sternum. She's so damn pretty. Her black hair falls in loose curls down her back, a little braid going around the top like a crown. She chose to wear her veil back, so everyone can see her face, the elegant lines of her jaw, her full lips, her thick, inky lashes and luminous, whiskey-colored eyes.

She pauses for one moment, as if waiting for everyone to take in the sight of her, all beauty and pure innocence in that flowing white dress. She doesn't look like a virginal, blushing bride, though. There's nothing delicate in her gaze when it meets mine. Hatred burns in her eyes, and she marches toward me with the determination of an assassin going in for the kill. I may not relish the idea of marrying a stranger or a lush, but her feelings are beyond that. A knife could be easily concealed by all that fabric…

Let her fucking try it. I have a job to do, and I'm doing it. I'm not going to be taken out by some mafia asshole, and I'm sure as fuck not going down by my own wife's hand. If she pulls a weapon on me, she'll see who ends up paying.

Mr. Pomponio kisses her cheek and leaves her with me. She's in my hands now. My wife. My responsibility.

She looks up at me with those big, doe eyes. The priest goes on for a minute while I stare back at her. God, she's so fucking pretty. Too pretty for a mafia asshole like me to put his hands on. Her skin is dewy, her cheeks glowing. She lowers her eyes to her bouquet, her long lashes curling against her cheek. She looks like some kind of fairy, too fragile to touch, too pure for any man, let alone one like me. I haven't been saving myself for her. I've fucked lots of girls, all of them meaningless. And now here is this girl who should mean something, the only girl who should mean anything, and I can't let her.

I can't give her what she deserves. I can't love her.

As I repeat the vows, I mean the rest of the words. I will give her what I can, making up for the missing parts of myself, the ones I can't give. I can't give her my heart or my innocence. I no longer have either of those things. But I'll give her everything else. I can still be a good husband, even without love. I will honor her, respect her, and value her. I'll listen to her. I will treat her as an equal. I will be faithful. I will provide for her. I'll take care of our children when that day comes. I will protect her heart by making sure she never loves me, even if she tries. Because the one thing I can't promise, the thing no made man can promise, is that she won't end up a widow.

Those things aren't in the vows, so I don't say them aloud. But I vow them to myself, and that's more binding than saying them to her or a priest.

Eliza hands her bouquet to her bridesmaid, the one who's been eye-fucking me every moment I'm in her line of sight since we met at the dinner last night, where she suggested we fuck before I began my married life.

I've been to enough weddings to know the bride usually hands off the bouquet before the vows, and I can't help but wonder if Eliza kept them between us on purpose, not wanting to be closer to me than she has to, not wanting me to take her hands as we repeated the vows.

I slid her ring on while she held the bouquet in her other hand, and now she slides mine on, shoving it into place with her slender fingers, cold despite the heat of a New York summer.

"You may now kiss the bride," the priest says.

Eliza gives me a look that says if I dare kiss her, she'll castrate me in my sleep. But she's my wife, and there's no use in an arranged marriage if we're not going along with what's expected. I step forward and slide a hand behind her head, under her hair. She goes stiff as a board in my hands. Her lips are plump and pink, ready to be kissed, but I hold back. I lean closer, so close I can feel the heat of that fuckable mouth against mine. "You will kiss me," I say, my voice so low no one else can hear it, not even the priest.

Her lips pull into a smile, not moving as she speaks through clenched teeth. "Touch me and die."

"If I don't kiss you, this is off, and we'll both die."

"Oh, I won't die," she assures me, her smile turning smug. "I'm a fucking princess. You're nobody."

"I'm your husband," I grit out.

I can hear the crowd getting antsy, but I don't take my eyes from hers. Someone yells, "Shut up and kiss her!"

Eliza smirks. "You'll never be my husband in anything more than name."

"In name, and in public," I say, curling my fingers into the hair at the nape of her neck and pulling her forward, so she stumbles against me. I clench my fingers tighter, so she has to go up on tiptoes, her head back and fury burning in her eyes as my mouth descends to hers. Her squeal of protest is muffled by the kiss. Our first kiss isn't tender or even passionate. It's rough and harsh. She struggles against me, but I force my tongue between her lips. It's not because I want to taste my new bride. It's not even to silence her muted denial. It's to show her that this is how it is.

Her father gave her away—literally. He gave her to me, and she's mine now. I swipe my tongue across hers, making sure she knows what I'm doing, that she gets the point. I'm the one in control here. Her teeth clamp down, biting into my flesh. I don't stop, though. I don't pull back. Let her taste my blood. It only proves my point more fully. We are bound in blood now, just as I'm bound to the Valentis after taking the blood oath that swore me in.

Eliza recoils, trying to break free when the salty warmth of my blood spreads through our kiss. I thrust my bleeding tongue against hers, our teeth clashing one more time before I draw back. People are laughing and hooting and clapping. I don't know how long I kissed her. Long enough to send a message, that's clear.

"I hope you die," Eliza hisses. "Then I won't have to marry you."

I smirk down at her, slowly releasing my grip on her hair. "Too late," I say. "I'm your husband, and you'll show me the respect that title deserves."

"You don't deserve respect until you earn it," she shoots back.

"I just did," I say. "Behind closed doors, do whatever the fuck you want. In public, you're my wife, and you obey me."

She stares at me, her nostrils flared and her breathing coming quicker. I notice her lip trembling, but I can't tell if it's anger or fear. That funny little tug starts behind my sternum again, but I crush it before it can get a good hold. It doesn't matter if she's pissed at me or terrified of me. Her feelings are as irrelevant as mine. For a second, we don't move. Something shifts in her eyes, though, and when the priest steps forward, she turns to face the crowd with me.

"It is my honor to present you Mr. and Mrs. King Dolce," he says.

I grip her hand in mine, and she doesn't struggle. Her fingers are soft and delicate against mine, and I feel the slight tremor in them, too. Ignoring it, I step forward, and Eliza follows my lead as we descend the step to walk back up the aisle.

I smile at my Dolce family, my parents and all my uncles, aunts, cousins in the first rows. My parents have been getting along this week, and even though things have shifted with my brothers, they're still my brothers. They were my groomsmen, up at the altar with me. I wouldn't have it any other way. Even though they're all here, I can't help the instinctive sweep of my eyes as they search for the last member of my flock, like I'm a fucking sheep dog.

I turn away, pressing my lips together and pulling Eliza toward the door of the church faster. I don't want to think about who's not here. My sister should have been up there with Eliza's bridesmaids. But she's not. She's not here. She's not anywhere. We didn't even get to bury her. And it's my fucking fault. If I had seen how bad she had it, that disease called love, I might have saved her. If I'd seen what it would cost her, what it would cost all of us, I would have found a way to put a stop to it. Even if I had to kill the asshole she fell for, I would have. He ended up dead anyway—and he took her with him.

I won't make the same mistakes.

As we make our way to the back of the church, I squeeze Eliza's hand, trying to calm whatever storm is brewing inside her. She leans into me like she's any bride excited to be starting a new life with a man she loves. With her free hand, she waves and blows kisses, suddenly all smiles, her performance worthy of a fucking Oscar. You'd never know she was spitting and hissing up there on the altar.

We pass the photographer, and then we're out of the church, blinking into the blazing July sun, trying to see. Light doesn't just help you see. It blinds you. It seems a fitting metaphor for the day, for love and weddings and all this shit. Suddenly, the charade feels exhausting beyond what I can bear.

And it's only getting started.

As soon as we step out the door, Eliza rips her hands from mine, grabs up handfuls of her skirts, and charges behind some shrubbery.

"Eliza," I say, a warning in my tone. This is too public a place for our first fight.

She doesn't come out, though I can see half her skirt still trailing from behind the hedge, so I know she's not doing the whole runaway bride thing on me. I sigh, rake a hand through my hair, and glance back at the church. People are going to come spilling out at any second.

I step behind the hedge and face my wife.

The moment she sees me, Eliza rears back a hand and slaps me. I balk, too stunned to react for a second. Only a second, though. That's the last time she'll catch me by surprise.

I grab her hand and squeeze her fingers together until her nostrils flare and her eyes go wide. She doesn't whimper, though. I can see her gritting her teeth together to keep from crying out as she glares at me.

"That was for kissing me like you own me," she snaps. "Now let me go."

"I do own you," I snap back. "I'm your husband. You may have gotten away with this shit with your parents, but not with me. Understand this, little wife. I'll let you go, but you *will* come back."

She snorts, but I release her hand anyway. If she tries anything, she'll find out how seriously I take those words. I wasn't making a smug prediction. I'm not arrogant enough to think she wants to come back to me. My words are a threat.

She rubs her fingers and stares up at me, her expression calculating as she weighs her next move. I can already tell I've underestimated her. She's probably used to that, and she's figuring out how to use it to her advantage. But I'm onto her now. She's not the spoiled, drunk party girl I read about in the gossip columns when I did a little research over the past month. Or rather, she's more than that. It'll take something beyond a curfew to rein her in.

Behind me, the church doors open, and I hear the first guests spilling out, talking about the beautiful ceremony, the kiss, Eliza's dress. I don't turn. I stare down my bride, resisting the urge to drop my gaze to her plump, pink lips.

Her eyes dart to the crowd, then back to me. "Did you mean what you said in there?" she says, her words coming out in an urgent rush. "That you won't control what I do behind closed doors if I'll be your wife in public?"

I have only a second to decide. In a moment, we'll be noticed. She'll scream I was hurting her and get me executed. Just because it's a wedding, that doesn't mean anyone's unarmed. You can bet your ass everyone is carrying, not to mention the number of nondescript guys hanging around the bosses, guys I know are bodyguards. This wedding is probably the FBI's wet dream—if they could pin anything on anyone. All the families are here. They could take down New York's entire Italian mafia. They could try, anyway.

Just as I know better than to refuse Eliza outright, I know better than to agree to anything binding. I can already tell she's sneaky as fuck.

"Show me what a good wife looks like to you today, and I'll decide tonight."

"Not good enough," she says, lifting her chin.

"Eliza," calls the woman I thought was her young stepmother until Little Al corrected me and told me she was Mr. Pomponio's *cumare*.

I grit my teeth and resist the urge to tell the woman to get lost as she waves and totters our way in her heels.

SELENA

"Be my good little wife today, and you can choose your reward tonight," I say to Eliza. "Act like a little brat today, and I choose your punishment."

Some unreadable expression flickers across her face. I could dissect all I saw in that one flash of her eyes, but I don't. It doesn't matter.

She slips her hand into mine, lacing our fingers like we're a real couple, but I know the gesture for what it is—a handshake. She's agreed to my deal. She smiles serenely at her father's mistress, and I can't help but wonder about the true feeling she harbors for this woman. She's too good at faking it, better than I am. But I won't be outmatched. I won't be outsmarted and manipulated.

My life depends on doing my one job—bringing our families together. So, that's what I intend to do. If I have to make a new bargain with my bride each day, so be it. I'll compromise, like a good husband. One bribe at a time, she'll give me what I want. If she doesn't, she'll get what she's asking for.

five

Eliza Dolce

"Girl, why are you still here?" Bianca asks, staggering against me and throwing an arm around my neck. We stumble a few steps into the water, which is frigid even in July. "That's what I don't understand. Shouldn't you be bleeding on that beautiful man's white sheets right now?"

Even in my drunken state, my heart lurches at her words. I know better than to believe the promise of a Valenti, to believe he'll leave me alone tonight because I was a good girl today. That's why I've postponed the inevitable, why I've gotten sloppy drunk with my bridesmaids instead of spending the reception next to my groom. If I take enough shots, surely it won't hurt too bad. If I drink enough, maybe I won't even remember it tomorrow.

I don't do well with pain. I live for pleasure. What really scares me is that once I do this, once *we* do this, it's real. The deal is sealed. There's no undoing it, no getting out of the marriage. Part of me knows it's already too late, but that's the rational part, the one that recognizes the ring on my finger and the marriage license in the safe.

Some other part of me, somewhere that doesn't care about signatures and official documents, the real Eliza, inside my heart, knows. It knows that once he's been inside me, he owns me. There's no going back from that, no getting out of it. Once it's done, King will control me. He'll have all the power. Maybe that's an illusion, but it's all I have to hold onto. The only bit of control left to me. My own body.

Because I can't control where I'll be forced live, who I live with. My whole life uprooted from the bedroom at Daddy's that I've slept in since I was a baby, when Mom went through an artistic phase and painted giraffes and lions and safari animals on the walls.

DANGEROUS DEFIANCE

The same room where I got my first period, and Mom wasn't there to ask, and I didn't want to ask Daddy, so I just lay there in bed bleeding all night, thinking I was dying, that something in my belly had ruptured and that's why my abdomen hurt so bad. The next day, the housekeeper found my bloody sheets and had to tell me about periods because that wasn't the sort of thing I learned about in Catholic school. Then she told the whole staff, and everyone knew, and shame burned in my cheeks every time I passed them, as if they could see what they hadn't before, that I was *unclean*.

But at least the nanny asked if maybe it was time we painted over the babyish safari animals still on my walls. It wasn't the kind of thing my father would notice or think to ask, and I was grateful when she offered me buckets of paint with a hopeful smile that I didn't realize was more about her bid to ride the Anthony Express than to help me.

When we opened the cans and I saw the paint was bright pink, I didn't have the heart to tell her I didn't like pink. Back then, I didn't understand Mom. I was angry.

Those animals had always made me feel like maybe one day things would be okay. As if knowing she'd once cared enough to hand paint each stripe and spot on every zebra and giraffe proved that she somehow loved me, even though she hadn't contacted us once in the years since she left.

But now that I was a woman, as the housekeeper informed me, I had to accept the truth. I had my dad and the nanny parade, and that was all the family I'd ever have. My brother was dead, and my mother might as well be. I told the nanny I loved the paint, even though it was hideously bright and looked like something an eight-year-old would pick. I even asked if I could help. I relished each stroke as I rolled the garish paint in wide swaths over the beautiful animals my mother had painted with love and care. It felt positively criminal—and I loved it.

I halfway expected her to walk in as we were doing it and scream at us for ruining her hard work. Or to call the very next day and casually ask, and I'd have to admit what I'd done, slathering on the pink paint so thick it ran like Barbie blood down the walls.

DANGEROUS DEFIANCE

I didn't understand Mom's decision then. Now I get it. Now I know why she left, what was worth so much that she'd disappear from her own daughter's life forever, not even showing up at her wedding, what people say is the most important day of her life. Mom knew. She had one when she was eighteen, too. She knew this day isn't the beginning of a new life to celebrate, my married life. It's a death to mourn.

"If you don't fuck that man tonight, I will," Lizzie purrs, swaying her hips in a seductive slow dance as she twirls at the edge of the water, her hands twining into the breeze above her head like silk scarves. I wonder if she's dancing for my husband, if he's watching her, wishing he could fuck her instead of the frigid bitch he ended up with. An ugly streak of jealousy darts through me, but I push it away. I don't want his eyes on me. If he's watching her, wanting her, he can have her. I hope he goes to bed, and she sneaks into his room and fucks him for me.

I glance at the bay windows overlooking the beach, but I don't see him there. I turn back to my bridesmaids—my friends, enemies, and competition.

"Like you'd bleed," I scoff at Lizzie.

The other girls break into a chorus of giggles.

"Oh, I'll bleed for my husband," Lizzie says. "You just have to know what you're doing. Let him rough you up a little when you're still dry, and you can bleed any time you want."

"Really?" Bianca asks, gaping at the other mafia daughter.

"Sure," Lizzie says, giggling. "It's not exactly pleasant, but it gets the job done if anyone wants proof on your wedding night."

"You should have told me that years ago. I would have slutted it up like you," I lie.

"Hey," she protests.

I've never met someone as in love with herself, with pleasure, as Lizzie Salvatore. I hate her out of envy as much as anything. She said a big fuck you to tradition and had sex when she wanted to, consequences be damned.

And she never looked back. The rest of us are simultaneously in awe of her and disgusted by her, but I'm sure the other girls are as envious as I am. For all our talk about carving our own paths and making our lives, Lizzie has really done it, in her own way. Even if all she owns is her sexuality, it's something.

"Like any guy will think you're a virgin," Bianca says, linking her arm with Lizzie's on the other side. "Everyone knows you spent half of high school on your back."

"I probably won't get lucky enough to marry a guy as young as Eliza's King," Lizzie says. "So it won't matter. No one past high school knows about my rep."

"I wouldn't count on that," Gianna says quietly. "My family keeps tabs on me everywhere."

"Oh, who the hell cares?" Lizzie says, the liquor making her braver than she is. We all care what our families think. They might love us, but that doesn't erase what they're capable of.

"To not caring," I yell, kicking at the little waves washing up at the edge of the water.

SELENA

"Hell, yeah," Bianca squeals, thrusting a fist at the sky. "Fuck caring!"

The other girls link arms, and we kick at the waves together like some kind of drunken chorus line, our laughter carrying up the beach to the house and over the water to the houseboat bobbing expectantly before us. I've avoided looking at it all night, the place I'm supposed to spend my wedding night with a stranger. Sylvia and some of the other women in the family spent hours setting it up, so the groom and I would have privacy and not have to stay in my father's beachfront mansion with the rest of the family. The thought makes me nauseous— or maybe it's all the champagne and tequila churning in my belly.

When I finally look up, I see a figure standing alone at the railing Sylvia twined with twinkling fairy lights. He's watching us from across the water.

My heart flips, and I swallow hard. I don't know when he went over to the boat, but then, it's three o'clock in the morning and most of the guests are long gone. Maybe if I stay long enough, if I put it off until it's no longer tonight, he'll fall asleep on the deck, and I can crawl into bed alone at dawn, as is the norm on party nights. And this isn't just a regular party night. It's the biggest party of my life. It's supposed to be the best day of my life. I tried to make that happen, even though the dread of tonight sat heavy in my stomach like a threat. I could still revel in the attention, feel beautiful, and have fun being young and dancing with my friends.

That's all I want.

But I know that's not all I'll get. King will want me to pay for the sins of my family, and he'll extract the debt he thinks we owe one punishment at a time. He's already threatened. If he's unhappy with my performance today, there will be consequences.

It doesn't matter how gorgeous the guy is. His eyes are casual but terrifyingly cruel, making my blood shrink away instead of longing for his touch. Mafia men are violent by nature. Sometimes it carries over into their marriages and sometimes it doesn't. Not two minutes after saying "I do," I had my answer to which one of those categories King falls into.

SELENA

I can feel his watchful eyes on me from across the water, and I know I'll be in trouble when I get there. That doesn't make me want to rush over and apologize. It makes me want to stay out longer, to milk every drop from this night, the last night that's mine. Yes, we're married now. I'm his, as he so bluntly pointed out. But everyone knows a wedding is for the bride. It's my party, and fuck crying if I want to. I'm going to *party* if I want to. I don't care that the salt is ruining my dress, that the edges are already stained and bedraggled from the water and sand. I just don't want it to end. When tonight ends, reality sets in. When tonight ends, so does my freedom.

So I stay a little longer, drinking in the night, running in the foamy salt spray of the waves, dancing at the bonfire, throwing down more shots. At last, light creeps into the sky, and I'm too tired and worn out to go on. I collapse onto the sand next to the embers in the firepit and lay back against Tommy Fatone, who passed out hours ago. A couple fresh bodyguards sit off toward the house, drinking coffee and not speaking in the silence of the morning. Vince, my bodyguard and human chastity belt, is not among them. My chastity is no longer in danger.

I rest my head on my ex's belly and close my eyes. This is a victory. One more night until I'll be tortured by a sadistic Valenti. I sigh and fold my hands on the bodice of my ruined dress. My stomach is sour and churning, the world is spinning, and my head is already pounding, but I made it to sunrise without giving in to the enemy. I smile to myself. He must have fallen asleep hours ago, waiting for me. The thought of him lying there waiting fills me with smug satisfaction. I know there will be countless nights ahead when the roles are reversed, when I wait for him to come home from doing a job or visiting a woman who isn't me, when I wait in terror for the sound of the door opening and my husband returning to brutalize me.

For this one night, I got to make him wait. It's not much, only one night out of the thousands to come, but I take what I can get, as tiny as it is. I'm lulled by the morning, the alcohol and exhaustion, the rise and fall of Tommy's belly under my head. The only sounds are the rush of the water at the edge of the beach and the sighs of a handful of people sleeping on the sand around the dead fire.

Suddenly, strong hands grip my wrists, pulling me up in one swift motion.

"Who the fuck is that?" King asks, glaring down at me.

For a second, I don't know what he's talking about. Then I realize he's talking about Tommy. "No one," I say, trying to wrest my hands from his punishing grasp.

"That's right," he says slowly. "That's no one. And I'm your husband."

He releases one of my hands and drags me to a little rowboat rimmed with roses, the one in which Sylvia thought my groom would romantically row me out to the houseboat. I stumble along after him, tugging at my arm. He stops after a few steps, scoops me into his arms, and carries me to the boat like a conqueror capturing his unwilling bride. That's what carrying a woman across the threshold represents, after all.

King unceremoniously dumps me into the rowboat, gets in, and starts rowing us across the water.

DANGEROUS DEFIANCE

This is it. I'm about to become his wife in the last way I want to. I grip the side of the boat, considering if I should jump. I might just drown in my drunken state, dragged down by the weight of my own dress in some poetic metaphor I can't quite form with my liquor clouded brain. Maybe that would be better. Anything would be better than what's about to happen.

A wave bumps against the little boat, and the rocking motion is the last straw. Between the alcohol and the abject terror of the impending events about to unfold, my stomach rebels, and I lean over and vomit out the side of the vessel.

We reach the houseboat, and King ties up the little rowboat and drags me onto the deck. I steel myself, ready for his words, his violence, his touch. Instead, he just looks at me. He doesn't even look angry. He looks tired and a little disgusted.

"Are you done?" he asks, his voice icy.

I nod, feeling suddenly vulnerable standing in front of him. We're alone. No one to save me. No bodyguards, no scary father. I'm on my own. It doesn't feel good or freeing. I feel like a scolded child. He's blurry to my vision, as if I'm seeing him through water, a bad girl being punished at the bottom of the tub when she didn't obey.

His lips tighten into a line, and he takes my hand and pulls me down a small set of steps. We turn and enter the bedroom, all decorated with flowers and candles, with a bucket of ice beside the bed where a bottle of champagne sits untouched. Red rose petals are strewn across the white bedspread like drops of blood. My heart lurches into my chest, and I'm so lightheaded I barely keep my feet. I wish I hadn't been sick already. I want to puke again, but my stomach is empty.

"You should get some sleep," King says, turning away.

"Aren't you going to collect your prize?" I ask, cringing at how childish and scared I sound even as I try for a taunting edge to my voice.

King lets out a quiet scoff. "Believe it or not, the last thing I'm interested in right now is your cunt."

I wince at his harsh tone and crude words, even as a swell of euphoric relief rises inside me. "You're not going to punish me?"

King doesn't speak for a minute. He loosens his tie and slowly pulls it free of his collar. "You think sex is a punishment?" he asks at last, not bothering to watch my response as he folds his tie in thirds.

"For a girl," I answer honestly.

He shakes his head but doesn't speak as he slides out of his jacket, turning his back to hang it over the back of a chair before he begins undoing his cufflinks. "You really are a virgin, aren't you?" he says, watching me in the mirror.

"I am, but..." My eyes catch on the gun tucked in the waistband of his slacks, and I swallow hard. He might be new to the Life, a lowly soldier, but he'll deal with things the way mafia men do. And he'll treat me the way mafia men treat their wives. He's my husband now, after all. He might spare me tonight, but no matter what I do or say, he's not going to spare me forever. Our families will expect a baby to cement this union. He's going to force me to do what good wives do no matter what I say. So why even try to explain my fears?

"What?" he asks, his hands going still. He stares at me in the mirror, and I sink onto the edge of the bed, avoiding his gaze.

He's a ruthless Valenti. The most mercy I can hope for is that he'll find a mistress soon, like my father did after marrying my mother.

"Nothing," I say. "Don't worry. You got what you paid for. I'm as pure as freshly fallen snow. Go ahead and ruin me."

He moves to the bed and sits down beside me, and I tense. He watches me for a long minute, then reaches to gather my hair and drape it over my shoulder. Without a word, he slowly begins to unbutton the long row of buttons down my back.

His fingers are gentle, but I know what they're capable of.

"You're shaking," he says quietly.

"No shit," I say. "You would be too, if you were the sacrifice to pay for all the murders your family had committed."

"I don't want to hurt you, Eliza," he says, his voice gentle but firm. "Whatever our families have done to each other, that's on them, not on us. I don't know about you, but I have enough sins of my own to pay for without paying for the sins of our fathers."

I don't answer. I can't absolve him of this. His family destroyed mine. If my brother had lived, everything would have been different. He could have saved us all if he'd lived past sixteen.

But he didn't have the chance—because of this man's family. How can I forgive him for that? And how do I know he's not lying through his teeth, getting me to let my guard down so he can hurt me even worse than when I'm expecting it?

King's fingers stop unbuttoning at my lower back. Their tips brush across the bare skin beneath my dress, and I freeze, a little hiccup of fear erupting even as warmth shimmers through me. The conflicting sensations, my body getting pleasure while my mind screams no, paralyzes me. I feel like I'm floating above, watching this and wanting to become a giant like Godzilla, to rip King away and crush him in my fist and hurl him across the ocean.

"Eliza?" he whispers. When I don't answer, he takes my chin gently and turns my face toward him. His dark eyes search mine, but I can't look. I squeeze my lids closed, my throat suddenly aching and tears stinging the backs of my eyes. "Are you okay?"

I shake my head.

He slowly reaches up with his other hand, brushing his thumb along the fringe of my lashes. Shame burns through me. He knows I'm crying. He knows I'm weak, and broken, and all the things I try so hard to pretend I'm not. "What's wrong?" he asks, his knuckles stroking my cheek.

I take a shaky breath. "I just… I'm not ready. If that's okay?"

He doesn't say anything for a long minute. So long that I have to know what's going through his mind, or at least a glimpse. I open my eyes, blinking away the tears. His brow is creased with a frown, but it's not an angry one. It's more... Confused.

That's worse.

"I did what you asked," I remind him. "I stayed by your side and acted like your wife, like I was happy. You said I could choose my reward."

"For your reward, you want me not to touch you?" he asks.

"I've just never had any desire," I say, trying to make him stop studying me like he wants to cut me open and expose all my feelings. "I think there's something wrong with me. It's like that part of me is frozen. I never developed those feelings."

"What feelings?" he asks, gently tugging the dress down over my shoulders.

"You know," I say, clutching the material to my chest and casting my eyes down. "Sexual feelings."

His hand falters only a moment. "Oh," he says. "Is that why you got hammered tonight? You think it'll make sex better? Because I assure you, it won't."

Is this self-righteous asshole really going down that road? I drank to escape his dumb ass. And what right does he have to judge me? I've dealt with more in my life than he's even imagined.

But I only nod, because this is going so much better than I could have hoped when he grabbed me off the beach. I don't think he's even going to rape me tonight. I'm not about to run my mouth and make him change his mind.

"Can we just… Wait?" I whisper.

"Okay," King says with a defeated sigh. "We'll wait as long as you need."

As long as I need. That sounds an awful lot like freedom. A thrill of triumph mixes with the shame I feel for manipulating him. I may be a horrible, fucked up person, but I do what I have to do to survive, just like everyone else.

"Let's get you out of this dress, and you can sleep it off," he says. "We can talk later."

It's all I can do not to get my drunk ass up and do a victory dance. Yeah, I cried in front of him and showed weakness, but hey, it's worth it to keep this heartless asshole off me. After all, I can't just let him lay down the law and then follow it like an obedient little sheep. I don't want to be someone's property. I want to be an independent woman, free to follow her dreams, like my mom was after she left the yoke of marriage and domesticity. The only way to do that is for *me* to lay down the law, to let him know from day one that I won't be owned and controlled. I just did what it took to make that happen.

King peels off my dress and lays me down in the bed in my underwear, and a shiver races over my skin when he looks down at me. As I stare up at him, feeling every bit as exposed and vulnerable as I am, I notice again how fucking beautiful he is, all angular lines and dark shadows. I shiver, my skin prickling into goosebumps as his gaze moves over me. For a second, there's nothing cold about him. His eyes are pools of molten chocolate, his gaze heated as it moves over my lace bustier and white panties.

I watch his Adam's apple bob as he swallows, and something swells inside me, a weird sense of pride at having a man who looks like him look at me that way, like he finds me every bit as sexy as I find him. I'll be damned if I'm ever going to love a heartless, sadistic bastard from the Valenti family, but it doesn't mean he's not attractive. It doesn't mean that when his gaze strokes across my skin, I don't feel sexier than I've ever felt in my life.

I can't delight in the sensation, though. It should be nice to be wanted, even if it's by a man I can never allow myself to want, but it's not. It's terrifying.

Because one day, he'll be done waiting, and he'll take what he wants. And there's nothing I can do to stop him, or to stop that day from coming. After all, every day of my life belongs to this man. He became my keeper and my owner the moment he put a ring around my finger like a brand, and he can do whatever he wants with me. I don't even get to be my own person, to keep my own name. He erased my identity. I am no longer Eliza Pomponio. I am Mrs. King Dolce.

six

King

The morning after the wedding, I leave Eliza sleeping and join the families for brunch, ready to make excuses for my new bride and take the inevitable ribbing. I enter the Pomponio's beach house through the back door, passing a handful of guards on my way. I'm still getting used to that part of the Life. Sure, Dad was rich, and we had a few crazies try to get to us, but we didn't use bodyguards. He's a businessman, not a celebrity. Now that I think about it, the mafia ties probably kept him safe. He's not involved enough to warrant his own guards, but everyone knows what happens when you mess with Al Valenti's most valuable associates.

"Where's the bride?" Duke asks, slapping my shoulder as we meet in the doorway of the dining room. "Don't tell me you wore her out already."

"Why not?" Baron asks. "We wore out our bridesmaid."

They crack up and shove each other like the idiots they are, too immature and sheltered for their own good. I let it slide, though, because they're the youngest, and they're only fifteen, and if you can't be an idiot at that age, you'll never get the chance. I envy them, in a way. I never had the luxury of being so carefree. It's a good look for them.

"What's this I hear about the lady of the hour skipping her own brunch?" Uncle Al asks, appearing at my side. I can see Dad just about popping wood at the sight of me and my great uncle, the famous mafia don, getting close. He always knew I'd work for Al, but this is even better. Now, he's really connected. I'm in with the Valentis *and* the Pomponios, and he hid none of his relish at the prospect of increasing his influence and standing when we talked before the wedding. He's determined to turn his biggest profit yet this quarter, so he can line the pockets of the Pomponios as well as the Valentis.

"I thought I'd let her sleep in," I say to Al.

"You keep her up all night?" Little Al asks, joining us.

"She's just not feeling too well this morning, that's all."

"I bet she's not, you dog," Little Al crows, slapping my back. "Probably couldn't walk if she tried."

Little Al is next in line for the Valenti throne, the grandson of Uncle Al and my partner. More accurately, he's the babysitter they assigned me as a new soldier, one who taught me the business of collecting payments and breaking kneecaps. He likes to give me shit about my fiancé so I'm grateful when Anthony Pomponio, who's holding court at the head of the table, waves me over.

"I expected to see my daughter here," he says, gripping my hand with his big, hard one. His fingers are thick and rough around mine, squeezing like a threat.

"She's fine, sir," I assure him, though I'm not too sure. "She just wanted to sleep in."

"I should probably warn you," he says with a slight smile. "Eliza's used to getting her way. I'll admit I was lenient with her growing up. After losing a son and a wife, I wanted to give my little girl everything. Raising a kid's hard—you'll know that soon enough. But raising one by yourself…"

He breaks off and shakes his head. I don't say anything, but I'm thinking, how the hell am I going to have a baby and bring our families together when Eliza won't even let me touch her? I didn't expect her to love me, but what's the point in joining the families by marriage if we can't have a baby? And yeah, maybe I'm a dick, but I expected sex. I'm not into the whole mafia lifestyle that lets a man have a mistress on the side. When I took a vow to be faithful, I meant it. If I can't fuck anyone else, then I damn well expect to be fucking my wife.

"A man's not cut out for that work," Anthony says. "Not when it's as much work as that girl. For the sake of all of us, you'd better pray for a son."

DANGEROUS DEFIANCE

He laughs, and I swallow the bile that wants to rise in my throat. My veins feel cold and slow, like they're filled with the ugly frozen slush left after snow begins to melt. How can I tell him there won't be any sons or daughters either?

I can't. It's that simple. Eliza will just have to find a way to get over her hang-ups, at least until she's pregnant. And then what? I'm supposed to live like some kind of monk while sleeping next to my beautiful, irresistible wife? I was a dumbass to think we'd treat our marriage as a business. I want sex. She probably wants love. And that's the one thing I promised I would never do to her.

"Life's short, you know?" Anthony says, releasing my hand and clapping me on the shoulder. "You never know when that day will be our last. I spoiled my little girl. She's got some growing up to do, but I'm sure you kids will figure it out together. Just don't you be afraid to show her who's boss. A man's gotta run his own family."

Run my own family. How do I do that when my own wife is scared of me? Or is she just trying to avoid me because she hates me? Is she scared I'll find out she's been fucking that guy on the beach, or whoever it is she's been with? If I tell her I don't care if she's a virgin, will she relax and give us the son we need to unite our families?

When one of Anthony's brothers slides in at his other side, I move away with relief. I find my way to the next table and take a seat next to Little Al. "Don't have too much fun on the honeymoon," he says. "You'll think that's what's coming for the rest of your marriage. Trust me, kid, it don't happen that way."

"Sure," I say.

"Just a fair warnin'," he says. "But guys like us don't have to worry about that, am I right? There's plenty of pussy out there. You don't have to marry it to fuck it."

"I think I'm set," I say, glancing at Little Al's wife, who's making her way toward us, a baby on her hip.

Al follows my gaze and turns to more wife-friendly topics as she reaches his side. "Don't be gone too long," he says to me. "I got jobs piling up startin' this afternoon."

"I could probably do a couple this afternoon," I say. "The flight doesn't leave until six."

"Forget about it," he says, putting an arm around his wife. "Go relax with your honey."

"I'll do it," I say, frowning. "As long as I'm back in time to catch the flight."

My things are already packed and back in the boat if Eliza hasn't thrown them overboard. Now that she's unburdened me of the delusion that sex could be a perk of an otherwise empty marriage, a honeymoon seems even more ludicrous. I don't know why we're even going through with it, other than my mother already planned the whole thing. I have no interest in a fucking vacation, but I don't want to make Eliza's family think I'm not making an effort, that the marriage is as meaningless and hollow as our words on that altar. So, we'll go through with it, even though neither of us have any interest in the other.

If there's one thing our families won't let go of, though, it's tradition.

I wait until we're on the way to a job that afternoon before broaching the subject with Little Al.

"You've been with a lot of women, right?" I ask, knowing full well that he has. If I've learned anything by working with the guy for a month, it's that he loves women just as much now as he did before his wedding.

He cracks up, and I immediately realize I sound like a fucking virgin. "Dude, you going to ask me how to fuck a firecracker like your wife?" he asks at last, wiping tears of laughter from his eyes.

Ignoring him, I get to the point. He's not a guy who needs a delicate approach. "You ever been with someone with... Issues?"

"All women got issues," he says, grinning like it's the funniest thing he's ever heard.

I frown. "Then maybe some kind of trauma?"

He snorts with laughter. "Eliza Pomponio's had dudes guarding her pussy since before there was hair on it. She's got trauma like my ass got trauma. And that's to say, none."

I don't say anything. I'd thought of that. I just don't know what else would make a girl so fearful about sex. She called it punishment, for fuck's sake.

Suddenly, a thought makes bile rise to my throat. She's only eighteen. The only person punishing her up until now would have been her father. That frozen, slow, ache builds inside my chest again, like it's filled with the dirty slush after a snow is scraped off the roads. Anthony Pomponio looked right into my eyes and told me I should handle his daughter with a firm hand.

And bodyguards don't protect a girl from her own father. Especially when that father is a mafia king who pays their salaries. Chances are, even if they found out, they'd look the other way out of fear for their lives. Just like I will, like a fucking pussy. Because there's not a goddamn thing I can do about it except sign my own death warrant by trying to kill the bastard. I'd probably fail, anyway, seeing as how the guy has about six bodyguards. Then she'll be right back where she started— at his mercy.

But I'm getting ahead of myself. There were other people in her life. Uncles. That boyfriend she was on the beach with last night. People who work for her father.

"What if one of the bodyguards did something to her?" I ask.

Little Al just shakes his head. "Dude, her dad's a don. Anyone touched her, he'd have them and their whole family executed with a quickness, you feel me?"

"I guess."

"Look, Kid, I don't know what she's trying to get out of it, but she's pulling one over on you. She may be smarter to the Life than some of the daughters, but that girl's so sheltered she may as well have lived in a bubble growing up. No way she's had any trauma besides reaching the credit limit on her AMEX."

"Yeah," I say, staring out the window without seeing. "You're probably right."

I know what I saw, though. Eliza was upset. She cried. I saw her tears. I heard her words on the shore with her friends. She wasn't lying.

Was she?

*

"So, this guy Luigi, he's behind a few payments," Little Al says as we stop in front of a walk-up apartment. "You gonna take out his kneecaps, or should I bring a baseball bat? I got one in the trunk."

"I'll handle it," I say, getting out of the car without waiting. My blood is still churning funny in my veins, like it hasn't quite thawed from the thoughts that hit me in the car, the ones I can't shake.

Al is probably right, though. It has nothing to do with her having some past that makes her have no desire. The present is what makes her have no desire. She hates me. She didn't want to marry me. She doesn't want to fuck me.

But if he's wrong…

It had to be her dad. Al's right about that part for sure—no one else would dare touch her.

When we knock on the door, a woman answers. Two little kids peer around her wide hips. She gasps and steps back when she sees us, tries to shut the door.

I wedge my shoe in before she can slam the door in our faces. My chest knots up when I see the scared eyes of those little kids, so I tear my gaze away. "We're here to talk to Luigi."

"H-he's not here," she says.

I glance at Little Al, wondering if we should come back later. I don't want to hurt a guy in front of his family.

Al nods, telling me to go ahead.

"Mind if we come in and confirm that?" I ask.

I hear a noise in the background, the squeak of a door or an old window opening. Without waiting for the lady to answer, Little Al shoves past her and charges in. The window is open, and a guy is silhouetted inside the frame like a picture as he gets ready to go down the fire escape.

I push past the lady, too, racing to grab the guy and help Little Al wrestle him back inside. He twists like an eel, wrenching free of our grip only to lose his balance and go sprawling on the floor on his back.

"Where's the money?" Little Al barks, his voice deeper and fiercer than when he's ribbing me. He grabs the guy by the collar and pulls back to punch him. The guy does the usual groveling and begging, making excuses. The first time, I had to convince myself that I could stomach it even while thinking, what would it hurt to wait one more day for the payment?

Now, I barely hear him. I know what it would hurt. Our reputation, for one. If we give one guy a day, he'd be asking for a week, a month, a year. If we did it for one guy, we'd have to do it for the next. They all have the same story, some sob story. Our job isn't to listen to their sob stories. It's to collect. That's it.

But when I look up, I see three pairs of terrified eyes watching. I put a hand over Little Al's fist, stopping him.

"Tell your family to wait in the bedroom," I say to Luigi.

"No," he sobs. "They need to see what you monsters do."

"You don't like the business, don't be in it," I say. "Now tell them."

"No," he howls, probably thinking we'll go easy on him in front of his wife and kids.

I turn to the wife. "Go in the bedroom and don't come out until you hear the front door close," I tell her. "You don't want your kids seeing what's about to happen."

The little boy is already crying and clinging to her leg. The girl is just staring with big, silent brown eyes that remind me too much of my sister's. Maybe she needs to see this. Maybe protecting her from it will turn out as well as protecting Crystal turned out for my family. Her family is in this, and at some point, she'll have to face the hard truth.

But I can't do it, and not just because she's only a child, and there are things no child should have to see or know. Maybe that's why I shielded Crystal for so long, too. I didn't want her to have to know the truth about our family, but more than that, I didn't want her to know that I was capable of something like this. That I was the bad guy.

"Go," I bark at the woman when she looks uncertain. Luigi keeps telling them not to move, but the woman is smart enough to want to protect her kids, and after a last, longing glance at her husband, she hustles her kids into a bedroom down the hall.

I grab Luigi by the front of his shirt, and when I look into his face, I don't see him. I see Anthony Pomponio, who might have ruined my wife. I see that guy on the beach she was snuggling with on our wedding night. I see Devlin Darling, who my sister fell in love with and died with. I see my father, selling the services of his unborn son to a crime lord. I see the face that looks back at me from the mirror each morning, so ordinary you'd never know it belonged to a man whose job is to make other men suffer.

I pull back and punch him in the face. I can feel his nose give way, and he howls in pain, flopping around and trying to hit back. I don't feel his blows that rain down on my shoulders, my head. I don't even feel my own fist connecting with the bones in his face. Little Al helps pin him while I hit him again and again and again, until blood splatters the floor and my arms, my hands, my face.

After a while, Little Al pulls me off. "A dead man can't pay his debt," he says, a phrase he used on my first job. "We made our point. Let's go."

I stand up, stumbling back. Blood drips from my battered fist. My skin is peeled back from my knuckles, already swelling and turning dark beneath the red. Luigi lies motionless in a pool of blood on the floor. Not Anthony. Not the man responsible for my sister's death. Not my father.

Not me.

"Yeah," I say. "Let's go. I have a plane to catch."

*

As I predicted, our honeymoon is anything but romantic. That's fine with me. I'd rather be at home working with Little Al than going through with this empty tradition. Still, I try to engage Eliza in conversation a few times, only to have my questions met with resentful silence or hostile glares. Apparently, sex is not the only thing we won't be having.

I suppose that's fine, too. I told her she only had to be my wife in public. Conversations aren't part of that.

Still, it's hard to spend a week in a room in all-inclusive resort without getting to know someone a little. Despite her sullen attitude toward me, Eliza isn't unhappy. She participates in the activities at the resort and excursions with excitement. She's got a big personality that can't be dampened by my presence. She makes friends with the boatmen, the dive guides, the waitresses.

She's never sloppy with herself. She gets up each morning and puts on nice clothes, ones befitting whatever excursion my mother planned for us. She's meticulous with the scant amount of makeup she wears, her hair, her outfits. She obviously respects herself and isn't going to let herself go or try to discourage my attraction by making herself unappealing. Her clothes are tasteful but on the alluring side—a silk shirt without a bra, a flowing dress that clings to her curves when she walks, tiny shorts that show every inch of her strong, toned legs.

Sometimes, I have to stop myself from reaching out and touching her. I remind myself I can't love her, that it's a good thing she hates me. It makes everything easier. At night, I turn my back and stay on my side of the bed, feeling every tiny movement she makes through the expanse of mattress between us, the tension in her body as she lies there, stiff as a board, barely breathing until I fall asleep. Despite what Little Al said, I don't think she was faking it on our wedding night. She's scared. And even though I tell myself I don't care about her, it fills me with rage to think of anyone hurting her. I hope she only hates me because our families were at war for the past decade.

We have dinner together each night, and each night, she wants to go to the bar afterwards. I go with her for the first few nights, though I have no interest in drinking. I sit and watch her make friends with other guests at the resort, and a dark feeling creeps between my ribs. Why is it that she can make friends with the bartenders, waitresses, and strangers she's just met, but she can't stand to even speak to me beyond the absolute necessities—asking me to hand over her toothbrush in the morning or pass the salt at dinner? A comment on the food is the extent of our casual conversation, but at the bar, she can throw her head back and laugh, swatting the arm of the waitress like they're best friends already.

I'm relieved when, on our fourth night, she calls me a psycho stalker and insists I stay in the room while she goes down to the bar. I fall asleep easily for the first night since we've arrived, without the dark tendrils of resentment licking at my ribcage or the cold, thick feeling crawling up my throat like it does every time I wonder why she's so frigid.

The end can't come soon enough. At last, it arrives. On the last evening, I start picking up random pieces of clothes and things left around the room, wanting my bag packed and ready to get out of here the moment I wake in the morning. I know being home won't change much, but at least I won't have to spend every day with a woman who despises me. I'll have a job to do.

SELENA

Eliza reclines on the couch in a silk robe that's parted over her knee, revealing her bare leg as she watches a show about a boy band breaking up. Cute little freckles randomly scatter across her olive skin, from the beauty mark on her cheekbone to the spot on her ankle just above the gold bangle she wore on our boat outing. From her position, I see new ones on her inner thigh I haven't seen before, and I wonder how many more I don't know about. I've seen her in her underwear just once, the morning after our wedding, and in a bathing suit several times on our trip, but I can't help but wonder if there are more hidden from my eyes. It seems like something a husband should know.

I push the thought away and snatch up some socks from under the bed. "Want to give me a hand with this?" I ask, tossing a pair of her sandals toward her suitcase.

Eliza tears her eyes away from the TV, some trashy gossip channel my sister used to watch on occasion, and scoffs. "I'm not your fucking maid," she snaps. "If you think I'm going to clean up after you and cook you dinner like some sad little housewife, you can forget about it."

"What exactly are you going to do?" I ask, thinking of my mother at home drinking herself silly and gossiping on her phone all day.

"Two things," Eliza says, counting them off on her fingers as she speaks. "One, whatever the fuck I want, and two, none of your goddam business."

I grit my teeth and yank the zipper on my suitcase closed. "I get that you wouldn't have chosen me for a husband, but remind me... Exactly why is it you hate me so much?"

"You're a nobody," she says, giving me a dirty look. "Why should I even bother explaining it?"

"That's it?" I ask. "You think I'm not good enough for you because I'm not some bigshot like an underboss or heir to one of the families' empires?"

"You really don't know anything about the families, do you?" she asks, staring at me. "It's not my job to fix that. You should have done your homework."

Her judgmental tone makes me want to shake her, but I remind myself she has a reason for the way she is. She may look like she has it all, like a spoiled mafia princess who needs a firm hand to guide her, but her life hasn't been easy. I'm the last person to believe the myth that money makes problems disappear. It only makes them disappear from the public eye.

"Then what is it?" I ask, bitterness creeping into my tone. "You had a boyfriend you wanted to marry? That asshole you were cuddling on the beach the morning after our wedding?"

Eliza just blinks at me a few times like she can't believe I'm this stupid. "You really don't know, do you?" she says. "King, you killed my brother."

I open my mouth to argue, to tell her I haven't killed anyone yet, but then I get it. I shut my mouth and turn away. So, that solves that. If I was hoping for a breakthrough with her, which I wasn't, I can stop now. It doesn't matter if I did it myself or if it was Little Al or Al Valenti himself or some random enforcer. My family killed her brother. It doesn't matter which one pulled the trigger. It might as well have been me. It's my family. We're all the same to her.

And if I was going to argue, all I have to do is imagine how I'd feel about her if she was a Darling, someone from the family responsible for Crystal's death. Just thinking about it puts an empty pit behind my sternum that makes it hurt to breathe, and I know I can't ask her forgiveness. Losing a sister is not something our family will ever 'get over,' and losing her brother will never be over for Eliza, either.

"Okay," I say, thinking it would have been real fucking nice if someone had told me that before. Not that it matters. If anything, this makes my life easier. I don't have to wonder if someone hurt my wife or think I did something to piss her off. "Okay. That's fair, then."

She gives me an incredulous look. "Fair? Is that what you call it? Fair would be if I killed one of your brothers."

"You're right."

She cocks her head to one side and studies me for a long minute. "Okay, your turn," she says at last.

"For what?"

"Why do you hate me?"

"I don't hate you," I say. "I just can't love you."

She looks like she might ask further, but then the commercial on TV ends and the show about the Wilder brothers comes back on, and she shrugs and goes back to that while I finish packing.

When I'm done, she stands up and flips off the TV before stretching her arms over her head, her tight little body draped in silk like a prize I can never touch.

"I think I'll eat alone tonight," she says. "I'd like to walk on the beach one more time before we go."

"Our flight leaves first thing," I say. "Don't stay out too late."

She rolls her eyes. "Not that it's any of your business, but yeah, I'll probably have a few drinks afterwards. You don't have to wait up."

She goes into the bedroom to get dressed, and I try not to dissect her words, but I can't help it. We're like two points on lines that look parallel but are actually moving infinitesimally closer, and one day, they'll intersect. I want to keep going straight, to stop it from happening, but I can't get off the line, can't prevent the inevitable collision.

DANGEROUS DEFIANCE

Eliza leaves looking like a girl who needs to get fucked, in a little black dress that barely covers her ass and looks like it's made entirely of elastic with the way it clings to her body. I bite back a comment, bite back the urge to forbid her to go out in that. I'm not her father. I have my life, and she can have hers, separate from mine. That was the deal we made. If she wants to go get drunk with her new friends, that's her business, not mine. I need to be sharp for a job as soon as I get home tomorrow.

But I can't help but wonder, are we already following in my parents' footsteps? Eliza is certainly no stranger to drinking too much, and she seems intent on doing only what she wants, on having fun and ignoring her obligations, just like my mother. And me, am I like my workaholic father who never had time for the family he created, so we had to fight each other for scraps of his approval? Not just by doing the regular things like being a football star or doing his job and looking out for the family, but by going to such extremes as colluding to fake our own kidnappings and fucking the wives of his enemies and rivals to ruin their families so we could pretend ours wasn't already ruined.

Yeah, I'm probably more like him than I want to admit, and it's not by accident. I made myself just like him because it was the only way to get a pat on the back. But I won't be like that with my kids. I'd rather spoil them with all the love they could want, smother them with attention, than the opposite.

Like Eliza's father. Is that the other option, the other script laid out for us? These are our examples. A hedonistic wife who escapes through the lid of a prescription bottle, or one who fled. A mother who denies reality or one who left her daughter to escape it altogether. An ambitious husband who always puts his wife last, or one with a reputation for all the mistresses he's taken. A father who uses his children as pawns, or one who's attentive and did his best.

That's the one good point in all of this. Our parents have plenty in common. Our fathers are unfaithful. Our mothers left. But out of the four of them, one of them seems to have gotten the parenting part right.

DANGEROUS DEFIANCE

I had a suspicion, for a moment, that he abused her. But now I know she's not scarred from that kind of trauma. She's scarred from losing her brother, just as I'm scarred from losing my sister. She hates me for it the same way I hated the family responsible for my sister's death. Her hang-up isn't about her. It's about me.

I think about what Little Al said about Eliza, how she's sheltered and spoiled and how she was trying to pull one over on me. I think about her dress that clung to her ass like a fucking advertisement for sex. Her words on the beach after our wedding, when I overheard her bragging to her friends. On the boat after that, her words to me, her crocodile tears. How different she is with me and with other people. She's a vivacious, flirtatious, sexy woman in public. In private, she's a frigid, hateful brat.

I understand why. If she was Eliza Darling, I would despise her. I would want to hurt her.

I don't want to blame her for treating me the same as I'd treat her if the roles were reversed.

But I do.

seven

Eliza

After a couple drinks, I know I should stop. I'm not looking to get wasted, and I'm too smart to get drunk by myself in a strange place. But, like, I know it will end. I know King won't let me go on like this forever, so why not enjoy every minute I can before he takes it all away? Tomorrow we're going back home, and he'll want to play house. So, I might as well make the most of tonight.

Some guys want to buy me and the waitress shots, and it's her night off, and we became fast friends my first day here, so why the hell not? No one knows who I am unless they read the gossip columns religiously. It's not like I'm famous. I'm pretty well known in New York, but outside of the city, I'm practically anonymous. And as much as I enjoy the attention I get at home, it's nice to be somewhere that no one will know me or judge me or take pics of my drunk ass and sell them to *Your Celebrity Eyes.*

So we take some more shots, and dance the night away, and it's nice. It's nice to lose myself, to not be myself. It's nice to be free and young and wild and take shots with strangers on a tropical island with my new best friend whose name I'll probably forget by my first anniversary. I don't even care that I'm not with a guy. I've spent most of my adult life making sure I don't get too wrapped up in a man and let it cloud my judgment and make me stupid. Marriage doesn't change that.

Sometime after midnight, the luster wears off, though. If King's not going to fight me on this, what's the point? Why bother rebelling if there's nothing to rebel against?

I keep thinking about my parents, and how hard I rebel while also working to convince myself they're heroes. Have I been living in an illusion all along? Maybe I've been holding onto the notion of freedom because it's the only one I can bear to look at, the only reason for my mother's leaving that I can stomach. At least she had something to run to, something worth leaving her family for. I have nothing.

I slide off the barstool and turn to the nearest guy, determination giving me strength. This isn't for nothing. It's not. If I keep acting, keep pretending, it will eventually be true. I'll figure it out if I keep going. Meaning will emerge eventually. It has to.

A few songs later, the guy I'm dancing with is all over me, his hands groping my body until I have to push him off me. A minute later, he's back at it. I'm about to push him away again when someone grabs him from behind, wrenching him away from me.

"What the—" the guy yells, reaching for me as he stumbles backwards.

Through the haze of smoke and pulsing lights, I make out my husband standing still in the crowd of writhing bodies, wearing low-slung sweatpants and a white T-shirt like he just got out of bed. The guy tries to shove him off, but King pulls back a fist and decks the guy. Several girls around me scream when the guy goes down like a ton of bricks, crumpling to the floor in a heap. King towers over me, his eyes flashing with rage, his jaw set tight.

For one drunken moment, pride snaps through my brain. My husband can throw a fucking punch. I smile before my brain catches up with my body, but King's not having any of it. He grabs me by the arm and marches me off the dance floor like I'm a bad little girl who snuck in on a fake ID, and he's my daddy coming to give me a lecture and haul me out of the bar. Not that my dad ever did that. I was partying from the time I turned thirteen, and he couldn't do shit about it. He didn't bother to, anyway. With his wife gone and his son dead and the families at war, he had enough on his plate. So he just let me do what I wanted as long as I kept my bodyguard and human chastity belt at my side at all times.

"Eliza," crows my waitress friend. "Where are you going?"

"My husband," I say, gesturing wildly toward King with my free hand, since he still has my other arm in a death grip.

"Oh," the waitress says, frowning from me to King. "Okay, then. Have fun!" She waves and disappears into the crowd of writhing bodies and pulsing music. King stares at me a second, then bends and scoops me up, throwing me over his shoulder.

"Put me down!" I yell, but he ignores me and strides out of the bar. I pummel his shoulders with my fists, but he pretends to be oblivious as he carries me kicking and screaming all the way back to our room.

He strides into our suite and slams the door so hard the pictures of sunsets on the wall tremble. Only then does he set me down, his eyes blazing with fury as he faces me.

"I told you at the wedding, you *will* come back to me," he says, his voice low and deadly.

"I don't think it counts when you fucking drag me," I snap, rubbing my arm where he grabbed me. "You didn't have to do that. I would have come back eventually."

He just stares at me, breathing hard, his chiseled jaw clenched tight. He may not say much, but there's plenty going on in there. Maybe it's the alcohol making me brave, but suddenly I want to poke him until he explodes, until he shows his hand, lets me know what he's really thinking.

"What's your problem, anyway?" I ask.

"You have no sexual feelings, but you can rub your ass all over some stranger's dick in a club?" he demands.

"So what?" I ask, raising my chin and glaring back at him. "It has nothing to do with you."

"Except it does," he says, his voice a dangerous growl. Suddenly, I realize how stupid it was for me to tempt fate, to push his limits when we're in another country where I have no real protection. "The deal was that I would let you do your thing in private, but you would respect me as your husband in public. I take my word seriously. If you want to survive this marriage, you'd better learn to do the same."

"That—that was for the families," I say, swallowing the tremor in my voice.

"Bullshit," King growls. "That was pretty fucking public, what you just did."

"No one at home will ever know."

"*I'll* know," he says flatly.

"What, I can never go out dancing again?" I ask, feeling an ache behind my eyes. I fucked it all up already. I should have been more cautious, not gone all out. I should have reined it in and taken it slow, working up to this. But of course I didn't do that. For me, it's balls-to-the-wall or nothing.

"You can dance any time you want," King says. "If you need to grind your ass on some guy's dick…" He breaks off and shakes his head, then lowers his voice. "I'm right fucking here, Eliza."

A snort escapes me before I can stop it. "What? I'm supposed to grind on you?"

We stare at each other for a long moment, neither of us speaking.

"Oh, you poor thing," I say at last. "That's what you meant, isn't it?"

"No," he says, scowling and turning away. Out of his usual suit and tie, he doesn't look so stiff. Now that I've had a week with him, I know he's not as dickish as he came off at first, but I still don't know him well enough to predict his next move, and that scares me.

"It is," I say, an incredulous laugh bubbling out as I bounce onto the bed on my ass. "You totally want me to rub up on you."

"Why would I want to dance with a frigid brat like you?"

"I'm not frigid."

King scoffs. "You literally told me your sexuality was frozen."

I stare at him a minute. But there's no way I'm going there with him, letting him know anything real about me. I'd rather just get it over with. He's going to fuck me eventually, anyway. I might as well learn to grin and bear it. And I'd rather him hurt me than look at me the way he did on our wedding night, like I'm some fragile, broken thing.

Broken? Yeah, I'll admit it. Fragile? Like a fucking grenade is fragile.

I'll take his wrath over his pity, and I know exactly how to get it.

"Yeah, about that… I may have exaggerated," I say lightly.

"You what?" he asks, his voice going low and deadly.

I shouldn't have said it, oh god, his eyes are glittering with a malice that says I'm treading in very, very dangerous territory. But once you say something like that, you can't just take it back. I don't want to, either. It's a relief to know this is finally happening. I've spent the whole week tiptoeing around him, hardly daring to breathe lest it draw his attention. I lie in bed each night trembling and petrified, sure each one will be the night he'll be done waiting.

"Yeah, I lied," I admit. "I don't have a problem with sex. I have a problem with you."

King just stares at me, his eyes incredulous and turbulent as a storm. "You *lied*?" he asks at last.

"Yep," I say. "I'm good at that. But it says something about you, too, you know."

"What?" he asks, not moving a muscle, just staring at me. But I can see the fury inside him, can see the way he's almost shaking with it. I know I should leave him alone, but the reckless animal inside me wants to keep poking the beast. Like I said, I've never been one to stop at halfway. I push limits. I want to see how far I can go, what I can get away with, what he'll do when he finally snaps. Maybe that's partly why I keep going out every night, waiting for him to put his foot down the way no one ever has. To demand answers. When I met him, I thought maybe he'd be a formidable opponent or even a match for me. But he's too scared of my father, like everyone else in my life.

"You know," I say. "It says a lot that a girl would lie about something like that just to keep from having to have sex with you."

"You're not a virgin, either, are you?" he asks.

I try to gauge his expression, his tone, to see how he feels about that. I don't see disappointment in him, but there's definitely an edge of jealousy in his voice. He does want me, despite his best efforts to pretend otherwise. The thought sends a tremor of triumph through me. I want to be wanted just like anyone else, even if it's by a man I don't want in return. I could lie to him, but I think of how important my hymen is to men and decide it will only make him want me more.

"I'm a virgin," I say.

"Prove it."

We stare at each other for a long moment. "How?" I ask, a challenge in my voice.

"I heard you talking on the beach on our wedding night," King says, prowling forward. "Voices carry across water. You should know that, having a house on the beach."

I scurry off the far side of the bed and find myself backed into a corner. Damn it. I dart forward, trying to get around the bed, but he's too fast. He grabs my wrist and backs me against the window. My heart is racing like a scared rabbit in my chest as I look up into his deep, dark eyes.

"You wanted me to hear, didn't you?" he asks. "You love testing me, but you don't know who you're fucking with, *piccola*."

"What are you talking about?"

"Just like you wanted me to know where to find you tonight." A little smirk forms on his full lips, and my heart skips a beat altogether. "You said I didn't *have to* wait up. You didn't tell me not to. You wanted me to wait up, to sit here wondering and worrying, didn't you? Admit it. You wanted me to come find you."

"No," I say, scowling. "Why would I want some asshole to come ruin my fun?"

"Because you get away with everything, but you don't actually want to," he says. "You want someone to stop you. You want someone to care enough to save you from yourself."

"Don't try to psychoanalyze me," I snap. "You don't know anything about me."

"I think I do," he says. "Did you want me to hear you on our wedding night, too, Eliza?"

"Hear me doing what?" I ask, genuinely confused this time.

"I think you did," he purrs, stroking my hair behind my ear with his free hand. "Is that why you said those things? Or was it because that's what you like? You want me to rough you up and fuck you dry?"

My heart flips. I realize then what's he's talking about, that he mistakenly thought those words were mine. All this time, he's thought I said those things about how you can fake being a virgin. Shame burns through me, that my husband thinks I'm a slut.

"That wasn't me," I say, my voice coming out breathier than I want. It's just that he's so close to me, his body almost touching mine. And even though I was just all over some stranger in the club, this is different. This is my husband. I've never been so close to him, and my body trembles at his nearness. He's standing so close I can feel the heat of his body crackling across my skin, can smell his scent, something spicy and salty at once that makes my mouth water. I feel electric, combustible, like I'm gasoline and he's a match hovering just out of reach.

I want to know what happens when the match is dropped.

"That was my friend Lizzie," I whisper, gripping the windowsill behind me.

DANGEROUS DEFIANCE

He hasn't spoken, hasn't moved, but his eyes are drinking me in, caressing me until I ache for just a whisper of his skin against mine.

"Prove it," he says again, his gaze heated. His fingertips brush the bare skin of my outer thigh, and a tremor goes through me. I bite my lip to keep from gasping, and his hungry eyes follow the movement, locking on my mouth.

I can't move. I feel like an animal, frozen with fear. My pulse races for a different reason when his fingers move up, slowly trailing across my skin and sending goosebumps blooming over my body. His gaze never leaving my face, he hooks a finger into the hem of my little dress. I shudder again, my own grip tightening on the windowsill. He adds a second finger, working it under the tight fabric. A shaky breath escapes me. My whole body is tight with anticipation as he slips another finger into the hem. When he tugs slightly at the stretchy fabric, my eyes drop closed, my nails pressing into the paint on the sill.

King draws a labored breath and drags my dress up with one slow, sure move. His hands fall to my narrow hips, and I suck in a breath, my eyes flying open at the sensation of his rough, hot hands on my bare skin. He thumbs the straps of my bikini underwear, swallowing hard enough that I can hear it in the silence between us. Nothing moves except his thumbs, toying with me as they move up and down over the thin straps.

"Show me," he murmurs.

"No."

After a pause, everything happens at once. His chest moves forward, pinning me against the window. His knee presses between my thighs, pushing me back so my thighs bite into the sill right below my ass. And he slides a hand straight down the front of my underwear.

I cry out in shock, my hands flying to grip his shoulders as my toes struggle to stay on the floor. King's head drops forward next to mine, so his hot breath fills the space between my shoulder and my neck, and his hand begins to move, gently massaging my mound. My fingers dig into his shoulders as I struggle in silence at the strange sensation of someone else's hand on me for the first time.

"Don't hurt me," I gasp out, although right now, it's doing anything but hurting. To my utter humiliation, I feel a tingling heat building between my thighs as his fingers keep moving against me in slow, gentle strokes. I go still, willing myself not to feel it, not to respond.

"Then get wet for me, *piccola*," he says, sliding his middle finger between my lips. "Men like me are never gentle."

"I can't," I say, shoving at his shoulders, suddenly aware of how close I came to giving in without a fight. "Not for you."

To my horror, my body disobeys my command to stay dry as a fucking desert. I hear his chuckle against my ear, a whisper that's only breath with no sound, as wetness springs to life, slicking over his coaxing finger. I squeeze my eyes closed, my face burning with shame. At least he can't see that, how humiliated I am that my body has taken his side, letting him take control not by force, but in the very reactions I have to his touch.

My only solace is that he's breathing as rapidly as I am, that I can feel his body straining, his shoulders trembling under my grip as he holds himself back, his free hand fisting in the curtain as he braces his elbow on the wall. His slick finger explores my folds, spreading my wetness until it coats my lips, inside and out, and his finger. He circles my clit with his thumb, varying the pressure until I'm gasping and squirming for more than freedom.

Then, without warning, he buries his hand between my thighs and drives a finger deep inside me. I cry out in pain this time, tears springing to my eyes as my walls spasm and clench around him. I've never touched myself, never put a finger inside for fear that I wouldn't be able to deliver on my wedding night. Now I regret that. If even a finger hurts, a cock will be torture.

"Fuck, you weren't lying," he groans against my neck, his other hand sliding down to grip my hair. He pulls back, watching my face while keeping his long finger buried knuckle deep in my untouched flesh.

I bite my lip, trying not to cry out again, trying not to let him see that it hurts. He'll only use that against me, hurt me more.

"Let those pretty tears fall for me," he murmurs, his voice a seductive purr. "You might have fooled me once, little wife, but you won't fool me again. No more fake tears. I want the real ones."

I fight to hold them back, but one escapes my lashes and trickles down my cheek. King watches, his gaze heated, as it slides over my skin. Then he leans forward and licks my cheek, his tongue leaving a wide, wet path from my jaw to my eye, taking every trace of my tear with it. He makes a little sound in his throat, somewhere between a moan and a growl, and presses his lips to mine.

This kiss is no more welcome than the one at our wedding, but it's different. It's not just business. King wants me, but the thrill of that knowledge is gone. I found out what happens when I poke the beast. His tongue slides between my lips, and I taste more than the salt of my own tears on his tongue. I taste his hunger, his dangerous desire. I tremble against him, bracing my hands against his chest to push him away. Before I can, he steps in closer, pressing his body to mine.

He begins to move his finger in rhythm with the stroke of his tongue, gently pressing against my walls in a slow, circling motion, hitting every nerve inside me with a pressure that makes my knees give way. A deep ache of pleasure builds in my core as the initial pain retreats. He strokes my slippery clit with his thumb, and I nearly cry out at the knife of pleasure that pierces through me. I've never had anything inside me, and it took a moment to adjust, but oh my god. I can barely register how much more complete my pleasure feels with his finger inside me and his thumb on my clit.

King groans and grinds his hips against me, and I feel the ridge of hardness biting into my thigh. An erotic thrill shoots through me, making me tremble with fear and lust at the same time. I have the absurd urge to reach out and touch it, but I stop myself, realizing I've been kissing him back without meaning to. His slick thumb massages my clit, and I whimper into his mouth, my resolve crumbling. Instead of pulling away, I bury my hands in his lush, dark hair and pull him deeper. I don't care anymore. I'm drunk, and this is our honeymoon. I'm his wife, and I want to experience this, and this is the only man I'll ever get to do it with. What does it matter if I hate him, if he hates me?

His hand is absolute magic. He draws his finger back at last, then drives it deep again, growling into my mouth. I moan in answer, and he begins pumping his finger into me, deep and quick. He fists his other hand in my hair, and I wince in pain at the tightness of his grip, but I don't stop him. I rock my pelvis against his hand, needing relief from the ache he's put inside me. At last, I feel myself cresting, and I break the kiss, letting my head fall back against the window as pure bliss grips my body and pulls me over the edge.

My walls clench around his finger again, and he stills, pulsing gently in answer to each throb inside me as I climax. My toes curl, and I grab onto the sill again, lifting my hips for him to push his finger as deep as it can go inside me. And I want more. I want his cock to break me open, to fill me fuller than his finger. I imagine it thrusting into me, spilling cum inside me, and I cum on his hand.

I'm breathing so hard I feel lightheaded, but at last I come down, uncurling my fingers and toes and opening my eyes. King is watching me, his eyes burning with intensity.

"Understand this, Eliza," he says, his voice so cold it shocks me back to reality. "You can have your own life, your own mind, your own friends. But this is mine."

I can feel how wet his hand is against me, that I've soaked his fingers and his palm, and embarrassment floods me. How could I let him make me lose control like that while he's still completely calm? I squirm to pull back, tensing and squeezing my thighs together around his hand, but he tightens his grip, fisting my pussy while his finger stays buried inside me.

"You're hurting me," I gasp.

"Do you understand?" he asks, squeezing tighter.

I suck in a breath, my clit so sensitive after his ministrations that even a touch hurts. "Yes," I gasp.

"Good," he says, slowly withdrawing his hand. He tugs the edge of my dress out and slowly begins wiping his fingers on it one by one. "You're my wife, and I take care of the needs no one else can. If you don't want to talk to me, fine. Talk to whoever the fuck you want. If you don't want to cook and clean and all that shit, we can hire someone. But I will be the only one paying the bills in our house, and I will be the only one who touches you. Understand?"

I don't even know what to say to him, how to respond. I knew he'd put his foot down at some point, but this… I don't know how to even answer him. He's giving me everything—almost. He's giving me so much that I want, how can I say no?

I nod, and King takes the edge of my dress and pulls it up over my head. I fight to bring it back down, but he yanks it off, tossing it to the floor and glowering at me. I wrap an arm around my chest, trying to cover myself.

"Let me see you," he commands.

"No fucking way," I shoot back. I push off the windowsill and try to step past him, but he puts a firm hand on my chest, pushing me back.

"Let me see my wife," he says. "I want to know what's mine."

"Oh, you want to see the goods you paid for?" I taunt. "Fine, look at them. Doesn't it make you feel so noble and proud to own such a pretty piece of livestock?"

I throw my arms out, letting him see the price I'm paying, letting him see what he bought like a fucking piece of furniture. That's the only thing that explains why my father picked this asshole to marry me off to. King is nothing, a lowly soldier, and a new one at that. He's never even killed a man. He's only been in the Life for a few months. My father denies it, but that's the only explanation. This asshole's rich and paid him off, basically buying me. Of course he wants to see what he got for his money. I'm surprised he hasn't claimed what's his already.

He stares at me for a long minute, his eyes moving over me with agonizing thoroughness, slowly stripping me of my dignity. I should be terrified, even repulsed.

Instead, my nipples harden under his gaze, and my cheeks go hot with shame that he can see what he's doing to me. That his gaze on my skin is like a caress, bringing me to life. That he can see that I like him looking at me, wanting me. That it turns me on.

Goosebumps sweep over my skin, and a shiver goes through me. My clit pulses when his eyes dip lower, raking over my belly, my hips, my soaked panties, down my thighs. I can feel a tingling heat gathering between them, wetness blooming to life again when he reaches my feet and begins his agonizing examination from the bottom this time. His heated gaze slides over my skin, up my trembling thighs, catching between them. I watch his Adam's apple bob as he swallows before continuing.

Finally, our eyes meet again. My cheeks burn hotter, but I don't drop my gaze. I want to see his expression, want to read what's behind those dark eyes. But I can't. I don't know him well enough to know what he wants, what he intends. I thought he was as into it as I was before, but when I came, when I lost control, he didn't. He was as cold an unfeeling as a monster, using my pleasure to his advantage the whole time. There is no passion in this man, only calculation.

That must be how he got me in the first place, how he negotiated for my hand and my body, convincing my father to give me up for his use.

"Turn around," he says at last.

I falter. My bravado is long gone, and my knees start shaking. Oh god. This is really happening. He's going to take me like the brute he is, from behind so he doesn't have to see my face.

I shake my head, and his jaw tightens, anger flashing in his eyes. He wants my obedience, but he doesn't require it. If I say no, he'll take what he wants anyway. Still, it's better to go down fighting than to let him think I agree to this, to any of this. I shake my head again.

King repeats himself slowly, and I grip the sill as he steps forward. "You will do as I ask, or there will be consequences."

"My dad will kill you if you hurt me," I whisper.

"We both know that's not true," King says with that little smirk that makes me want to slap his face.

I meet his eyes, and a tremor of pure terror goes through me. I'm around killers daily, but this man is more terrifying than any mafia boss. He has permission to whatever he pleases with me, to wreck me in unimaginable ways. He can use me until I'm as dispirited as the other mafia wives, until I don't even want to fight because I know it's useless. Until I pray he'll fuck his mistress, so he won't want to touch me when he gets home. Until I forget freedom because it's too painful to dream of something that will never be.

"What are you going to do?" I ask. "Do I have a choice?"

King slides a hand behind my head, gripping my hair gently. "You always have a choice, Eliza," he says. "Obey me, or accept the consequences."

I try to pull back, but his grip on my hair tightens until I wince, until I can't move my head. The sting brings tears to my eyes. I gather all my strength and spit in his face.

He spins me around so fast my hands fly out to brace against the window. I cry out, but he doesn't touch me beyond his grip on my thick bundle of hair. I can hear him breathing behind me, can feel him moving slightly, but I can't see his face. I'm glad he can't see mine. Tears of fear and pain trickle down my cheeks, though I breathe through my mouth so he won't hear. Steam forms on the cold glass around my fingers as I stand there, tense with terror as he readies himself.

"Let those pretty tears fall for me," he says. "I like knowing you give me the real ones, not faking it like you did on our wedding night."

He hooks his fingers into the back of my underwear, letting the tip of his fingers trace the line of my crack softly as he draws my underwear down over my thighs. A whimper escapes me, but I bite my lip to hold back the hiccup of terror. My whole body is shaking when he straightens, leaving my underwear around my ankles. He stands there for a long minute, not moving, just looking. My nipples harden and another sweep of goosebumps shivers across my skin while he looks.

"Why don't you want me to look at you?" he asks, his voice husky. "You're… Flawless."

How can I even begin to tell him all the fucked up reasons I don't want him looking at me? How can I tell him that I don't want it because he doesn't deserve to see me, but that when he looks at me, completely bared to him against my will, heat pulses between my thighs?

He steps forward, the soft fabric of his sweats barely grazing my skin. He slides an arm around me and tucks his fingers between my thighs, cupping my mound in his palm. "You were telling the truth about one thing that night," he says. "You're not ready. When the time comes, I'm going to bury myself so deep in this tight little cunt that you never forget my claim. All you'll remember is that you belong to me, and you'll like it that way."

I try to slow my breathing, feeling the wetness pooling between my thighs at his touch, hoping he can't feel it yet.

"For tonight," he murmurs into my ear, his voice a sexy rumble against my back. "You'll sleep like this. I want every part of your beautiful body bare for me to see when I wake. If you're good, you can have your underwear back in the morning."

"What?" I breathe.

He pulls me to the bed and tosses back the blankets before picking me up and laying me down on the sheet. I think he'll force me to do something obscene for him, but he only lies down next to me, pulling me into his arms. I tense at his touch, but he rolls me away from him, fitting his body around mine like the bigger spoon, and slides his hand back between my legs. Then he reaches for the remote and switches off the light.

Like I can sleep right now. I lie awake, trying not to squirm as heat pulses between my thighs, where his hand remains. I'm completely naked, but he's still wearing sweats and a t-shirt. That comforts me a bit, even as it makes me feel more vulnerable. He's making it clear he's the one in control, that I'm at his mercy. But he doesn't take anything else. He doesn't give it, either. His hand covers my mound in a relaxed, possessive way, like he's just putting a hand on my knee. Like he knows it belongs to him, and he's not worried about how I feel about that.

I want to go to sleep like I don't even feel it, like it's an offhand gesture to me, too. But I feel wetness increasing in my core with each minute as the heat of his hand, the gentle pressure of his fingers, builds my arousal. It's all I can do not to squirm against him, beg him for another orgasm. By the time I realize he's fallen asleep, I'm so worked up and frustrated I could scream. I wonder what he'd do if I started riding his hand. A strange mixture of arousal and fear mingles inside me, and I realize one is fueling the other.

This is not good. I'm so fucked up in the head.

I love risk. I love danger. And this man is all of that.

He terrifies me.

And I think I like it.

eight

Eliza

King is as quiet as usual on the flight home. I glance at him every few minutes on the plane. I'm quiet too, but I'm brimming with questions, worries. I don't want to feel any kind of way towards him, but I do. I'm scared and confused, furious, ashamed. I wish he'd just fucked me and gotten it over with. Now I have to wait, not until I think I'm ready, but until he does. In truth, I'll never be ready. He's going to have to take what he wants one way or another. Not knowing when is worse than just getting it over with.

When we reach New York, I'm relieved. All I want is to go back to the way things were. Instead, King gets my bags, and we head for his car in the same heavy silence that's hung between us all day. He slides around to open the door for me like he's some gentleman, not the guy who forced me to sleep naked next to him last night.

"I like your car," I offer when he's done loading the suitcases into the Lotus and has slid behind the wheel.

"Thanks," he says, switching it on. "You drive?"

"I know how." I don't have a car—most people in the city don't—but I have a license and I've driven Dad's car. He wanted to make sure I was capable in case our house was ever ambushed, and I needed to make a getaway.

We leave the parking garage before I decide I've had enough of this weirdness. I'd rather just talk about it and clear the air instead of pretending last night never happened.

I turn to King as he pulls out into the stream of taxis and other traffic. "Listen," I say. "About last night…"

"I'm sorry," he says immediately. "I got pissed when I saw that man with his hands on you. I know you hate me, and now that I know about your brother, I understand why. I shouldn't have handled you like that."

I'm so surprised that he's apologizing that I don't even know what to say. I figured he'd wake up in the morning and force himself on me, but he barely said two words to me all day. I'd never in a million years have guessed he was feeling guilty. It makes me like him more, see him differently. He's not some callous mafia guy yet. I could have done a lot worse.

I clear my throat and glance at him. "I'm sorry, too. Sorry we were both forced into this. I know it's not fair to ask you to wait for me to be ready. Even I don't know how long it'll take, or if I'll ever want to. So, I think you should find a *cumare*."

He shoots me a scowl. "I don't want a mistress, Eliza."

"I know," I say. "You want a wife who isn't a frigid bitch, as you put it. But unfortunately, neither of us got to choose that."

"I didn't call you a bitch," he says. "I called you a brat. And that was wrong of me. You're not a brat. You just act like one."

I close my eyes and thump my head back against the headrest in frustration. "It's not an act. I'm a frigid brat who's not sleeping with you because I hate you and I want to hold out on you and drive you crazy."

"Then why are you telling me to take a girl on the side?"

"Because I know you need that," I say. "If I can't give you what you need, then I have to be okay with you finding it somewhere else."

"I don't want anyone else," he says. "I want you, Eliza."

His words hang between us, heavier than the silence. The honeymoon was only a week, but it seems all that time alone together made this happen faster than either of us wanted. If he made me vulnerable last night, he's putting us on even footing again. I don't even have to figure out how to do it. He's doing it for me, showing me his own vulnerable side, admitting he wants me when I haven't done the same. He may have forced me to show that I do, that my body responds to his touch, but my heart will never want him, and I haven't admitted it the way he's doing. I admire him for putting himself out there when he knows I won't reciprocate.

"I don't want you," I say quietly. "I'm sorry."

This time, he sighs, adjusting his grip on the wheel and reaching over to lay a hand on my knee. "No, I'm sorry," he says. "I shouldn't have pushed you last night. I don't want to put pressure on you if you're not ready. But I only want my wife. No one else. So if I have to wait a month, or a year, or ten years, until you're comfortable with me, then that's what I'll do."

Ten years. A thrill of pure triumph goes through me. What if he means it?

"Then let's negotiate how this marriage will work," I say. "I want you to have all your needs met. It's just like… Like I don't want to clean, so we'll hire a maid. I don't want to have sex, so you can hire someone for that. There's nothing wrong with sex workers, King. Dad has a club where a bunch of them work. They're really nice. I'm sure you can find one you like."

He gives me an incredulous look. "Are you fucking serious right now?"

"Well… Yeah," I say. "I know you think I'm setting you up or something, but I'm not. I may be inexperienced, but I know men. It's in your biology. My father might have gotten me a human chastity belt, but he didn't shield me from much. I've been sitting in on poker games since I was five. I've heard the talk. I've met the kinds of guys who do this job, and you need a way to relieve stress."

"Stop telling me what I need," he grits out.

"I'm just being reasonable. If you need sex, I'm fine with you getting it. I'll look the other way. And you don't have to worry about me. I won't have my picture taken with men at clubs or make you look bad. I won't be with anyone else. I'll be your good little wifey, and you can be a good husband by getting what you need from someone else and not putting that burden on me."

"How would you like it if I was over here lecturing you on how much you need sex because it's natural and biological…"

I shudder, wrapping my arms around myself at how close those words come to the ones I've heard before.

"You're right," I say. "I'm just trying to make this easier for both of us. I'm giving you the freedom to do what you want, to live your life however you want. All I ask is that you just let me live mine the way I want. This is a marriage of convenience. Even if we don't love each other, it doesn't have to be miserable."

We drive in silence for a while. At last, King moves his hand from my knee to shift, glancing at me from the corner of his eye. "Maybe we can work through it. Maybe if we get to know each other…"

I snort. "I don't think so."

We're quiet for another minute.

"Okay," he says at last. "But I'm not going to fuck anyone else. I promised to be faithful, and I told you I take my word seriously."

I can see the man has his pride, and his word is part of that. Still, it seems a waste. He's so fucking beautiful. It could be years before I want intimacy—if I ever do. He's in his prime, and I'm holding him back, smothering him with my demons.

Shit. I'm *his* human chastity belt.

"You also said you can't love me," I remind him. "If you're with someone else and never with me, it'll ensure that we never become close. Isn't that what we both want?"

"Yes," he concedes at last. "I want us both to stay alive."

Something in my chest dies a little at his words. Is he agreeing to find a *cumare* because he can't have me, and he feels bad about pushing me past my limits?

I tell myself it's a good thing. Even though it makes me feel weird to think about him with someone else, I'd rather he find a mistress than come at me, making me feel the terrifying things he did last night, things I had no control over, just like when I was a kid. Taking my body over as if it really does belong to him, even more than it belongs to me.

If he finds a *cumare,* maybe he'll be too caught up in the honeymoon phase with her to want one with me. I couldn't stop the wedding, but maybe I can stop the worst part. It's all arranged, a contract signed by two families, a marriage in name only. If he gets his needs met elsewhere, it can stay that way.

The families want us together, but they don't require love. I'm doing my duty to them, just like Dad wanted. One day, my biological clock will start ticking and I'll want a baby. We can try then. If I still don't want to touch him, don't trust myself with him, they have doctors for that now.

I know it's not ideal, and maybe it's even selfish. I know what people would say. It was a long time ago, I should just get over it. I should go to a shrink. I'm being selfish.

But it's more than a memory, more than something that fucked with my head. I don't even think about it that much, but it's always there, as if it sank into my being, became part of me. It lurks inside me even when I don't feed it with attention or conscious thought. It feeds off me like a parasite, like a cancer, living in every cell that makes up my body. I can't just forget about it, can't get over it and move on, any more than someone with a disease can get over it by willing it away. All I can do is ignore it, not let it control my life, and live hard and outrageously, prove to myself that it doesn't define me.

It only defines one part of me, and that part is hidden and private, tucked away safely, never to be touched or awakened. That part made me a victim. If I don't have those feelings, don't acknowledge that part of me, it can't hurt me, can't make me a victim again. And I won't be a victim. I'm strong now, coated in armor, dipped in the river Styx like Achilles. I have a chink in my armor, but luckily, it's a lot harder to access than my heel. I'm stronger than Achilles, stronger than anyone knows. Strong enough that I don't need sex, even if it is biology. I control my body, not the other way around. And no one will ever control me again.

nine

King

"You're going back to work today, right?" Eliza asks, sitting at the vanity, her hair tumbling to one side as she tilts her head to watch herself put in a big, gold hoop earring.

"Yes," I say, standing behind her and adjusting my tie in the mirror above her head.

We don't meet each other's eyes. Things have been different since returning from the honeymoon a few days ago. I can't tell if they're better or worse. There's a wariness in both of us, as if we're both watching the other from the corner of our eyes, waiting to see our partner's next move. We tiptoe around each other, overly respectful of the others' physical space.

"Does that bother you?" I ask Eliza.

"Of course not," she says. "I know how much you men love your work."

I don't know what she means by that. Hurting people is not exactly a job I'd say I loved, but I am dedicated to my work, it's true. I have to be.

"What about you?" I ask, lingering to watch her even after I've checked my reflection. Looking the part is important. Appearances reflect on a person's character, family, and everything else. Eliza is beautiful with or without makeup, but I like that she puts herself together to go out in public, that I'm the only one who sees her bare face.

"I'm not sure," she says, lightly.

"No plans?"

"Look, I've always done whatever I wanted," she says flatly. "My mom followed her dream, and I'm following mine."

"I'm sorry," I say.

She stares at me, her lips pursing as she swallows. "For what?"

"That your mom's not around," I say. "That she didn't come to the wedding."

Eliza drops her gaze and messes with the makeup on her vanity for a few seconds before lifting her face and shaking her hair back, leaning in to powder her skin with a brush. "My mom's my hero," she says. "She risked her life to be free and follow her heart. Not many women have the balls to stand up to a mob boss."

I want to say I'm sorry again, to insist it still sucks, but I hold it back. I'm no stranger to complicated feelings about shitty mothers. Ma laughed at me when I voiced my fears about joining the Valenti mafia family, laughed at the thought of me killing a man. But she's still my mother.

"She sounds brave," I say after a second.

"She is," Eliza says. "And I won't have any man controlling me, either. I did as my family wanted and married you. My duty is done. No one is going to tell me what to do now. I'm going to keep doing what I have been, whatever the fuck I want, and you can't stop me."

"Okay…"

"I mean it," she says. "If you mess with me, if you hurt me, you'll see just what my father is capable of."

"I'm not interested in being your surrogate father or telling you what to do," I say. "You're an adult. We've been over this. Act like a married woman when you leave the house, and you can do whatever the fuck you want when you're at home."

"Good," she says. "I just wanted to make sure we're still clear about that."

It's the first time we've really talked since the car ride home, when we came to a shaky peace. I got carried away when I saw her dancing with a stranger on our honeymoon, and that's it. When I saw his hands on her, the frustration boiled over. She's my fucking *wife*. Only my hands should be on her.

And yeah, maybe the week of sleeping next to her and seeing her and not touching her, maybe it caught up with me. Finding out it was all a lie, that she just didn't want to fuck me, pissed me off. I shouldn't have treated her like that, though. I shouldn't have let my anger and resentment bubble over. I shouldn't have let my lust get away from me, shouldn't have touched her at all. I shouldn't feel any of those things, period.

I don't have the time or inclination to argue with Eliza today. What am I going to say, anyway? If I fuck with her, she'll make sure I'm killed in some unimaginably horrible way. And why should I care what she does with her days? I won't be there. Just because I can't afford to love her, that doesn't mean I don't want her to be happy. I want her to do whatever she pleases.

I just need to get better at not feeling for her, for the people I have to get money from, for anyone. I can't help but want to take care of her, but that doesn't mean the feeling is mutual. I need to remember that and be careful. Just because I won't fuck someone else, that doesn't mean I get to fuck her. Just because I can't love anyone else, that doesn't mean I love her. She's better at this than I am, and I should be grateful she's keeping the distance between us when I fuck up. One day, I'll get better at it, and it'll be easier.

"Well, enjoy your day," I say, leaning down to kiss the top of her head. It's one of those offhand gestures that wasn't planned, but after I do it, it makes the place behind my sternum tighten into an ache. That's something a man would do with a wife he's comfortable with, a wife who loves him, who cares whether he comes home that night.

When I get to Al Valenti's, his guards check the car, including the trunk and underneath it, as if someone could be clinging to the bottom of the Evija. I almost laugh.

"Gotta check everyone," the guard says, giving me a friendly salute. "Can't be too careful."

"I know," I say, saluting back before heading around to park. Little Al's car is there, too, and after being stopped by two guards at the back door, I'm allowed to enter.

One more guard is stationed outside the dining room where I find Uncle Al, Little Al, and Al's consigliere having lunch.

"There he is," Little Al crows when he sees me, dropping his hoagie and holding out a hand for me to slap. "You been working on your tan?"

I shrug. "I've been at the beach for a week."

"How was Bora Bora?" Uncle Al asks, looking up from his food and fixing those watchful eyes on me. The guy doesn't miss anything.

"You better not have seen any of it," Little Al says, winking at me and biting into his sandwich. "Why were you on the beach, bro? You should have spent every minute in your hotel room."

I've had about enough of this conversation, so I steer it in a different direction, though I notice Al Valenti watching me like he knows something's up.

"What'd I miss?" I ask, taking a seat and scooting in next to Little Al.

"Nothing important," Uncle Al says. "I'm meeting with Anthony Pomponio this week. If that wife of yours hasn't checked in with him since the honeymoon, make sure she does that."

My stomach clenches at the unspoken threat in those words. Make sure she gives him a glowing report of our marriage. Of me.

That's not gonna happen.

Guilt flares inside me when I think of the last night of our honeymoon, when I all but forced her to cum for me. Considering her aversion to sexual contact, god knows what she'll tell her father about me.

Both Als are watching me, and I give my head a little shake to clear it and grab a sandwich off the tray in the middle of the table. "I'll see what I can do."

"Hey, why doesn't he go with you?" Little Al asks his grandfather. "He can give Anthony a first-hand account of the honeymoon."

I want to punch the guy when I see the glimmer of humor in his eyes, like he has some idea that things aren't too peachy between Eliza and me, and he thinks it would be just hilarious for Mr. Pomponio to grill me about my treatment of his daughter. He did seem to know an awful lot about her upbringing when I asked him about her, even the goings-on of her family. Does he know more than he let on?

Maybe they have a history I don't know about. Or maybe he's just being a garden variety asshat and knows exactly how uncomfortable that situation would be.

"Not a bad idea," Uncle Al says.

Is he fucking serious? I could strangle the shit out of my partner for suggesting it.

But I'm not going to argue. I'm responsible for bringing peace between the families, and if I fail, I always knew what would happen. Might as well get it over with. The question is, will he chop off my head, or just my dick?

I try not to think about it for the rest of the day as Little Al and I make our rounds, collecting payments. When I walk into the penthouse that afternoon, Eliza is on the sofa, the celebrity gossip channel playing on the flatscreen TV, her phone sandwiched between her ear and her shoulder as she picks through a bowl of mixed nuts. I notice she got a new set of nails today, and I wonder what else she got up to when she was out, who she went with.

She barely glances my way before going back to her call, giggling to her friend. I try to be glad she's happy, even if it's not with me.

I leave her and go into the other room, but pretty soon, it's time for dinner and she's still on the phone. I stick my head into the sitting room and wave my phone at her.

"I'm calling out for dinner," I say. "What do you want?"

"Oh, I'm about to meet Bianca for dinner," she says, covering the end of her phone to speak to me. Why she needs to go eat with her friend after talking to her on the phone for over an hour, I don't know.

"Then can you get off the phone for a minute?" I ask. "I need to talk to you."

She rolls her eyes and sighs. "What could we have to talk about?"

"You seem to have plenty to talk about," I say, cutting my eyes at the phone.

She rolls her eyes again, then puts her phone back to her ear. "Hey, I gotta go. The ball and chain wants to *talk.*"

She scoffs, giggles at something Bianca says, then says goodbye and hangs up. She faces me with barely concealed annoyance. "What?"

"I'm meeting with your father in a few days," I tell her. "You need to call him tonight."

She smirks. "You want me to give you a five-star review?"

"Yes."

We stare at each other for a long minute. Eliza could get me executed with a single word. That's probably what she wants. Sure, she'll be a widow at eighteen, but that can't be too rare in this line of work. And she'll be free to do whatever the fuck it is she's so passionate about—if she can find another husband to finance her lifestyle, put up with her attitude, and be content getting nothing in return except a piece of arm candy when he has an event to attend.

"Fine," she says at last. "I'll call him later."

Irritation flickers inside me. I'm not asking too much. I'm literally asking for the bare fucking minimum—to keep my life. I force myself to address her calmly. "Do it now, and you can go out to dinner with your friend."

She just her chin out, her eyes flashing a challenge. "You can't tell me what to do."

My hands tighten into fists. This little brat has been traipsing around doing whatever the fuck she wants all day, while I've been working to keep the truce, which keeps our extended families alive. I ask nothing of her except to not get me killed, but apparently that's too goddamn much. Someone's going to have to teach her how this works, though, and I'm the one the families nominated for the job.

I step up behind the sofa, taking her hair gently in one hand and wrapping it around my palm. She starts to twist away, but I grip her hair a little tighter and tug her back against the couch. "You'll call now, *carina.*"

She lets out a huff, but she thumbs her phone on and calls. "Are you going to stand there looking over my shoulder like an overprotective dad monitoring a phone call to his daughter's boyfriend?"

"Yes," I say, stroking her hair with my free hand. "If you don't want me treating you like a child, don't act like one."

She starts to pull away again, but I squeeze my hand closed around her silky rope of hair and hold her still. Her father answers, and she puts the phone to her ear.

"Hi, Daddy," she says, turning her head just far enough to glare up at me from the corner of her eye.

"Behave," I mouth, giving her hair just a gentle tug, just enough to remind her of the night in the hotel. She turns forward again, but I catch her squeezing her knees together for just a second.

Does she like it when I treat her like a child? Or is it the threat that's got her squirming and adjusting her skirt before she responds to whatever her father is saying?

"It was great, Daddy," she assures him. "The beach was gorgeous, the weather was perfect, and the hotel was great. I got a massage every day. I'm so relaxed."

I smile, loosening my hold on her hair and stroking her head. She goes on, describing the beach and the excursions and the meals for a few minutes. I release my hold and stroke her neck, letting my hands rest on her shoulders. While she talks, I gently knead the muscles. It's not so hard to get her to obey. I just have to promise her what she wants. Dinners with her friends, luxuries at home, my complete disinterest in her as a wife.

She pauses while her father speaks, and I feel her tense just as she bursts out, "He's horrible, Daddy! I hate him! Please let me come home. I can't live with a Valenti. He's a monster!"

Fury flares in my chest. This bitch is going to get me killed, and I haven't done shit to her. I've barely touched her. Any other man in his right mind would have fucked her on day one, no matter her excuses. He would have told her she couldn't go out dancing on their honeymoon. He would have told her to get off her ass and do something while he was at work, not offered to hire help so she could go wherever the fuck she wanted, with whoever the fuck she was with today. He would have wanted answers, accountability, a wife who acted like one.

I went too easy on her. Bargaining isn't going to cut it with her. I won't make that mistake again.

I grab her hair and yank her head back so hard she gasps, struggling to free herself. I try to swipe the phone, but she keeps it to her ear. "When is that?" she asks, then waits for him to answer. "I don't know if I can make it three more days. He'll kill me by then!"

"Give me the phone," I growl.

"Fine," she snaps into the phone. "But if he doesn't show up at *Jean-Jean's,* it's because he killed me and went on the run. I hope you'll be happy when I'm dead!"

I grab the phone from her hand and hang it up before shoving it in my pocket. "What the fuck is wrong with you? You trying to get me executed?"

"Why shouldn't I?" she shoots back. "You executed my brother."

"Is this a game to you, Eliza? Your whole fucking life is a game, isn't it, just to see what you can get away with?"

She snorts. "Hypocritical much? That's what everyone in the Life's trying to do."

I've never thought of it that way, and it takes me off guard yet again. I keep thinking I have her figured out, and then she goes and says something like that. She may act like a shallow party girl, but there's more to her. I need to stop forgetting that.

"You're a smart girl," I say calmly. "You disobeyed me. You knew there would be consequences."

I watch her throat working as she swallows. "What are you going to do, spank me?" she asks, the sass back in her voice.

"I told you to tell your father I was good to you, and you could go out with your friend. You didn't do that, so you'll be staying in for dinner with me. What do you want?"

She jumps up off the couch, all her smug bravado gone. "You can't stop me from seeing my friends."

"There are consequences to your actions," I say. "It's time you start facing them. You knew the terms, and you chose to lie."

"I didn't lie," she shouts. "You *are* horrible. Keeping me from my friends is abuse!"

Now it's my turn to scoff. "You've been with your friends all day. I don't think it's abuse to ask you to have dinner with me."

She juts out her lip and glares. "You can't stop me."

"Who pays for your credit card?" I ask. "It's not your daddy anymore, Eliza."

Her mouth falls open in an expression of shocked disbelief, her eyes going wide with indignation. "You're cutting me off?"

"I'm buying you dinner."

"You'll have to go downstairs to get food," she says. "I'll leave."

"You have money for a taxi? An uber?"

"I'll call Bianca."

I raise a brow at her. "Will you?"

She glances around on the couch and coffee table before turning back to me. "Give me my phone."

"You mean my phone?"

"You didn't buy me that."

"I pay the bill."

We stare at each other a long minute. "I'll message her online."

"Good luck guessing the wi-fi password." Today's her first day at my place, so I know she doesn't have it already. Considering she doesn't want to know anything about me, she probably doesn't even know I have a sister, let alone her name and birthday.

She huffs, staring at me with blazing fury. It's hot as hell.

"You really are a monster," she says at last, her voice calmer now.

"Then maybe we are meant for each other," I answer. "How's pho?"

Forty minutes later, the driver calls up to tell us the food has arrived. Eliza has been suspiciously quiet the whole time, fuming in silence and no doubt plotting my death. I'm not the only one who underestimated my opponent. I like knowing I'm impressing her, even if it's in a negative way.

"I'll go down and get it," she says when I tell her dinner is here.

I can't help but chuckle. "Nice try."

"What, you think I'm going to trade a blowjob for our dinner? I don't have any money, as you so kindly pointed out."

"I think you're going to tell him some sob story and probably go to the cops, which will ensure your family or mine gets rid of me."

She gives me a look of pure loathing. "I would never go to the cops," she says flatly. "I'm a mafia daughter."

"I'll get the food," I say. "Thanks for offering. Maybe another time, if you're home all day and get bored, you can learn to make something. Or look up a recipe. Or hire a cook if you're so dead set on avoiding the kitchen. Or hell, just do what I did, and call in an order for food."

She rolls her eyes. "I had a busy day, okay?"

"Yeah? Doing what?"

"Not that it's any of your business, but we went to a show, and I had to get a mani-pedi after all that sand in my toes, and we had lunch and met up with some friends."

"Sounds rough," I say. "I bet you could have fit a phone call in there somewhere."

"I did," she says. "Before you took my phone."

"You're an adult, Eliza. Act like one. You should know how to feed yourself."

I don't know why I even argue with her. I shouldn't let her get to me. But her entitled little brat attitude makes me want to teach her a lesson. I'm out there forcing myself to beat up guys with families, with wives who actually love them and kids who won't eat if we take all their money. I hate what I have to do every fucking day to earn that money she spends like it's nothing, like it rains from the sky instead of my pockets. It would all be worth it, and I'd be happy to give my wife everything she could want and more, if she wasn't trying to fucking kill me in return.

I'm just handing the driver a tip when Eliza comes racing out of our building past the doorman, waving her arms wildly at the driver. She's barefoot, and her buttoned blouse is halfway untucked, as if she just fought her way out. "Help," she yells. "This guy is holding me hostage!"

"Eliza," I bark. "What the fuck are you doing?"

"Take me with you," she says to the guy, all desperation. "He's going to kill me!"

The delivery driver looks between us like he's unsure what to do. The poor guy probably thinks he's supposed to call 911. She's so damn convincing I halfway believe her.

She runs for the car, trying to open the back door. I grab her arm and drag her back.

"Hey!" the guy protests in a heavily accented voice.

"Get the fuck inside and stop acting like a child," I growl at Eliza, who's flailing in my grip like I really am her kidnapper and not her fucking husband.

I pull her back toward the building, but the driver gets out of the car and comes toward us.

"Hey," he says again. "Let go."

"Fuck off and mind your business," I say. "This doesn't concern you."

"Take me with you," Eliza wails to the guy as we reach the doors to our building. The doorman is watching with slight amusement. This is Al Valenti's territory, and the guy knows who I work for, so he's not going to interfere. He also knows Eliza is my wife, and he must think we're playing some kind of game. He watches with a little grin as I try to maneuver myself between Eliza and the delivery guy, a bag of takeout containers swinging from one arm.

"He's abusing me," Eliza howls. "He took my phone!"

That's it. I've had it with her shit, with the scene she's making, with all of it. The delivery guy reaches for her, but I step between them and punch him in the face. He crumples to the ground, out cold.

No one fucking touches my wife.

Without a word, I throw her over my shoulder and carry her inside, straight into the elevator. I set her on her feet only once the doors have closed and the car is moving.

"What are you going to do to me?" she asks, sounding half defiant and half scared as she brushes her hair out of her face, apparently done with the histrionics.

Not nearly as much as you deserve, baby girl.

I don't say the words aloud, though. I watch her, wondering what she wants me to say, and what she *needs* me to say, and if those are very different things. The bratty, spoiled princess I married wants something very different from what I suspect the scared, insecure girl inside her needs. The question is, can I give her that?

I promised myself I wouldn't. But if I could teach her to be good, if I could show her she's worth teaching, she might learn to live with me. She's my fucking wife, after all, not some random girl whose name I forgot two days after she spread her legs for me. It would be worth it to try, if she'd let me. It would be worth it to see what makes her tick, though I suspect I already know. From the rare glimpses I've caught of something beneath the glossy surface, I think I know how to give her exactly what she needs.

"Well?" she asks as we reach the apartment.

I push her inside and close the door before answering. "You acted like a child, so you get treated like a child."

"What are you going to do, punish me?" she asks, rolling her eyes. Even when she acts like a brat, there's something so incredibly innocent about her, as if all that bravado and sass is just a cover to hide the fact that she's scared, and broken, and too naïve for her own good. Her eyes are wary, her hair a mess after her tantrum outside, and damn if she doesn't look too fucking sexy for her own good.

"If that's what you want," I say. "You need discipline, Eliza. Punishment can be part of that, if you like that."

"What the fuck does that mean?" she demands.

"It means the same thing I said before. If you behave yourself, you get your phone back. If you throw a fucking tantrum on the street, you get punished."

"Oh," she says, swallowing.

We stare at each other for a long minute, measuring each other. I've never punished a girl before, never even thought about it. The thought is… Hotter than it should be. I've never been with a girl long enough to warrant games like this. If I didn't like something a girl did, I walked away and never looked back. But there's no walking away from Eliza Dolce. She wears my ring and carries my name. She's family, and I don't walk away from family.

ten

Eliza

"Sit down," King says, gesturing to the table.

I don't know what I was expecting, but it wasn't that. I thought he'd bend me over the table and make me pay for what I did. Instead, he stares at me with dark, expectant eyes that leave no room for argument. I can see the fury inside him, behind the sheen of control. I can see the glittering malice, the sadistic monster who would love nothing more than my disobedience. I can see him itching to put me in my place, to hurt me. He probably thinks I'm going to do what I did before, but there's no point now. Why throw a fit for only him to see?

That's a performance, something a girl does to get her way. It usually worked with Daddy. I'd start making a scene, and he'd give in, not wanting the public spectacle. The only time it didn't work was when he told me I had to marry a Valenti.

He's not here to rescue me now, and King's the villain, not my knight in shining armor. So I placate him because I want to survive this as much as he does. I sit at the table and fold my hands expectantly. Waiting for whatever horror he's about to serve up. And even though my heart is racing and my nerves fluttering, I won't let him see. I show him only attitude, though I'm beginning to think he's onto me. He may be young, but he's not dumb. He may not be able to see through me yet, but I bet he knows he's only seeing the surface just like I know there's more to him than meets the eye. And not just because the handsome face hides a devil underneath. No, King has walls even thicker than mine. We may put up different facades, but I'd bet they serve the same purpose.

What's he hiding behind those dark, smoldering eyes? What made him a sadistic Valenti man at only eighteen?

King retrieves a set of Asian-style soup spoons we got as a wedding gift and sits down at the head of the table. He opens them carefully, neither of us speaking. In the same slow and methodical way, he unpacks the bag of food. For a minute, I think he's just going to make me eat with him in silence, like we did on our honeymoon. I have nothing to say to a man whose family killed my brother. If it weren't for the Valentis, my mother would still be here, too. She wouldn't have decided she couldn't take the Life anymore. True, she wouldn't have realized her dreams, either. But she'd be here to tell me what to do, to advise me. I don't have the first idea of how to be some man's wife, let alone a stranger's.

"You behaved like a child, so you will be treated as one," King says, setting a bowl in front of each of us. "I will feed you, and you will eat, but you will not speak."

What the fuck?

This is definitely not what we did on our honeymoon.

I open my mouth to argue, then decide it could be a lot worse. If he has some weird fetish about feeding people, whatever. At least he's not starving me or raping me or beating me. He could do any of that if he wanted. I'm at his mercy. If the worst he'll do is burn my mouth a little, I'm getting off easy.

"That's it?" I ask. "That's the only punishment? If I let you feed me dinner, you'll give me back my phone?"

"You're not to speak until I say so," he reminds me.

"Fine by me," I mutter. "I don't have anything to say to you, anyway."

King picks up my spoon and feeds me a bite of soup before taking a bite of his own. The first one isn't so bad. The soup's not even that hot after the ride here and the commotion since arriving, so it doesn't come close to burning my mouth. Still, King takes another scoop from my bowl and blows on it, like I really am a fucking child, and he has to cool off my food because I'm too dumb to know how to eat. I glare at him as he brings it to my lips. This time, I don't open my mouth.

"Open wide," he says, his voice a quiet taunt.

"This is fucking ridiculous," I snap. I start to rise, but King's hand shoots out and clamps around the back of my neck. His grip is firm, just short of painful. Hard enough to let me know the pain he could cause if he wanted.

I still in his grip, and he strokes the side of my neck with his thumb. "I appreciate your obedience," he says. "Now open your mouth like a good girl."

A funny little shiver wraps itself around my spine, and I open my lips. This time, when he guides the spoon inside, I find myself holding my breath. His gaze moves from my lips to my eyes when I close my mouth around the spoon. I try not to move my mouth too much as he slides the spoon out, his eyes following its path back to the bowl.

Then he sits back and takes a bit of his own soup. I find myself chewing self-consciously, wondering what's going on in that mind of his. He's so quiet. What's he thinking? Is he disgusted by the way I acted?

Thinking about it, I'm disgusted with myself. I threw a tantrum like a child, and for what? To prove a point? It's not like I actually expected the delivery guy to whisk me away to a better life. I live in a fucking penthouse.

Even if he'd taken me to Bianca's, I couldn't have stayed. I didn't have a plan. I just didn't want King to win.

He finishes chewing and picks up my spoon again, raising it to his lips to blow on it. I stare at his mouth, his lips full but masculine, all lines instead of curves. He brings the spoon to my lips, and I meet his gaze. It's strangely, horribly intimate.

When he goes back to his own food, I try not to squirm with anticipation of the next bite. Is this doing strange things to him, too? Did he already know what it would do to me? If this really is a fetish of his, that means he's done it before with other girls. Were they weirdly, erotically charged by the way it made them feel so completely vulnerable, and helpless, and almost violated?

I'm thrilled when it's my turn to have another bite. A little twinge of excitement runs through me and lands between my thighs. I find myself staring at my husband's lips as they curl to blow on the soup, wondering what they'd feel like against—

No.

I cannot allow myself these thoughts. I let myself go with him once, but I was drunk and my defenses were down. That won't happen again.

And he's feeding me soup, for fuck's sake. It's not even a sexy food. It's not like he's feeding me chocolate covered strawberries. It's a punishment, treating me like a child, not something that's meant to turn me on.

He obviously doesn't think it's sexy. He doesn't look turned on at all. He watches my lips with burning intensity each time, but then he just goes back to his food like it was nothing.

He brings to spoon to my lips, and all I can think about is how clumsy and helpless I feel when a drop of broth escapes the corner of my mouth. I try to catch it with my tongue, and King's eyes light on the movement. My heart stutters in my chest, and I hide my tongue inside my mouth, feeling suddenly ashamed, like I made a lewd gesture. I pull my lips in, pressing them together as the drop slides down my chin and dribbles off.

King picks up a napkin and gently wipes my chin, his fingers lingering, his eyes drinking me in. Then, slowly, his gaze moves to where the drop landed, right on one of my breasts. Still holding the napkin, he reaches out and dabs gently against the spot. I hold my breath, not daring to let my chest rise against his touch. When his gaze rises to meet mine, I don't know if I'm relieved or terrified to see the desire in my own eyes reflected back in his.

"King?" I whisper, my throat tight, a delicious, sick feeling swimming in my belly and sinking lower, settling into a dull throb between my thighs. "Feed me more?"

"You're a greedy little thing, aren't you?" he murmurs, the corner of his mouth quirking up in a haughty smile.

But it's a smile of approval.

Much to my annoyance, a swell of pride threatens to rise inside me. I like that I pleased him. Worse, I want to do it again. I want his approval, his appreciation, that smile that says I did something he likes.

"I spoke," I say quietly when he gets a bite for himself. "Are you going to punish me?"

"You're doing so well, *carina mia*," he says, reaching out to stroke my hair behind my ear. "I don't think you'll need it. You'll do better next time, won't you?"

I tuck my hands under my thighs and try to get myself under control. Everything is going wrong inside me. My body is on fire and cold at the same time, like I've had a fever that's finally breaking. My heart is beating erratically as I watch him reach for my spoon. I notice for the first time how long and fine his fingers are, strong and masculine but beautiful, too. How did I miss that when I put on his ring?

And why do I care?

My emotions are as haywire as my body. I'm grossly aroused by his feeding me, treating me like something less than him, an invalid, almost less than human. It's offensive.

And it's shameful that I'm taking it like an obedient little lapdog, and even more shameful that some part of me enjoys it, even craves more.

I'm ashamed that I have to squeeze my knees together as I accept his next offering, my lips caressing the porcelain spoon as they wrap around it. I find myself hoping he'll notice how full my lips are, how pink they are without lipstick. That he'll notice the flush in my cheeks when his knuckles brush my skin, the curl of my lashes as I look up at him through their fringe.

I find myself wondering what the punishment would have been. And most humiliating of all, I find myself disappointed that I won't find out.

eleven

King

Eliza obeys my every command for the rest of dinner. By the time I'm done, I've gotten more than I asked for, more than I expected. It must be a testament to how long it's been since I've fucked a woman, but I'm hard as a rock watching her suck on my spoon like that. When the last bite is gone, I push the bowls away and turn her chair to face me. I don't care if she can see my cock straining against my pants. I fucking hope she can.

"Look at you," I say, lifting her chin and examining her face. "You got food on yourself, *bambina*. What a messy little eater you are. I hope you swallow my cum better."

Her lips part in a silent gasp, then snap closed. She swallows, her eyes swimming with fear. She shakes her head, her plump lower lip trembling. "You said dinner."

"You slopped your dinner on your pretty blouse," I say, brushing my knuckle lightly over the stain on her tit. Her nipple pebbles against the fabric as if eager for my touch. I want to peel off every layer of her clothes, lay her on the table, and suck her cunt until it turns inside out.

Instead, I brush my knuckles in a slow circle around her nipple, my skin just a whisper against the soft fabric. She sucks in a breath, her knees spasming together for a second. I chuckle. "I think we'd better get that off, don't you think, *piccola mia?*"

"King," she whispers.

I love the sound of my name on her tongue. I want to be her king. I want to see her kneeling at my feet, worshipping me the way I want to worship her. Without meaning to, without knowing it, I've begun to want her to be my queen as much as I want to be her king.

But she doesn't need to know that. Not yet. Not until I've got a handle on her.

"That's right, baby girl," I say. "I'm your king. Don't forget it again."

I grip the front of her shirt in both hands and give a swift tug. Buttons fly, clicking against the table and floor as they fall. She lets out a little cry as I spread her shirt open, baring her bra. It's black lace, and I don't like thinking about who she's wearing a sexy bra for. Was she really just planning to go out with her girlfriends?

"Who are you wearing this for?" I demand, hooking my finger in the center, between her tits.

"No one," she protests, her eyes widening.

"Take it off."

"What?"

"I don't like it," I say. "Take it off. Go out tomorrow and get some plain white ones. Not ones that makes me think you're showing them to someone else."

"Oh, now you're jealous?" she asks, her voice hardening in a way I don't like. I like her when she's soft and vulnerable.

"Fuck yes, I'm jealous," I say. "I'm your husband. I don't want to think about anyone else even looking at you."

She hesitates a moment before slowly unhooking her bra and pulling it down her arms, dropping it to the floor beside the table. I stare at her, bared to me like an invitation. She makes no move to cover herself. Her tits are round and perfect, her nipples small and whiskey-brown like her eyes, hardened by arousal already.

I duck down and take one of her them in my mouth, sucking it between my lips. She gasps and grips my head, but I can't tell if she's pulling me closer or pushing me away. I don't care. I want to taste her skin, to make her moan. I run my tongue across the tip of her nipple, groaning at the softness of her skin, the tightness of her nipple, like a puckered little pebble. I suck harder, drawing her tit further in, filling my mouth with her flesh. She whimpers, and I bite down just a little, squeezing with my teeth. She sucks in a breath, squirming in her chair.

SELENA

I know when a girl needs her cunt filled, and I don't waste any time. I push my hand under her skirt, running it all the way up to the apex of her thighs. Her panties are as wet as I suspected. She lets out a little cry, and I pull back on her tit, closing my teeth around her nipple and biting down gently while I flick the tip of my tongue against it. She's panting and squirming when I release her tit and open her knees. My cock throbs against my pants when I touch her, the heat of her need burning through the wet fabric between her legs. I push up her skirt and tug aside her panties, opening her lips so I can see the glistening pink flesh of her slit.

"I'm going to need you to shave this," I say.

"What?" she demands, still breathless but sounding pissed all the same.

I take a pinch of her pubic hair and tug it hard enough to make her lift up in her chair, sucking in a breath. I didn't know there was a girl left in New York who hadn't lasered the hair off her pussy by now. "Shave it," I say. "I want to see you, Eliza. All of you."

"This is all of me," she protests.

I scoot my chair back, grab her around the waist, and lift her onto the edge of the table. I take her hands and wrap them around the edge. "Don't move your hands from there," I order, standing over her.

Her eyes are filled with uncertainty, that innocence shining from her as she wonders what I'll do to her, how far I'll go. It's addictive.

I strip off her panties and spread her knees, stroking her wetness while I slide a hand behind her neck, pulling her face closer to mine. I gaze into her eyes, watching them while I sink a finger into her. She's so tight I can hardly get a single finger in. I have to force it through her slick, clenched walls. Her lips fall open, her eyes widening, and she takes a long, shuddering breath, her hands clamping around the edge of the table.

That's right, baby girl. Obey, and you get to cum.

I pump my finger into her hot little hole, loosening her up. God, I can't wait to wreck this beautiful, perfect, untouched part of her. I want to feel every moment of her tearing open, feel my cock rip through the barrier and sink into her, taking something from her no one else ever will. I want to feel her cunt clutching me like a slick pink vice from every side while I bust deep inside her, where no one has ever been and no one else will ever be, leaving my claim in the deepest part of her.

"I want to see this tight cunt spread open and bared for me," I murmur, my mouth inches from hers. "With nothing covering it. I want to feel your soft skin against my cock before I break you open, not this." I grab a handful of her pubic hair and yank on it so hard she cries out.

"If I have to shave, then you should, too," she manages, her words coming out around panting breaths.

I smirk at that. "Trust me, I know how to keep myself groomed for fucking."

She tries to push me away, but I'm not done taking what's mine. Showing her that it's mine. I work a second finger against her opening, and she whimpers and tries to close her legs. I push them apart and twist my fingers together, working them both in at once. She sucks in an unsteady breath, squirming against me as I stretch her tight little virgin opening further than it's ever been. I push my fingers all the way in nice and slow, marveling at how fucking tight she is. I don't know if I'll ever be able to get my cock in.

My cock throbs so hard I think I'm going to cum in my pants like a fucking virgin just from fingering her. But she needs to know I'm the one in control here, and how can I show her I can control her if I can't even control myself?

I steady myself and then begin to move my fingers, drawing them out and thrusting them back into her hard and deep, making her gasp and shudder and jerk her hips as I plunder her slick entrance. Finally, I can't wait any longer.

"Fuck it," I say, shoving her back on the table. "I can't wait for you to be ready. Your dad will kill me for your lies, and I'm not going to die without fucking my wife."

She catches herself on her palms, then glances up at me with trepidation when she realizes she released the edge of the table. "No," she whispers. "That doesn't count. You pushed me."

I prowl forward, dipping my lips toward hers but stopping just before they touch. I squeeze her knees, holding them open as wide as they'll go, leaving her juicy cunt open for whatever I deliver. I brush my lips across hers. "I'm going to destroy this tight little cunt so thoroughly no one can ever wonder if your husband claimed his rights to it."

"Please," she whimpers. "I'll do whatever you want. I'll—I'll give you head. Anything you want. Just don't hurt me."

"Do you even know how to give head?" I ask, raising a brow at her.

"No," she admits, her eyes downcast. "But I can learn how. You can show me."

I lean close again, running my nose across hers gently, teasingly, while I ease my fingers back into her. I can't stop touching her, fucking her with my fingers. I want to fuck her in every hole with my tongue, my cock, my fingers. I want to hear her scream my name when she cums. "Tell me you don't want this," I murmur. "Tell me you don't want me to tear that virgin cunt in two. I'll turn your pink pussy red and fuck you in the pool of blood."

She shudders, but I feel her cunt throb around my fingers. She wants it, even if she can't admit it. "No," she whispers. "Please. You said dinner."

"Dinner's not over until we've had dessert," I tell her. I reach for one of the spoons, the ceramic utensil gleaming white under the kitchen lights. Slowly, I lick both sides of it clean, sucking it into my mouth. Eliza watches me, her face flushed, her eyes locked on my mouth.

I slide my fingers out of her and press the rounded end of the spoon against her cunt. She gasps when the wet ceramic touches her hot flesh, but I catch her knees when she tries to squirm away. I push them open again, my cock throbbing as I watch the smooth white instrument slide through her wetness. I push it against her opening, and she gasps, her thighs quivering as I put more and more pressure on the handle until it breaches her entrance and slides inside her.

A shudder goes through her, and heat ripples through me. I spread her open with my other hand, stroking around the swollen, pink bud of her clit while I begin to move the spoon, fucking her with the smooth instrument. She watches as if transfixed, her breath rapid as I slide it in and out of her cunt, slicking my thumb back and forth across her clit until she's letting out soft little cries with each stroke. At last, she drops her head back, her wild hair tumbling down her back as she lifts her hips in an invitation.

I'm tempted to push the spoon further, but I don't want anything to break through the barrier of her virginity but my cock. So I draw the spoon out, leaving Eliza panting and staring at me with disbelief and desperation. She was close, and she needs me to finish her off. There's only one thing I'd love more than to fuck her right here, right now, on the table with takeout soup containers around us.

"Only I can taste this cunt," I say. "Only ever me."

I slowly lift the spoon to my mouth and slide it between my lips. Eliza's expression goes from gaping indignation to a mixture of heated desire and embarrassment. Her cheeks pinken, but she can't take her eyes away. I lick the back of the spoon, tasting her on it, then turn it over and lick out the inside. By the time I set it down, I think she's going to launch herself off the table and wrap herself around me. I take her chin in my hand and pull it up, pressing my lips to hers before sliding my tongue into her mouth, letting her taste herself on it.

I draw back after a few seconds. "Know this, *piccola*," I say. "I control your pleasure. I can give it, and I can take it away. I tell you when it's enough. Tonight, you'll think about what you did. If you do better tomorrow, I'll let you finish."

twelve

Eliza

I stare up at King, trying to comprehend what he's saying. My brain feels foggy and slow to engage.

"Are you fucking kidding?" I ask, hating how breathless I am.

He pulls my phone from his pocket and sets it on the table. "Text your father and tell him you didn't mean that, and I'll finish what I started."

Then it snaps into place. He's trying to bribe me with orgasm.

And yeah, the one he gave me in Bora Bora was the best feeling I've ever had in my entire fucking life, but I'm not going to be controlled by lust and pleasure—at least not the kind he gives me.

DANGEROUS DEFIANCE

I pick up my phone and hop off the edge of the table, pushing past King. I'm painfully aware of the air against my bare skin, that I'm wearing nothing but a short skirt now. I spot my damp panties lying discarded on the floor, and shame burns through me. I save whatever dignity remains by stepping over them and walking away, ignoring them and the swollen ache waiting between my thighs.

"I'm going to meet Bianca for a drink," I call back over my shoulder before ducking into the bedroom.

I wish I could watch his reaction, see the shock on his infuriating face. His stupid rules and games won't stop me from doing what I want. He needs to know that.

I strip off my skirt and stand in front of the mirror. How dare he tell me to shave?

Still. I do look like a virgin, a teenager who's never had a man see her naked and therefore had no reason to shave. I'd look more like a worldly woman if I shaved it all off.

That must be what he's used to.

SELENA

The thought bothers me more than it should, just like it pissed me off when he said he kept himself ready for fucking. Who says that to his wife? How many women has he fucked? How many has he given the kind of pleasure he gave me, and more? He talks like a guy who has gotten his share of pussy. How many have his fingers been inside? His tongue? His cock? How many sluts have gotten down on their knees and worshipped that cock I've never even seen? I've only seen the outline straining against his pants, but other girls have seen it bare, have seen it "ready for fucking." Other girls have had it in their mouths, buried inside their core.

Jealousy burns through me, and I feel sick at the thought of those girls touching him, sucking him, spreading their legs for him, coming on his cock. The thought nauseates me, but it also makes the ache between my legs pulse stronger. I slide a hand down my belly, opening myself to the mirror. My slit is pink and shiny with arousal. I stroke my clit, imagining King's lips on it the way they caressed that spoon. I move my fingers around it, the way he did, until I find the rhythm and pressure he used that took me right to the edge. When I picture his cock pushing up into me, my core squeezes, and relief floods through me as I cum.

The moment I finish, regret floods in. I hurry away from the mirror, stepping into the closet to pick out something for tonight. Shame burns along my limbs, through my blood, in the satisfied pulse between my thighs. I won't think of him when I do that again. He doesn't deserve my undivided desire. Not when he's wanted, and given in to his desire for, probably dozens of women.

I slam the door shut on that thought, that ugly emotion. I don't care how many people he's fucked. It means nothing to me. And so does he.

When I emerge from the bedroom, the table is clean. King stands at the sink, washing the spoons. I bite my lip when I think of where one of them has been, how he used it. Watching him fuck me with it, watching it come out of me slick with my arousal, watching him suck the taste of me off it like it was the rarest delicacy...

Fine, I can admit it was fucking hot, even if I don't tell him. I can't deny the truth to myself, and besides, it kept him from touching me, which is always the goal.

He doesn't turn when I go to the door.

"I'll be home by morning," I say.

I want him to say something, though I don't know what. Maybe I'm expecting him to stop me. Maybe I even want him to. Not because I don't want to go, but because I want to force his hand. I want him to show weakness like I did, to put us back on even footing.

But he doesn't even look my way.

I wait a long minute before turning and walking out. I missed dinner with Bianca, but I call her as soon as my driver picks me up, bodyguard in tow.

"He's the absolute worst," I rant to Bianca after telling her the basics, leaving out the spooning incident and everything related.

"I can't believe he took your phone," she squeals through her laughter. "What is he, your dad?"

A flash of irritation hits me. I open my mouth and then close it again. I'm annoyed at her for talking shit about him, as if he's my family, someone only I can talk shit about. I'm even more irritated with myself for wanting to defend him. I force a laugh and pretend he's just some pathetic guy chasing us, like Tommy Fatone. "The sad thing is, I think he's trying to be."

At the bar, I have a margarita and dance, but something feels off. I just can't seem to get into it. After an hour, I find myself sitting at the bar, just tipsy enough to talk to the stranger beside me. He offered to buy me a drink, but I don't even want one.

"The thing is, I think I'm done going out clubbing," I say. "I just don't know what to do instead. Like, this is boring."

"So, let's go somewhere else," he says with a little smile.

I roll my eyes. "I'm serious. I want freedom, but what's the point, if I'm just going to be free to go dancing? I want to do something big, something important, like my mom did."

"What'd your mom do?"

"She's an actress."

"Anyone I've heard of?"

I shake my head and sip my water. I realize it sounds stupid when I say it like that. Why am I even trying to explain it to this stranger, anyway? He's not going to understand. He doesn't know what it's like to sign a contract that signs his whole life away, giving it into someone else's hands.

I could just go home. It's not admitting defeat exactly. It's doing what I want, which is freedom. Much to my irritation, I know that I can't go home so soon, though. To King, it will look like I want to be there with him, like I don't want this freedom I've fought so hard for. I want him to think I have a glamourous life that he can't touch, one worth fighting him to get. But as I look around, it all feels empty.

"This scene really is tired," the man says. "Want to go back to my place?"

"No," I say, giving him a dirty look. "I'm married."

He draws back and glances around. "Then why the fuck are you here?"

"Haven't you been listening to anything I say?" I ask, straightening on my chair.

"Well, yeah, but that's because I thought I'd be taking you home," he says. "Why am I here wasting my time with you if we're not hooking up later?"

I shake my head and push my glass away in disgust. "What, so I'm not worth talking to if I won't sleep with you? For all you know, I'm the most interesting person you've ever met."

He snorts. "You're not. And even if you were, it wouldn't matter if you're not giving it up. Trust me, there's not a guy in this place who cares what you have to say. We just pretend to listen until we get to the good stuff."

My mouth drops open in indignation. "You're a pig."

He shakes his head, pushes his glass away, and slides off the stool, disappearing into the crowd in moments. I sit there for a minute, confused by what just happened. I never go home with men, but they love buying me drinks and flirting.

It must be the ring on my finger.

Even when he's not with me, King is ruining everything.

No one here knows me or wants to know me. I'm not even sure my own husband would care what I have to say, and I'm damn sure none of the guys here do. Why would they? They're just here to make a connection, have a little fun and find someone to go home with.

Obviously I can do that. I'm not wild and free anymore. I'm tied down, married, for fuck's sake. Maybe I'm not being fair. That guy had a point. This club is a meat market, and I'm off the market. Why am I here?

If I can't assert my freedom this way anymore, though, what am I supposed to do? The point of freedom is to follow a passion. The point of life is passion. And if I don't have a passion for anything, I have nothing to fight for, which means I've been fighting my husband for nothing all along.

But that's not quite true. I've been fighting for freedom. For control of my life, my body. I'm terrified I'm already losing that battle. King does things to me that are beyond my control, things I crave even as I despise them, things that terrify and thrill me in equal measure. What terrifies me most, though, is that every day I come closer to forgetting why those things matter. Why I need freedom. Why I need control over myself. Why I need to keep my distance.

It's better to turn him down first, so he can't reject me. It's better to let him hurt my body than to let him hurt the parts inside me that are already so broken they can never be healed. That part of me would die altogether if it were finally exposed, the truth laid bare, and he was incapable of loving me then. And he would be.

Somehow, it's better to choose it for myself, to make sure he never loves me as I am now, without knowing. Because if he knew, he'd run screaming, demanding an annulment. And if there's one thing worse than knowing I'll never love someone because of what happened to me, it's knowing that no one could ever love me if they knew.

thirteen

King

Since Uncle Al decided I should report to Anthony about our honeymoon, I accompany him to *Jean-Jean* in the early afternoon on Friday, as arranged. No one else is in the place, as it's a sweet spot between lunch and dinner. A bored-looking college student stands behind the counter, waiting for customers. Uncle Al and I order and take our seats near the windows while two of his men take theirs outside at the table directly on the other side of the glass. They'll see anyone coming in, but we'll have privacy to talk to Anthony Pomponio, who chose the bistro as a meeting place.

We're halfway through our paninis before Uncle Al speaks. "I'm glad we got here before them," he says. "Gives us a minute to talk."

I nod, my throat tightening. "Oh yeah?"

"How you liking things?" he asks. "You doin' okay?"

"Yes, sir," I say. "Job's good."

"How you liking your partnership with my grandson?"

"Good."

Little Al is not my favorite person, but it could be a lot worse. I'm not going to complain to his grandfather, that's for damn sure.

Uncle Al nods, taking a bite before speaking again. "I know he's somethin' else. You kids… This generation." He breaks off and shakes his head, smiling ironically. "I sound like an old man now, don't I?"

"Nah, he is something else," I agree, and we both laugh.

I'm just starting to relax when he asks, "How's things with the wife?"

"Fine."

"Marriage is hard even for people already in love when they start out," he says, his watchful gaze on my face. "It can take a while to figure out your places, your roles, how you fit together."

I nod. I'm not used to talking about this kind of thing. The only time Dad talked to me about women was when he needed me to seduce one. But Uncle Al is the closest thing to a confidant I have now, and he's asking me to open up. Truth is, I've never a long-term relationship, and I'm not sure how to handle one with a woman like Eliza. I could use some advice from someone who's been successfully married.

"It's been tough," I admit. "Eliza stays up half the night and sleeps half the day, and I'm working all day. When I come home, she's getting ready to go meet her friends or they're all at our place when I just want to relax. Once we get used to each other's schedule, it'll be easier."

Al cocks a brow and takes a drink of his coffee. "She's not a kid or a free woman anymore. It's not outta line to expect her to act like your wife."

"I know," I say. "She's had some hard times, and she blames me. Our family, anyway."

He shakes his head. "Her brother dying, her mother running off. Can't be easy."

"Yeah," I say. "Death's a bitch."

"That's right," Al agrees. "You got some sad history in common."

"I guess so," I say, though mine seems trivial in comparison to hers. My mother didn't leave us, at least not in the physical sense. I stayed with her for a few weeks when I came back to New York, while I was looking for a place of my own. She lives in our home, and we're always welcome. We visit on holidays. She came to the wedding. And my sister wasn't murdered.

"How you doing with that?" Al asks, his eyes serious. "Your ma says you took Crystal's disappearance pretty hard. It's only been a few months. You okay?"

I shrug, avoiding his eyes. "Like you said, it's never easy."

"You talk to Eliza about that?"

"No." It's not something I want to dwell on, and she has enough ammunition. The last thing I need is for her to know that I got my own sister killed. That Dad entrusted me to watch out for her, and I didn't. I left her with her boyfriend. I didn't want to, but I told myself he'd look after her. But it wasn't his job to watch out for her. It was my job.

I failed.

And she died.

It's as simple as that.

Al seems to get that I don't want to talk about that anymore. He wads up his napkin and drops it on the plate before reaching for his coffee. "You settling in since you got home?" he asks. "How's she like the new place?"

I shrug. "To be honest, she hasn't mentioned it. We don't spend much time together."

Al cocks a brow and takes a drink of his coffee. Before he can answer, I see one of Al's guys slump over the table outside.

I don't think. I just act.

DANGEROUS DEFIANCE

I dive across the table, tackling Al and crashing to the floor with him. At the same moment, the sheet of glass beside the booth fractures into a million pieces, raining down over the table and the floor around us. Al curses and rolls away, leaping to his feet with his gun already in his hand before I can even scramble up. The dude may be past fifty, but he's still fit as fuck and quick on the draw.

He fires as a figure dressed in all black jumps through the window onto our table, a ski mask pulled over his face and a gun with a silencer aimed at us. Outside, I can see two figures on the ground, and the remaining Valenti man aiming to fire again. The masked guy on the table crashes to the floor, and I yank my gun from my belt and release the safety, aiming at the window as two more men duck into view, both of them with guns raised. I pull the trigger without thought, without hesitation, and one of the men falls. A bullet ricochets off a nearby table and buries itself in my thigh, but I hardly feel it. Steadying the gun with one hand, I turn it on the other guy, but he falls before I can squeeze the trigger.

Al pivots toward the edge of the building, where the guys appeared from. We wait, our guns cocked and ready. The only sound is the gurgle from one of the bodies on the floor as he tries to speak. I swing my gun in his direction and squeeze the trigger, putting a bullet in his head before turning back to the corner. This time, we see the guy edging around the side of the building. I fire, but he ducks back, and I can't tell if I hit him.

Al leaps up onto his seat, takes one step on the table, and is out the window in another. I glance back toward the counter. There's no trace of the guy working there, which means he's smart enough to have ducked behind the counter or gotten the fuck out through a back door when shit started going down. That, or he knew ahead of time.

I don't have time for maybes, though. Leaping onto the table, I propel myself through the window and land in a crouch. Outside, I follow Al around the corner. I scan the area, on full alert.

Al jerks his head in the direction of a black SUV parked on a side street. He creeps toward it, gun at the ready. I follow, a few steps behind him. We're almost to the vehicle when I hear the scuff of a shoe on pavement. I spin and see a man with his hands up, wearing plain clothes instead of the black disguises the others wore.

"Don't shoot," he says. "I ain't involved. I—I got a family. I'm just going to my car."

I almost drop my weapon, but then I see the pile of black clothes discarded behind him in the little nook he stepped out of. In the instant it takes me to glance there and back again, he snatches a gun from his belt. I squeeze the trigger instinctively, without taking the time to aim correctly. The man grunts as the bullet buries itself in his belly. Two gunshots ring out at the same moment. A bullet grazes my shoulder, and one makes a hole right in the center of his forehead, so clean and crisp it almost looks fake. He crumples to the ground, and I turn to see Al behind me.

He grabs my arm and hustles me down the street and into his car. We sit there for a minute, both of us breathing hard and cursing plenty.

"What the fuck was that?" I ask after a minute.

Al claps a hand on my shoulder. "That was your first shootout, son."

I start laughing like a fucking idiot, and I know Al's going think I'm unfit for the Life and put a bullet between my eyes like I've got a fucking bull's eye painted on my forehead, but I can't stop even when I try. Al looks at me for a second, and then he throws his head back and starts laughing, too. We just sit in his SUV letting out big guffawing belly laughs that make us look like we're crying like a couple of pussies.

Finally, Al wipes his eyes and shakes his head. "You know, I fucking needed that right now, King," he says, turning on the car and lowering the visor against the afternoon sun. "You're a good kid."

"You get hit?" I ask.

Al's got blood splattered all over him, but he shakes his head. "Not a scratch."

I wipe my face, then pull off my shirt to wrap my arm where I got hit. My thigh hurts like the devil, but it doesn't seem to be losing much blood. I use my tie to secure my shirt in place around my shoulder, then press my palm down on my thigh, gritting out curses until I get used to the pressure.

"How bad's that one?" Al asks.

"Didn't even feel it," I admit. The adrenaline was too much. The pain's only now setting in.

We drive in silence for a minute, back toward home. My stomach knots up, and I glance at Al from the corner of my eye. "Was that a set-up?"

"Had to be," he says. "It isn't like Anthony to be so sloppy, sending guys in broad daylight. He's making a statement."

"Fuck," I say, clenching my hand around the door handle. This is my fault. Eliza told him I was going to kill her, that by the time we met at *Jean-Jean*, it would be too late. I should have done more than fuck her with a spoon. She's trying to end my life. I underestimated just how dangerous she is.

I shouldn't say anything, it will spell my doom, but Al should know why. I have to know for sure before I tell him, though. "How fast can you get me home?"

Al grimaces. "Not fast enough, kid. If he went after us, the deal is off. He won't have made a move without getting his daughter out first. If he did, she'd be left to answer for it."

"She told him I wasn't good to her," I admit quietly. "That must be why they attacked."

Uncle Al doesn't say anything for a long minute. He's probably deciding whether to dump me in the river while we're out.

"You told her about this meeting?" he asks at last. "The details?"

"Yeah. I had her call her father."

"Anyone else?"

"No."

The Life is my life now. I don't have friends here, or a girlfriend, or anyone to tell besides Eliza. Obviously that was enough.

"They might not have known you were coming," Al says. "They could have been planning it before we decided to involve you. They're not going to pass up a chance to knock down one of the families if they can get me alone."

"Maybe." He's definitely a more desirable target than me. As Eliza likes to remind me, I'm no one. But I did tell her we were meeting today. Her father told her where.

Or maybe it wasn't him at all. He gave her to me, after all. He entrusted me to take care of her, and he didn't seem convinced by her pleas the other day. It's not like the mafia to get involved in private affairs between a husband and wife, even if it's a don's daughter.

If it wasn't him, does she hate me enough to have set this up herself? I thought we were past that, but maybe she was faking it. I've seen how good an actor she is. And she loves to talk about her obsession with freedom. What better way to attain it than to get rid of the one person she perceives as an obstacle?

"So, Eliza knew we were meeting," I say. "Some of the other Pomponios obviously knew. On our side, there's the two of us, your consigliere, and Little Al."

My mind circles back to my "innocent" little wife, who I put on the Pomponio's side without even thinking.

Did she try to fucking kill me? I shouldn't be surprised. Rage swells inside my chest, closing off everything else, even the pain throbbing in my shoulder. If she did this…

This week, the house was a fucking disaster of dirty dishes and takeout boxes and wine bottles from her friends coming over and hanging out all day. When I told her to clean up after herself or hire a maid, she played dumb and said, "I don't know how to hire a maid."

I know she's not dumb. She may not know how to hire a maid, but I'd bet she knows how to hire hitmen.

"It had to be Eliza," I say quietly.

"Look, kid," Al says as we approach my place. "Anthony wouldn't do something like this just because his daughter complained. If you were hurting her, he'd hurt you. But he wouldn't come after both of us like that—not for a personal matter. This has business written all over it."

"I'll call home," I say. After confirming with her bodyguard that she's home with her friends like usual and not off with the Pomponios waiting to hear if their assassination plot worked, I hang up. Eliza hasn't gone out since this morning when she visited the salon. That puts my mind at ease a bit, and I relay the news to Uncle Al.

"It don't look good," he says. "The Pomponios don't show up, and we get ambushed? It's got all the makings of a setup. I just don't know yet, kid. Why come after us, knowing the war would be back on? And why leave Eliza with you?"

"To throw us off," I say. "To make us think it wasn't them."

"I don't see the benefit," Al says, frowning at the road ahead.

"Who benefits from our families going back to war?" I ask, turning to him.

He nods slowly, his eyes narrowing as he thinks through the possibilities. "One of the other families. Luciani's messy like this."

I nod, hoping it's that and not my father-in-law, even though I don't believe it. Anthony set up the meeting, and then he tried to kill us. Is he so confident that I'd be dead after the attack that he didn't bother getting his daughter out?

Of course he is. I'm the new kid, green as fuck, with no experience. What chance do I have of making it out alive when a half dozen seasoned killers ambush us?

Uncle Al pulls up to my building and scans the area before stopping. "Let me worry about this," he says. "You take care of that shoulder and leg. Have your wife take a look at them. I know a man has his pride, but don't be too proud to let her take care of you when you need it. It might help things between you."

I don't think looking weak in front of Eliza, being at her mercy, is going to make things better, but I nod and thank him before reaching for the door handle.

"Oh, and King?" Al says, putting a hand on my good shoulder.

I turn back.

"Thanks," he said. "You saved my life back there. I won't forget that."

"I just did what anyone would do," I say before climbing out of the car.

As much as I'd like to take the credit, I'm no hero. I acted on instinct alone. And in the end, when there was one guy left, I shot too soon. I was sloppy the whole time. But it's nice of Al not to mention that, to focus on the one thing I did right, even if it's not entirely true. I pushed him to the floor when the first shot came, but that doesn't mean it would have killed him. Hell, if it was Eliza's doing, the shooter wasn't even aiming for him.

I ask the doorman for a report, since he's Al's man, and thinking my wife is trying to kill me has me a little paranoid. Her bodyguard came with her. He's on my payroll now, but he might retain ties and loyalties to the Pomponios. After hearing the doorman confirm the details Eliza's bodyguard already gave, I head upstairs.

I walk into the usual circus. The kitchen looks like the aftermath of a party. The blender sits half full of red slush. Pink liquid dribbles down the cabinets in front of it. Pools of melted ice dot the floor. Bags of frozen fruit sit melting on the counter, along with cups sweating their condensation, snack bags left open, and other detritus of Eliza's hedonism left scattered across every surface. Five or six girls sit around the living room drinking colorful slushie drinks, along with a new addition to the endless party—two guys.

"What the fuck are they doing here?" I demand, glaring at Eliza.

One of her girlfriends giggles, covering her mouth with the rim of her drink to disguise it.

"Damn," says Bianca Luciani, one of the other mafia princesses. She elbows Eliza and lowers her voice, but I can still hear her when she murmurs to my wife, "Remind me why you not hittin' that?"

Her eyes remain on me as she speaks, and suddenly, I'm so fucking done with all this shit. I don't know what Eliza is telling them, but obviously more than they have any business knowing. And it's a fucking mystery to me, too. Why am I not fucking my wife again? Obviously her friends all think I'm plenty fuckable.

Why did I get stuck with the frigid bitch who wants to kill me? The one who'd rather spend the afternoon making a disaster of our house than hiring a fucking maid to clean up after her. She goes out shopping and does her nails and sees shows and gossips and has lunches, and she can't even find time to make one fucking phone call.

I walk in and snatch the drink out of Eliza's hand. Glaring down at her, I speak to the rest of the room.

"Get the fuck out," I say, my voice quiet but leaving no room for argument.

Bianca giggles again. "Is he serious?" she asks Eliza, as if I'm not standing right here.

Eliza rolls her eyes. "I told you. I might as well have married an eighty-year-old. He's like a stuffy old man who ruins all the fun."

"Get out," I say between clenched teeth.

"Oh, relax," Eliza says. "We're going."

"You're not going anywhere," I say, my eyes burning into hers. "They are."

"O-kay," says one of her friends, letting out a nervous giggle. She picks up her bag and edges toward the door. "I'll just be going…"

Eliza glances at my shoulder, where my shirt is tied, and then back at my face before heaving a burdened sigh. "You really need me for that? It doesn't look too bad."

"Get them out of my house," I growl. "Or don't. Let them watch. I don't care. But you've got some explaining to do, and you're not leaving until I get the answers I'm looking for."

Her chin rises in that defiant little brat expression, but I only stand over her, my gaze boring into hers, my body trembling with rage. Is this the party she threw in celebration of getting rid of me? Did she throw me a wake before I'm even in the fucking ground?

When I don't flinch, she sighs. "You guys go on. I'll meet you later."

"Don't fucking count on it," I say, grabbing one of the guys as he starts to rise. I recognize him as the guy Eliza was sleeping on after our wedding. "You got a lot of balls showing your face here."

"We're just friends," he says, holding up both hands.

"Make other friends," I say, shoving him roughly toward the door. "If I see you in my house again, or anywhere near my wife, you won't have a dick left to fuck her with when you try."

"King," Eliza snaps as I shove her little boy toy out the door. "Don't threaten my friends."

I slam the door behind them, lock it, and turn back to her. "Then don't have friends who want to fuck you."

"Tommy doesn't—"

Before she can finish, I grab her arm and spin her around, pinning her to the door. I wrap a hand around her throat, pushing her head back against the door. "Now you're going to answer my questions about what happened today."

Her eyes widen, and I relish the real fear I see written on her face. "I don't know what you're talking about."

"I think you do," I say, leaning in until our noses almost touch. "Now I'm giving you one more chance to tell the truth, you little liar. What did you do?"

fourteen

Eliza

"I didn't do anything," I swear to King. "I don't even know what you're talking about."

"Bullshit," he growls, his fingers tightening around my throat. I've never seen him this angry, too angry to even toy with. "What did you do?"

"I don't know," I say again.

"Your father told you where we were meeting," he says. "You knew we'd be there. Did you hire those thugs to shoot us? Or was that his doing?"

My mouth drops open in shock. "What?" I whisper. "No. I didn't—it wasn't us. Whatever happened, we didn't do it."

"If it wasn't him, then who was it?" he asks. "Who did you tell?"

"No one," I say, shaking my head. I did tell Bianca, but she wouldn't do that. We have a love-hate relationship, sure, but things have been good between us for a while. Surely she wouldn't try to kill my husband just because she's jealous that I got someone hot and young and her family won't even tell her who she's going to marry.

King's thumbs tighten painfully on my throat, and I suddenly feel lightheaded.

"My family wouldn't do that," I manage. "We made peace."

"Until you told your father I was going to kill you, so he tried to kill me."

I stare at him, unable to comprehend. Someone shot him, and I should be used to that, living the life I do. I *am* used to it. But this is my husband. He could have died. And he was never anything but someone to fuck with, toy with. I don't know the first thing about him. I never tried. Our marriage has been nothing but a game to me.

"I'm sorry," I whisper at last. "I didn't think he'd do anything. I mean, I don't think he did. But…"

King stares into my eyes with so much hatred it makes me recoil. "But his men fucking shot me," he says. "I had to fucking kill someone today, Eliza. Do you know what that feels like? Do you think I like doing this shit?"

"No," I whisper.

"I do it because I'm your fucking husband, and that's what's expected of me. It's my fucking job."

I nod mutely, not daring to even speak. His fury makes me tremble all the way to my core. He vibrates with it, with rage and danger and a force I can't begin to fight.

"The last thing I want to do when I come home from work is deal with this shit," he says. "I don't want to see your friends around here, or your boyfriend, or anyone else. This is *my* house, Eliza. Until you do some work for it, it's not your house. You just live here. Because I let you. And you can't even respect me enough to clean up your shit or hire a fucking maid to do it."

"I'll hire a maid."

"You have one job as my wife," he says slowly, his eyes burning into mine. "Your job is to spread your legs and let me relieve some tension, and you can't even do that. I thought you were a prize, Eliza, but you're less than worthless."

I shove at his chest, his words hitting me somewhere too close to home, too close to pain. He doesn't move, even when I push him as hard as I can. His fingers only tighten. But I'm done being scared.

"I'm not the one who's worthless," I shoot back. "And I can spread my legs and relieve my own tension. You should try it. Or get a whore and get all the diseases your dick can carry. I don't care because it'll never be inside me. You might think this sucks, but at least you've had your whores. You can fuck a different girl every night, and no one will blink. I'll die a fucking virgin."

He smirks, but it's a cruel, cold expression. "Don't count on it."

I swallow hard, past an ache that's growing in my throat. "You're the one who likes to brag about all the women you've fucked. So go fuck one. I'm sure it'll be easy to find one. Get yourself a little *cumare* like all the men do. I don't care. I don't want you. I'd rather die a virgin than fuck the most vile man on earth."

"I don't want to fuck a *cumare*," he growls. "I want to fuck my wife."

We stare at each other a moment, both of us breathing hard. He knows I want him. He's made me show him; he's made me cum. But he's never showed me the same. I could feel it when he pressed up against me, could feel that hardness that made my throat tighten and butterflies tremble in my belly, but I didn't think he'd ever say it after I turned him down on our honeymoon. I thought I'd feel more triumphant if he ever admitted it, but all I feel is scared. His eyes burn with something more than anger, and I know he's going to take what he wants. There's nothing I can do to stop him.

"What are you going to do to me?" I whisper at last. I know what happens to people who rat out their family. And as much as I like to think otherwise, King is my family now. If he wants to cut out my tongue for this, it wouldn't be out of line. My father can't protect me anymore. That's what he's been telling me. I belong to King now.

"I'm not going to do anything to you, *carina mia*," he purrs, stroking my throat gently with his thumbs. "You're going to do something for me."

I swallow hard. "What?"

"You're going to get down on your knees and wrap those pretty lips around my cock and suck me until I cum down this lovely throat. And you're going to remember what that mouth is for next time you open it."

I nod mutely and sink down on shaking legs. It could be so much worse.

King chuckles. "Not here, *piccola*."

He takes my arm and leads me into the bedroom, closing the door behind us. My whole body starts shaking, as if I wasn't at his mercy before, as if we were less alone when we weren't in a bedroom.

He leads me over to the closet, stopping when I'm right in front of the mirrored closet doors. He stands behind me, my nervous gaze meeting his cold stare in the mirror.

"Take off your clothes," he says, his voice hard and emotionless.

I knew this day was coming, that he'd eventually take what was his, but that doesn't make it any less terrifying. I nod and reach for the button on my jeans, but King holds up a hand to stop me. He steps back, stopping at the foot of the bed to watch me undress.

"Your shirt first," he says.

I swallow hard, the aftertaste of alcohol sour on my tongue. Then I turn to face him, reach for the hem of my shirt, and peel it off over my head, letting the soft fabric flutter to the floor at my feet. King's eyes drop to my chest, his gaze locked on my breasts as I unhook the white bra he demanded I buy. I let it drop to the floor on top of my shirt. The heat in his gaze makes my core tremble, and I find my body responding to the hunger in his eyes even as I fear the consequences.

My fingers tremble as I undo the button on my jeans and slide the zipper down. I watch him, biting my lip, wanting... Something. Some reaction. I feel so alone standing halfway across the room from him, my bare skin on display while he's still in his clothes, a pair of black dress slacks and a white undershirt stained with blood. He holds his dress shirt on his shoulder, and I can see blood soaking through that as well.

I gulp, my gaze roaming over the outline of his sculpted shoulder muscles, the hint of his washboard abs I can see through the thin fabric of his undershirt, the pebbles of his nipples in his strong pecs. His arms are beautiful, brown and strong, the muscles standing out even when he doesn't tense, lined with thick veins. He's so young that he doesn't usually intimidate me. But with blood on him, he looks like what he is.

Dangerous. Deadly. A killer.

A chill goes through me, and my bare nipples tighten painfully.

"Are you wet?" he asks.

I shake my head.

"Touch yourself," he orders.

"What?"

"You said you like to spread your legs for yourself," he says. "I don't know if you're lying to piss me off, or if you're really taking what's mine. I want to see you do it, if you're really stupid enough to touch that cunt after I told you no one but me was allowed that privilege."

"That includes me?" I ask incredulously. "I can't touch my own body?"

"You can touch your body," he says. "Except there. Your cunt is mine alone. If it needs attention, I will touch it, and taste it, and fuck it. That's my job as your husband. Not anyone else's, and not yours."

"It's my body," I protest. "I don't tell you when to jerk off."

"Fine, I won't jerk off," he says, a cruel smirk on his perfect lips. "When my cock needs attention, you'll provide it. Better?"

"That's not what I meant."

"It's only fair," he says, still smirking. "Now, let me see how you've been touching what's mine."

His words send a little erotic thrill through me. I gulp again, swallowing the bratty words that threaten to come out. Instead, I obey, sliding my hand into my jeans on top of my underwear. I'm wearing underwear that matches the bra he told me to buy, white cotton ones with just a little red rose on the front. Through them, I can feel how deliciously smooth my skin feels after getting my hair lasered off.

A tremor goes through me when I imagine him seeing what I did for the first time.

"Go on," he says.

I begin to move my fingers, touching myself the way I did the other day. He was right. It feels so much better without anything in the way, my skin smooth and bare. I watch him watching me, his dark eyes riveted on my hand as it moves. The heat of his gaze burns into me, shivering along my arms, settling into an ache between my thighs.

I can feel my panties getting damp, and then my gaze moves down his body again, and they get wetter. This time, I let my eyes move further, over his belt to the long, thick ridge in his pants. My clit throbs, and suddenly, my panties are soaked, and I have to swallow the saliva pooling in my mouth at the thought of what he said he was going to do to me.

"Put a finger inside your panties," King says, his voice husky.

I jerk my eyes from his pants, my cheeks flushing with shame. Slowly, I draw aside my panties and touch my bare skin, the lips already slick with my wetness. I suck in a breath, my knees squeezing together, my clit throbbing when my fingers swipes across it.

King's eyes are blazing now. "Tell me what it feels like."

"Wet," I breathe.

"Does it feel good?"

"Yes." I whisper the word, my voice trembling with shame as I stroke faster, wanting to stop, to hide this most intimate act from him. At the same time, I know that doing this in front of him is what makes it feel so good, so dirty.

"Good," he says. "I want you to remember exactly what it feels like to know I'm watching, because from now on, you will only touch yourself with my permission."

His commands are sharp and direct, and feeling like I have no choice, like I'm utterly at his mercy, is humiliatingly addictive. I rock my hips, panting for relief, sliding my finger deeper into my slit.

"That's enough," he says, the hard edge in his words cutting through the fog of arousal. I don't want to stop. But he's unpredictable when he's angry, and I don't want to push him right now. Frustration makes me nearly cry out as I draw my hand from my jeans, leaving the heavy pressure of arousal thick between my thighs, needing to be fulfilled.

"Now take off your jeans."

I hook my fingers into the waistband, easing them down over my hips. King's eyes drink in my hips, his gaze dipping between them with a heavy stroke that's nearly tangible. I bend to pull off my jeans, my cheeks heating when I realize he can see that the white fabric of my panties is soaked through, clinging to my bare skin.

I wait for him to comment, to praise me for getting rid of the hair. I realize how much I was craving his approval when he doesn't give it.

"Turn around," he orders.

I turn to face the mirror, but I can't meet my own eyes. I shouldn't like this. I shouldn't be turned on by his command over me, by the fact that he treats me like a possession, a child, a plaything to use and bend to his will. I should hate it.

"Take them off," he says.

My fingers tremble, and my shame burns even hotter as I bend to slide my panties over my thighs, knowing he's watching me bend over, seeing everything, seeing exactly how wet I am.

When I straighten, a gasp escapes my lips. King is standing right behind me, his dark eyes an inferno as they meet mine in the mirror. He slides his arms around me, one of them across my breasts, gripping me firmly to him. His shoulder wound is shallow, a long streak across his deltoid that cuts into the muscle, the skin around it purplish as blood pools under it. As if he's forgotten his injury, King takes my nipple between his fingers and begins to squeeze as his other hand dips between my slick thighs. "If you want to cum, I'll make you cum so hard your eyes bleed," he says, spreading my outer lips to expose the pink, wet flesh inside. "Is that what you need, *piccola?*"

He gives my nipple a squeeze, and my clit throbs visibly. He chuckles and tightens his grip on my nipple until it's all I can do not to gasp out loud. I can only manage the slightest shake of my head at his rough words, so incongruous with the way his middle finger slowly, sensually caressing my swollen clit. Slippery wetness coats his fingers, and he presses his hips against mine, letting me feel how hard he is. The threat of his cock makes my knees tremble and my core clench.

I watch in the mirror, transfixed by his movements, every soft touch a taunt, every gentle stroke carrying the threat of violence as he crushes my nipple with agonizing strength. I can't imagine the pain he's in as blood begins to leak down his arm, but it's me who finally breaks. Even as my hips rock against his hand, trying to get there before I beg for mercy, his torment of my nipple reminds me this is no game to him.

Finally, I can't take it, and pain overtakes pleasure. "Stop," I gasp, going up on tiptoes, as if that will break his punishing grip on my poor, bruised nipple. "Please, King."

He drops his hands from me, sliding one up and under my hair, gripping it and spinning me toward him in one motion. He bears down, forcing me to my knees.

"Now you'll suck my cock," he says. "Take your time. Do it nice and slow. I want to feel that mouth for a good long time. You'd do well to get used to this position, because you'll be here a lot from now on."

I stare at the ridge in his slacks, swallowing hard. My mouth waters, and I feel the thick pressure between my legs heighten at the thought of taking it out of his pants, seeing it for the first time. Touching it. Tasting his skin.

I reach up with trembling fingers, but King pulls my hair, drawing my head back until I'm looking up at him. "Don't even think about trying anything funny, my little wife," he says. "If you want to keep your teeth, you'll keep them off me. Understood?"

DANGEROUS DEFIANCE

I gulp, my heart leaping into my throat. What made me think I could outwit or outmaneuver or even escape this man? The moment he slid that ring on my finger, he might as well have clamped a bear trap closed on my foot. And this is just the inevitable conclusion, the culmination of all my bratty behavior.

I knew this was coming if I kept going, but I did it anyway. I knew he'd put his foot down, that he'd lay down the law and force me to do his bidding. Maybe he was right on our honeymoon. Maybe I always wanted him to. Maybe that's why I didn't fight harder tonight, why I don't stand up and walk out of the room right now. Yes, I'm scared of what he'd do. But part of me wants to know, even now, if I could push him further, if I could get him to do more.

When I reach up and unbutton his pants, I feel my heart racing with not just fear but anticipation. I slowly ease down the zipper while King stands over me, tall and proud, looking down at me like I'm a whore, a servant whose only job is to bring him pleasure. And I want to.

SELENA

I want the shame that burns in my cheeks, the overwhelming thudding in my chest that makes me lightheaded, the ache between my thighs. I reach into his pants, my fingers shaking, tentative. I don't know how to do this. All I know is that I have to be careful, to make it good. As ridiculous as it is, I want to be good. I don't even want to do this, and yet, I want him to think I'm good. Which is ridiculous, since I've never done it before. But no one wants to be bad at *this*.

I shift on my knees and glance up at him. He's watching me, but I can't read his expression. I can't tell if he's still angry, if this is still a punishment. I only know it's a punishment I deserve, one I worked hard to earn.

I take a deep breath and run a finger along the ridge of his erection, tracing the outline of it through his boxers. I gulp, suddenly feeling lightheaded with terror. His cock is hard and thick, and as I follow it down to the base, it seems to go on forever.

My throat constricts, and I start to rise, but King's fingers are still gripping my hair, and he won't allow it. "What's the problem?" he growls.

"I—I can't," I admit, my eyes aching with unshed tears. "It's too big."

"You'll get used to it," King says, of course having no mercy for me, for the fears of a dumb virgin.

I lower my face so he won't see, blinking back the tears that blur my vision. Without another word of protest, I pull his cock free of his boxers. Biting my lip, I stifle a gasp. I've never seen one in real life, never touched one. I've only seen the ones in porn clips Lizzie Salvatore found on the internet and sent when I admitted that. In person, it looks huge. All I can think is, how the hell is this enormous thing going to fit inside my tiny opening?

I'm grateful he's only asking for my mouth. I lean forward, sliding the thick head in. It throbs against my trembling lips, as hot as an animal and just as savage. Tears blur my eyes as I push it further back, trying to remember all the things Lizzie told me about sucking dick. I run my tongue over the head, marveling at how soft his skin is, softer than I imagined it would be. Something warm and salty spreads over my tongue, and I start to draw back, wondering if he's already about to cum.

"Go on, *carina*," he says, his voice low and husky, his hand cradling the back of my head instead of gripping my hair now. "Just like that."

I glance up at King and find his eyes fixed on me with such heat, such lust, it makes my core quiver. My gaze moves down the sculpted, solid muscle of his lean body, down to the V of muscle that leads to where my mouth is. Veins bulge in the skin above his cock, rough and masculine despite his impeccable grooming.

I push away a sharp stab of jealousy when I see how neatly he's kept himself trimmed. Who is he keeping himself fixed up for? We've been married a month, engaged for six before that. Of course he hasn't been celibate all that time. I hate that I even care, that I wonder if he's been with women since he told me he wouldn't. But I told him to take a mistress, and I can't expect him to wait forever just because I'm fucked up.

I focus on the task at hand, shoving all other thoughts away. His hair is trimmed short, but just enough not to be prickly. It's soft against my hand as I grip his cock, sliding it deeper into my mouth, feeling the delicious way my mouth stretches to fit him. He gives a little moan, stroking my hair, and pleasure coils through me. I'm doing a good job.

And as I continue, I feel heat pulsing inside me when another little burst of salty liquid coats my tongue. Now that I've stopped fighting it, accepted that it's happening and I can't stop it, I let myself go. I let myself enjoy the impressive size of my husband, of my first cock. I want to explore it. My mouth waters as I lick and suck, running my tongue around it like an ice cream cone, sucking it deep into my throat, kissing the tip and along the length of his shaft.

When my jaw tires, I sit back on my heels. "I don't think I can do more," I admit.

King looks down at me with cold eyes. "Did you cum?"

"No."

"When you touched yourself, did you cum?"

"Yeah, but…"

"If you can make yourself cum, you can make me cum."

"I don't think that's how it works," I mutter.

King's eyes rake over my naked body, and I shiver. "I make you cum," he says. "No one else. Not even you. I told you that, and you disobeyed me. So now you'll make me cum. If you can't do it with your mouth, then do it with your cunt."

I shake my head, my heart racing. "No, I'll try again."

He takes my hair in his hand again, gripping the rope of dark strands behind me. "On your hands and knees," he says, his voice hard. "I want to watch your cunt in the mirror while I fuck your mouth."

I balk at the obscenity of his words, but he drags down on my hair, and I have to drop to the floor as he asked. He shifts us so he can watch me in the mirror, then lowers his cock to my mouth.

"Remember what I said," he warns. "I'd hate for you to lose those pretty white teeth."

Without waiting for an answer, he thrusts deep into my mouth. His cock hits my throat and I gag, tears springing to my eyes. "Relax your throat," he orders. "I'm going to be fucking it for a while."

He drives into my throat again, holding my hair to keep control of my head as he continues to fuck my mouth hard and deep, plundering my aching throat with each punishing thrust. I'm too scared to choke for fear that he'll punch out my teeth, so I focus on relaxing my throat even as tears course down my cheeks and his cock slams into my throat again and again, using my mouth with no regard for my comfort.

At last, his grip tightens painfully on my hair, making a muffled whine escape my tortured throat. "Open your knees and spread your cunt for me," he growls, his voice coming through labored breaths.

I do as he says, all fight gone from me. I just want it to be over.

"Put a finger in," he says a minute later.

I slide a finger through my wetness and work it into my entrance. King lets out a guttural grunt, and warm liquid hits the back of my throat, shooting down it until I choke, my whole body constricting. King jerks out, yanking my head back and shooting the rest of his load all over my face. I choke out a gasp as sticky, hot cum runs down my face, mixing with my tears. I see blood on his hand, and for a second, I think it's from my throat. It hurts enough for me to believe it. But then I see the blood has trickled all the way down his arm onto his hand from his shoulder.

"Clean that up," King says, still holding my hair. He pulls my face to his groin, pushing his wet cock against my cheek. It's still hard, slick with cum and spit, and I want to bite the whole fucking thing off, but I'm too scared to even try. My face burns with humiliation and hatred as I kneel up and begin to lick him clean. I run my tongue along the vein on the bottom of his shaft, over the soft skin, the oozing tip.

"All of it," he says, pressing my nose into the soft carpet of short pubic hair at the base of his cock. I run my tongue over it, onto the bit of white cream dribbling onto his full balls. At last, he pulls me back, releases my hair, and pulls up his pants. I sink down from kneeling to sitting on my heels, bracing my hands against the floor and letting my hair fall forward while I try to catch my breath. I'm shaking uncontrollably, but King doesn't give me time to recover. He hooks his hands under my arms, pulling me to my feet and then scooping me up into his arms like a conquering groom. He lays be down on the bed gently, but terror reams through me. I tense, ready to fight, but he only pulls the blankets over me, leans down, and kisses my forehead tenderly.

"Don't worry," he says, stroking my hair behind my ear. "You'll get better with practice."

fifteen

Eliza

I'm going to kill him. I'm going to fucking murder him. I bury my face in the pillow and bite down as hard as I can so I won't scream, but I picture his dick while I do it. I didn't plot to murder him today, but now I want to.

A shooting wouldn't be horrible enough for him, though. He deserves torture.

Five minutes later, just as I've nearly cried myself empty of the humiliation and rage inside me, the door opens, and King appears again. He's holding a cup of tea on a saucer like he's the fucking Prince of England and not a sadistic bastard. He sits on the edge of the bed and sets the saucer down on the nightstand. "For your throat," he says.

"Oh, now you fucking care," I snap.

He smiles a little and hands me the cup. I swipe angrily at my face and slump back on the pillows, accepting the cup in defeat. Somehow, this is worse than him crushing my defiance. Offering me comfort afterwards is a slap in the face.

It does feel good on my bruised, sore throat though.

King kicks off his shoes and sets them under the bed neatly before swinging his legs up and settling on the other side of the mattress. He crosses his arms over his chest, and I see that he taped a bandage on his shoulder while he was in the other room. Blood is already soaking through.

"You know that's not going to stop bleeding until you stitch it up," I tell him, staring sullenly ahead so I don't have to look at his obscenely beautiful face. It's not fair that a monster can hide behind a face like that.

He shrugs. "It might take longer, but eventually it'll heal."

"You don't know how to sew it up, do you?" I ask.

"I'm righthanded," he says, flexing the hand on the side with his wounded shoulder.

"I know how," I say smugly. It's nice to have the upper hand for once, even if I just debased myself for him. For once, I know more than him, can do more than him. And he can't do shit about it.

"How would you know?" he asks.

I shrug. "I just do."

"How?"

"Maybe if you stop being a stubborn asshole and ask for help, I'll take care of it for you," I say, glancing over at him. As sick as it is, I want him to see that I'm good at something, to admire how skilled I am at removing bullets. I want him to see that I'm not some simpering little obedient wife, that I'm tough, too.

King studies me for a minute, until I'm squirming with discomfort and wishing I hadn't said anything about his arm at all.

"Why would you do that?" he asks after what feels like an eternity.

I sigh and set the cup on the bedside table. "Because you're hurt, and I'm a very nice person."

King looks at me for another long moment, like he's trying to figure me out. "You're going to drop some poison into my blood while you stitch me up, aren't you?"

"Don't give me ideas."

"The bullet's still in my leg."

"Sucks to be you."

He grits his teeth and glares. "Can you help me or not?"

"I can," I say, picking up my tea again. "I don't know if I will. You're not asking very nicely, King."

His nostrils flare, and this time, I'm happy to see the hatred burning in his eyes. If he can drive me insane, it's only fair that I do the same.

"Will you please get the fucking bullet out of my leg?" he asks.

"Hm, I suppose," I say. "Since you said please."

"Thank you," he grits out, the words sounding more like a curse than gratitude.

SELENA

I leave him seething while I wash up, throw on some clothes, and grab my surgical kit. I won't tell him the whole truth. There's ammunition in the truth—that not only do I want him to admire me, but that I can't stand to see anyone hurting. I'm softer than anyone in this business should be, and more than that, I respect all the men who do the jobs that have to be done every day. Begrudgingly, even King.

He watches dubiously while I open my bag and spread out my instruments. "Why do you have that?"

"I used to stitch up my dad and his guys all the time," I say with a shrug. "I mean, we have a doctor on the payroll. I'm not that good. But I can do little stuff." While I talk, I set a towel on the bed and settle onto my knees beside him. When I pull off the bandage on his shoulder, he doesn't react outwardly. But when I start to clean the wound with alcohol, I see the muscle in his jaw tense as he clenches his teeth.

Apparently he's human, after all.

"That's why you offered, isn't it?" he asks, staring straight ahead with a stone face. "You know it hurts like a son of a bitch."

"Why else would I help my husband after he'd been shot?"

This time, I get a whole grunt in response.

"Look, I know I'm not a good wife," I say. "I'm not so self-absorbed that I don't know I'm hard to handle. And even though you're a grade-A asshole, I'm sure you could be worse."

He looks away. "How?"

"Oh no," I say. "I'm not giving you any ideas."

The corner of his mouth lifts the tiniest bit, and I think maybe he has a sense of humor buried somewhere deep down in there.

"I'm sorry you got shot," I say. "I know you won't believe me, but I really didn't have anything to do with it."

He doesn't say anything.

"And I'm sorry I haven't acted like we're in this together. I know you hate being married to me as much as I do. It's not just you, King. I never wanted this. To be a wife. I was sure you'd try to make me into something I'm not. I know what mafia wives have to put up with. So I was making sure you knew I wasn't giving up my friends or my life. But I'll do more around here. I live here, too. I want it to be my house, *our* house, not just yours. I'll act like it from now on."

"I don't expect you to be the maid," he says, watching me run the thread through his skin.

"I know," I say. "But I can hire one."

"I thought you didn't know how."

"I'm sure I can figure it out," I say, tying off the ends of the thread and sitting back. "All fixed up."

"Yeah," he says, glowering at the window. "Thanks."

So, I may be able to bandage a wound, but I can't fix what's wrong with his head. And that's okay. I don't expect him to fix me, either. I smile at that thought. There's way too fucking much wrong with me to fix.

"What are you smiling at?" he asks after a second.

I dart a quick glance at him. I didn't know he was looking.

"Nothing," I say, shaking my head as I reach for the bandages to cover the gnarly stitching. "I was just thinking I could fix you, but I don't think anyone could do that."

"You're probably right about that," he says after a pause.

"And that's okay," I say. "I won't try to fix you if you don't try to fix me. Deal?"

He hesitates again, grinding his teeth back and forth. Finally he nods. "Deal," he says, but he doesn't sound very happy about it.

"This one's going to hurt more for a minute, but it won't last as long," I say, reaching for the needle-nosed plyers. "Lie down."

He swings his legs up onto the bed and crosses his arms over his chest. I straddle his shins and lean down over the bullet that's still lodged in his quad.

"We don't need to love each other," I say as I work. "We have to make this marriage work, though. There's no out for either of us. This is how it works. There's no divorce. We have to coexist in the same house. We don't have to be enemies, though."

"What are you getting at?"

"I just think maybe we've been selfish," I say. "We're both miserable and we both hate each other. But I'll be the first to admit I haven't really considered how much it sucks for you to be stuck with me when you could have gotten someone like Bianca or Lizzie."

"And what would you rather have gotten?" he asks. "Someone who lets you walk all over him?"

"Well, yeah," I say with a little laugh.

He sucks in a breath when I hit the end of the bullet. We share a minute of silence as I carefully dig to get a grip on it. "I remember the first time I did this," I say with a little laugh. "I must have been, like, eight. I woke up in the middle of the night, and I heard all this screaming and yelling, so I went to see what it was all about. Daddy was hauling my uncle in, and he was cussing like... Like no eight-year-old should hear." I break off, shaking my head.

King doesn't speak, so I go on.

"He was shot in the back of his leg, below the knee. A few other guys were there, too, but they couldn't get the bullet out because Uncle Bert kept kicking every time they started digging for it. But then Daddy saw I was up, and that I'd seen all the blood already, and heard all the cussing, and I hadn't run screaming. And I had tiny fingers that could get in the bullet hole and get the bullet when no one else could." I laugh softly and deposit the bullet onto my tray. "My mom was so pissed when she found out."

It's been so long since I thought about that night. Sewing up injuries just became part of my life at some point soon after Mom split.

King doesn't say anything, but I know he's listening. He's watching me with… Something new in his eyes. Respect, maybe. I realize that's the longest conversation I've had with my husband about the way I was raised. I don't really know anything about his life, either. Suddenly, I feel weird about having shared that memory, as impersonal as it is.

I get the needle ready to sew up the tiny opening from the bullet. "Just a few more stitches," I say. "You can keep that bullet as a souvenir. I hear it's memorable—the first time being shot."

I glance up at him, and see his eyes are glassy with pain. He's been amazingly still considering the pain he's in. The injuries are pretty minor, but they've gotta hurt like hell itself. I respect him for his stoic response. Once, I told him that he had to earn my respect, but I didn't think much about him respecting me. I assumed no mafia man really respects his wife, but King's not like most of the men I know. I'm proud to be able to help him, to maybe earn his respect the way he's earning mine. It's hard not to respect a guy who barely winces after being shot.

He jerks when I poke the needle into him, but he doesn't say anything. When I dart a glance at him, he's laid his head back on the pillow, eyes closed, nostrils flared.

"Want me to shut up?" I ask, putting in another stitch.

"No," he grits out. "Keep talking."

I want to ask him about his life, but he probably doesn't want to talk right now, so I try to think of something else to say. "My friend Bianca thinks you're hot," I say, remembering her teasing at the salon.

That thought brings me to the conversation I had with Dad on the phone while I was there, which leads me back to King's accusation.

"I know you think this was a setup, but that's because someone wanted you to think that," I say. "Someone who wants us to stay at war. If it was my dad, he would have gotten me out before anything went down. Trust me, King. He would think of me."

I have no doubt about that. He's always thinking of me, even in this marriage that seemed like a curse. I may not have seen it at first, but now I do. Now I know he gave me what I needed, that he was thinking of not just an alliance with the Valentis, but of my happiness. He didn't want me to be left a widow at twenty-five, so he gave me someone young. He didn't want me to be in the heart of danger at all times, didn't want my husband to be in the most dangerous positions, so he gave me a soldier. He didn't want me to marry someone callous and unfeeling, so he gave me someone new to the Life.

So, who would want to take out the Valentis besides my father?

Well, that answer is too easy. Everyone.

"Our families made an alliance, but that doesn't mean the other families are all going to be peaceful forever," I say. "Or it could have been one of the Irish or Russian organizations. And for all we know, someone thought both Anthony and Al were in there. They could have meant those bullets for both our families."

King nods, his brow knitting into a frown.

"It could have been random, someone who just saw Al going in and took the opportunity."

"It wasn't random," King says. "They were wearing ski masks. They had silencers. It was premeditated."

I nod and carefully place a bandage over his wound. "Does anyone want you dead? If we can rule that out, we'll know they came for Al."

King pauses, his eyes searching mine. "What did you tell your dad about me?"

"Nothing," I say, scowling at him as the guilt sets in. He knows what I said. "Just that you were horrible and you were going to kill me."

He looks at the window again. "Would he come after me for that?"

I sit back on my heels. "Yeah, if you actually killed me."

"You told him I was abusing you."

"My father wants us to work things out, just like I'm sure your parents do. He would never leave me a widow. He loves me, and he wants what's best for me."

"Getting rid of your husband might be best," he mutters. "Especially if he wants the alliance ended."

"I know what people say about him," I say. "That he's a monster, all that, but it's not true. I mean, maybe when it comes to women, the rumors are true. But what's he supposed to do, be celibate for the rest of his life because his wife won't talk to him? And maybe he had his little things on the side before that, but it's not like they

259

were happy, anyway. It was arranged, just like this. My mom never loved him, never wanted him."

We stare at each other for a long minute, and I realize I've said way too much. He doesn't need to know all that about my family.

"Like you," he says quietly. "That's why you think I'm going to fuck around. Because you don't want me, the same way your mom didn't want your dad. And that's what he did."

I raise my chin and glare at him. "He's a good dad, King. As good as he could be, under the circumstances. He had plenty of girlfriends, yeah, and he might have a violent temper, but he'd never, ever lay a finger on me. And he wouldn't get rid of my husband without telling me."

"Okay," he says.

For a minute, we sit there in silence, our wills battling each other. I need him to know that I'd never lie about this, that my father is a good man, even if he's also a violent monster with a temper when it comes to his job. But never to me. To me, he was the stressed out, overworked dad who had so many obligations that he had to choose between leaving me with more nannies in the evenings or taking me along. I wanted to be with him, and he loved me, so he made the choice that maybe wasn't ideal, but it's the one that made me happy.

He chose to take me along, hence the poker games and emergency meetings to talk strategy, the bullet removals at two in the morning, and the certainty that he would never, ever leave me behind if our families were going to war. He wouldn't send guys to do a job in broad daylight. He'd never have his men cover their faces with masks, either. King may not be convinced, but I can say with complete confidence that this was not my father's doing.

"You can get cleaned up now," I say. "But try not to get it wet for a few days."

"I guess it's good you fixed me up," King says, swinging his legs off the bed. "I'd probably have gotten blood on the sheets."

The image catches in my mind, the comments people made about our wedding night. I'm the one who's supposed to bleed on the sheets. Maybe he's thinking the same thing, because he quickly heads for the bathroom to clean up while I put my things away.

He stops in the doorway of the bathroom, turning back. "Eliza?" he says.

"Hmm," I say, not looking at him as I set aside the bloody instruments that need disinfecting.

"Thank you."

I shrug. "It's nothing."

Our eyes meet, and his dark gaze is so intense it makes me squirm. "It's something."

This time, I'm the one who looks away. Sometimes it feels like those espresso eyes pierce straight into my soul.

He hesitates a moment, then steps into the bathroom and closes the door. I'm glad he's gone, that he doesn't see me close my eyes to collect myself, doesn't guess at the shivery, fluttery feeling turning my insides all around.

It's been a long day, and an even longer evening, and I decide to just go to bed and be done with it. A while later, King comes out of the bathroom wearing nothing but a towel around his waist. I close my eyes and pretend to sleep, but tonight I peek through my lashes. King's not especially modest, but he doesn't parade around naked in front of me, either. I've only ever seen his cock once, and I'm ready for more. Not in a sexual way, like when he gave me the orgasm. I want to see him, all of him. I want to know him in a way I haven't bothered to do.

His hair is wet and his body clean, little droplets of water clinging to his skin where he washed, lit up by the golden light filtering into the bedroom from the open bathroom door. He glances at me as if to check if I'm sleeping before he drops the towel and turns to the dresser. He has a scar on his side, above his hip, and if I had to guess, I'd say it's less than a year old. It looks like another bullet wound, though he didn't correct me when I said today was his first. It makes me wonder because I thought he was new to the Life. I watch the curve of his ass, how nicely muscled his butt is, the strong, lean muscles of his thighs. When he turns away from the dresser, I can just see the shape of his cock hanging down, and it makes fireworks explode inside my belly.

I had that inside my mouth. Warmth shimmers through my lower belly, and my mouth puckers with saliva just looking at the shape of it. Even when it's not hard, I can see he's big. And not just big, but nice looking, all smooth and straight and well-groomed. I wish the light was on, that I could see more. I know I shouldn't, that I'm spying, but it makes my heart race in a familiar, exciting way. It's all I can do not to let out a sigh of disappointment when he pulls on a pair of sweats, wincing when he drags them up over his injured thigh.

A minute later, he sinks onto the edge of the bed and strokes my hair back with his good hand. "Eliza?" he whispers. "You awake?"

I don't move, don't answer. I let my lids relax closed so he won't see a glint between my lashes. My heart is beating so loud in my ears I think he'll hear it, that he'll know I'm awake, that I was watching, that butterflies are swarming in my belly and warmth coiling beneath it. I want to scream in frustration. I want him, but I hate him. I hate that I want him. I hate that I want him to want me. And more than that, to respect me, admire me, and praise me. I want his approval. Even though he took over and fucked my face earlier, humiliated me at the end by making me lick the cum off him, it still turned me on. That's how fucked up I am.

And beyond all that, I hate that I can't just ask for what I want. I can't tell him how hot it makes me when he tells me what to do, when he forces me to do it. If I told him, he'd stop. So I have to just keep poking him, pissing him off and making him hate me more, just to get what I want. Which isn't freedom or for him to leave me alone. It's for him to prove he cares, to prove I'm worth something. He said I was worthless, but if I was, he wouldn't keep trying. He wouldn't keep coming back to me because he can't help himself any more than I can help myself from responding to it, craving it.

He stands beside the bed a long moment, watching me pretend to sleep. Then he leans down and presses his lips gently to my forehead. "I'm sorry," he whispers. "I'm so fucking sorry about everything."

I can't tell him that I don't want him to be sorry, that I don't want him to stop. I don't even want him to feel bad about the way he treats me. I want more. But I can't ask for it, at least not with words. I'm only learning what I need as he gives it, and maybe, if I'm lucky, he'll learn, too. Without me having to tell him, to ask for what I want, to spill my fucked up past with its ugly secrets, he'll learn to be a good husband—and make me a good wife.

sixteen

King

"I haven't found a couple of them," Little Al says. "They haven't released their names because the cops haven't talked to their families, but we've got some inside intel, and three of them were on the news. They're from the Bronx, and they obviously weren't our men, which means they're Anthony's."

"Why would they attack us right after they made a marriage pact?" I ask. "It doesn't make sense."

He shrugs. "Had to be a setup. They were trying to get Al. You're lucky you got out alive. Both of you."

"Yeah," I say. "Is he looking into the other guys?"

"No point, really. They're from Anthony's territory."

"I might look into it," I say. "There's gotta be a reason."

"I know a guy over there," he says. "I'll ask around. But Al thinks it's them, so there's really no point."

"Thanks." I'm at a disadvantage in every fucking thing because I didn't grow up here. I don't know anyone outside Manhattan unless they're related to me. But at least my family has connections—we've got a barber, a cop, and a lawyer on my dad's side. Of course, we've got the whole Valenti family on my ma's side, including Little Al, who's a distant cousin to me.

We do our rounds, collecting money, breaking fingers, and report back to Uncle Al just before I head home. I hate that I have to ask my own doorman if anyone is at my place, but I don't want to wind up with a bullet in my brain, either. I thought Eliza and I made a sort of peace last night, but today blew that all to hell. Now that I've confirmed that the attack was most likely the Pomponios, I don't know what I'll walk into at home. It would be nice if I could trust my own wife to be on my side, but it's not like I've given her a reason to want me around. I guess I should be glad she doesn't cook, so I don't have to wonder if my food is poisoned every night.

When I ask if anyone's been up today, the doorman nods. "The usual."

I stew all the way up to the apartment. After last night, I thought we might make progress. I thought I'd figured out a bit of what Eliza needs, and that maybe she was accepting it as well. She didn't fight it when I was forceful with her. She asked me not to hurt her before, so I didn't, but I didn't let her get her way this time. She was dripping wet for it, and afterwards, she rewarded me by using her expertise to patch up my bullet wounds.

Maybe she just brought Bianca over after lunch today. She's definitely one of the usuals.

I turn the key in the lock and push the door open, only to be hit with a wave of nauseating chemical smell. When I step into the living room, I'm greeted with the usual, extravagant mayhem. Eliza is lounging sideways over a chair, he dress riding so high up I can see half her ass. A dozen other girls and a couple guys sit around on pillows or the couch, wine glasses next to most of them. They've set up what looks like a salon in our living room.

Nail polish bottles, cotton balls, and bottles of remover sit all over the coffee table. A bottle of remover lays toppled on the hardwood in a pool of liquid. Blue nail polish is smeared over the surface of the coffee table, a few drops running slowly down the stainless-steel leg. Lotions, glues, and a dozen other products are strewn around the room—the little foam things girls use to separate their toes, lava stones, packages of fake nails, something that looks like colored sand, salt scrubs, essential oils, and things I can't begin to identify.

Music thuds through the room as I stand there thinking I can't win. It never ends. This girl is going to push me over the edge. After spending the day looking over my shoulder, not knowing if someone is after me and if they'll make another attempt on my life, not knowing if I'll be able to respond quickly enough with a thigh that hurts like the devil himself is lancing it every time I move and a bandage on my shoulder, I come home to this shit. The same as every other fucking day.

DANGEROUS DEFIANCE

She promises to do better, to hire a maid, to contribute, only to go back to her hedonistic extravagance the next day like it never happened. Every time we take a step forward, it's erased the very next day when she steps back into her chosen world, the one where she's a pampered princess who gives zero fucks about anyone but herself.

Why can't she go to one of their houses?

Of course, that wouldn't work. She's doing this shit on purpose. She wants me to know what she's up to. She's proving a point—that I can't tell her what to do. That she will do whatever the fuck she pleases. She won't keep her word, and she wants me to know it. She wants me to think she's a terrible wife so I won't expect her to fulfil the role the way anyone else would. She wants me to be afraid of what she'll do, what sway she has with her father, what power she wields in our marriage.

Well, fuck that.

When she's in my house, I'll tell her what to do, and she'll fucking do it. I won't sleep with one eye open the rest of my life because I can't trust my wife not to murder me, won't order every dinner out so she won't poison me. This shit has gone on way too fucking long, and I'm done.

I stride over and yank the plug from the wall, and the music comes to a thudding halt.

"Oh, no," Eliza says, rolling her eyes. "Daddy's home. Guess the fun's over now, girls."

She gives me a saucy look, as if she's daring me to contradict her, to put her in her place in front of company. She thinks I care what her friends think. She thinks I give a single fuck about spoiling her fun. But I don't.

"Get the fuck out of here," I tell her friends before turning to her. "And you. What the fuck is this, Eliza?"

"This is called fun," she says, gesturing around the room. "You should try it sometime."

Bianca giggles into her drink, used to the spectacle by now.

"I told you I don't want to come home to this shit anymore."

"What are you going to do?" Eliza asks, rolling her eyes. "You're my husband. You're not my father. You can't ground me."

"Try me," I say. I grab her arm and drag her up, pulling her toward the bedroom.

"Stop," she shrieks, waving an arm at her friends, as if they're going to rescue her. "You're hurting me!"

Bianca is still giggling into her drink, and the others look like they're just waiting for her to leave so they can gossip about our fight. Not one of them looks the least bit concerned. They must know Eliza as well as I'm beginning to.

"All of you better be gone when I'm done with her," I warn the others before I wrestle Eliza through our bedroom door and slam it behind us.

"Are you crazy?" she yells. "My father will kill you for treating me that way!"

"He already fucking tried, remember?" I snap. "I'm so fucking done with your shit. I thought I'd made myself clear last night, but apparently, you need a harsher lesson."

"What are you gonna do about it?" she taunts.

"I'm going to make you my wife," I growl. "I'm fucking tired of you acting like a bratty child. It's time you became a woman."

I stalk toward her, rage pulsing in my brow. She tries to dart past me, but I grab her around the waist and throw her back on the bed. Her dress flies up, and the red lace panties under them make my head nearly explode.

Was she planning on going out after her little spa day, or was that asshole Tommy coming over, but I got here first?

I plow on top of her before she can get up. She tries to pull her dress down, but I pin her hands. "Who the fuck are you wearing these for?" I ask, reaching down and grabbing the crotch of her panties. I wrench them from her body, tearing them off and crumpling them in my hand.

"No one," she says, struggling under me. "They're for me. Now get off me. My friends will hear."

"Let them listen," I say, dragging my cock out of my pants. "Then they'll know that you belong to me, not them."

Being between her bare thighs is too much. I've been celibate as a fucking monk for months, since hearing about our engagement. I'm done. If she's going to do whatever the fuck she wants as my wife, then I'll do what I want as her husband.

I spit on my hand and slick it over the head of my cock before I rub it through her slit, feeling her tremble even as she gets wet for me. I ignore her protests and rip her dress off over her head, leaving her delectable little body bared for me, her shaved cunt on full display. She wants this. She pushed me on purpose, knowing we'd reach this point if she didn't stop. She tested me, and she found my limit. She wants me to take control, to put her in her place, to give her boundaries where she's never had them. To do that, I have to show her what happens when she pushes me too far.

"You are my wife, Eliza," I growl, pushing her flat on her back. "It's time you became one in more than name."

I promised our families I would end her party girl ways and teach her how to be a wife. We're both doing our duty tonight. I let her distract me before, but now I'm focused. I obey my bosses, and she obeys me. It isn't about love. It's about duty.

"No," she cries, her struggles becoming frantic under me. "I'll give you head again."

"I don't want your mouth," I say, wadding up the lace panties and pressing them to her face. "I want your cunt. It's mine, and tonight I'm taking it."

"You're too big," she cries, turning her face away. "I'm tiny. It'll never fit."

"I'll make it fit," I growl. "I'm going to ram my cock so deep inside you that you can't breathe, and then I'm going to fuck you so hard you never forget who you belong to again."

"Please," she cries, her pretty tears glistening in her eyes. "I already belong to you. You said I could have my own life, do what I wanted when I was at home."

I know she twists things, fakes it to get her way, and I'm done letting her have her freedom only to pay for it later. I'm done waiting to claim what was mine all along. It's time for her to accept that every part of her is mine—especially this one.

"You can be your own person, but your cunt is mine," I say, grabbing my cock in my free hand and forcing the head into the vicelike grip of her virgin opening.

"You're hurting me," she cries, tears springing to her eyes.

"I told you I wouldn't be gentle."

I pull out and enter her again, nearly losing my mind with the exquisite sensation of stretching her virgin flesh around my cock. She cries out in shock this time, and I push the panties between her lips, shoving them into her mouth to muffle her. She might be fighting me, but her slick cunt tells me she wants this, even if her stubborn mind can't admit it. I push a little deeper this time, shaking with the effort of holding back. It's been so long since I fucked a woman, and I want her so fucking much, that my body threatens to cum before I've even torn through the barrier inside her. I'll only get to take her virginity once, though, and I'm damn sure going to make it last.

"Fuck, you're tight," I breathe, easing my cock in deeper, opening her untouched cunt for my passage. "It feels so good."

She bucks under me, crying out behind my hand. I release her face, leaving the panties stuffed in her mouth, and thrust deeper, into the woman who has tested my patience every day until she found my limit. I'm done playing her game. That's what this is to her, a game to see if she can make me snap.

Well, she's finally gotten her wish.

My cock meets the barrier or her virginity, and I pause, feeling it stretch deliciously around my tip.

I draw back an inch and then give a quick, sharp thrust, tearing through her virginity. She shrieks, writhing under me. I still inside her, stroking her hair back and kissing her tearstained lids.

"Give me those pretty little tears," I croon. "Cry for me, my virgin bride. You don't fool me. You can take it. I know how tough you are."

When she lifts her hips, trying to push me off, I drive deeper into her, watching her pretty tears fall as finally I take what's mine, what's been mine all along.

"That's it, *piccola mia*," I whisper. "Get it all out now because you're going to get used to this. Since you need reminding who you belong to, I'm going to be fucking this sweet little cunt of mine ever night until you stop fighting it. You'll always be mine. You might as well accept it and learn to take me like a good little wife."

As I speak, I slowly push against the clench of her walls. She cries out again with each inch I move deeper into her virgin cunt, opening her flesh for the first time, fitting it to my cock's size. I don't hurt her unnecessarily, but I don't give in to her tears, either. I go slow, letting her adjust, but I don't stop until I'm buried to the hilt inside her, claiming every inch of her to the very depths.

She's so tight, so slick and hot, I can barely see straight. "This is mine," I growl, pulling back and thrusting deep inside her again. "You're mine. Understand?"

I draw out and then drive into her so deep she moves up the bed with the force of my hips. I grip her hips, holding her in place to receive the next blow. I bury my cock to the hilt, grinding my pelvic bone against her clit. She makes a sound, muffled behind the panties still stuffed in her mouth. Her eyes are pools of shining hate as she stares up at me. I slam into her again, loving the way her eyes widen with shock when I hit her depths.

"Look at you taking every inch of me," I growl, thrusting to her depths again. "Just as I'm taking you. I'm yours, Eliza. Every part of me is yours. Every inch. Just as you are mine."

I have staked my claim to my bride at last. She is truly mine. Her cunt, her virginity, her body. It's been saved for me. It's not a prize I've won, but a reward for all I've been through. It's my right, what was promised to me for putting up with her. I gave her time to get used to the idea, to come around on her own terms, and she didn't. Now she learns my terms.

This isn't a game. I could have died yesterday because of her little tantrums. I've realized just how real this is, how real the consequences of her despising me are. Now it's time for her to take the same dose of reality, time for her to learn the price of her betrayal. More than that, it's time that I did my job and showed her what it means to be a mafia wife.

I move faster, watching her tears fall and her jaw clamp down on the panties in her mouth. Her cunt grips me in its slippery vice, and I pump into it, punishing her for her defiance with each rough thrust. I'm proving a point, but I'm also letting myself go at last, letting myself take what's mine without worrying about our future. She already hates me. It makes no difference if I fuck her or not. It makes no difference how I fuck her. So I do it the way I want, unleashing my fury and frustration each time I slam my cock to the hilt inside her.

Each thrust brings a muffled sound from her throat, her sweet cries of pleasure and pain keeping me going. I pound into her hot, slick cunt, pushing up to watch my cock owning her, the blood proof that she's a treasure that only I will ever claim. She's perfect, the most beautiful woman I've ever seen as she lays under me, her hair spread out around her, glistening tears clinging to her wet lashes, her face flushed. Her full lips tremble around the red lace stuffed inside, but she doesn't spit it out.

At last, she's surrendered.

She knew this was coming. She sure as fuck knows how to provoke me, and if she didn't like the consequences, she wouldn't do the same thing every goddamn day. She might cry her fake tears, but she wants it as much as I do, wanted me to put her in her place and show her how to submit. She wants me to show her how much I want her, how completely I own her. She wants to see how far I'll go to claim her, how hard I'll fight for her, that I will never give up and walk away just like she'll never give in. She can't admit it, but she needs this as much as I do. She needs to be claimed by force if necessary, to be dominated and owned.

DANGEROUS DEFIANCE

She's no longer tense, no longer fighting it. Her highs are open to receive my claim, and I claim her. I claim the gift that was mine to take all along, that I should have taken the very first night. I drive into her harder as she gets looser, wetter, until I'm pounding her into the bed, driving my cock to the hilt inside her bloody cunt with each brutal thrust until I can't hold back. I slam into her one last time and hold, claiming the depths of her cunt with my cock, staking the final claim inside her body with each spurt of cum. This is mine to take, to fuck, to punish and own in whatever ways I see fit. She is not her own person. None of us are.

We are husband and wife, whether we want it or not. I'm a soldier who breaks people every day, whether I want to or not. But this... This is what I want. To be truly together, husband and wife not only on paper but in the physical sense, our bodies joined as one, our hearts beating against each other as I lie on her, the aftershocks of my orgasm still squeezing drops of cum into her cervix every few seconds.

At last, I pry myself away from her and climb off the bed. Before I go to the shower to wash the blood away, I turn back. "Now that we've gotten that out of the way, it's time to get a maid to start coming in and changing the sheets."

seventeen

Eliza

I hate him. I hate him with all the impotent rage burning through my limbs, with every crashing beat of my hurricane heart, with the helpless fury of all the mafia wives ever sold into the bondage of marriage. And there's absolutely nothing I can do to stop him. He proved that tonight. I'm his, and he can do what he likes with me. He's mine, too—my punishment, my torture to bear.

I curl around myself, furious at every tear he forced from my eyes, the tears that still soak my cheeks, dripping onto the pillow like the cum I can feel still dripping out of my wrecked body, leaking onto the sheets with my blood. I want to kill him, to kill every Valenti who's ever hurt my family, every person who's ever hurt me. I want them all obliterated, burned to nothing more than a stain in my memory.

I hear the shower running, but I don't move. There's no use. I'm trapped, a broken animal in a cage. So I just lie there and fume, and I cry. I cry for my mother, for what she had to endure that brought me into this world. For my brother, who died before he could inflict this torture on anyone else. I cry for myself, for what I have to look forward to for the rest of my fucking life.

The water shuts off, and King emerges, all steamy and wrapped in a towel, proud of his conquest. He looks at me, his gaze moving from my shivering, naked form to the spot behind me where he fucked me. I know there's blood, but I don't look. It's enough to feel it, the destruction he wreaked inside me, the pain when I move that feels like he left razor blades inside me.

"Fuck, El," he says, coming over and sinking onto the bed beside me. All his anger and gloating washed away with my blood in the shower. Lucky him.

I don't say anything. I don't even have it in me to hide my tears. He's already seen them. He likes them. The sick fuck likes to know he's hurting me, that I'm crying for him.

He shifts around, pulling the blanket over my huddled form. "I'm sorry. I should have been more gentle."

I still don't answer. What is there to say?

He strokes my hair back, then pauses. Tilting my chin up, he hooks a finger into my mouth to tug the wet lace from it. Using his thumbs, he dries the tears from my cheeks, as if he can erase the pain that easily. It must be nice, to be able to believe that it's gone just because he can't see it.

"How badly have I hurt you, *piccola mia?*"

"I'm fine," I manage.

"I'll—I'll make it up to you," he says, sounding a little desperate, like he really is sorry. Like he's only now realizing that I wasn't playing, that it wasn't a game to me.

"You can't," I say flatly. "Go away."

"Let me make you feel as good as you make me feel," he says, moving onto the bed in front of me.

SELENA

I don't say anything, because there's no point. I tried so hard to take control of my life, to have something of my own, but it was all an illusion. I've never had control of anything, least of all my own body. It was never mine. It's always been the property of others, and when I tried to refuse, it's been bent to their will.

King moves closer, bringing my body into his warm, strong arms, his skin still damp from the shower. He kisses my forehead, stroking my hair with his thumbs before reaching for my face, tipping my chin up. The cruelty is gone from his eyes, but I'll never forget he has that inside him, the capability to brutalize me that way.

"Let me make you lose your mind the way I do when I see how beautiful you are," he whispers, cupping my cheek in his palm. "When I remember that you'll always be mine."

I shiver at his words, the promise that's a shackle around my ankle. He kisses my cheeks, my lips, then along my jawline, his hand falling on my breast. Tingles shoot through me when his mouth reaches my ear, but my body is shaking too hard to enjoy what he's doing. All can think about is what comes next. I grip his shoulder, my nails digging in.

"What are you doing?" I whisper, panic coiling inside my belly. This wasn't supposed to happen. I keep thinking that over and over. Where did I go wrong? I gave in. I let him have me. How is he still going? Why isn't he done?

"I want to kiss every inch of you," he murmurs into my neck, his voice low and rough. "I want to taste your cunt. I want to make you cum over and over until that's all you remember."

He rests his weight on one elbow, leaving soft, warm kisses down my neck while his other hand strokes my arm, my side, my thigh. His breathing his coming hard, sending shivers through me as he kisses down the column of my neck, nudging my chin up.

It feels good. It does. I keep telling myself that.

I did fine with the blowjob, with his fingers, even with the sex. Great, in fact. He said only good things. And if I could do that, then why can't I do this?

I can. I can do it. I let him do his thing, moving down my body, kissing my breasts. "You're so beautiful," he says, and his hands are everywhere, his words, his desire. I'm drowning in it, and I can't find the surface, so I just lie there while he lets out a soft moan, taking one of my soft nipples in his mouth and sucking gently. My breath hitches, and my clit throbs in response. He sucks harder, and a little whimper escapes my lips. He caresses my belly, moving lower until he's brushing the edge of my bare mound, lasered bare for him. I knew he'd fuck me. I thought I was ready. But I will never really be ready.

I jerk back to myself, shocked to the surface with the throb he sends straight to my core with each suck. I wish I felt nothing, but I can't help myself. He releases my nipple and blows a stream of air across my wet skin, watching a shiver ripple over my body. He must like that, the feeling that he can fix everything, that it wasn't so bad because my body responds to his touch. But no one can fix me.

He tugs the other nipple into his mouth, moaning around it, which makes it even worse. I can feel heat and wetness pooling between my thighs, the pressure from earlier returning full force, the blood throbbing in my torn flesh, swelling with arousal.

And then he's pushing me back under the water, because it's too much, what he's doing and how much he wants this, how much he needs... How can he want more? I've been destroyed, given him everything, and he's still going. I can't handle it, can't fight it, so I let myself sink down to the bottom, wishing it was so deep he couldn't touch me. I can hear the voice that haunts me, distorted like something out of a horror movie when really it was a kind voice with an edge of steel under it.

Don't be afraid of your own body, Eliza. Don't fear your own pleasure.

He slides a hand between my legs, his touch so gentle it brings tears to my eyes again. I squeeze my lids shut and take a shaky breath as he parts my lips and begins to slowly stroke my clit with his thumb. His mouth moves back to my other nipple, where he licks and sucks and nibbles until my whole body is tingling with heat and his fingers are slick with my arousal.

Then he moves lower, and his mouth is on my stomach, and I'm shaking so hard he has to feel it, but he doesn't stop. Each time his thumb slides over the swollen bud of my clit, it throbs in answer. He flicks his tongue into my bellybutton and then sits up, his hand still between my legs. He spreads my thighs and kneels there, looking down at me, no longer a virgin. Shame slams into me and I try to close my legs, but he pushes them open further, his nostrils flaring and his gaze going molten hot.

"You're so fucking perfect," he breathes, massaging my thighs to ease the tension.

"I'm not," I whisper. I stare up at him. I can see the light above, blurry as if through water.

I try to close my knees, but he keeps them open, sliding down the bed so he's between my legs, staring at me from only inches away.

"Let me look at you," he murmurs, his voice thick with lust. "I want to memorize your freshly fucked cunt so I can picture it forever. It's the most beautiful thing I've ever seen."

I squirm, my face heating with shame at how dirty I feel with him so intimately close. I'm torn open and wrecked, leaking blood and cum.

"Are you okay with this?" he asks, looking up at me, a stitch pulling between his eyebrows.

Of course I'm not fucking okay with it. How can I be okay? I'm drowning, screaming inside my head, but if I open my mouth, the water will rush in, so I only nod.

"Have you ever done this?" He pulls my legs onto his shoulders, running his hands from my ankles and along my calves, cupping my knees before he runs his hands down the front of my thighs.

I don't have the strength to worry what he'll say, if he'll be mad. I nod again.

"Good," he says, giving my legs a reassuring squeeze. "Then you know it doesn't hurt. I'll never hurt you again, Eliza. I promise. Just relax and let me make you feel good."

Don't be afraid of you own body, Eliza. Don't fear your own pleasure.

It's like a taunt inside my head, the chants of a hundred cruel bullies on the playground. But there was only one bully, one bully and a bathtub, and the water was too cold, and I can't stop shivering.

I nod.

King slides down closer, spreading my lips and taking a deep breath. "You smell amazing," he says, his voice husky.

It's not so bad, I tell myself. It feels good. But I'm not sure, because I'm not here, I'm somewhere else, and the feeling good part is not connected to my brain, only my body. King strokes my swollen clit with his fingertip, murmuring again how beautiful I am as he opens me with his fingers.

"What are you doing?" I manage, my whole body tensed even as I try to calm my racing heart, my quaking limbs.

"I'm tasting my bride," he says, and he buries his tongue in my raw cunt.

And I...

Shatter.

eighteen

King

Eliza shoots out from under me like she's propelled by something inhuman. I don't even know how she gets out of my grip, only that one second I'm taking the first taste of my wife, and a split second later, she's tumbling off the bed. She spins on her heel to face me when she's halfway across the room, her stance defensive and ready, like she might bolt in either direction if I move a muscle. She stares at me with her bourbon eyes incomprehensible, wild and animal and filled with what can only be described as instinctual terror.

"Whoa," I say, kneeling up on the bed and holding up both hands. "What's going on?"

My words seem to bring her a little closer to reason and she crosses her arms over her tits. "I—don't—like that," she says, grinding out her words between heaving breaths.

"Okay," I say slowly. "Then we don't have to do it. Jesus, Eliza. You could have said something."

"Like I said something when you were about to fuck me?"

I swallow, feeling that blow down to my soul. "I'm sorry," I say again, sinking down on the bed. "You're right. I just wanted to make it better."

"That doesn't make it better," she says. "It makes it worse. I hate that. *Hate it.*"

The vehemence in her voice and the fierceness in her eyes tells me she's not playing, not testing me. I fucked up, and I know it. It's finally sinking in just how serious a crime I've committed against my wife. The moment my head cleared, guilt started to creep in, but I'm still not sure how badly I hurt her. I was supposed to be getting her to trust me, not making sure she never would. I don't know when she stopped playing, when it became real to her, too. I only know I realized it too late. I got her to submit, yes, but submission that is forced and not willingly given isn't submission at all. It's defeat.

"What do you need?" I ask.

Without a word, she steps into the bathroom and closes the door.

Fuck. I fucked up, and this time, I'm not sure how to fix it. I know one thing for sure—I'm not going away. She can try to push me away all she wants, but I'm here, and I'm making up for what I did.

Her attitude drives me over the edge, but I don't want her to lose it. I don't want her defeated. I'm not supposed to win against her. We're supposed to be a team. We win and lose together. Her defeat is my defeat. I'm supposed to be the man, to be in control. I'm not supposed to lose control and hurt her, erasing all the progress we might have made. The last time I lost control, my sister wound up dead.

I think about all the movies I've seen where someone slits their wrists in a bathtub, and I know I'm not going to let her out of my sight until I know she's okay. I'll fight for this, fight for her until she's willing to fight beside me for it. Until she sees it as something worth fighting for.

I turn the knob and step into the bathroom. Eliza whirls on me from her position in front of the mirror. "Get out!"

"I'm not leaving," I say. "I know I fucked up, Eliza. I'm not going to do it again. But I'm not leaving you alone right now. If I can't make it up to you, let me make it better."

I plug the clawfoot tub and turn on the water.

Her eyes move to the tub and back to me. "You think a bath will make it better?"

"It won't make it worse," I say. "Talk to me, Eliza. Tell me what I can do to fix this. To show you I'm sorry."

She blinks at me a few times, like she wasn't expecting that. And why would she? She already hated me, and now she knows exactly what kind of asshole I am.

"What are you apologizing for?" she asks, narrowing her eyes.

"For fucking you even though I knew you didn't want to."

She stares a me a minute, and then her shoulders slump. "You can't fix that, King."

What the fuck is wrong with me? Yeah, it's been a while since I've had sex, and I was frustrated as hell that I can't fuck my wife, but that's no excuse. She was obviously not okay. I told myself she wanted it, but did she really?

That was the absolute worst way I could have gone about it. I already knew she was scared of sex, and taking her virginity so roughly isn't going to help that any. I should have treated her like a princess, like something precious, because that's what she is. I've screwed up during sex before, but not like that. If I start to doubt it, all I have to do is replay her reaction. She all but screamed behind the fabric I used to muffle her when I entered her. She was crying the whole time. When it was over, she couldn't get away fast enough.

SELENA

The drunken mistakes or married women who woke up and took one look at me and realized they'd ruined their marriage for a taste of youth were bad enough.

Okay, so I've always been a complete dick, not just tonight.

But this woman...

This is my wife, and I treated her like... Like an enemy.

Just when we'd started to have some kind of breakthrough, I managed to immediately fuck it up beyond repair. Because she's right. There is no going back from this. I took her virginity, something she can never get back, and I claimed it for myself, with no concern for her.

I rake a hand through my hair as I sit on the edge of the tub, watching her dab a tissue between her legs. It comes away red. I can see my face in the mirror beyond her. Blood rings my mouth like a fucking cannibal from how deep I drove my tongue into her cunt. I don't want to wash it away, though, to erase the only taste of her I'll probably ever get. It wasn't enough.

I'm beginning to realize I'll never get enough of her. Knowing it now, when she's done with me, is a torment oo cruel even for the likes of me.

"Get in the bath," I say, turning off the water when he tub is full enough.

She meets my eyes in the mirror, her expression guarded. "You won't touch me?"

"I promise. I won't even get in if you don't want."

She nods, and to my relief, she steps into the tub. Then she slumps down, sliding into the warm water. Her whole body looks defeated, smaller and more fragile than it was before, as if I've broken the spirit that animated her. My stomach twists, and I know she's right. I can never undo what I did, can never take it back, can never make it right. It's not fair of me to ask her how I can repair the damage. I fucked up. I have to figure it out myself, figure out how to move forward after a violation like that. The truth is, there is no moving forward. We'll be stuck here forever.

A warm bath to relax her and ease the soreness is so inadequate it's almost insulting.

She sits in the tub, staring miserably at the first swirls of red threading through the water. "I just… I'm messed up, King."

I crouch next to the tub, but I don't touch her. I lost that right when I forced her to take me when she wasn't ready. "That's not true," I assure her. "I'm the one who fucked up."

"Yeah, maybe," she says quietly. "But I never would have been ready. It was the only way."

"I don't understand."

"I just… Don't like to be touched."

"Anywhere?" I ask.

"Not if it's going to lead there," she says.

"You said you were lying about that," I remind her. "On our honeymoon, you said you'd made that up."

"I said I was lying about not having those feelings," she corrects.

"So… You have sexual feelings, but you don't want sex or even for me to go down on you?"

She shakes her head, mumbling into the water. "That's even worse."

It's one thing if she likes to be forced, if it's part of the game, the way I thought it was. My brothers dated a girl like that last year. But she's saying she doesn't want it at all. I don't know what to say, what to think of that. I knew she was scared of sex, but this is different. How can a girl not like her pussy licked? I mean, if she hates me, I get her not wanting *me* to touch her, but I can't deny that having my dick sucked feels good. It's biology. I've fucked lots of girls I don't care about—because it feels good.

And I've made her cum before, gotten her wet plenty of times. So what's the hang-up?

We sit there in silence for a minute.

"I understand I hurt you," I say. "But oral doesn't hurt."

"I'm sorry," she says, picking up a bottle of bubbles and dumping some in the tub. I turn on the water so she won't have to move.

"Can we talk about this?" I ask.

"I'm not going to change my mind, King. I hate it and I will always hate it. The only way I'll ever let you do that is if I don't have a choice."

"Like today," I say, swallowing the knot in my throat.

She sinks back into the water. "I'd rather you do what you did today than make me do the other thing."

"If you hate it that much… You said you've done it before. Is that how you know you don't like it?"

She swallows, moving the bubbles to cover her in the tub. "Yes."

"Because… You didn't want to that time, either," I guess. "Someone forced you."

She takes a long, shaky breath.

"Who was it?" I ask, my voice so quiet, so calm and still, she'd never guess the murderous rage gripping my heart. If my mother doubted I was capable of murder, I could give her a real clear answer now.

Eliza shakes her head. "It doesn't matter," she whispers. "I don't want you to do anything. That's why I didn't tell you."

"So you just let me fuck you when you didn't want to, just like some other asshole? You couldn't have told me beforehand that's why you're fucked up about it?"

"I didn't let you," she whispers, and a tear falls from her lashes into the water.

The shame that burns through my veins is like poison, like nothing I've felt before, not even when we came back from the party and saw that my sister was gone. I didn't just fail Eliza. I actively destroyed her.

My hand fists at my side, but I keep the other one relaxed as I reach over the side of the tub to gently take hers. She cries quietly, but she doesn't pull away. I don't know if this is the last time I'll hold her hand, so I don't let go. It feels so small, so delicate, in mine. It makes me want to massacre anyone and everyone who ever hurt her.

"Who touched you?" I ask, my voice low and more menacing than I meant for it to be.

"It doesn't matter," she says, wiping her cheeks with her free hand. "I was still a virgin for you. You know I was. You felt it. I wasn't lying. Look." She points to the bloody water from how roughly I fucked her, not knowing she was anything other than a brat who needed a little rough treatment to put her in line.

I measure my words carefully. "Do you really think I fucking care about that right now?"

I want to murder someone, but at the top of the list of people who hurt her is me. What I did is a thousand times worse than some asshole eating her out when she didn't want it. The blood in the water is a testament to how much she didn't want it, to how badly I fucked up. It didn't just stain the linens in our room. It's a stain on us, on our bond. I didn't just violate her. I hurt her.

That blood is a stain on my fucking soul.

She looks at me and then away. "I just wanted you to know. You still got someone who'd never been fucked, just like you were promised. They just did… Other stuff."

My heart is hammering with rage inside me. "You'd better tell me who did that to you, so I can take care of him."

Them.

Fuck. She said '*they.*'

"You can't," she says, pulling her hand from mine. "There's nothing you can do. It was a long time ago, and t's already been taken care of."

"You told your dad?"

She doesn't say anything.

Fuck. My heart freezes in my chest, and I remember my earlier suspicions. "It was your dad," I say flatly.

"No," she says quickly.

Too quickly. Too emphatically.

Who else would have access to her... *And* not be terrified of what Anthony Pomponio would do?

"Look, King," she says, turning her face to me at last. "I'm sorry that you got a wife who's broken, but I didn't tell you because I didn't want you to know and react exactly like this. I wouldn't have told you at all if I hadn't freaked out like that and given it away. I would have just endured it like a good little wifey and kept my mouth shut, just like I did when you fucked me. That's how much I didn't want you to know. So please, please respect my wishes and just drop it. I don't want revenge. I don't want to talk about it. I want to forget it happened and move on with my life. *Please*."

I don't know what to say to her. I can't just forget it. I can't drop it and let it go and pretend I don't know especially after what I did to her tonight. But it's her body, her experience, and I've already violated her enough. I have no right to ask for anything else. I have to respect her wishes, even if it feels wrong to the very core of my bones.

"Okay," I say at last.

She shakes her head. "I'll do my duty to the family. I know we have to have a baby. Maybe it worked this time, and if not, I'll find some way to get through it if it happens again. Maybe I'll just get really drunk, so I don't even feel it."

"I'm not going to do that," I say, adjusting my position where I'm kneeling on the tiles. I relish the ache in my knees, the pain reminding me that I hurt her so much worse. She didn't hurt me, though. She never did anything but act like a brat. I'm the one who fucked up, and now I'll live with the consequences. I'm glad when she sweeps a mountain of bubbles over her body, so I can't see her anymore. Looking only reminds me what I can never have again. It reminds me what someone took from her, and the immensely more devastating thing I took from her.

Maybe it's not too late. Maybe I can still make it right.

"Can I get in?" I ask. "I won't touch you. I won't make you do anything you don't want, Eliza. Never again. No matter what. I don't care how you act, or what the families expect. I'm going to make this up to you, no matter how long it takes. I know you might never trust me, but I'll work the rest of my life to prove to you that you're safe with me. That I'll never hurt you again."

She looks up at me, her eyes all question and vulnerability. "Promise?"

"I promise." I lean forward and kiss her forehead.

"What happens when they ask about a baby?" she whispers.

"We tell them we're trying. And when that stops working, we can tell them you couldn't get pregnant. As long as we're married, the families are united. A baby would help solidify it, but even without one, they have us." I squeeze her hand, and she nods, a tear sliding down her cheek.

"Thank you," she whispers.

I climb over the side of the tub and sink into the water with her. Instead of scooting to the far end, I open my arms, giving her a questioning look. She swallows, then slowly scoots over, giving me space beside her. I sink down next to her and pull her into my lap. She tenses, and I curl my body around hers, kissing the back of her neck. "Can I just hold you?" I ask. "I don't want anything else."

"Okay," she whispers, and I feel her begin to relax. I hold her gently, like a fragile thing, though I know she doesn't want that. No one wants to be thought of that way. But the burn of my anger has cooled into something warm and fiercely protective, and I keep my arms around her, as if I can protect her from myself after what I did to her.

I don't know when I stopped thinking I would never care about this girl. Maybe it happened sometime during the honeymoon, when I was counting the freckles on her skin, watching with envy as she laughed at everyone's jokes but mine, admiring the fearless way she dove into the water from a cliff. Maybe it was in the weeks since then, when I earned her obedience, fed her from a spoon, licked it clean after being inside her. Maybe it was when she stitched me up even after I demanded her submission on her knees. Or maybe it was tonight, when I came inside her and then saw inside the cracks in her armor that look so much like mine, even if the cause of our brokenness is so very different. Even if I put the cracks in her armor tonight that let me see through to the real girl inside the brat.

I only know that I've already broken the vows I made on the altar. Not the ones to her, but the ones to myself. I promised I wouldn't let her love me, but I forgot to worry about my own stupid heart.

My sister once told me that I'd make a good father because I want to protect people, to take care of them. I may never be a father, but the other part is true. I didn't ask for it, but I'm cursed with an instinct that makes the life I'm bound to even more dangerous.

I know what it's like to hurt, and when I see someone hurting, I want to take that hurt away. It binds me to them in some way, a way that has nothing to do with the vows I made to Eliza or the rings we put on each other's fingers. I can't help but care about what's mine, and I will go to the ends of the earth to protect it. And the instinct isn't just for family, for a girl I vowed to protect. It's more than that. She found my weakness. When I know a girl is hurting, something primal inside me awakens, an instinct to protect her, to care for her, to heal her, even if I'm the one who caused the damage.

I know how dangerous that is, not just because someone could take her from me, but because I won't be able to protect her from all the hurts that come with being a made guy's wife. I can't promise her I'll always be here. I wasn't there to protect her in the past when she was hurt, and I can't protect her from the effects of her past on her life now. The truth is, I can't even promise I'll protect her if I'm here. I've failed before. How could she trust me to take care of her when the last girl I was supposed to protect ended up dead?

Even worse, I've made sure she can never trust me. That I won't protect her from the monster in her own house. I don't deserve what I took from her. I proved myself unworthy of the wife the families chose for me, the one they entrusted me with. I didn't protect her and cherish her. I lost control of her, lost control of myself. I ruined her, wounded her in a way that can never be healed. And for that, I can never even ask forgiveness.

nineteen

King

I'm standing in the kitchen looking out over the neighborhood when I hear footsteps behind me. The August sun is murky in the east, the heat visible over the buildings even at eight in the morning, but I turn away, surprised Eliza's up so early. She usually sleeps in. Then again, she went to bed early last night, turning in after our bath. I lay awake all night, tormented by guilt, unable to shut off my thoughts and find peace in sleep.

Eliza picks up the coffee pot and pours some into one of the tiny teacups we got for our wedding. "I'll get a maid today," she says, gesturing around the kitchen, which I cleaned up sometime in the middle of the night, when I couldn't bear to lie beside her any longer.

"Is that why you're up so early?"

"You're working today?" she asks, watching me adjust my tie. It's too hot for this shit even with the air on. There's not enough AC in the Bronx to cool a penthouse apartment on a day like today.

"Do you need me for something?" I ask.

"No," she says.

Of course she doesn't. I fucking overpowered her last night, took what was mine with no regard for her wellbeing. I should have been more careful, at least gentle. I knew something wasn't right with her, that she must have some trauma, something behind her behavior. But I let her bratty attitude get to me, thought I could fuck it out of her.

"I work every day," I point out. "Did you want me to help you interview for the maid position?"

"I'll figure it out," she says. "I'm meeting Bianca for lunch, anyway. I need to ask her about something."

I watch her swallow a mouthful of coffee, her cognac eyes meeting mine over the rim of the cup. She smiles shyly, and a twist of guilt tugs inside me. When we got in bed last night, I stayed on my side, with an ocean of space between us. I wanted to hold her again, but I didn't ask. I know I don't have that right anymore.

So instead of holding her, I lay there alone, thinking about what she said about me finding a woman on the side. I know my frustration with not getting laid is getting to me, but I'm not about to hire a prostitute like it's the same as hiring a maid. Not when my wife sleeps next to me. But I can't push her to do something she doesn't want. I'll never do that again.

If I'd kept my promise to myself, felt nothing for her, it might be easier. I wouldn't want her for more than what a whore could give me, for more than fulfilling a basic need.

I shouldn't need more. But I do.

And the fucked up part is, I'm never going to get it. Not from her. But I can't even conceive of taking a mistress because my wife has been abused. So I guess celibacy is my penance for what I did to her. If I was a better man, I'd wait forever with nothing but patience and understanding. I want to be that man. But in truth, I want to fuck my wife. Once was not enough. I want her every night. And not the way I did last night. Not the way it would be if she agreed to it, like she did afterwards, when I tried to go down on her.

I don't want her lying there stiff as a board and shaking, letting me get off on her like she's a blowup doll. I want her to want me. I want her to grab me when I walk in the door and start ripping my clothes off. I want to throw her down and ravish her, make her cum with my name on her lips and my cock so deep inside her she can't remember her own. I want to make her lose control and cum for me like she did in Bora Bora, before I knew.

And then I feel like a piece of shit for wanting those things from a girl who's had those things stolen from her. I took that from her, and I have no right to expect her to ever give it willingly after that violation.

"What?" she asks, jerking me back to reality. I realize I've been staring right through her for two minutes straight.

"Have fun today," I say. I set my cup in the sink and turn away, but her arms snake around me before I can take a step.

She drops her cup into the sink, the coffee splattering against the stainless steel as she squeezes me hard, like she thinks she could crush me with her tiny arms.

She said she doesn't like touch. What does that include? I let her set the terms, standing there while she hugs me. She presses her cheek to my back. "Be careful," she says quietly.

I pry her arms loose and turn to face her, wrapping my arms around her gently, so she can pull away if she wants. "I will."

She stands on tiptoes, lifting her face to mine and looping an arm behind my neck. She pulls me down for a kiss, and I'm so surprised I don't even react for a second. She's about to drop back onto her heels when I grip her tighter against me, cradling her head in my palm and kissing her harder. I want her so much I think I'll explode from a single kiss, and I have to rein myself in to keep rom backing her against the table, spreading her legs, and devouring her. I swear I can still taste her, that single lick I got last night.

I kiss her gently instead, my lips pressing against her soft ones, and fuck, she's so soft, so delicate, it makes me ache. I want to hold her like a fragile flower, never bruise her petals again. When she opens her lips, I almost don't want to taste her deeper. It will only make it worse.

But I'm weak, and I slide my tongue between her lips, taking everything she'll give me. She shivers against me, and I pull her closer even though she's already flush against me. I can feel her soft tits pressing into my abs with each breath she takes, her pulse fluttering like a moth trapped against a windowpane when my thumb caresses the side of her throat. She makes a soft sound of pleasure into my mouth, halfway between a moan and a whimper, and I want to fucking die.

She breaks off, her eyes flying wide. "You're hard," she whispers.

I curse and jerk away from her so fast she stumbles back, catching herself on the edge of the table. She's staring at me like… Well, like I'm the asshole who forced her to take my cock the last time it was hard.

I sink back against the counter and rake both hands through my hair and grip handfuls of it, squeezing my eyes shut and trying to get my raging hard-on under control. I should never have let myself kiss her back. I should have known she makes me lose my fucking mind when she touches me. She deserves someone else, someone better, someone who can control himself and doesn't act like the horny teenager he is.

"It wasn't a *bad* thing," she says. "I was just surprised. Don't be embarrassed."

"I'm not fucking embarrassed," I say, lifting my head. Ashamed, yes. Not embarrassed.

"You're not?"

"And why would you be surprised?" I go on, too pissed at myself to hold back. "I haven't had sex in months, and I sleep next to you every night, and you're about the most beautiful, desirable, irresistible woman I've ever seen. I fucked you one time, and I can never have you again. So yeah, kissing you makes me hard, and if that makes me a fucking monster, then that's what I am."

She stares at me another minute, the air so still between us that I can hear the honk of a car on the street below, a dog barking, someone yelling. "You still want me?" she asks at last. "In that way? How?"

"Did you not hear the part about how you married a monster?" I ask, pushing away from the counter.

"It's just… After what I told you, I didn't think you'd see me like that. You were looking at me like I was damaged goods. Something to be pitied. Not…"

"Not fucked?" I ask.

She swallows, dropping her gaze.

"That *happened* to you, but it's not you," I say. "It doesn't change how much I want you. I'm sorry. You don't want to be anyone's sex object. I know seeing you that way makes me no better than the people who did that to you, but you already know I'm not. I did the same and worse just last night."

She just stares at me with those clear, whiskey eyes all wide and shocked, like she's just realizing what she's stuck with for the rest of her life. I can't stand it any longer, so I turn away and go to our bedroom. I grab my gun, check the chamber and the safety, and shove it into my belt. When I turn, Eliza is lingering in the doorway.

I don't want to push her aside, but I can't be here with her. I thought I could be a better man, that I could do this job and still be a good man, but now I know that being a good man has nothing to do with this job. I thought the sum total of a man's worth was whether he chooses right or wrong more often, but maybe it's not. Maybe it's a single moment, a single choice. The choice to hurt your wife. The choice to stay even knowing you can't be anything other than what you are, or to walk away before you hurt someone who's already been hurt more than anyone should.

We stand there staring at each other for a long minute. My chest tightens, my throat, my hold on myself. I lost myself for a minute, lost sight of what I had to do.

"Say something," she says softly, an edge of pleading in her voice.

"I'm going to work," I say. "When I get home, you should be gone."

"What?" she asks, her eyes widening with shock and... Hurt.

I swallow before forcing the words out. No one ever said doing the right thing was easy. Usually, it's the opposite.

"You should go home," I say.

"I am home."

"Back to your father. I hurt you, Eliza. You said it yourself. I can't fix it. It's too late. If he's not the one who hurt you before, that's where you'll be safest. You shouldn't be here. I'm not safe."

"You're wrong," she says, stepping into the room.

I move away, edging toward the door. But then I stop. I won't run like a coward. "I'm sorry," I say, facing her squarely. "I thought I could be the man you deserve. You deserve someone who thinks only of you, not himself. But I'm not that man."

"I never asked for a saint," she says. "And don't tell me what I deserve."

"You deserve love."

"And you can't do that?" she asks.

It's the hope in her voice, her eyes, that destroys me. I promised I'd never hurt her by letting her love me. Last night, I hurt her in another way, and I won't add love to the list of ways I've wronged her. It's time to stop it before I hurt her more. Because I will. I press my lips together, my sternum aching like I just took a punch to it, and I shake my head. "No."

She stares at me. "Not even if I could?"

"Tell your father you want an annulment," I say. "Tell him I can't get it up or whatever you have to say to get out of it. Al owes me, so he'll be okay with it. He'll find someone else, someone better for you, so the families will still be united. And it'll be like this never happened."

She opens her mouth like she's going to argue, but then she closes it. She blinks a few times, swallows, then nods. "Okay. If that's what you want."

It's the last thing in the world I want, but it's what she needs. What I want to do is close the distance etween us, sweep her into my arms, and kiss her. But then what? Then I'll want more, and I can't have it. I'll be ashamed of how much I want her after what I did, and he'll feel bad that she can't give it, and I'll hate myself more. I've fucked up so many times, but I don't want to be the same man I was six months ago. I want to learn from my mistakes, to see more clearly. I couldn't save my sister. I couldn't save Eliza from what happened to her before we met. I didn't save her last night.

I attacked her.

But I can save her now. I can save her from myself.

I stand there for a minute, not knowing what to do, how to say goodbye. Or maybe the truth is that I don't want to say goodbye at all. I've never cared about a girl the way I care about her.

At last, I hold out a hand. "It's been an honor being your husband."

She stares at my hand, then turns her face up to mine, her eyes flashing in the familiar way that fills me with relief even though it's always driven me insane before. I didn't want to break her spirit, to turn her into someone else. I just wanted to claim her, to remind her she was mine, that she couldn't do whatever the fuck she wanted. But I took it too far. Knowing she still has some fight left in her puts my mind at ease. I know I've made the right decision, that she's strong enough to move on, that she'll be fine without me. And Al will know better than to use me for such an important job again. I'm too young to be trusted with a job this big, with something so precious as Eliza Pomponio.

"Are you fucking kidding me right now?" she demands. "You want a *handshake?*"

I drop my hand.

"You know what?" she says. "Fuck you, King. This isn't about what I deserve. This is about the fact that you can't survive without having someone to stick your dick in, and now that you fucked up, you can't stick it in me because you feel too guilty. But I told you all along I didn't want that to be part of our marriage. I told you I didn't like sex. I told you to get a mistress. It's not my fault you're too proud."

My own temper starts to rise, but I hold my tongue. This is my fucking fault. Not for what I did last night, but for falling for her. I wasn't supposed to care. But I didn't protect my own heart, and now I'm fucking paying for it. My one consolation is that she shows very few signs of returning those feelings. I can handle the pain if I know I did right by her.

"You're right," I say. "You're right about everything."

"Ugh," she says, grabbing a shoe off the floor and hurling it at me, barely missing my head. "You're impossible."

I twist off my wedding ring and set it gently on her vanity. "Goodbye, Eliza."

I turn and walk out of the bedroom. I hear another shoe hit the wall, and she yells after me, "Don't worry, I'll be gone when you get home, and you won't have to deal with my shit ever again!"

I close my eyes and take a breath. "That would probably be best."

A lamp flies out the bedroom door and crashes to the floor beside me. I wince, every instinct telling me to turn around, to go back and tell her I can handle all of her, the damage and the crazy, the brat and the wild girl. That we'll work through it together. That it's going to be okay, that it isn't her fault. That after last night, I will spend the rest of my life making up for what I did.

But this isn't about what I want. It's about the fact that I fail, and it's better to just get it over with now than wait until she cares. I will never be the husband she wants, one who's satisfied in a marriage where we live two separate lives. I'll never be a husband who's happy to cross paths once a day because he has no interest in her as a person. I've already failed in that. She was forced to be my wife, but she never wanted this, never wanted me. I was supposed to change her mind, but all I did was prove that she had every reason not to trust me from the start.

I want her, and I'll never stop wanting her, and that's dangerous for both of us. I can handle putting myself in danger. I do it every day. But I can't put her in danger.

The least I can do is take her out of harm's way, out of danger, and that means letting her go live the life she always wanted—one without me in it.

twenty

Eliza

I hurl the other lamp out the bedroom door into the living room with a scream of rage when I hear the front door close. He left. He fucking left me. After everything he did, I should be the one leaving. I grab his shoes, all lined up neatly under the edge of the bed like he's in the military instead of his own fucking home, and I hurl them at the wall, the mirror above the dresser. The mirror tilts, reflecting the surface of the dresser, where his wedding band sits like an accusation.

It's over. I should be happy. I'm finally free.

I snatch it and hurl it at the mirror. It bounces off, barely making a sound. The rage wells up inside me. I open my mouth and let out a roar of fury. Grabbing the dge of the tilted mirror, I heave it with all my strength. It otters, then topples over with a splintering crash as it hits the floor. I jump back, but I'm filled with a gleeful satisfaction. A hysterical laugh bubbles up inside me. I grab the wooden frame and kick the glass out, not feeling the cuts on my bare toes.

I tried. Even this morning, after what he did last night, I played nice. I tried to appease him, telling him I'd hire a maid, even giving him a goodbye kiss. Because the truth is, he only did what every other man would do. I knew it, but I also knew he was different, and it pissed me off. It pissed me off that he was so above everything, like he thought he was better than me and everyone else. He left me alone, and when he did touch me, he was too fucking good at it. It's not fair.

I slam the frame of the mirror on the floor again and again, pounding the pieces of glass into smaller fragments until the wood splinters and cracks, and I'm left with only one long piece of the frame. I'm too mad to care that there's glass in my feet. I stomp across the floor, gritting my teeth against the pain as new shards cut me.

SELENA

It's like walking over hot coals. Mind over matter. I control my body. Just me. Not him. Not the face in my nightmares, my memories, distorted through water like in a funhouse mirror.

I catch sight of myself in the mirror above my vanity. I look insane, my hair a wild tangle, my face flushed with exertion, my gaze desperate and unhinged. I rear back and swing the wood like a baseball bat, shattering the mirror above my vanity. Glass rains down over the makeup scattered over the surface. I swing again, sending the bottles of nail polish flying. King must have brought them in from the other room sometime last night after I fell asleep. Taking another swing, I clear the top of the vanity. Then I pick up the chair, smashing it on the floor and letting out a primal scream of pain and rage. How could he fucking leave me?

Everyone leaves. First my brother, then my mother, then every single nanny I ever had until Sylvia, then my own husband. The only person who never left is my father.

DANGEROUS DEFIANCE

When the chair is destroyed and my throat is sore from raging, I sink into the shards of mirror on the floor and let myself cry. It's all so fucked up.

My feet are bleeding. Between my legs is still shockingly painful from King's rough treatment. And inside my chest feels hollow but hot at once, raw and aching.

I did this. It's not his fault. It's mine.

The truth is, I didn't just know it was going to happen. I wanted it to happen. Not because I wanted sex, but because I just had to prove to myself that he's not special, that he's the same as every other guy. I had to win, to prove myself right, to prove he was no better than me or anyone. He's a common man, with common needs, not someone who's too good to get a mistress even though I won't let him have me.

I pushed because I wanted him to snap. I wanted him to take me, to get it over with. I wanted him to take me so I didn't have to give in myself, so I didn't have to feel anything scary. I was pissed that he kept making me lose control, kept making me want him, while he stayed in complete control. It was my turn to push him past his breaking point, like he did to me on our honeymoon and again on the table. I didn't care if it hurt. I know it makes no sense, but somehow, making him lose control let me feel like I held the power, even when he took control of me and had his way with me.

If he took me by force, I could keep hating him. I'd have a reason.

I do have a reason. I have so many reasons, so why does it hurt so fucking much that he left?

Things were just starting to get better between us. I thought we really had a moment the other night, when he let me take care of him. But then I had to go and push him the next day, because I loved what he did to me the night before when I pushed it.

Worse than anything he did is secret I told. It's the truth, but it's a truth no man could handle. Why did I tell him? I've never told anyone. I didn't want anyone to know, didn't want them to look at me differently. That's why he really left. Of course it is. No one wants to know that about his wife. Maybe he didn't even consider me a virgin. Did he leave because he felt deceived, because he didn't get someone untouched after all? Or because he thinks I'm tainted and scarred in the worst imaginable way? Or because he realized he'd been consigned to a life without sex?

Now he's run off to probably find some slut who will want to fuck him all the time and make him feel like a man again.

I know that's totally unfair. A girl who wants to fuck him isn't a slut, she's normal. I only call girls that to make me feel better about myself instead of feeling like I'm broken for not being able to do what they can. The truth is, I'm jealous as fuck of girls like Lizzie. I mean, look at my husband. It's so unfair. When I remember kneeling in front of him, looking up at his body... It was like some kind of marble statue come to life. What girl wouldn't want to fuck him all day, every day? Even I halfway want to fuck him, and I've never wanted to fuck anyone. I've never even gotten wet for a guy before him.

Sure, I made out with a bunch of guys in high school, but it wasn't about getting turned on. It was for the rush of saying no, of knowing I was the one in control this time. Kissing boys let me explore that while knowing I was safe, that if anyone ever didn't want to stop, I had a safety net in the form of a two-hundred-pound bodyguard with a gun.

But King… God, what is wrong with me? I had someone good, better than any other guy I could have gotten.

No wonder he wants out of this. He deserves someone who wants to fuck him, someone who lets him fuck her, not a frigid mental case like me. I couldn't just appreciate that my father married me to a young, hot guy. I didn't try to make it work. I had something to prove—that I was in control, not him. But I didn't just do that. I was a total bitch, and I kept being my bratty self, intentionally disrespecting him.

But not everything is my fault. He fucked up worse than I did.

He hurt me. He deserves to suffer for that. He deserves all the guilt, not me.

He's the one who went too far. He took me with no remorse. He wasn't gentle. He knew it would hurt, and he didn't care.

And after he's ruined me, now he walks out.

Maybe I always knew he would do that, too. Some part of me has been waiting for it all along. Not so I could be free—in truth, what do I need with freedom? To party and get drunk?—but because I knew that he wouldn't stay. If my own mother wouldn't stay, why would anyone else?

I sit there and pick the glass out of my feet for a while. Then I get dressed, not bothering with makeup today. When I bend to retrieve a shoe, I see the wedding band gleaming from amid the shards of mirror on the floor. I'm so mad I can't think straight when I see it. How dare he kick me out?

I shake out my shoe in case of glass shards, then pull it on before snatching up the ring.

I should have been the one to take off my ring. I should have been the one leaving. After what he did, he has the audacity to tell *me* to leave? Even after what he did, I was going to make it work. I was going to get a maid today.

Well, fuck that. He can clean up this mess himself. As for his ring, he didn't want it.

I storm into the bathroom, throw it in the toilet, and flush.

Still not satisfied, I storm around the apartment throwing shit again until I'm too exhausted to go on. If King wants me gone, fine. I'll leave his fucking ass just like he wants. Of course that's what he wants. He wants someone like Lizzie, who knows what she's doing, who owns her body and her sexuality and drowns him in it. So let him go find her. I'm fucking done.

I pack my bags, throwing everything in without folding it. I leave my wedding dress in the closet. Let him look at it for the rest of his life the way I had to look at his ring today.

I'm startled by a knock, and when I look at the time, I realize it's already time for my lunch date with Bianca. I'd forgotten all about it. I sigh and open the door.

She comes strutting in with her bag swinging on her wrist and her heels clicking on the floor, only to pull up short. "Damn," she says, glancing into the kitchen, where I took great pleasure in shattering every single one of the wedding dishes we got. If he doesn't want the bride, he sure as fuck isn't keeping the presents. "Did a hurricane come through here last night, or were you and that delicious man of yours doing it on every surface in the apartment?"

I snort. "Hardly. We got in a fight."

"Makeup sex, then?" she asks, wiggling her brows. "How is he, anyway?"

"A complete brute," I say, filled with a smug satisfaction that I'm telling the truth. I always knew he would be, and I was right. I wanted to prove something, and I did. In the end, that means I won, even if he is the one who ended it.

I won't think about that part.

"That bad?" Bianca asks, looking delighted. "Oooh, let's burn his clothes."

"Tempting," I say. "But I can't do that."

"Why not?" she asks. "What happened? Did *you* fuck up?"

I look at her eager face, just waiting for the juicy gossip, and I know I can't tell her. Bianca isn't the kind of friend you tell your darkest secrets. And even though I didn't mean to tell King, I did. And somehow, that brought us closer.

Or so I thought.

In truth, it just scared him away. I expected him to think I was tainted, even to pity me so much he couldn't think of me in a sexy way because every time he tried, he just thought about me being molested and lost his desire. I didn't think he'd leave me altogether. I also didn't expect him to still want me. But this morning, he did. I felt it when he kissed me, and god… A little shiver goes through me when I remember it stretching me open last night.

But there's no way I can tell Bianca any of that.

I can't tell her that I've changed my mind, that being on my own isn't the best thing in the world. Now that he's given me the freedom I wanted all along, it only tastes bitter. I told myself that's what I wanted, to be a young widow, free of all obligations. But maybe all along, it was just an excuse to keep people at bay, to keep anyone from getting close enough to know the truth.

Now that someone knows it... In a way, I was relieved. Last night, when he held me in the bathtub until the water got so cold we were both shivering, when he didn't try to touch me or press the issue, I felt closer to him than I've ever felt with anyone. For a moment, I didn't have to carry the burden on my own. For a moment, someone knew even the worst parts of me, and he helped me hold up the sky.

Until he fucking left, that is, leaving me to hold it all on my own. Only now do I realize how heavy it was all those years, that I was weakening, slowly crumbling under the weight of it. I was wrong all along. I needed help, not freedom. I needed someone to accept it, to love me anyway.

Now I have everything I've ever thought I wanted, everything I fought for. He gave me a way out. I'm standing on the edge of freedom, but it no longer looks like the end goal. It looks terrifying and isolating. That isn't what I want anymore.

But I only realized it too late.

"Yeah, I fucked up," I say to Bianca. "We both did. Mostly him."

I don't add the rest of it, that I should never have told King, that I should have just sucked it up and lain there and let him fuck me every night for the rest of my life. If I'd never told, never let him take part of that weight off me, I'd never have realized it was crushing me. I'd have gone on forever without thinking about any of it too closely.

But then what?

"What'd you do?" Bianca asks. She looks different, though, not as eager and more… Guarded. And this is why I can't trust her with anything. I never know when she's a friend and when she's going to use something against me.

"We're just so different," I say, knowing how lame that sounds when she can see the devastation all around us. This is not from any irreconcilable difference.

"You might have more in common than you know," Bianca says, picking her way over to the couch.

That makes me snort. "Like what?"

"For starters, you both have a dead sibling," she says.

Some people might call a comment like that insensitive, but when you've grown up the way we have, it's just the way things are. There's no point tiptoeing around the truth. We've all lost people we care about, and plenty of us have lost family. Which means it's hardly something to bond with my new husband over.

Still, jealousy rears its ugly head when I think about him telling her something painful from his past. When did they talk about this? And why didn't he talk to me about it?

"Did he tell you that?" I ask.

Bianca shrugs. "You'd be surprised what you can learn by reading the news."

I don't want to be interested, but I'm way past that. I want to know everything about my infuriatingly proud, stubborn husband. I just wish he'd told me. I accused him of not doing his homework, but to be fair, I don't know anything about him. Not that I can blame him for not telling me something personal. I haven't exactly made it super easy for him to talk to me. I've been too busy being a brat and provoking him for him to trust me with anything. I would have thrown it back in his face.

"How'd she die?" I ask.

"I guess she drowned in a flood," Bianca says popping open her compact and examining her lipstick. "They never found her body."

"When was that?"

"Like, this year," she says. "I don't remember when. I can't believe he hasn't told you."

She snaps her mirror closed, looking smug, as if he's the one who told her and she wasn't internet stalking *my* husband. I want to smack the sloppy lip gloss right off her face, but I'm too preoccupied with thoughts of King. I remember how I felt after my brother died. How numb I was, like I was in shock for months. Which means King is still probably in the grieving period, and instead of being there for him, I've been a total brat. And not just a brat, but so hateful that he actually thinks I'm capable of arranging a hit on him.

I haven't cared up until now. I haven't wanted to talk to him or know him. I didn't want to risk getting close. But that's all gone now. There's no way to go back, now that I've spilled my dirty secrets to him. And there's no way to feel distant from someone after telling them something like that, something you've spent your life hiding, and compensating for, and ignoring. Something you've never told anyone. I bared my soul, my shame, my brokenness. I don't even know why I told him. Maybe some part of me recognized a brokenness inside him, and it called out to me that we are the same, that he could be trusted with this, that he could bear it.

But I was wrong, and he's gone. And it's time for me to be gone, too.

"What's with the bags?" Bianca asks when I go to get them.

"I'm going home for a few days."

"That bad?" she asks, barely hiding her glee that my marriage is falling apart after only a few months.

345

"Yeah," I admit. "I might have to skip lunch today."

She sighs. "Seriously? I came all the way to the Bronx to see you."

"Sorry," I say, though I'm not. I was getting tired of the parties and gossip anyway, but now it's lost all appeal. I'm too worried about my husband leaving me to think about the most exclusive new lunch spot we need to hit to stay relevant. I don't give two shits about being relevant. I want my marriage back. The realization shakes me. Am I turning into one of those pathetic women we hate? The ones who serve their husbands like slaves?

"It's fine," Bianca says with a huff. "It would take you forever to get ready anyway."

"We'll do it another day, okay?"

"I need to pick up something for my dad, anyway," she says dismissively. "But if you turn into one of those boring old housewives who never goes out, I'm telling everyone you're hiding because you got fat and have stretchmarks all over your ass."

Best frenemies to the end.

When she's gone, I just sit there for a few minutes, working on not going to pieces. I don't know why I care about this stupid apartment. It's not my home. It's King's. He bought it for us, a new place for us to make into our home together. But now I can't stop seeing him taking off his ring, laying it so carefully on the dresser, and walking out.

I have no more tears. There's no one to cry for. No one but me, and the little voice inside me who says we knew this was coming, I can't count on anyone to stay. It's just us, just me and my demons.

At last, I grab my bags and walk out, out of King's place, out of my marriage. I leave his place as wrecked as our life together. Maybe he was right. Maybe this is for the best. I was starting to have feelings for him, and that's something I can't afford to have. It wouldn't be fair to him. I'd start being jealous if he found another woman, and I can't give myself to him the way he deserves. Leaving is the best thing I can do if I really care about him. He deserves more than a broken wife who wastes his youth, his prime, his beauty. His heart.

I call the driver and take the elevator to the lobby. I think about King coming home, walking into the ransacked, empty apartment. Will he think for a fraction of a second, before it sinks in, that I'm just out with my friends like usual? I've been purposely selfish. I don't blame him for wanting me gone. But I know how it feels to open a drawer that used to be filled with the clothes of someone you love, only to find it empty. To stare into it and not quite believe it, even though you know they're gone.

Not that King loves me. He made it clear he can't, that he won't. That I was nothing more than a business deal for him, a way to advance his career. I was his possession, and he made sure I knew it, putting me in line every time I tried to rebel and then tossing me like trash when he found out I was defective.

"Ready, Miss?" the driver asks, climbing out of the car. He puts my bags in the trunk. I watch, numb. I wonder if this is how my mother felt when she left us.

"I'm ready." I climb into the car with one last look at the building that was my home for the summer. I've ained my freedom, but I don't feel triumphant. I feel defeated.

I always imagined Mom was happy, full of hopes and dreams, a lifetime of promise ahead as she drove away, waving and smiling, to her new shiny life of fame and excitement. How could she do it? And not just to her husband, but her daughter?

"Where to, Miss?" the driver asks. His eyes in the mirror are sympathetic.

I sit up straight and take a deep breath, trying not to look like a failure who's crawling home in defeat. This is for the best. If I stayed, King would have questions.

I don't want him to go digging, to unearth the past. I don't want him thinking he can be some kind of hero, save me from myself. I want him to leave it alone, to pretend it never happened, just like I do. But for the first time, I wish I knew him better, that I hadn't spent the last few months keeping as much distance from him as possible, locking him out, telling him I hated him, that I didn't want to know him.

Because now I don't know him, and I need to. I need to know what he's thinking, planning, feeling. Will he tell my father what I told him? Will he tell him how he found out, what he did to me last night? Who will end up dead because I couldn't be a wife, couldn't keep my mouth shut, couldn't bring peace between families?

And on a more personal note, I want to know what is down in the depths of those deep, brooding eyes, what pain was reflected back when I shared mine. Was it about his sister, the one I didn't even know was dead? That's the most basic thing, something huge in his life I should have known. I saw his brothers at the wedding, and I envied their closeness, and I think someone even mentioned something about a sister, "Too bad she couldn't be here." But I was so wrapped up in my own worries that I didn't ask. I didn't care to know.

Now I wish I had. I wish I'd known him better, asked him what he wanted, tried to be some kind of wife to him. I wish I knew how he sees me now, if he can't help but be repulsed by me and my fucked up trauma. Even more fucked up, now that I know he won't see me as his sexy little wife anymore, that's all I want. I want him to want me, to still think I'm desirable and fuckable instead of delicate and broken.

Which is ridiculous, since I didn't want him to see me as sexy or fuckable before he knew.

It's too late for that now, though. What's done is done. He did what he did, and that damage cannot be undone. I opened my mouth and let him in, and I can't undo that. All I can do is crawl home in shame and beg Dad to let me stay, to take pity on me, and maybe, to find me a new husband, one I know won't be half as patient or understanding as King was.

twenty-one

King

"You ready?" Uncle Al asks, drawing me toward the room where I first met his men, the room where I took the oath.

I'm not ready. How could I be ready? My head's been a mess for a week, since the evening I came home and found the apartment completely trashed and my wife gone. I'm ready to take my mind off her for a few hours, though, and that's going to have to be good enough. I'm starting on understand my father better, to know what would make a man throw himself into his work with such single-minded focus.

"Yes, sir," I say to the don.

"Your shoulder all healed up?"

"Yeah," I say, rotating my arm. "Good as new."

Al steps into the room, gesturing for me to follow. Around the table sit five of his seasoned men and his consigliere. Besides them, a guy stands in the corner like a six-and-a-half-foot marble statue covered in ink from his chin to the backs of his huge hands, which he holds crossed in front of him as he waits, staring into the room with blank eyes.

"What's up?" I ask Al, turning away from the unnerving giant. I'm suddenly running over what Little Al told me about the attack at *Jean-Jean*. My throat tightens as I think how easily someone could throw my name out there, and it would be me walking the plank. But that's stupid. Why would I set up an ambush, especially one where I could have been killed, too? Unless someone made it look like that was my cover. You can never trust anyone in this business.

And then there's the small matter of me breaking the pact with the Pomponios. Eliza went home. She must have told her father what happened by now. I hurt her. I failed in my assignment. This could very well be my execution. I've already resigned myself to that end, but my heart still picks up speed at the abrupt realization that the day has arrived.

"We're going to pay Luciani a visit," Al says. "I normally wouldn't take a rookie, but since you were shot, you might like a chance to see justice served."

"Luciani?" I ask, thinking of the cold-eyed mafia don from our wedding. The one whose daughter spent every afternoon in my apartment with my wife until she left.

"We got some intel that he was working both sides before the deal with the Pomponios," he says. "Other families could have benefitted from the war, too. But we know he was profiting, and that's a good motivation to try to disrupt the peace before it could be established."

"It wasn't Anthony's men?" I ask, for some reason relieved that it wasn't Eliza's family, even though it doesn't matter anymore.

"The shooters were hired men, all from the Bronx. Made it look like they were Anthony's men. Whoever set this up was trying to start the war over."

I nod and square my shoulders. "Eliza had lunch with Luciani's daughter the day of the ambush. She must have talked."

I don't want Eliza in danger, but I won't keep my part in this from Al. I'm grateful it's not my head on the chopping block today, but if I lie, it will be.

"Even more reason to suspect Luciani," Al's consigliere says.

I wonder what Eliza's told her father when she went home to him, why I haven't faced the penalty yet. Of course the marriage isn't the sole reason for the peace between families, but it's a symbol of goodwill, and now that symbol is gone. It's the first thread to unravel, and I can't help wonder what they'll do about that. Will they find Eliza another husband, or will they consider her ruined since I fucked her?

The idea sends a knife of guilt down deep in my belly. I should never have touched her. Then she could have remarried and started from scratch. Now, I don't know what they'll do about her. I hope I haven't ruined her prospects, blocked her from finding someone else.

Just the thought of someone else marrying her makes me want to destroy him and his whole family. But I know have to let her find someone else, have to make a clean break like she did. Maybe they won't marry her off at all and she'll finally get that freedom she wanted so badly.

"This is Divo Bertinelli," Al says, cutting his eye toward the giant but not stepping toward him. "He'll be joining us."

I realize in that small gesture that even the great Al Valenti himself is ill at ease with the man I've heard of but never met. His name precedes him, as Little Al and the other guys refer to him by his nickname, *Il Diavolo*. If my job is breaking fingers, his is breaking necks. His specialty is getting men to talk, so it makes sense he's coming along, since we still don't know who tipped off Luciani and his men. If Al's going after Lou Luciani himself, he must have found enough information to be sure that the men who ambushed us were sent by Bianca's family, hired goons who weren't supposed to make it out alive or lead us back to them if they failed.

DANGEROUS DEFIANCE

Of the eight men paying Luciani a visit, I'm by far the youngest, though it's hard to tell about Il Diavolo. The tattoos and hardened expression make him look older than he probably is. The rest of the guys range from around thirty to fifty, all seasoned veterans whom Al trusts with his life.

"Lou's house has four guards," Al says, grabbing a paper from the table and making a few quick lines to sketch out the house, pointing to the rear and front entrances. The house is a row-style one, he explains, so there's no chance of entering through a side window. A few minutes later, we're all strapped and piling into a pair of black SUVs. Al takes the passenger seat of one, another of his men driving while Il Diavolo and I sit in the back. Conversation is limited to a few small comments.

We reach Luciani's building without issue. It's a three-story townhouse style that stretches as long as the street, each home with a different colored exterior. The front of the building has a small, wrought-iron fence with arching gateways leading to the steps, which lead to the entrance on the second level. Luciani's place is set apart by the grey exterior and thick, wooden double doors without windows. One guy stands outside, but we don't stop. We follow the street and double back around to the rear of the building.

A security guard stands outside the privacy fence, and when he sees us, he grabs for his radio. Al pops him before he can hit the button to call, his gun making a quiet *pffft* sound with the silencer on. Then we're all out of the vehicle and racing through the gate onto a slate tile patio with a square of sod, an outdoor fire pit, and two enormous grills built into the brickwork. The entrance on the back of the building is at ground level, though there's a set of stairs to a second-floor terrace with a second entrance. The terrace partially protects us from view on the second level, but the third floor offers us up for the picking. The large windows give an easy view of us—for Luciani and for anyone in the adjacent homes on either side.

They haven't realized we've breached their guard, or they'd be shooting already. Al's men fan out in pairs as instructed. Al and three of his men go in the back door while I follow Il Diavolo up the iron staircase to the second floor with two more guys. Just as my foot touches the terrace, I hear the muffled shot from a silenced gun, and a bullet pings off the stairs behind me.

"Fuck," I mutter, drawing my own gun and aiming upwards. The terrace is exposed, with no cover, which means I'm all that stands between the shooter and the three other lives at risk right now. My eyes sweep the windows on the floor above us, all closed.

"No fire escape," I mutter to the others, jerking my eyes at the top floor. "They have roof access."

Another shot rings out, and I just spot the head of the shooter ducking back before I can get off a shot. But I know his position now, so I wait. One of our guys is cursing up a storm, and I know he's hit. Il Diavolo races across the terrace in a crouch before lowering his shoulder and crashing into this thick glass. It splinters, raining down around him and crunching under his boots as he ducks inside. Another guy follows, then the last guy, cursing and bleeding from his arm, where he was hit. For a few seconds, I'm alone.

I wait in silence, adrenaline spiking through me with every heartbeat. When the head peaks over the edge of the roof, I get off another shot. I hear it connect, the cry that goes with it, and the guy slumps over on the roof. I take off, getting inside to some cover. For some reason I was expecting bedrooms, but this is the entry floor from the front of the building, so I'm in a long living room with an exposed brick wall and a kitchen at the other end of the open floor plan.

At least it limits hiding places. The area is empty, but I hear the shouts of men downstairs and bursts of gunfire. Il Diavolo appears from a doorway at the far end of the kitchen, gesturing for me to follow. I run through the long living room crowded with overstuffed chairs, wincing when the wooden floorboards squeak underfoot. But it's not like we're being stealthy at this point. I duck through the white tiled kitchen with white-and-black marble countertops and duck through the doors into a small entry hallway. A guard lays face down on the floor, pool of red spreading across the white tile. From there, we have access to the front door and the stairs.

Il Diavolo turns to the stairs, leveling his gun in front of him as he creeps up, his back flattened against the wall as he goes. I follow him up, covering the stairs behind us. The house is suddenly silent, the gunfire having ended below. I don't know if they've already gotten the Lucianis, but we have to check the top floor, anyway. We don't know how many people were in the house to begin with.

We reach a small landing, and Il Diavolo extends the silencer of his gun a few inches past the corner. Nothing. He edges forward, peering around. A gunshot sounds, and he jerks back. The bullet sinks into the wall behind us. I hear a creak and level my gun on the bottom of the stairs. A guy ducks around, his gun pointed straight at me. I almost shoot, at the last second realizing it's one of our guys. I turn to Il Diavolo, who edges past the corner and squeezes off one round after another.

He ducks back into the hall. "Cover me," he says, stopping to shove another magazine into his gun. Seconds later, he motions me forward. Together we step

into a second kitchenette area. A man lies slumped over
the counter, another two on the floor. To the left, a small
den sits empty. To the right, we can see into a bathroom
and beyond that, two closed doors.

We turn that way, but a slight rustling behind us
catches Il Diavolo's attention. He spins and shoots
without time to even aim properly, and my first thought is
that he shot the guy coming up behind me—one of
Valenti's guys. But the piercing scream hits my ears just as
I turn. The Valenti guy is on the floor, and a pretty
fortyish woman huddles behind the rocker in the den
covering her mouth.

Il Diavolo aims and fires before I can say a word,
and all I can think is that I'm next, that he's going to take
out any witnesses that he killed one of our men. The
woman's scream is cut off, and her body thuds back
against the wall behind her before sliding sideways to the
floor, leaving a streak of blood in her wake.

"We're killing everyone?" I grit out. "Even the
women?"

Il Diavolo strides into the den, kicking aside a chair, and drags the body up by her hair. A gun falls from her lap to the floor, and I see the hole in the rocker. It takes a second for me to put it together. *She* shot Valenti's man. Il Diavolo shot her through the chair, and she screamed and dropped her gun. And then he killed her.

The way he tosses her body aside like a bag of trash and strides past me turns my stomach, but at least I know we're not killing innocent bystanders. Il Diavolo gives me a disgusted grunt before heading for the closed bedroom doors.

Not a sound comes from either one. "Cover me," Il Diavolo says before swinging open the door on the left.

A girl is kneeling in front of a safe, shoving bundles of money into a duffle. I know it's Bianca by the cascade of wavy hair, but she doesn't turn to show her face until Il Diavolo strides into the room. He grabs her by the hair and yanks her backwards, sending her sprawling on the floor. "Would you look at that," he says, a cruel smirk twisting his lips. "It's the mouthy bitch who got you shot."

"I didn't do anything," Bianca retorts, her tone defiant even as she struggles to rise while Il Diavolo drags her backwards across the floor, her body sliding on the hardwood.

"Want to cut her tongue out?" he asks me, shoving her head toward me.

"Not now," I say. "We still need Luciani."

"Where's your father?" Il Diavolo barks at Bianca, shaking her by the head. He maintains his grip on her hair as she flails and tries to pry his hand loose.

"I'm not turning in my dad to you monsters," she snaps. "You can kill me first!'"

"He's in that room, isn't he?" Il Diavolo asks, a triumphant gleam in his eye as he drags Bianca to her feet. She looks like a doll against his giant form as he holds her in front of him.

As if in answer, a rain of bullets splinters the door from within.

"Unless you want to hit your daughter, stop shooting," Il Diavolo shouts, ducking back into the adjacent bedroom.

"You sons of bitches are setting me up," Luciani yells. "You don't have my daughter. I told her to get out."

"Tell him you're here, or I'll put you out of your misery right now," Il Diavolo says, pressing the silencer of the gun to Bianca's throat, still holding her pinned to his chest.

For the first time, fear writes itself across her face, as if she's just realizing this is real. She can see out the open door to the handful of bodies spread across the kitchen.

"I—I'm here, Daddy," she calls. "I was getting money from the safe. They caught me."

"Good girl," Il Diavolo growls, shoving her forward as he turns to the bedroom. I step in front, kicking down what's left of the door and then jumping aside. No bullets come. Il Diavolo steps through the door, still holding Bianca in front of him, the muzzle of his gun pushing her chin up as he presses it to her throat. I step in behind him, edging in with my gun raised.

The room is small, probably meant to be a bedroom, but it's set up as an office with a thick leather armchair near the window and a heavy walnut desk to our left. Lou

Luciani is sitting in the armchair, an automatic rifle lying across his lap. Bianca start sobbing and choking out apologies to her father. I lean around my partner, aiming carefully at the man sitting in the chair. While his eyes are on his daughter, I squeeze the trigger.

The bullet rips into his thick torso, and he curses savagely.

"Daddy," Bianca screams, flailing in Diavolo's arms.

"Shut the fuck up and stop squirming unless you want my finger to slip on the trigger," Diavolo says, squeezing her until she whimpers.

"She had nothin' to do with it," Luciani says, his voice thick with a Jersey accent and edged with panic. "Let her go and I'll put the gun down. See?"

He raises both hands, leaving the gun in his lap.

"You think we fucking trust you?" I ask, cradling the Glock in my palm, keeping one finger on the trigger and the barrel aimed at his face as I stride across the room.

"Don't kill him yet," Il Diavolo says behind me.

Right. Dead men don't talk.

"How'd you know where we'd be that day?" I ask, pressing the gun to Luciani's temple.

He lunges out of the chair, his arms clamping around my torso as he tackles me to the floor. My finger convulses on the trigger, sending a bullet into the ceiling when I hit the floor, the air knocked from my lungs by the larger man. I bring the butt of the gun down on his temple, and he slumps on top of me, groaning. I heave him off and frisk him quickly, tossing his pistol into the corner and kicking the rifle away.

"Don't kill me," he wheezes when I roll him onto his back and press the muzzle of my gun to the underside of his chin. I grab his tie, pulling his face up. Blood is coursing down his face from where I struck him, and his eyes are small and teary as they roll around in his head.

Even the most powerful men are reduced to nothing in a moment like this, so much like the ones I see every day with Little Al. Lou Luciani may be a sneaky bastard, and he may have tried to kill me, but at least he loves his daughter. So much so that he's giving up his life for hers, letting us walk in on him. He must know it's over. He may have executed a sloppy ambush in broad daylight but he's not stupid, and he's not heartless. There are worse people in the world, at least.

"Answer the fucking question," I demand.

"I'm no rat," he spits back at me, his lips coated with saliva and trembling as he tries to get the words out.

Il Diavolo spins Bianca and pushes her face down on the walnut desk, yanking up her skirt and pushing the muzzle of his gun against her panties. "Answer the fucking question, or we'll know your daughter is the rat," he barks.

Bianca screams out a sob, her terror palpable as she writhes on the desk, begging for mercy.

"Don't touch my daughter, you sick son of a bitch," Lou yells, bucking under me.

Il Diavolo pulls aside her underwear and rubs the tip of the silencer against her entrance, his other hand flat against her back, pinning her down. "Oh, but I bet she's never been touched," he taunts. "It's such a shame to waste good virgin pussy."

"Is that necessary?" I growl, glaring over at him while I wrestle to keep Luciani down. If I thought I could let go of Lou without him going for his guns, I'd take down the devil himself. But if I did that, Lou would kill me, and Eliza would be left a widow, and that's one thing I promised I'd never do. I may not be her husband much longer, but until we sign divorce papers, I'm responsible for her.

I could kill Lou and go after Il Diavolo, but then I'd never find out who tipped him off, and the blame will fall on Bianca whether she's guilty or not.

Besides all that, I don't even want to think what this guy will do to me if I try to take him down and fail. And even if I succeed, there's no question about leaving Eliza a widow then. If I killed one of our own men, Al's inner circle no less, to protect an enemy who could be responsible for the attempt on Al's life...

I force myself to hold onto Luciani's throat, my fingers digging in while I kneel on his chest, the gun still shoved against his chin. This asshole needs to talk, and fast.

"Please," Bianca sobs. "I didn't tell anyone anything."

Il Diavolo grins at Luciani, who's going nuts in my hold, and forces the tip of the silencer into Bianca's hole. "You got one more chance to talk, or I'm going to shoot and then fuck this tight little cunt while she bleeds to death."

I ram the gun into Luciani's jugular. "You're going to die anyway," I snap. "If you love your daughter, you better talk right fucking now."

"It was Al," he howls, his voice high with panic as he tries to rise, to go to his daughter. "Little Al De Luca. He tipped me off."

I pull the trigger and jump up, grabbing Il Diavolo and shoving him. He grins at me and slides the tip of the silencer out of Bianca, who is sobbing uncontrollably on the desk.

"Works like a charm," he says, wiping the gun on his pants. "Too bad he talked. I wouldn't mind a few minutes inside the bitch. She's tight."

I pull Bianca to her feet, and she collapses into my arms, clinging to me like I'm some kind of savior, her body convulsing with sobs. "We'd better go find Uncle Al," I say.

"Bring her along," Il Diavolo says, gesturing lazily with his gun for me to follow as he heads for the door. "To the victor go the spoils, right?"

I follow him out, Bianca hanging off my neck. "What are you going to do with me?" she wails as we start down the stairs.

"Nothing," I say firmly.

"Al can keep you until we check out your dad's story," Il Diavolo says. "If he was lying, you'll die like the rest of your family. If he was telling the truth… You're Al's problem then. Maybe he'll put you to work at one of his clubs until you've paid off what Lou owes him."

Damn. Luciani owed him money. No wonder he tried to take us out. He must have thought his debt would be erased if he got rid of one of the other families.

The remaining men gather in the little fenced yard. Al is bleeding from a cut on his cheek but otherwise fine.

Three of the guys were killed, and one more is seriously injured. Il Diavolo has a cut on his side that I didn't even notice, as he showed no reaction whenever he got it. The rest of us got away without injury. We pile into the SUVs, anxious to get out of there before more Luciani men show up. With the head cut off, either the family will fall or more likely, someone will rise to take his place immediately, and we don't want to be there when a bunch of thirsty heirs show up to duke it out.

I end up in a car with Al, Il Diavolo, and Bianca, who has fallen silent and stares out the window with mascara running down her cheeks from her blank eyes. She's probably in shock.

"You need to get that looked at?" Al asks Il Diavolo, who sits up front with him.

"I'll stop by the chop shop later," Il Diavolo responds.

We don't discuss the findings until we're back at Uncle Al's. His housekeeper takes Bianca off to clean up, I assume, and the rest of us head into his office space

ownstairs. When we're all seated around the table with
ne consigliere, Al speaks up.

"What information did you get from the late
uciani?" he asks, crossing himself.

I wait for Il Diavolo to speak, but he gestures a giant
and at the me, his other mitt holding a towel to his side.
"It's your moment, rookie," he says. "Tell him."

I clear my throat, not wanting to deliver this news
nd unable to keep from wondering if this is a shoot-the-
nessenger situation, and Il Diavolo knows it and doesn't
vant to be the one to tell Al that his beloved grandson
onspired to have him killed.

"He said Little Al tipped him off," I say quietly.

Uncle Al doesn't even bat an eye.

"I'm sorry, sir," I add.

"Were you aware of this?" he asks.

My blood runs cold. I'm Little Al's partner. Of
course scrutiny falls on me. "No, sir."

"Then don't apologize. He set up the meeting and
wasn't there when shots were fired. You joined at the last

minute and took a hit for me." He studies me a second then tips his chin. "I'm going to let you deal with him."

I nod, gulping down the protest. It's one thing to shoot the bastard who tried to have me killed and set up my wife's family, trying to pit us against each other. Luciani's another family. Little Al is a Valenti. And not only is he family, he's my partner. Sure, he's kind of a tool, but we've worked as a team for the past three months, since my first day on the job. It might as well have been my whole life. I've grown, learned, and hardened to become a man who gets shit done, who does what he needs to survive. A lot of it is thanks to Little Al.

He taught me well.

So I use what he taught me. I give the only answer that lets me live another day, go home to my empty apartment, and try to be a better man tomorrow. "Yes, sir," I say.

"He's not answering his phone," the consigliere says with a frown. "I'll try his old lady."

One of the men at the table grunts. "You think someone tipped him off?"

"We didn't leave anyone alive to tip him off," says Joey One-Eye.

"Did anyone take Bianca's phone?" I ask.

There's a long moment of tense silence while the consigliere calls Mrs. De Luca. After a brief conversation, he hangs up and shakes his head. "She says he left early this morning and she hasn't heard from him since."

"Son of a bitch," Uncle Al curses quietly. "He was here for some of the planning to take down Luciani. He must have known he'd talk, and he ran like the coward he is."

"He'll be lying low, waiting to see if we succeeded," the consigliere says.

"Need me to find him?" asks Il Diavolo, his voice a low rumble.

"We'll find him, alright," Al says, grimacing. "He's a threat that needs to be eliminated."

As we leave the room after a few more minutes of discussion, Al lingers, putting a hand on my shoulder to keep me after everyone leaves. "Brother killing brother is just another day in the Life," he says. "You seemed a little shaken in there. It's just business, son."

"I know."

"Good," he says. "You've had enough excitement for tonight. Go home to your wife."

"Thank you," I say, just managing not to stammer. He doesn't know she left. I'm not sure if that's a good thing or not.

Al gives me a long, shrewd look. "Is that going better?"

I hesitate, and then, because he's the only person I can talk to about this, I stay a minute longer. "Can I ask your advice about something?"

"Sure," he says. "Does this need a drink?"

He pours a couple glasses of whiskey from a decanter on the liquor cart in the corner.

"I fucked up," I admit. "She's been back at her father's for a week."

Shame weighs down every limb in my body as I stand there admitting the worst mistake of my life to someone I admire.

"You hit her?" Al asks, squinting at me above the rim of his glass.

"No," I say. "I did worse. She's... Headstrong. I lost my cool, and I... Forced her to submit."

I swallow the sick taste in my mouth with a sip of burning liquor. I can't even look at this man while I tell him what I did. But it affects him, in some way. Our marriage affects everyone in both the Valenti and Pomponio families.

Al nods slowly, sinking back down into his chair and leaning back, swirling the liquor in his glass and watching me. "I see," he says.

The longest minute of my life follows, the room silent as I stand there waiting for his verdict.

"I'm sorry," I say at last.

"You'll get through it," he says. "There's no other option, King. You might have to work harder to earn her submission after this, but if you show her you're worthy... Submission is earned, not taken."

"What if she doesn't want that? She doesn't to be dominated. She wants her own way in everything."

"It can be taught," Al says. "You'll find the way to teach her to submit and do it willingly, to want it. But it's a balance, never forced. She has to get what she needs most if you want what you need most."

"Then it seems we're at an impasse," I say. "We both need the same thing."

"You'll find a way to work things out, though. That's your job."

"Yes, sir," I say, the weight inside me settling heavier. There is no divorce, not even when there was never really a marriage. My lifelong assignment was to bring the families together, and I failed, but he's not letting me off the hook. The problem is I'm *not* worthy of her submission. If I were, she would have given it willingly.

I don't know what to do to fix it. She's already gone. So we'll go on as we did when we were married, except she won't live with me. It won't be so different. Really, I should be thankful. There's no chance of feelings getting involved when we're not sleeping next to each other, not even texting. I'll be the solitary soldier I envisioned when joined the Valentis, before Al told me my fate was to be ed to hers. I won't care about her, and therefore, no anger will come to her.

I thank Uncle Al for his advice and trust in me, and hen I leave. As I drive home, I think of what Little Al id, about how much it must hurt to be betrayed by your wn family—and not just far extended family or people ho work for you, but your own grandson, whom you've roomed to take your place. Uncle Al may not show it, ut he's got to hate that. Which means if I want to show ny loyalty to him, I have to kill the guy who betrayed im.

I thought pulling the trigger on a stranger would be he hardest thing I'd ever have to do, but this is so much arder. I don't hate Little Al. And he's not a stranger whose face I can pretend I don't see when I can't sleep at night. He's a friend. I don't know how the hell I'm going to go through with it. I'll find a way, though. I've already failed Eliza, fucked up my first assignment beyond repair. This is probably the last chance I'll get. My second strike.

SELENA

It's time to put what I've learned to use. This wi
make or break me, put me in a grave or maybe in Uncl
Al's inner circle. And more than that, it'll prov
something to myself. I need to know if I can survive thi
life when it's not just easy jobs, or if I choke in crunch
time. Time to prove that I can do the right thing ever
when it's hard. I thought I'd done the right thing with
Eliza by letting her go, but now I'm not sure. This time
I'm sure.

There's no easy way out of this one. The mafia rule:
are clear. He violated them. He knew the risks, the
consequences. Those are clear, too. It may have been my
job to worry about my partner's life when we were
working side by side, but he's not my partner anymore.
He's the fallen heir to this empire. He chose where to put
his loyalty, and I choose where to put mine. He made his
bed, and it's my job to make sure he sleeps in it—
permanently.

twenty-two

Eliza

A knock on my door interrupts my glum evening.

"Someone's here to see you," Sylvia says, sticking her head into my room.

"Who is it?"

"Come see," she says, a knowing smile on her lips.

I sigh and climb off the bed. I'm sure it's Bianca, and she'll probably tell me I look like a slob. To be fair, I am wearing drawstring sweats and a t-shirt with no bra, and my hair is barely contained in a messy bun. The last time she saw me, I was at least wearing jeans, and she still told me it would take me forever to be presentable for the lunch date I cancelled. I haven't felt up to socializing since, but I know I need to be there for her, since her dad just got taken out and her family is in ruins. I should be smug about that—she would be if the situation were reversed—but I can't summon the cruelty.

"Aren't you going to change?" Sylvia asks when I step past her into the hall.

"No," I say. "She'll just have to see me in my natural state."

I'm halfway down the stairs before my visitor steps into view. Not Bianca.

My husband.

My stomach does a funny little flip, and my throat catches. Suddenly, I wish I'd fixed myself up. But he's already seen me, so it's too late to run back and freshen up. At least I showered this morning, so I'm not totally feral. I pause on the steps and take a breath, my pulse fluttering in my throat.

"What—what are you doing here?" I ask, slowly descending until I reach the bottom step.

"I'm here to woo you," King says with a little smile.

"What?" I ask, recognizing the words I threw at him on our first meeting.

He shifts on his feet, looking as stiff and uncomfortable as he did that day. "I fucked up," he says. "I know that, and I know I can't ask forgiveness. I thought letting you go home and have your freedom was the best way to protect you from me and my…"

He glances behind me, and I know Sylvia's there. It makes me feel weirdly proud of her for sticking by me. I haven't told her or Dad exactly what happened, but they let me stay. They're wary around me, as if they're waiting, but they haven't pressed the issue.

After all, the Pomponios are the least traditional of all the families. My father is the man who let his wife leave him. He's probably the only don in New York who wouldn't force me to go back to my husband.

King clears his throat and returns his gaze to me. I know he wants me to send my father's mistress away, but I don't. I'm not going to make it easy for him. He crossed a boundary, broke my trust. If I want someone present during our visits, I'll do it.

"I wanted to see you," he says. "I was wrong to treat you that way, and I know that. But you are still my wife, and I want you to know I'm still honoring our wedding vows. I will never break them again."

"You broke our vows?" I ask, my heart tearing inside my chest. I don't blame him if he went to a whore that day I left or any time since then, but it still crushes me inside.

"I didn't honor you," he says. "That night... The night I forced you to submit. I should never have done that. I should have treated you like the princess you are. From now on, I'm going to. I won't ask you to come home, but I hope one day I can earn your trust, and you will."

I swallow hard, relief mixing with some other feeling, one that's too dangerous to name, that swells in my heart and makes me want to sit down. "That's why you came?"

"Yes," he says. "I want to try again. I'll do whatever it takes, Eliza. If that means waiting for a year, or ten years, or forever, I will. I'm not giving up on you. I won't leave you the way your mother did."

A lump rises in my throat, and instead of getting defensive, I want to cry. I wave Sylvia away and lead King into the bar. I don't want to get drunk today, though. I get a hard seltzer from the fridge and hand one to King, too. He hesitates, not sitting until I slip onto one of the barstools and pat the one next to me. "I don't know if I can trust you again," I say. "You said you'd never hurt me, and you did. Not just that night, but the next day. I don't know if I'll ever forget seeing your wedding band lying there."

"I know," he says, looking so miserable it aches in my chest. "But I never stopped wanting to be your husband. I just wanted to protect you."

"From what?" I ask. "You can't protect me from the past."

"From me," he says, looking at me like I'm missing something.

"I thought... I thought you left because of what I told you."

He draws back. "What? No. Eliza, I told you to leave because I hurt you. Because I didn't know if I could be trusted not to do it again. But I swear to you, I won't. I want you to be my wife, El. Even if it's just to hav

dinner with me in public, and I never touch you again."

"It wasn't because you think I'm damaged goods?"

ask, my voice barely above a whisper.

"Of course not," he says, reaching for my hand o

the edge of the bar. He hesitates, then lays his hand ove

mine. "I told you. That happened to you. It doesn

define you."

He's wrong, though. It does define me. It shaped my

whole life.

"What happens now?" I ask.

"Can I take you out?" he asks. "We can get to know

each other, like we should have from the beginning."

"You want to… Date me?"

"Yes," he says. "But I'll do whatever makes you

comfortable."

I watch him from the corner of my eye for a minute.

"Why?" I ask at last.

"What do you mean?"

"Why would you want to date your wife? You

already have me. We're married. You fucked me."

"Because I want to know my wife," he says. "And yes, I hope that one day you'll want to come home. I won't pretend that's not the goal. I'm ready to do whatever it takes, to wait as long as you need, before that happens, though."

"You're just going to take me out, and then drop me off here afterwards?" I ask carefully.

"That's generally how dates work," he says. "Unless you want something different. I want you to be happy. But I'm not giving up on you, El. Not ever."

"Okay," I say, nodding. "If you're really going to respect me and go slow."

"I will," he says immediately.

"Thank you," I say. "And if you need relief before then…"

"If you tell me to get a side chick one more time, I'm going to tattoo a stop sign on my forehead with the word *cumare* on it."

I can't help but giggle at that, the tension between us easing. "I was going to say, I could text you a picture or two," I say, sipping my drink. "You lost your chance at a mistress when you took me."

"That's fair," he says, sliding off the bar stool and leaning in to kiss my forehead. "I'll pick you up at eight on Friday."

And that's how I start dating my husband.

For the month, King takes me out twice a week, to dinners, shows, concerts, galleries, movies, and even a club. Sometimes I can forget what he did, and we just have fun together. It's truly the best of both worlds—I maintain my freedom, but I get a partner, too. I don't have to obey him, but I have someone to do things with, a guy who wants me, makes me feel beautiful and sexy and wanted but not pressured. We kiss in the car when he drops me off, which progresses to making out, but I never invite him in. Sometimes, I send him nudes to tease him after he drops me off, but he doesn't push things.

I know I should go home, but I'm having too much fun with this, and I'm afraid he'll go back to being his dominant self, and that I'll want that too much. I don't want to lose sight of who I am, to disappear into our marriage. He's patient, but I know he won't be forever, so I revel in the honeymoon phase, living it the way I lived my party days before the wedding—diving in with both feet, committing with abandon. When he's not around, I'm working up the nerve to do something I know I have to do before I can be a good wife.

twenty-three

King

It's an odd thing to be a single, married man in New York. I no longer go to parties like I did in high school, but I don't have a family to go home to, either. I'm a bachelor but not. Before now, I've only lived alone for a few months before the wedding. Before that, I had my brothers to look after. It leaves an empty place, a restlessness, as if I have no purpose. I know it's good for me, though. Ma said she went from her father's house to her husband's. It's not much different for me. Being married so young means I've never really been on my own.

I'm not made for that kind of life, though, and I soon realize it. I want Eliza home. I worry about my rothers, about what they're doing down in Arkansas and about the fact that they've pulled away, not talking to me as much as they used to. I need someone to take care of, someone to put my energies into. When I don't have it, I end up working until well past dark most nights. Al gave me a new partner, and we're both eager to prove ourselves.

With Eliza, things are strained at first, but they get more comfortable as we get to know each other. I want to take care of her, but she won't let me, and I never know when I'm going to piss her off or what she'll do if that happens. She's learning to trust me with her body, though, even if she's still moving slow. I'm okay with that. She's worth the wait.

When I take her to the club, she even dances with me, grinding on me until I'm ready to take her right there on the dance floor. Of course I can't do that, though. I'm respectful, and she doesn't freak out about my hard on this time. She grinds on it like teasing me is her sole purpose in life.

I don't push for more. Between what happened to her when she was a kid and my violation, she's slow to trust. I don't mind waiting. She's worth it. I'm going to keep showing up for her, showing her that I'm not going to hurt her. Eventually, she'll learn that I'm a man of my word, that she can let her guard down and let me help her heal. I may have failed the last girl I had to care for, but it won't happen again.

This time, I'll save her.

We kiss goodnight each time, but nothing more happens. It's funny how I've begun to notice other things now that sex is off the table. When I know it's not coming later, I can relax and feel physical pleasure apart from sexual pleasure. It's almost deeper, the pleasure I take in her soft, small body curled against mine in a booth; the heat and weight of her head when she rests on my arm while I'm kissing her dizzy in the car; the buttery smoothness of her skin under my calloused hands. Touching her feels fucking amazing no matter where it is or where it's leading.

Finally, she starts to invite me in after our dates.

DANGEROUS DEFIANCE

I've never been selfish enough to get off without making sure I got the woman off, too. I thought that meant I wasn't a selfish lover, but with Eliza, I realize that's not true. Making a girl cum has always been a point of pride to me. I was doing it for my ego, to prove that I was a good lover. Or because I knew she would tell her friends that I was good in bed. But I was still doing it for myself.

With Eliza, I don't think about myself. She makes me take things slow, think about only her—what she wants, what she needs, what feels good to her and what is triggering.

For a few weeks, we go slow, and it's hard to see progress, but we're intimate in the ways she's comfortable with. We kiss, and I let her explore my body, which she likes so much it kinda goes to my head. I've never been with a girl who was so painfully innocent, so curious, so fascinated by my body, not just my dick. Maybe the girls I've been with were as selfish as me. We were always both just thinking about getting off.

But Eliza isn't thinking about that. Whenever she gets close, she freezes up and backs off. She seems more interested in me, which I have to admit is hot as hell. She's fascinated by things no one else has ever paid attention to, like the fact that guys like their nipples played with, too, or how to touch my balls. She likes to lie her head on my belly and breath on my cock and watch it get hard. And she seems pretty intent on learning to excel at blowjobs and hand jobs both.

Still, it's frustrating. I want to touch her the way she touches me, with freedom and wonder. I want to spread her open and sink my fingers into her hot little cunt and make her moan for more. I want to taste her, to fuck her with my tongue until I push her over the edge, and I want to feel her lose control and cum in my mouth. And I want to fuck her hard and deep, to cum inside her while she screams my name.

But we're a long way from there. Instead, I spend a lot of time with the nudes she texts me.

One night after a Halloween party, we arrive back at her father's house and stumble in, both a little tipsy.

"Come here, my bride," I say, scooping her up in my arms with a growl.

She gives a little shriek and kicks her legs, but she's laughing as she links her arms around my neck and leans up to kiss me.

"Shhh," I say. "I may be your husband, but I still don't want your father waking up and hearing what I'm doing to his daughter."

She giggles and buries her face in my neck, kissing and licking and driving me crazy as I carry her up the stairs to her bedroom and lay her down on the bed.

She kicks off her red heels and squiggles out of her Dorothy dress, tossing it onto the nearby chair and pulling off her bra. Her tits are mine for the taking, so I push her back and suck on one and then the other, running my hands over the incredible smoothness of her skin until she's panting and squirming against me. I move up to her lips, sliding my tongue into her willing mouth as she pulls up my shirt to run her hands over my ribs.

"Take this off," she says, breaking the kiss to tug at my Scarecrow costume. I undo the overalls and kick them off, then unbutton the flannel and toss it aside so I can press my bare skin to hers. When we're back on the bed, lying face to face, I slide a leg between hers as our mouths meet again. After a while, she rolls over onto me, pulling her knees up to straddle my hips as she runs her nails over my skin, making goosebumps rise and my nipples harden. She smiles down at me, and my cock throbs against her center.

This is my penance. As much as I love seeing her enjoy me, giving up control is the hardest thing I've ever done. I need to be the man in the bedroom, to be the one who holds her down and fucks her until she can't see straight, until she cums so hard she blacks out. But for her, I'll give that up. It's a sacrifice I would never make for anyone else, but after what I did, I owe her this— giving up the one thing I need most so she can have what she needs most. And what she needs is to feel safe.

Leaning down to kiss me, she covers my pecs with her palms, and I reach for her tits again. I roll her nipples between my fingers until she's squirming against me, her hips rocking on mine. I sit up, holding her body against line with one arm while I keep squeezing her nipple with my other hand. She throws her head back, riding me in a way that makes me imagine the clothes between us gone.

The sensation of the softness between her thighs against the hardness of my erection makes me want to cum in my pants like a fucking virgin. But this is for her, so I ignore the ache in my stiff cock and let my lips play over her throat in that way that always makes her sigh with pleasure. I help her keep rhythm, gripping her hip as she moves faster, her hips rolling against my cock.

I massage her tit, pinching her nipple a little harder. She gasps, tensing like she's going to jump off me the way she always does.

I release my grip on her nipple and wrap my arms around her, cradling her close but not too hard, so she'll feel comforted, not trapped. "It's okay, you're safe," I say quickly, stroking her hair back from her cheek. "We can stop if you want, but you can let yourself go with me. I'm here, *carina*. I won't hurt you. Can you keep going?"

Her eyes clear, and she relaxes. I begin to move her against me, adding a little motion in my own hips to rub my cock right at her center. After a minute, she closes her eyes and drops her head back, her beautiful hair falling in waves down her bare back to brush my hand that holds her hip. I watch her rock, her tits rising and falling, the little freckles that dot her skin like a constellation on full display. I take her nipple between my fingers again, squeezing it gently while I massage her breast with my palm. When I apply pressure, a stitch pulls between her brows and her pink lips part in a little "o." Her fingers dig into my skin, and she tenses up, but this time, it's not fear gripping her. I can feel her cunt throbbing against my cock, and I can't help myself. I explode with her, cum rushing from my cock as she lets out helpless whimpers of pleasure, her hips jerking against mine as she rides out her orgasm against me.

I watch her cum, and it's everything I thought it would be. Breathtaking. Triumphant. Agonizing.

twenty-four

Eliza

As I come down, I'm terrified by what just happened, by what I felt for King in that moment. I'm past thinking he's the enemy, but I realize as he's holding me that he's something much more dangerous than an enemy. He's a lover. And a lover can destroy you in ways an enemy can't even begin to imagine. You know better than to let an enemy in, after all. A lover is already in. They may not even mean to cause you harm, may not hold any ill will toward you. And yet, you can see their soul like the trap that it is, open and ready to pull you and swallow you whole, drown you in pleasure, trap you in bliss like a fly in amber.

I love him. The realization shocks me. Sometime in the last few months, he didn't just earn my trust—he earned my heart. I'd rather spend an evening doing nothing with him than an evening clubbing with anyone else. Hell, I'd rather stay home stitching up his wounds than doing anything else, no matter who it was with. Instead of showing him that, I let him walk out the door thinking he was somehow undeserving of my love. He's more than deserving of my love, respect, and my time. But if I tell him that, I lose all power, all control over this relationship.

"What's wrong?" King asks, smoothing my hair back and looking at me with those dark eyes like wells I could fall into and no one would ever find me. His brows furrow with concern that could drown me.

I push him away and roll toward the far side of the bed, trying to get away from his caging hands.

"Why'd you do that?" I demand. "You know I didn't want to do that."

"I asked if you wanted to keep going," he protests, sitting up.

I jump up from the bed and turn to face him. "You made me want to do it!"

He gives me a look that says I sound just as crazy to him as I do to myself. "You didn't want to orgasm?"

"No," I say, throwing my hands up. "I knew once I started to believe in this marriage, once I started to feel something, I'd never get away. That's why I don't want to come home. I don't want this tiny life. I don't want to be a maid or a cook or a sex slave. I want my own life, my own freedom. And I can't have that and this, too."

It's everything I always feared about sex. Like when he made me cum in Bora Bora, it makes me weak, makes me need it, craving it already like a junkie needing a fix already after the first hit. I knew it could trap me, I just didn't know how fast it could happen, or that it could happen without me even noticing. Maybe that's why I kept holding back, why I stopped every time King got me right to the edge. I knew once I went over, once I began to depend on him for that pleasure, I'd want more. Less than that will never be enough—never again.

After the first time, I knew it was a trap, but it felt so good that I let myself be caught. And now he holds me in his arms so gently, as if they aren't teeth waiting to snap shut on me, consuming my life until I don't even remember what it was like before, until I want to stay home and make him spaghetti and clean his house, and one day I'll look back on the big dreams I never had a chance to even imagine, and I see that all that's left on the path behind me are little shards of bone that he picked clean and spit out.

I want to go back in time ten minutes, to take it all back. I want to stop myself from coming so I can stop myself from realizing my heart already belongs to him, that it's too fucking late. I want to go back to the life we had before I left, before we dated and he made me fall for him, trust him, without even realizing it. That life wasn't ideal, but it wasn't scary like this. I'm vulnerable now. I've let him see too much, know too much. I need to know his secrets, balance the scales.

I can tell he no longer thinks of me as just a bratty, spoiled princess. I'd rather be that than damaged and sad.

can't unsay what I said, take back my secret like I took back the lie I told on our wedding night to make him leave me alone. I can't make him forget my trauma or that he still wants me. How do I do damage control when the damage is so deep and irreversible I don't even know where to start? How do I make him stop pursuing me when even telling him the most shameful thing about me didn't kill his desire?

"Eliza," he says, looking so earnest it makes my heart twist. I turn away so I don't have to see him when I hurt him. I don't want to hurt him. I already care about him way too much. But I know this is my last chance, and it makes me desperate. I'm falling in a way I'll never get up from. This is worse than when he forced me to lie there while he fucked me. That was just my body. Now he's tricked me into giving up my heart.

"What?" I snap, hating the sympathetic tone in his voice. I don't want pity. I want a life where I'm in control of my own choices. Why didn't I run when he gave me the chance? Why did I let him back into my life, let him win me over, let him so much deeper inside me than he ever was before? Why didn't I realize that this was where it would lead? I love him, but it doesn't feel good. It's terrifying, and even though I know I'm sliding backward into the way I was at first, I can't stop it. The instinct for self-preservation is too strong inside me.

"I never asked you to be any of those things," he says. "After everything that's happened over the past few months, you're really going to accuse me of wanting you for a *sex slave?*"

"That's what marriage is," I say, repeating the words I've been saying since I was too young to understand their meaning.

"Obviously it isn't," he says. "And I don't want it to be. Our marriage can be whatever we want, whatever makes you happy. Only we can define what it will be."

I don't want to hear his promises because they sound too rational, and I'm not rational right now. I'm shaking with emotion. I don't want to think about marriage as protection and support, the way it's felt lately, because then I'll need him, and what happens when he walks away?

from me then? It's easier to fall back into the ingrained ideas I've held so long.

"It's the end of freedom," I say, clinging to the empty words I heard so many times, and now I've repeated so many times like a mantra.

"What do you want the freedom to do?" he asks. "I've given you freedom, Eliza. We don't even live together, for fuck's sake. If you want to go to school, or get a job, or travel… Eliza, I'm here to support you in that, or work through whatever you're going through, or figure out what you want to do. Just let me be part of it."

"I don't know what I want, okay?" I say, fresh tears springing to my eyes. "I just want to be free."

"As long as it's not the freedom to fuck other guys, you can still have whatever freedoms you want. Just talk to me, Eliza. You seem obsessed with this idea, but how can I give you that when I don't know what you want the freedom to do?"

"To live my life," I say, throwing my hands up. "The life *I* choose. As I please. Just like my mom did."

A life not controlled by him or my father or anyone, not even my own body. Most of all, I want to be free of my demons. But they're clawing their way out of me, tearing me apart from within, and I can't stop them. I know I'm ruining this, all the progress we've made, and it's not even his fault. It's mine. But I keep on doing it because I want him to go, to show me that he's one more person who wants to use me in the name of love, to hurt me and twist my heart around until I don't know what's right and wrong, what I want, how I feel, because *everything* is wrong.

King is quiet for a minute. "The freedom to leave your daughter to grieve both you and her brother because you can't handle the child you chose to have?"

"You don't know anything about my mother," I snap. "She was protecting me."

"I know that if one of your parents is a hero, it's not your mother."

I don't want to hear his words, don't want to think about them. I can't. I have to hurt him more than he hurts me, hurt him before he can destroy me. So I give a derisive snort. "Of course you'd think the killer is a hero," I say. "Because you're a pussy, and you'd rather follow in a monster's footsteps than admit it."

I don't know where the words are coming from, it's like they're someone else's, the last words of that wounded animal that lives inside of me with one instinct, the instinct to protect me, to keep the secret, to keep others away because if they know, they'll destroy me. It's telling me that I don't need anyone else, that they'll always leave, and it's all I will have left. It's been with me since I was a little girl, this little monster of my own, born in the bottom of a bathtub where there was no air, because I was a bad girl.

Good girls obey. Good girls get to breathe.

Bad girls get fingers around their throats, pushing them down, and lungs that burn for oxygen, and a head that thunders like waves crashing against the shore in a storm, and the yearning for one abstract idea that worms from the back of their black eyelids into their brains and makes a home there until it takes shape when they're old enough to understand what they've wanted all along.

Freedom.

"Your father might be a killer, but he also raised you on his own," King says quietly. "I know how fucking hard that is, trust me."

I take a deep, shaky breath and give my eyes an angry swipe before I turn back to him, so relieved for the opening that I could cry all over again. "How would you know that?"

He pauses for a moment, his dark eyes troubled. "I wouldn't," he says at last.

"What, you're a dad?" I ask. "Where's this kid you raised all alone?"

"I'm not a father," he says, turning away.

"Then how would you know?" I press. I can feel I've hit a sore spot, and I want to keep poking it, the way my thumb will keep finding a bruise, worrying it. Poking it to make sure it still hurts, that I can still feel something, that I'm still part human. I've spent half my life proving to myself that I'm still alive, that I'm not numb anymore. I've drank and partied and danced and fought with my friends and made out with guys, all in a quest to prove

hat I still feel, because I'm not a monster, and that I still
ontrol myself, because I'm not an animal.

"I don't," King snaps. "Forget it."

"Who are you talking about, King?" I press. "I heard
ou and your brothers moved to the South with your dad.
'hat means you're talking about him. He's such a big
ero for leaving your mom alone in the city?"

"You don't know what you're talking about."

"See how it feels when someone acts like they know
ou?" I ask, though I want to ask about his sister, his
arents, his brothers. I want to know everything about
im. There is more to this man than I know, so much
more. But it's dangerous to go down that path, because
nowing someone means caring about them, and I can't
are more. It brings us too close, brings him too close to
he truth that I swore I'd never tell. I don't get close to
eople for this very reason. My secrets are too dark, too
orrible. If I let someone in, I'll care, and when they find
ut the truth, they'll leave, and I won't survive another
low like that. At least King had the decency to let me do
he leaving. I'm the one who walked out, just like she did.

I bend and pick up my clothes, turning away from the bed before pulling on my bra and reaching behind me to hook it closed.

"It was your mom, wasn't it?"

My hands freeze, and I just stand there with my fingers paralyzed on the clasp, the hooks an inch from engaging. "What?"

"It was your mom," he says. "That's why you aren't triggered by touching a man, even in the most intimate ways. You're only freaked out when I touch you."

"So?" My voice is small, like a little girl's when she's sitting on the tile floor, refusing to stand up, to unwrap her arms from around her knees, even though she knows she'll be punished, but she can't do it because she knows she'll fly apart if she's not holding herself together so, so carefully.

King's hands are tentative on my hips, tugging me back with gentle insistence. My body tenses, and he stops pulling, but his hands are there, warm through my underwear. He doesn't push. He just sits there, not making me do anything, not even look at him. The tears on my face are silent this time. They come quick and steady, like a rain that could wash away the pain and the dirt and the glue I've used to patch myself up every time I start to break, the glue that holds every jagged edge together.

He doesn't say a word, but he's there. And I'm too tired to run away, to hide and lick my wounds and take a shot and dance and pretend I'm happy or strong or free. I'll never be free until I stop pretending. And I'm tired of pretending that I believed her when she said she loved me or that she did it for me; tired of pretending that she's a hero for striking out on her own as if that made her brave and not just a coward who knew her life would be over if her husband found out the things she did to his daughter in the bathtub. I'm too tired to patch myself up even one more time.

So, I let myself fall, and this man, my husband, my king, he catches me. His hands are rough, but his touch is gentle as he takes me in his arms and holds me. And I know I don't have to hold myself together alone anymore. Or pretend I'm whole, that I'm not scarred and cracked and dirty like the pavement on the streets outside. I can break apart, fall into a million pieces. I know that he will catch me every time I fall, that he will pick me up and hold all my pieces together as long as I need him to, and he won't break or drop or lose a single one. He'll just hold them until I'm ready to start the slow and painful process of building myself back into the girl I once was, before the person who was supposed to love me broke me instead.

That wasn't love. This is love.

twenty-five

Eliza

I sit in the back of the car, clutching my purse in my lap and staring out at the city bathed in November sun. Every few minutes, I thumb open the bag's closure and peek inside at the gun nestled there, and my heart does a funny little flip. I glance up at the driver and my bodyguard, busy discussing the Yankees, before checking my phone to make sure King hasn't texted. Some stupid part of my heart sinks when I see that he hasn't. He stayed the night with me for the first time since I left him, holding me until morning, when he had to go to work. I didn't tell him what I was doing today. I know he'd try to stop me, and this is something I have to do before I can go home.

But then I think of my husband going to work every day, facing the most dangerous men in New York and then coming home to an empty house because his wife is wife still broken despite my best efforts to move on.

I take a deep breath and reach for the door. "I'm going in."

My bodyguard gets out first, but I step in front of him, leading the way. After scanning the tall buildings of the Jefferson Housing project and rechecking the address on the sticky note where I scribbled it after secretly contacting King's uncle with connections, I head for the doors. A couple guys stand out front smoking cigarettes and watching us with calculating, suspicious gazes. I hurry inside and start up the stairs. I have to pull my shirt over my nose halfway because the smell of urine is so strong it brings tears to my eyes.

When we reach the fourth floor, we exit into the hallway. An old man lies against the wall, hopefully sleeping, though I don't stick around to see if he's breathing. I head for the door to the apartment and knock. I can hear loud music thumping from down the

1all, and I have to knock a couple more times. Someone in the next apartment yells for us to shut the fuck up, though they don't bother opening the door.

At last, the door opens a crack, and a bloodshot, unfocused eye blinks at us from inside. "Yeah?" a woman's deep voice asks. I can just make out brown skin and frizzy hair in the dim lighting from within.

"I'm Eliza Pomponio," I say, using my maiden name. It sounds strange on my tongue already. "I'm looking for my mother. Is she here?"

"And who's that?" the woman asks, her eye moving to my bodyguard.

"This is my friend," I say.

"Nuh-uh," she says. "That's the DEA."

"He's not DEA," I say. "He's here to protect me."

"You gonna need it around here," she says. "A pretty little thing like you, shit. Won't last an hour."

"I just want to see my mom," I say, my voice steady despite the trepidation growing inside me. "I haven't seen her in ten years, and I heard she was living here. Her name's Margaret, or Maggie, Pomponio."

"Maggie, baby," the woman calls behind her. "You got a kid?"

I hear a quiet voice speak, but I can't make out the words.

"She says she don't have a kid," the woman tells us, looking me up and down with suspicion.

"I told you, I haven't seen her in ten years," I repeat. "I need to see her. Just this once. Then I'll leave you alone, and I'll never bother you again. Can you just get her to come to the door for one minute? Please?"

The woman sighs and steps back from the door, yelling that this isn't her business, and she doesn't want to deal with it. A minute later, another face appears for just a second, and then the door closes, and I hear the chain lock rattle, and then it opens fully. For the first time in ten years, I stand face to face with my mother.

I wish I could say I hate her, or that when I see her, I feel nothing. That I could take out my gun and shoot her and walk away.

Instead, I stare at her, and I feel sad and sick and shocked.

"Come on," she says quietly. "Your bodyguard can wait out here. There's just a bunch of women in here, and most of them's asleep."

I nod to my guard, but he insists on checking the apartment before he'll agree to stand outside and let me go in with her. When we step inside, it's so dim I can barely make out the two figures lying on the floor in the living room, the carpet around them threadbare and stained, with holes from cigarette burns and who knows what else. One more woman lies sprawled on a sagging couch with the springs exposed, matted blonde hair covering her face.

Mom gestures for me to follow her into the kitchen. A cracked, plastic dish rack holds clean dishes, and the room itself is clean, though it's literally falling apart. Strips of linoleum are missing, as well as half the ceiling, so you can see up to the floor of the next apartment and bits of insulation hanging down. The counters are burned and stained and missing chunks of the Formica or whatever they used for the counters when this place was built.

My mother sits down at the table, which is in similar condition to the rest of the place.

"Mom, what are you doing here?" I ask, trying to keep the horror out of my voice.

"What are *you* doing here?" she asks.

When I pictured this meeting, I thought I'd come in guns blazing. I thought I'd be so angry, that I'd punch her teeth out and put a bullet in her head for ruining me for the one person who should have been able to love me. But I can't imagine anything I could do that would punish her more than this.

Once, Mom was a mafia princess like me. She grew up rich, and she married a mafia king.

Or maybe she never grew up at all. Maybe that's why she thought she could do whatever she wanted, and it would never come back on her. That she could run off and become an actress and everything would go her way, the way it always had. Just like me.

But now, as we sit across a wobbly table from each other, I look at her full in the face for the first time. I have to admit that as bad as this place looks, it's just a

ace. Just as they keep it clean even though it's a
ithole, good people can come out of the worst
rcumstances. People can come from nothing.

The opposite is also true. Bad people can come from
very opportunity, every privilege. Someone can grow up
ch, with everything handed to them, getting away with
verything, and then marry a rich man who doesn't watch
1em in the bathroom with their own kids. And they can
nd up like this. Her once lustrous chestnut hair hangs in
hin strings from her scalp. Her clothes droop off her
ody, her shoulders so thin I can see knobs of bone
ticking up against her shirt. Her cheeks are sunken, her
eeth stained and broken, her eyes lifeless.

"Mom, what happened? I thought you went off to
ecome an actress."

"I did," she says. "Just—give me a minute. I can't
elieve this is real. Am I dreaming?"

"Not dreaming," I say. "I came to talk about what
1appened when I was a kid."

"Let me get a smoke," she says, getting up and
ulling open one drawer and then the next, muttering

curses. At last, she comes back with a pack of cigarette and sits down, lighting up with a shaking hand. Sh immediately coughs, a deep, wet, rattling cough. "Yo want one?"

"No, thanks," I say, making a face before I can hel it.

"That's right," she says. "Don't want to stain thos pretty teeth. Looks is all a woman's got at your age. Gott keep up appearances until you can be auctioned off to th highest bidder."

"Mom," I say, my voice hardening. "I'm alread married."

She coughs again, waving smoke away with one han as she stares at me in the dim lighting of the kitchen. can see track marks on her arms from whatever she' shooting up. "Is that why you came?" she asks, her voic bitter, like I'm selfish for not coming to see how she is.

"Yes," I say, anger building into a hard knot in m chest. She didn't even ask about him, about the weddin that she didn't attend.

"Well," she says. "Congratulations."

"I didn't come for congratulations," I say, my voice hard. "I don't need anything from you, not even your best wishes."

She snorts, then holds in a cough. "Don't tell me you need money."

"No," I say. "I came to kill you. You ruined me, Mom. How could you do that to your own daughter? What kind of sick fuck does that?"

Her fingers tremble as she holds her cigarette, staring at me like she's shocked that I'd bring it up, that I'd dare speak those things aloud. After all this time, she probably thought she'd never have to answer for what she did in the bathtub.

"I never wanted to marry your father," she says, her voice trembling. "I wanted out, but he wouldn't let me. My father wouldn't, either. Women are just pawns to them, pretty playthings to use and sell off when they tire of them."

"That's your excuse?" I ask. "Your father sold you into marriage with Daddy?"

She goes on speaking without acknowledging my words, sucking angrily at her cigarette every few sentences. "They just want to breed you like an animal and make more pretty playthings for them to use. And then once you've made them an heir and another piece of meat to auction off, they have no interest in you. Your usefulness is gone by twenty-five, and they don't need you anymore. They go find a new little whore and leave you at home to raise their kids so they can use them to their advantage all over again."

"Don't you dare speak badly about my father to me," I say, gripping the edge of the table so hard I think it'll crumble. "He's the only person in my life who did the right thing."

She snorts smoke out both nostrils. "Your father's a monster, Eliza," she says, and I remember that she's the first person I ever heard call him that. "You really think that other family killed your brother? No, sweetheart. It was your own beloved father. He found out what Johnny'd been doin' to you, and he killed his own son."

"What *he'd* been doing?" I swallow hard, staring at her through the haze of smoke. I don't want to believe her. If my father found out but thought it was my brother hurting me, not Mom, he might have killed him.

But she's lying. I know she is. Dad would have gotten me help. And my brother's death was too hard on Mom, and that's why she left.

Or maybe she left because she was afraid Jonathan had talked before he died.

"That's why you left, wasn't it?" I ask. "Not to protect me, not because you loved me but couldn't stop and you wanted to keep me from what you were doing to me. You weren't even conflicted about it, were you, Mom? Are you even sorry?"

"You look like you're doing fine," she says. "Come in here looking all pretty. Expensive clothes. That handbag probably cost a year's rent in a place like this. Am I supposed to feel sorry for you, Eliza? Would you rather I'd taken you with me?"

"No," I say, horrified at the thought. I don't even want to imagine what I'd have become by now if she'd taken me from Dad. But he'd never have let her. He might have let her leave him, not gone after her like most mafia men would. But if she'd taken his daughter? He would have hunted her to the ends of the earth. I may not be a son or an heir, but he's never once expressed even a word of disappointment, never treated me as *less than*.

"Then I did a good thing by you," she says. "You'll see soon enough. Marriage takes the best years of your life and leaves you with nothing. You're too young to believe me, but you will."

"You're wrong," I say quietly. My voice is firm, though.

Her words played on a loop in my childhood, cursing marriage and men and my father. I didn't even realize how much of my objection to marriage came from her until now. She's the one who told me over and over, when I was way too young to understand, that marriage was a trap, a curse, a pit of quicksand to be avoided at all costs. As she splattered my little plastic plate with dinner, she cursed my father for not being home, cursed her life, her marriage, and the institution in general. Somewhere ong the way, my impressionable little brain internalized

Maybe marriage was a trap for her. But that doesn't mean it has to be for me. For me, it was the net that aught me on the way down when I was falling off the ghtrope she put me on all those years ago. It was a upport system even when I didn't realize I needed it, when I didn't even notice it was there—that *he* was there, aiting to pick me up if I fell, willing to do anything to et me back and show how sorry he is. Because he knows 's never over, he'll work harder than anyone else ever ould. That's what he was doing all those days before I eft, trying to work things out. And ever since he came ack into my life, he's been proving himself to me.

I was the one who refused to try from the very first day. Being forced into this with him doesn't make him he enemy, though. He didn't pick me, either. And he's no older than me. Neither of us had a clue what we were doing. But being bound together forever means learning o think of someone else's needs, to stop being selfish and running from reality, because this reality never end

It means growing together, being there for each other.

Like he was for me last night.

My husband didn't ruin me. Even after I told hir

what she did to me, he didn't hate me. He wasn't angry c

disgusted. He just wanted to protect me, and I wouldn

let him. If our marriage was a trap, it's because I made :

one.

He threw me a lifeline even when I refused to take i

He tried to pull me from the quicksand she pushed m

into when I was too young to understand what it was, toc

young to take a step and get out. Her toxic beliefs ar

hardwired into my brain, screwing me up for life. That'

the curse. Not marriage. She's the one who taught me tc

cut the lifeline even if it meant I would drown. To her

that was better than being stuck with someone she didn'

choose. And when she had her freedom, look what sh

chose.

"You buy into it, don't you?" she muses, watching

me. "All your father's lies. The Life. I'm too smart foi

that. I wasn't going to be part of it. They're all sick

bastards, every one of them. My father, your father—they're all the same. I wanted my own life."

"And it looks like you fucking found it."

We stare at each other across the table for a long minute. Mom gets up to get an ashtray and crushes out her cigarette before sitting back down.

"Your father's the monster," she says again, a familiar refrain from my childhood. "All of them are. The way they treat us. We're nothing but a conquest, some dumb thing to stroke their ego and their dick. You think you won't wind up that way, but mark my words, as soon as you've served your purpose, that new husband of yours will trade you in for a younger model. See, once you have kids, you're not so tight anymore, and he'll want a young one again so he can show his prowess, make him feel powerful when she worships him, make the other men admire how many sluts he can get to spread their legs for him."

"Not every man is like that," I say. "And not every woman does what you did when a guy cheats on her. I'm sorry Dad was unfaithful, but that doesn't excuse the fact that you hurt me."

"Don't judge me," she snaps. "Once you see what you'd do to get his attention, how you lose your mind sitting home night after night, knowing you have nothing to look forward to for the rest of your life, living on nothing but the fuel of your own rage while some teenage whore at one of his clubs gets his affection, the gifts, everything you once got. You'll convince yourself that maybe it's because he didn't get to pick you, that it was all chosen for him. That if he'd gotten to choose for himself, he would have chosen her. Everyone deserves love, after all."

I shiver, remembering King's words.

Mom laughs. "You already know it's true. You'll be a fool once or twice, but pretty soon you'll see the truth. He doesn't love the first one or the fortieth. He just keeps shoving his dick into more of them in desperation to fill the empty cavern inside him where his heart should be. He can't love those girls any more than he loves you. He an't love anyone. That's what the mafia does to you. It makes men monsters, and women into empty shells."

"Stop," I say, slamming my palm down on the table. I let her control me for too long, not just my body, but my mind. She told me lies, and she knew I wanted to trust her so badly I'd believe them. No more.

Mom jumps, licking her lips nervously and glancing around like she forgot where she was, who she was talking to. She reaches for her cigarettes and pulls out another one.

"I'm sorry if Dad cheated on you, though I'm guessing it had at least something to do with you not wanting anything to do with him. He shouldn't have done that. But I didn't come here to hear about what a monster Dad is. I know what people say. He likes women. He's killed people. He's far from perfect. But he doesn't abuse children. Nothing excuses that."

She smirks and lets out a stream of smoke. "How old's his current *goomah*?"

"Twenty-seven," I say. "Yeah, she's young. But she's not a child."

She sits there smoking for a few minutes before speaking. "I thought I'd strike out on my own, you know. Have a glamorous life. Be a Broadway star. You know what they told me?"

I shake my head.

"They told me I was too old. That I should've started earlier. I wanted to take acting classes, you know, but where was I going to get money? My father wasn't going to give me money. If I contacted him, he would have been furious, would have sent me right back home. And your father, of course *he* wasn't going to support me. At thirty-five, I was already done with life. I had no purpose in my marriage, no prospects as an actress, no skills to get a job…"

"What have you been living on the past ten years?" I ask. "Welfare?"

She gives a mirthless laugh. "I'm still married to your father," she says. "I wouldn't qualify for help. I did things… The things a woman with no prospects has to do to get money."

I close my eyes for a second. I don't want to feel for this monster, but I do. She's my mother, after all. She may be a monster, but she's a human one. I have compassion for her the way I would if a stranger told me this story. Because that's what she is. A stranger.

I never knew her then. Kids don't know their parents at that age. Parents are rulers, providers, protectors, jailers, and sometimes heroes. They are not complex human beings who make mistakes and have flaws and opinions and dreams that they gave up. Even having parents who talked to me about those things didn't really make me see them that way, as someone with internal struggles equal to mine.

I'm just starting to want to know my father as a person, now that he's not in control of my life. I could stay in contact with my mother, try to get to know her, too, with all her hurts and failures. I could help her.

But then I think of something King said. That people make their choices, and that makes them who they are. They do right or they do wrong, and each choice adds to the sum of their character.

My mother made her choices. She hurt me. Mayb
she hurt my brother. If she's telling the truth, and Da
somehow found out, and she made him think Jonatha
was the one hurting me, then she got him killed. And ye
she has a horrible life now, but it's one she made fc
herself. I won't invite it into my life. After all, I want kid
I want to be a good mother. And a good mother woul
never have someone in her life, and one day her kid:
lives, who's made the choices and done the things m
mother has done.

There's one thing that might have swayed me. Mayb
that's the real reason I came.

To see if she'd changed.

And now I know.

Because the last choice she's made, the one she mad
today, the one that lets me know she'll never change.
That was her choice not to apologize.

I didn't come here for that, didn't even expect it. Bu
she could have offered. She could have taker
responsibility, told me she'd made a horrible mistake, tolc
me it haunted her every day of her life. She could have

:ried and begged forgiveness. Or even just acknowledged vhat she did and that it was wrong, that it hurt me.

I may never have forgiven her, but she could have ısked. Maybe that's why I came. Just to hear her excuse, :o see what she'd say, as if anything she could say would ustify what she did. Still. Maybe I wanted that, the ımpossible. I wanted her to have a reason good enough to make me understand how you could do such a thing to a child who trusted you, a child you should have protected.

I push back from the table, the chair nearly dumping me on the floor with the uneven legs before I catch myself and stand. "I think I've heard all I need to hear."

"That's it?" she asks. "I thought you came to kill me."

I sling my bag over my shoulder and face her squarely. She doesn't stand, just looks up at me through the smoke, her strung-out face framed by the linoleum-striped floor and the gaping hole where a cabinet door is missing behind her. She doesn't sound like she'd mind if I killed her.

"I think you're doing a bang-up job of that on your own," I say. "Guess karma's a bitch."

"If karma were real, we'd all be living like this," she says, gesturing around with the stub of her cigarette. "You think you'll be different, but I was there once, too. Just married to some big shot, I bet. I was just like you. Thought I'd have it all. Now look at me."

"You left," I say. "That was your choice."

"Stay in the Life, do what they do, and you'll become a monster, too," she says. "You just watch."

"No," I say firmly. "I'm nothing like you."

"And watch those babies around that big shot husband," she says, tapping her cigarette. "Your father killed his son. Would have killed you, too, if he found out."

I just stare at her. "If he found out what? That you were abusing me? No, Mom. He wouldn't have killed me. He would have killed you."

Mom crushes out her second cigarette without taking her eyes from mine.

DANGEROUS DEFIANCE

"You know, despite everything, I admired that you left," I say. "I really believed you when you said you were protecting me. I admired you for having the guts to leave such a powerful man. For going off on your own, to find your way, do your thing, and take your daughter out of harm's way, even if that harm was you. You told me you left to be free, and I really believed it. All these years, I believed it. But you never really had a choice, did you? You weren't leaving to protect me. You were leaving to protect yourself."

I don't wait for her answer. I got all the answers I wanted and more today.

twenty-six

Eliza

When I hear the jangling of keys in the door, I don't know what to do with myself. I have the ridiculous urge to pose somewhere, like he's going to walk in and forget that I haven't lived here in months. I shove the thought away just as the door opens and my husband walks in. He stops short, blinking at me like I must be a mirage.

"What are you doing here?" he asks carefully, turning to push the door closed behind him.

Suddenly I wish I had posed somewhere. Better than standing awkwardly in the middle of the room, clasping my hands in front of me like I'm waiting for his fucking approval.

"You told me on our wedding day that I have to always come back to you."

He sets down his leather bag, the one that looks professional, but if I had to guess, probably contains a Glock, a few extra magazines, some rope for tying up uncooperative suspects, and maybe a handful of instruments of torture thrown in for good measure.

"And you made it clear you do whatever the fuck you want and don't obey me," he says, the corner of his mouth tilting up so I know he's just giving me a hard time.

"Yeah," I admit. "But maybe I sort of like it when you get all bossy and dominating."

He arches a brow. "Is that right?"

"It was pretty hot when you fed me that time," I admit, biting at my lower lip.

His eyes follow the movement, but he returns his gaze to mine quickly. "I'm going to clean up," he says, snagging his bag and heading to the bedroom.

A minute later, I hear the shower running. He always showers when he gets home, even when I can't see blood

on him. It must suck for a guy like him to have to hu
people all day. He's not like Dad's men, who joke about
over dinner. He'll get there, but he's not desensitized t
violence yet. I'm probably more callous than he is, fc
fuck's sake. But I can't help but wonder if he's excite
that I'm home, if he's taking a cold shower so he doesn
get his hopes up. I want to tell him that he can, that I'r
ready to try again, but I don't want to lead him on. I don
know if I'll make it all the way this time, or if I'll freak ou
again.

Dinner's not supposed to arrive for an hour, so I g
into the bedroom and sit on my side of the bed and lea
back on the pillows, waiting for him to come out. A few
minutes later, he emerges trailing wisps of steam, wearin
nothing but the water droplets clinging to his skin and a
towel wrapped around his hips, hanging low enough tha
I can see the V of muscle leading downward.

I swallow hard, trying not to ogle him. But god, he's
so beautiful. I'm not even an artist, and he makes mc
want to draw him. All those angles and long lines. Was
Michelangelo gay? Because it would be a damn shame tc

ook at something like that and not see how sexy it is. Or maybe that would be a good thing. I don't know how long it took him to carve David, but it would probably be the longest hard-on in history.

King goes to the dresser and opens the drawer to get his boxers.

"Are you just visiting?" he asks.

"No," I say. "I realized that I'm doing just what my mother did. I don't want to do that to anyone. I want to fight for this. For us."

"I've been a terrible husband," he reminds me.

"I probably deserved it," I say. "I was a total bitch to you."

"No one deserves what I did. I want you to know, I don't think you owe me your body. Not ever. If you give it to me, I'll honor it the way I always should have."

I shrug. "It's okay. I think I wanted you to force me. To get it over with. I just didn't know how to say it."

"Well, I'm happy to boss you around a little," he says with a little grin. "But I don't want to cross that line ever again. I don't want to risk losing you."

"Maybe I was testing you in some way to see. In my world, people don't stick around. I push them away because it's easier if I'm the one who makes them leave. Eventually, they always do. No one stays."

King's expression turns pained, and he comes over to sink onto the other side of the bed. "Eliza... Fuck. I'm sorry."

"I'm the one who left. You just let me."

"I thought you wanted freedom from me."

"I wanted freedom," I agree. "Now I have it, and this is what I choose to do with that freedom."

He reaches for me, pulling me to him. I curl against him, relieved for the contact. That surprises me. I've gotten used to his touch, and on our nights apart, when he's not there to hold me, I miss him all night.

"If this is what you really want, I'm so fucking happy to have you back. But I want you to make sure it is. Am I really good enough, or is this just another one of your self-destructive tendencies, like the drinking?"

"No," I say, stroking the brown skin on his ring finger. "I think it's the exact opposite of that."

He pulls me into his arms again, and I hold onto him, feeling the damp cool of his skin above the delicious heat of his body underneath. He's wrong about not being good for me. This is exactly what I need. Someone who makes me want to be better, to get better. Someone who challenges me and puts me in my place. Someone who makes me feel scary things and still want to go on, for him and for me, too. I deserve to feel good. I deserve to enjoy my own body. I deserve the same pleasure other people feel when touched.

I've tried for so long to push those feelings down, to shut off the sensations of my body. But now I'm mad. I'm mad that the chance to feel uncomplicated pleasure was taken from me. Yes, I want to give myself to King, but more than that, I want it for myself. It's not fair that the most basic, simple pleasures fill me with terror. I'm ready to change that.

I twist around in King's arms, throwing my leg over him and straddling his hips so he has to brace himself to stay sitting, his palms flat on the mattress and his legs extended along the side of the bed where he sleeps. He looks up at me, his expression guarded, but I don't hesitate. I take his face between my hands and kiss him hard. He reacts, but his kiss is tentative, careful. He keeps his hands on the bed instead of touching me. But I touch him. I run my hands over the hard, knotted muscles of his shoulders, the scar left from the bullet wound, and down the lean, taut muscles of his biceps, his forearms, and onto his sides. His skin is hot and damp, and his body shivers against my cool hands as they run over his skin.

I delight in the sensation of his body responding to my inexperienced touch, the little shiver that goes through him, the hardness growing in his lap as I press against him. A shiver goes through me, too, half fear and half arousal. He's pressed up against me, but through a towel and my jeans, it's not too much.

It's not enough.

I slide my hand down over his abs, still running with a few little drops from the shower. When I reach the knot in his towel, King grabs my hand, breaking the kiss.

"I can't," he says, gripping my thighs and scooting e back on his lap. He's breathing hard, but he looks iserable. "I want to be respectful, but I can't help yself. You turn me on so fucking much, Eliza."

"I know," I say, linking my fingers through his and aning forward to kiss him through the smile on my lips. I love it."

"You do?"

"I'm not scared of you, King."

"You should be," he says. "You drive me out of my icking mind."

He turns sideways, cradling my body and sliding me ff him, then adjusting the pillows so we're lying face to ace. He runs a hand up the side of my thigh from my nee to my hip, his thumb pressing into the crease in my eans at the top of my thigh. Nervous excitement vibrates hrough my body.

I reach for the knot on the towel again. "Can I touch ou?"

He nods slowly. "How does this work? You can lease me, but I can't even touch you?"

"You can try," I say, my voice sounding so stup:
and scared I want to bite my tongue and take it back.

"What if... ?" He breaks off, his brow furrowed wit
concern.

"I freak out again?" I ask. "I might. I'm sorry. But
want to try. That's something, right? And hey, maybe it
a good thing. You won't have to wonder if I want to c
not."

He scoffs quietly and adjusts his head, folding hi
arm under it. "You can say that again."

Suddenly, I'm so nervous my fingers are shakin,
again, and I want to call the whole thing off. "Is tha
okay?" I whisper. "You said you wanted me home, but i
you don't anymore…"

He tips my chin up gently, his troubled gaze meetin;
mine. "I want you to trust me again. Anything you need."

I nod, dropping my gaze. "You said we could wor!
through it together," I whisper, laying a hand on his hip
on the damp towel still wrapped around him.

"And you said you didn't want to," he reminds me.

"Now I do," I admit, searching his eyes, begging him for understanding.

"What changed your mind?"

"You did," I say, my voice barely above a whisper. "When you said that I don't deserve you. You're right, but not in the way you meant. You're so good to me, and I want to be good for you, too. It takes a lot for me to trust, but I want to trust you, and I want you to trust me. I want to know you, King. And I want you to know me—all of me."

"I want that, too," he says quietly. "So much."

"And... Maybe because you said it was okay if I didn't want to, and you've held up your end of that. You've been patient, and I want to show you how much I appreciate that. I don't want to live my whole life controlled by something that happened to me when I had no choice. Moving past it is my choice."

"That's... Really fucking brave," he says quietly, sliding a hand over the side of my neck, cradling the back of my head in his big hand.

"Will you help me?" I ask. "Please?"

He swallows, his eyes so deep I could drown in their darkness. "Yes," he answers. "What do you need?"

"I need you," I admit. "I need you to not treat me like I'm broken. Be bossy. Tell me what to do. Push me a little—just not as much as you did the first time."

"You're so fucking beautiful I'm scared to touch you. I don't want to break you."

"You won't," I whisper. "I'm not fragile. You won't hurt me. You can only heal me."

I reach for the towel again, slowly pulling it open. I swallow hard before slipping my hand around his cock, hot and damp from the shower and straining against my palm.

"Eliza," he says, his voice rough as I kneel up and crawl back down the bed. "You don't have to—"

He breaks off when I flatten my palm and run it along the shaft of his cock. It throbs against my palm, and a tremor goes through me. I shift my position to press my knees together against the ache growing there. But I won't pay attention to that. I'll pay attention to servicing my husband. I want to satisfy him.

I know I'm not great at this, but it feels good, xciting and dangerous but not too scary. I swallow hard t the size of it, my pulse fluttering in my throat. It's so ig, and so hot in my hand. Suddenly, a thrill of nticipation goes through me at the thought of it inside ne, bare and straining to fit in.

I slide my hand back down it to the base, until I feel he lump of his balls. I stop, still not sure how much I'm upposed to touch them. Something about them feels embarrassing, like I went too far. Obviously I know guys have balls, but even when I saw porn, I don't remember hem. I never paid any attention to them, and now I'm not sure what to do about them. They're so… *visceral.*

King clears his throat, running a hand over the back of my head and lifting my face. "You don't have to do that," he says, his voice low almost choked. If I couldn't tell by the hardness against my palm, his voice lets me know exactly how much he wants me to do it, even if he's giving me an out.

Our eyes meet, and I gulp down my trepidation. There's so much in those eyes, but I can't read what it all

means. I want to, though. I want to know what's mixed
into that longing in his gaze. "Let me?" I ask. "I liked it
last time."

He looks like he might protest, but I slip off the side
of the bed before he can. I sink back on my heels to
admire the raw beauty of his naked body, all chiseled
angles and lean muscle as he stands. I want to trace the V
of his hips, run my fingers along the sculpted muscles of
his abs. But most of all, I find myself staring at his cock,
standing tall and proud against his lower belly, straight
and deeper in color than the rest of his skin.

A hot thrill races through me, adding pressure to the
ache between my thighs. His cock is so... Animal. It
looks rough and brutish and wild, so unlike the
calculating, reserved man it belongs to. It makes me
tremble with fear again as I lean forward and gingerly
wrap my fingers around it.

He sucks in a breath, his hand circling the back of
my head, stroking my hair. I tense, expecting him to
shove his cock down my throat and fuck my mouth again.
But he doesn't pull me forward, instead letting me look at

m, explore him with my fingers at my own pace. I wrap
y hand around his shaft, sliding it down his thick length.
art of me wants to pull away, to turn and flee, like I've
one before. But another part is fascinated. I thumb the
ick vein that runs the length of his stiff cock, then run
y fingers over the ridge around the head. His skin is
elvety smooth, but beneath it, I can feel the steely
uscles straining for relief.

I almost wish he'd be a dick about it again, just force
e to do what he wants whether or not I want to so I
on't have a choice and can't back out. It's hard to deal
ith his kindness, especially when it's so undeserved. I've
een a horrible wife. A horrible person. I hardly gave him
he time of day since our wedding, and he's been nothing
ut respectful of my need for space since he took my
irginity. And yeah, okay, he was barbaric that night, and
ometimes he's cold and haughty, but compared to the
other men my father could have given me to?

There is no comparison.

I've met a lot of made guys, and if I'm honest, King's
he best one I know. Yeah, he's new and low ranking, but

that means he hasn't had years to become a hardene
heartless brute like a lot of mafia men. I don't know of
single one who wouldn't have demanded I fulfill n
wifely duties on our wedding night, that's for damn sur
He could have made me service him every single nigh
could have overpowered me from my wedding da
onwards, but he didn't. He did it once, and he showed n
how sorry he is for that even though he had every right t
demand that I become his wife in more than name.
recognize that, and I'm more than willing to thank hir
for his patience in this way.

I lean in, angling my head to kiss along his shaft fron
the base to the tip. He's breathing hard by the time
reach the head, and I feel a swell of pride rise inside me
His cock throbs against my lips, demanding more, and
open and lower my mouth over his salty tip. He lets out
soft groan, his fingers tightening in my hair. I'm not sur
what to do next, so I begin to lick and suck gently.

I keep going until my cheeks start to ache from the
work. When I slow, King begins to move his hips a little
keeping my rhythm going.

"Let me take over," he says after a few minutes. "Just relax your throat and keep your teeth off. I won't hurt you."

I remember the last time, when he threatened to knock my teeth out. We've come so far.

I nod, but when he grips my hair and starts to move my head, I tense up. I still get nervous about losing control.

He pulls out, his hard cock slick with my saliva, bumping against my cheek as it stands up straight again. King takes my chin and lifts it, his dark eyes searching mine. "It's okay," he murmurs, stroking his thumb across my wet lower lip. A shiver goes through me, and I press my knees together. "If it gets to be too much, pinch me, and I'll stop. No questions asked. Okay?"

I have to admit, I have no clue what I'm doing. I've only done this once and he said I was bad at it. If I let him show me, I can see what he likes so I can do better next time. I nod, and he grips his cock and lowers it back to my mouth, pushing it between my lips and over my tongue.

"Fuck, *piccola*, I want to cum down this pretty throat," he purrs, his smooth voice so seductive I don't care what he's saying to me. I think he could say he wanted to murder me in that tone, and I'd agree. I wonder how many other girls he's gotten to kneel for him by using that voice.

Stroking the side of my throat with his fingers, he begins to move my head in rhythm with his hips, rocking them forward and back, his cock sliding deeper with each shallow thrust. My pulse flutters against his fingertips, and a burst of nerves shimmers through me, making me quake. I raise my eyes to his, holding his gaze while he slides his cock deep into my mouth. Another tremor goes through me, clenching in my core.

I feel… Powerful. Somehow, even though I'm on my knees just allowing him to do as he pleases, I feel alive and excited and… Sexy. I can imagine myself through his eyes, on my knees at his feet, my mouth open for him to fuck while my eyes hold his, begging for him to have mercy on me as he takes charge. But that's the key. I'm *allowing* him to take control. I see the complete surrender n his eyes, that he's lost to his lust while I'm still in ontrol of my senses, even as he uses my mouth for his pleasure.

After a minute, I adjust to the new sensations, spreading my knees on the floor and arching my back, aking hold of the base of his cock and adding a little suck with each thrust of his hips. He knows what he's doing, so I let him do it while I take note of what he likes. It also lets me pay attention to the things I was too absorbed to notice when I was worrying about what I was doing wrong. I cup his balls in my hand, moving them inside his soft skin. He groans quietly and thrusts harder, hitting the back of my mouth, his cock straining against my throat.

Tears spring to my eyes and I gag, pulling back. He slows, stroking the back of my head, but he doesn't pull out this time.

"Baby girl, your mouth feels so good," he says, gliding in and out slowly until I recover. I can taste salt and a musky flavor, and saliva fills my mouth as his soft skin slides against my tongue. I want more. I kneel up higher, wrapping my hands around his thighs and pulling him closer again. I suckle greedily at him, and he moans and pumps deep into my mouth again, his thick cock throbbing as salt spreads over my tongue.

"I'm going to cum," he says, gripping my hair hard enough to make tears fill my eyes again. "Can you swallow for me, *piccola mia?*"

I bob my head in a nod, feeling naughty at his blunt words, but in a good way, one I didn't know I could feel. I inhale, filling myself with the scent of him, noticing the hardness of his muscular thighs as he thrusts deep into my throat. I force my throat not to constrict, fighting the urge to choke as he fucks my mouth hard for a minute, his cock battering my throat like it did the last time. Reaching between his thighs, I cup his balls again, now swollen and hardened, and give them a little squeeze.

He curses quietly, but before I know if that was a good or bad thing, his hips jerk forward and his big hand cups the back of my head. His vein throbs against my lower lip, and the next second, salty cream explodes into my mouth and down my throat. I choke, tears streaming om my eyes, liquid dripping from the corners of my outh.

"Keep it open for me, *carina*," he growls, stroking my ir as his cock pulses more into me, spasms wracking his dy every few seconds. He doesn't move, though, which ves me time to swallow what I can and relax my throat ain.

"Did I hurt you?" he asks, wiping my tears with his umb.

I shake my head, swallowing past the ache he left in y bruised throat. I don't care if I'm a little sore. I feel… riumphant. He wants me, *desires* me, so much, it makes e feel almost high. I may be kneeling at his feet with my outh around his cock, but I don't feel degraded. I also on't feel like I'm trapped, the way I felt after orgasm. I eel… Free.

At last, he pulls back, gripping the base of his cock nd slowly dragging it over my tongue until he reaches my ps. "Suck out those last drops," he croons, stroking my heek with the back of his other hand.

A naughty thrill goes through me. I love that he so... Dirty. He's a mess of contradictions—tender yet nasty-mouthed, considerate yet dominating, gentle but forceful.

My throat aches, but I obey, giving his cock a little suck. He draws a sharp breath, spasms going through his body every few seconds for another minute. I keep going until he draws away. At last, he grabs me under the arm, lifting me to my feet and laying me down on the bed.

"I'm going to get you jewelry for that one," he says with a grin, kissing my salty lips.

"Speaking of," I say, tracing a finger down his chest. "I sort of flushed your wedding ring. So we're going to need to get another one of those."

"Naughty girl," he says, giving my ass a playful swat. "I was wondering what happened to that."

"How long did it take to clean up the apartment?" I ask.

"Not too long," he says, cracking a grin. "Since I know how to hire cleaners..."

"Jerk," I say, but I throw my leg over him.

He runs his hand up my thigh and palms my ass. "At least you left the utensils alone. One of the soup spoons is very special to me."

"King," I scold, burying my face in his chest.

He slides his hand between my thighs and starts to troke me, sending tingles through me as he fingers the fabric, now damp from my arousal during the blowjob. 'If that's the only way I get to taste you, you better get ready for it to be inside you regularly," he says. "But tonight, I'll be content with licking you off my fingers. Now open your legs and let feel that pretty cunt fill my hand with your sweet cum."

twenty-seven

Eliza

"What's wrong?" I ask King, sliding a hand over his cheek. He's lying on the bed staring at the ceiling, the same as he's done for the past three nights. I don't think the guy ever sleeps.

He gives me a distracted smile and covers my hand with his. "Nothing."

"Talk to me," I plead, snuggling up next to him. "You can tell me anything."

"It's not you," he says. "It's just… Work stuff. The less you know about that, the better."

"King," I say. "I know all about your job, the families, the Life. I know you want to protect me, but you don't have to do that."

"But I want to," he says, turning his face toward me. "I'm your husband. It's my job to protect you. And I couldn't do that when you needed it most."

"You didn't even know me then," I point out.

"I knew you when I hurt you," he says quietly.

"I've forgiven you," I say. "And I know about this stuff, King. I'm not fragile or helpless. I'm an asset. Have you ever thought that's why Al picked you?"

"I want to do something for you now," he says. "She should pay for what she did."

"She's paying," I say. "I saw her, and I'm seeing a therapist. I wanted to make peace with it before I came home. That's why it took me so long."

"You saw her?"

"Yes," I admit. "I'm making peace with the past. I want to be better for you. I want to be everything you've ever wanted in a wife."

"You are," he says. "You're that and more."

I smile. "I want to be better for me, too. I want to be the person I was supposed to be, that I could have been, if none of that had happened. I think I just need to get clear and learn to move on, you know? From my brother's death, my mom, and my issues. I want to work through it, not hold onto it forever. I want to be a good mom when that day comes."

King turns back to stare at the ceiling again. After a few minutes, he asks, "What about your brother?"

"He's dead."

"I meant… Was she abusing him, too?"

I swallow hard and roll onto my back. I never wanted to confront any of this, but some part of me knew he'd keep asking, that he'd want all the answers. And he deserves them.

"I don't really know," I admit. "He was a lot older than me. I remember sitting on the floor in the bathroom one time, and she'd left me there, but I knew she was coming back. And she was trying to get Jonathan to come in, but he wouldn't. I don't remember the reason she was giving for why he needed to. I just remember that I was scared he'd come in and know. I remember him saying something like, 'I don't want to be a part of this house of horrors anymore.' A week later, he was killed."

King's jaw clenches, and I cringe back, imagining that he's thinking of me. "Where was your dad?"

"He was at work," I say. "He was always gone. I don't know if anything happened to my brother when he was younger, but he was old enough to refuse then. He just walked away. But she always made me feel guilty, like I'd let her if I loved her. She always said it was good for me, that I should enjoy it. And she'd get mad when I didn't, like there was something wrong with me."

"Eliza, you know that's not true, right? She was a sick person. And you were a kid, and she was the person who was supposed to love and protect you."

I nod, unable to meet his eyes. "I know. And the fucked up part is, she only did the right thing once in her whole fucking life, and that's when she left. So I kept focusing on that, on the one time she protected me. And I convinced myself that meant she loved me, even after everything else she did. I kept telling myself that, until it grew like a tall tale into this legend. She didn't just protect me one time, didn't just love me, but she was a hero."

"I wondered why you admired her."

"I don't," I say. "You know that. I just…I guess was a defense. I kept repeating it until if I didn't thin about it too hard, I could believe it. But I never thoug about when she was here. I only thought about h leaving. It's like she was only here to do one thing—wa out. There was nothing before or after that day. That's a she was. The mom who left. Because if she was that, sh didn't have to be the mom who molested me."

"And your brother?"

"Dying was his one act. He was only fifteen. When do think about him, before he died, I remember he wa so angry all the time. I was a little scared of him. S maybe Mom did hurt him, too, and that's why he was lik that. And then when he said that he didn't want to live i her house of horrors… I don't know, maybe they jus said he was shot to cover up how he really died. I alway thought some things didn't add up. Mom said Dad kille him, but now I wonder if maybe he did it."

King is quiet for a minute. "I've thought about tha with my sister, too. I don't want to, but sometimes wonder."

"If she killed herself?"

"Yeah," he says quietly. "She was seeing this guy my family hated. My father was set on destroying his whole family. And we're family, so we go along, the way you hate the Valentis because your family does. It was like that."

I swallow hard, knowing he doesn't talk about this to just anyone. He's never really opened up to me before, but he's finally letting his guard down, letting me in. I wish there wasn't painful parts of his past, too, but I'm glad he's sharing them now. Those are the hard parts, and when we can tell each other even the ugly things, there's nothing left to hide.

"Your family wouldn't let her see him?" I ask.

"We tried to stop her. I knew she'd get hurt, that if she loved him, and we hurt him, it would hurt her. I tried to make her see that, to make her stop, but it was like she couldn't. Like she was addicted or something."

"She was in love," I say softly, running my fingers down King's chest.

"Yeah," he says. "I guess."

"So, what happened?" I ask.

"We had this big fight with their family," he says. "She wasn't supposed to be there. But she insisted on coming, and even though I knew I shouldn't, I let her. I…I was supposed to watch out for her." His voice catches a little, and he looks away.

"I'm sure it wasn't your fault," I say softly.

"It was," he says fiercely. "I was worthless that night, Eliza. I got myself shot, and then I couldn't even fight when things went down. Crystal ran off, and my brother was so mad at her, he said we should leave her. I argued with him, but I didn't stop him when he drove off and left her."

I run my finger over his hipbone to the scar above it, soft and still slightly pink with freshness. I remember Bianca telling me how recently his sister died. "You were shot," I say. "You weren't in any condition to be stopping anyone from anything."

"But I should have been," he says. "It wasn't my brother's fault. He was her twin, and she chose her boyfriend over him. Over us." He's quiet for a minute,

466

taring off. "I told myself she'd be fine. We left her with her boyfriend. We went to this stupid party, and there was a big fight, and my brother started a fire. By the time we went back for Crystal, she was gone."

"Gone... How?"

"It was in the middle of this storm," he says. "We looked for her, but by the time we did, it was too late. The river rose and took her boyfriend's car with both of them in it."

"Oh my god," I say. "I'm so sorry."

"They found the car a couple days later," he says.

"They were... Stuck in it?" I ask, swallowing hard.

"No," he says, shaking his head. "They never found them. But they found... Evidence... in the back seat that they'd been there that night. I guess too busy fucking to notice the water rising. Part of me thinks... What if she didn't care that it was? She never thought things through in the long term. She was impulsive and sort of fragile, too. In that moment, she had him, and she didn't want us interfering. We'd pretty much told her we were going to kill the guy. She probably thought it was the only way not

to lose him. If she couldn't have him, they'd go ou
together. That's the sort of thing she'd do. Dramatic
Romantic. Tragic."

"That's all very Romeo and Juliet," I say. "But di
you ever think maybe she's still alive?"

He shakes his head. "We hired private investigator:
and looked for her for a few months after the cops gave
up, but the river goes right to the Mississippi, and we
were just a little above Louisiana. I like to think she's in
the ocean somewhere. She loved the ocean when we were
kids."

We're quiet for a minute, two. Then I hug myself
around him. "It wasn't your fault," I say again. "And I
know you don't want to hear this, but maybe that's the
best way to go. With someone you love."

"We could have stopped it," he says. "I could have. I
could have convinced my dad to leave him alone. To
leave his family alone. I'm sure I could have."

I shake my head. "If they're anything like mine, then
you couldn't. Wars between families are bigger than two
people."

"But I should have tried," he insists. "Instead of trying to keep them apart. Maybe if I'd understood what love is like…"

"I think I understand," I whisper, my heartbeat picking up speed. "Nothing could keep me from being with you."

He turns in bed to face me, his hand falling on my waist. "That's why I didn't want to fall in love with you. I didn't want you to fall for me, either. If anything happened to me, at least your heart would be safe."

"Too late," I whisper, cupping his cheek and leaning in to kiss him. "I think you stole it, King Dolce."

He smiles into our kiss. "I think you're the thief, Eliza Dolce."

I shiver at the way he says my new name. I was so insistent on keeping my independence, not belonging to him. But when he says my name like that, I know I already belong to him, and not because of any agreement between our families. My heart is his. He's treated it so carefully, I know he'll always protect me.

"I love you," I whisper, pressing my lips to his again.

He pulls back gently, his gaze finding mine, his eye
so deep and dark they seem bottomless. "I love you, too
he says, his voice thick with emotion.

"Make love to me," I whisper.

He searches my eyes, then leans in and kisses me
"You're ready?"

"I want to try," I say. "You deserve a wife who give
you everything. I want to be that for you. And for me."

We kiss for a long time, until my lips feel hot an
swollen, and my body is tingling all over. We undres
each other, and I marvel in his body the way I always do
the ridges and smooth lines of muscle, the dips an
points of bone. He runs his hands over me, too, adorin
me without touching me in a sexual way. Still, his touch i
electrifying as well as reassuring, and pressure ache
between my thighs. When he slides his hand down my
belly, I tense, though.

He touches me, and I lay frozen, my heart racing in
my chest. I tell myself it's not so bad, that it feels good. I
does feel good. I'm wet against his fingers. But my head is

470

creaming for me to get the fuck out, to fly off the bed like I did the last time he made me cum.

"Tell me if it's too much," he murmurs, his mouth on my neck, sending chills of desire through me.

Why can't I just fucking enjoy it like a normal person? I want to scream at myself, my mother, the world. It's so fucking unfair I want to cry.

He pushes a finger into me, and I let myself breathe, force myself to. I won't let someone evil define me, won't let her rob me of this.

It's my body. My choice. I can reclaim it, take back the experience, replace it with this. With a good man who loves me, and I can feel how much he wants and needs me in every part of his body, in the trembling of his restraint, in the thick, hard ridge of his cock biting into me as he pushes against me, in his rapid breaths, his heart hammering under my fingertips when I touch his chest.

"Fuck, you're so tight," he breathes, slowly sliding his finger in and out until I think I'll scream with how badly I want him. I open my knees, pushing my hips up against his hand, whimpering for more.

"You like that, don't you, my little wife?" he teases, pushing his finger deep and slowly circling it inside me. "Your cunt is so fucking hot, Eliza. I want to feel you milking my cock while I cum inside you."

"I want that too," I breathe. "Please. I'm so ready."

He moves on top of me, pulling back to look down at my face, his eyes searching mine with concern and desire blurring the lines between us. Reaching down, he grips his cock, rubbing the head slow and hard through my wetness while his gaze stays locked on mine. Pleasure ripples through me, and I open my legs for him, giving myself over even though fear is still pumping through me with each heartbeat. He hurt me so badly last time. I keep telling myself I'm safe, that he won't do that again.

"Tell me what you want," he murmurs, his cock straining against my entrance.

I can only manage one word. "This."

"I'm going to put it in," he whispers. "I'll be gentle. If it hurts or you need to stop, just say so."

I nod, biting my lip. He pushes harder, and I wince as he breaches my entrance with the slow, steady ressure. He begins to sink deeper, and I gasp as I feel im straining against my walls, filling me until I think I'll ip apart.

"You ready for the rest of it?" he asks.

No, I'm not ready. But I may never be ready, and if I lon't do it now, it'll just get bigger and scarier in my head until I can never do it. And I want to. I want to give myself to him fully, with every part of myself. So I nod my head.

King pushes against the resistance inside me, then lraws back when I gasp in pain. "What's wrong?" he asks, a stitch pulling between his brows.

"You're too big," I whisper.

He pulls out and then enters me again, the thick head of his cock fitting right inside my entrance, stretching me. It feels so good I think I'll explode. He grips his cock, pulling out and pushing just the tip back inside me. Groaning, he rubs his cock through my slippery folds the next time before sinking just a few inches inside. He watches as he begins to move, breaching my entrance again and again as he fucks just my opening until his cock is so slick it passes easily through the stretched flesh.

"Deeper," I moan, rocking my hips.

"I don't want to hurt you again."

"Just do it. I need you to go hard, like you did last time."

"I hurt you."

"I don't care. I need you inside me."

With a growl, he guides his hips forward, his thick cock stretching me deeper, until I can't hold back tears. I suck in a shaky breath, trying to blink them away before he sees. He pushes in to the hilt, his hips locked to mine, and rocks his pelvic bone against my clit while he rests on his elbows with his head hanging down beside mine, his breath hot and quick against my neck.

"You feel fucking amazing," he whispers, kissing my neck, my ear. He doesn't move, waiting for me to adjust, so I force myself to relax.

"Keep going," I whisper. "I'm ready."

He pushes in a few more times, slow and deep, until all I can do is remember the last time. My whole body bels, as if we're the wrong ends of magnets being forced together, and at the last second, I just can't. The pain is still there, and oh god, the sensation fills me with paralyzing terror and dread, and tears begin to pour from my eyes.

"Eliza," King says, sounding alarmed. He stops moving, using his hands to smooth back my hair. "You didn't tell me to stop."

"It's fine," I say, gripping his shoulders, wrapping my legs around him. "Just finish."

"You're crying."

He says the words gently as he rolls away, as if that's all the reason anyone needs to stop, as if what my body is showing is more important than what my mouth is saying. His strong, long arms wrap around me, and he holds me against him, and I can feel the hard, wet ridge of his cock pressing into my belly, and it makes me cry harder because I can't satisfy it. I want to scream and scream and scream until I can't breathe and can't speak and can't feel anything. He stopped, and I'm so angry at myself because I'm just. So. Broken.

He just holds me and doesn't say anything. No about how hard it must have been to stop, or how once again he wasn't satisfied, or that his wife failed him y again. He strokes my hair and kisses my forehead whi shame and fury pour from my eyes. I know I'm saf That's the worst part. I know I am, but my body st reacts like I'm not, and I don't know how to fix that.

At last, my tears run dry, but I can't look up at King This feels like the worst failure yet, confirmation of m worst fears—that I can't have sex.

"I'm so sorry," I whisper at last.

King takes my tearstained face in his hands, raising to his. He kisses my salty cheeks, my puffy eyes, my re nose. "No, I'm sorry," he says. "I should have known."

"What are we going to do?" I ask, clinging to him with all the desperation I feel. I've never told anyone th things I've told him, my deepest darkest secrets. Now those secrets are pushing us apart, that they'll continue to grow between us until there's no way back to each other My mother was right. There's no way to make it work. can't have sex, and no matter how understanding he is ow, one day he'll meet someone who can give him everything, with nothing held back.

"We'll get through it," King says. "I promise. We have our whole lives to try."

I nod, another tear slipping from my lashes. I want to ask how he can promise that, how he can know. How we can get through it. But it's my burden to bear.

*

A few days later, we're cuddling in bed when King tells me they still haven't found Little Al DeLuca, his partner who almost had him killed. I swell with pride that he's trusting me, that he's letting me into the business side of his life, too.

"You'll find him," I promise King, throwing a leg over him and cuddling closer. "And you'll make sure he never gets a chance to leave me a widow. I know you'll do it. You have everything it takes to fight and win."

"And what's that?" he asks, adjusting his arm to pillow my head before smiling down at me.

"You're a good man, and you have loyalty to your family and a reason to make it home at night."

"I think I'm starting to get it," he says, squeezing me against him. "I thought love was the enemy, but it's just what you make of it."

"Sure, love is dangerous," I agree, turning my head to kiss his shoulder. "But isn't that what makes it worth it?"

"It must be," King says. "Because I'd risk anything for you, Eliza. Whatever I have to do to keep you, to make you happy, to be your man, that's what I'm doing to do. And it's so fucking worth it."

"I know you miss her, but maybe that's what your sister wanted, too," I say. "To die for love. Maybe that was worth it for her."

"I wish I could have saved her," he says quietly, pressing his lips to my forehead.

"I know," I say. "But maybe she didn't need you to. Maybe she didn't want that. You can't be a hero to everyone."

He snorts. "I'm no hero."

"Maybe not," I admit. "But maybe a hero doesn't have to swoop in wearing a cape and save everyone. Maybe you can be a hero just by showing up, by being there for someone when anyone else would have walked away."

"Eliza, I'm never leaving you," he says, turning my face to his. "You're my wife."

"People leave their wives all the time."

"I'm not one of those people," he says. "When I make a promise, I mean it. Remember?"

I nod. "Then you're already a hero in my eyes."

"Hey," he says, kissing me lightly on the forehead again. "Anyone would have to be crazy to walk away from this."

"And that's why you're a hero," I say, twisting to press my lips against his palm. "You save me a little bit each day just by staying."

"Then get ready to be rescued, my little mafia princess," he says, pressing his lips to mine. "Because you're never getting rid of me."

"Good," I say. "Somehow I don't think I could find someone else to love me even when I'm unlovable."

"You're not unlovable," he says, pulling back to gaze into my eyes. "You are worthy of love, Eliza Dolce."

Hearing him say my name makes my heart melt every time. I fought so hard to keep my old life, but maybe I'm done being Eliza Pomponio, party girl fodder for the gossip columns. I'm ready to be someone else, someone better. Mrs. King Dolce. I'm all in with my whole self, and I can't think of anything better than letting him take me over, possess and own me, dominate me, tame my wild ways and make me his.

"I know," I whisper. "I must be, or you wouldn't love me. You don't love just anyone."

"I've never loved anyone," he corrects. "You're the only one, Eliza. There was only ever you."

I look away, my throat tight. "I just don't know what I did to earn it."

"You don't have to do anything to earn it," he says. "You're worthy just by existing."

I lean in to kiss him, and I don't pull back. I run my
nds over his chest, his abs, his thighs. I love that he's so
eral with his body, that he lets me have my way with
m however I want, as if it's my body as much as it is his.
love touching him, exploring every inch of his skin.

I want to give him the same in return. Someday, I'm
ing to do it. I don't know how yet, but I vow I'm going
make it happen. I will be worthy of him. He may think
am now, but I'm going to prove it to myself, the way he
roved himself to me. After what we've been through, we
oth deserve it. We deserve to have everything we need. I
eed to be treasured but also tamed. And he needs the
ift he gives me every day, the one he desires and
eserves most of all—me.

twenty-eight

King

"It's time," Il Diavolo says, nodding for me to get out of the car. We're parked under a bridge with nothing but warehouses behind us. The river crawls sluggishly by in the other direction. I climb out of the car, pocket the keys, and join the others. The night is windy and crisp, and as I cross the lot, lit only by security lights, I scan the building ahead for signs of life.

As quietly as we can, the four of us creep toward one of the darkened warehouses. Al may have promised this one to me, but he's not taking any chances. A guy with enough balls to make an attempt on a don needs to be taken out—now. We've spent the last month searching for the bastard, and we're not going to lose him again.

We pull up short at the front of the warehouse, and I look to Joey One-Eye, who gives the signal for two of us to go ahead while he waits outside in case we flush Little Al out. Il Diavolo heads around the corner to watch the back door. I step inside with Arthur, one of Valenti's other guys.

Any chance at stealth disappears when we find the door locked and have to crack it with a crowbar. After that little delay, we open the door and peer into the darkness. Little Al will be armed, and one of us has to take the first step inside. Since I'm the new guy, it falls to me.

I fight the urge to cross myself before stepping into the darkness. Silence greets me, and I gesture the okay for Arthur to come in. He swings his rifle in an arc, aiming the mounted light around the cavernous space. Around us, light pine boxes sit in giant stacks, with shelves containing boards in the same color along the walls.

A coffin warehouse.

If this isn't the perfect place to die, I don't know what is.

Arthur gestures for me to go right, and he goes left. His light bounces off the pale coffins, and shadow stretch across the room. I edge along a towering stack o the body-sized boxes, wondering how the hell we're going to flush Little Al out of a place like this. I think abou everything I know about him, everything he's told me. A coward runs out the back. Only a desperate man, or a stupid one, fights when he knows he won't win.

Little Al's obviously got balls to set up a plan agains the head of one of the most powerful crime families in New York. He's no coward. He's not stupid, either. But he is cocky. Again, no one else would orchestrate a plan like that. As far as how desperate he is, I'm guessing he's gotta be pretty fucking close to the edge by now. He's been on the run for a month, but he hasn't gone far. He must be sticking around for a reason. Either he's out of money, or he's stayed for someone he cares about.

I creep along the wall, waiting for a sound, a sign that he's here. Maybe he saw the car arrive and slipped out. He was feeding the Lucianis information, and if that family's leadership hadn't changed hands and made fast lliances with us, I'd think they were protecting him. But e doesn't have anyone in his corner now. He's alone, nd that's a bad place to be when you've pissed off a riminal organization.

Suddenly, I see a shadow move. I spin that way, my inger steady on the trigger. At first, I don't see anything. But then I see what caused the flicker in the corner of my eye. It wasn't a person. It was a stack of coffins.

I shout a warning to Arthur, but it's lost in the enormous crash. Coffins tumble and cascade, bouncing off each other and splintering as they smash against the concrete floor. The roar is so loud I don't hear Arthur, so I don't know if he screamed. I only know that I see a dark shadow streak for a small door in the side of the building, a fire exit that's unguarded outside. Joey is at the front entrance, where the workers come and go, and Il Diavolo is at the back, where the shipments go in and out.

Unless one of them is prowling and happens to be on that side, Al's going to have a good head start. I'm lucky to have been against the wall, unharmed by the toppling coffins, but I have to scramble over the debris to get to the fire exit door. By the time I shove through, see his figure retreating toward the bridge. I take off at a dead sprint after him.

He's almost to the supports on the bridge when I see that he's got nowhere to go except into the river. I imagine him plunging into the polluted water disappearing under the scummy surface. I pull up short take careful aim, and get off one shot before he disappears behind the pillars supporting the bridge. I hear cursing behind me and know that at least one of the lookout guys saw him run, and they're behind me.

Without waiting for them to catch up and give me backup, I run for the spot where I saw him disappear. My chances of hitting him are slim once he's in the water. He won't go down without a fight, though. He's probably behind the column, taking aim right now, so I weave in and out as I run, hoping he won't hit me, that the guy behind me will cover me well enough. Dust and grit from the concrete sloping down toward the river blow into my face, but I blink it away, ignoring the stinging in my eyes.

When I'm nearly at the supports, I hear a crack, and the bullet comes so close to my cheek I swear I can feel the air move. But I'm still standing, so I keep going. I could pull up and aim and wait for him to peek around his hideout. Instead, I go full force, pushing myself as hard as I can, until my thighs burn and my feet thud against the pavement. I don't slow as I reach the massive structure. I fly around it and slam into Little Al so hard he goes hurtling through the air. Together, we hit the ground with bone-splitting force.

Lucky for me, Al's on the bottom, and he takes the brunt of that force. He groans, cursing and wheezing as he tries to hit me with his gun. Before he can recover himself or get air in his lungs, I grab his wrist and twist. He howls, the gun skittering from his grip as his bones snap. While I'm still holding his right wrist, he delivers a crushing left hook to my jaw. It knocks me backwards, and he scrambles up, but I'm just as fast. I jump to my feet and level my gun at him.

"Don't fucking move," I warn before he can take a step toward his gun. He's dirty, his clothes ragged, his hair unkempt and greasy, a beard darkening his jaw. Guess he's not visiting a special someone in the city after all.

"I should have known they'd send you alone," he snarls in disgust. "They don't care about you, King. You're disposable to them."

"Is that why you tried to fucking dispose of me?" I snap. "You're the motherfucker who sent me into an ambush, after all."

"Don't get all butt-hurt," he says. "It wasn't personal. I didn't even know you'd be going when I tipped Luciani off."

"But you sure as fuck didn't discourage me from going," I remind him. "In fact, if I remember correctly, you thought it was a splendid idea for me to go. I thought you were just being a dick because you knew I'd have to face Eliza's father, but it wasn't that, was it? You wanted to get rid of me and Al in one shot. You're a sick bastard, you know that?"

"Give me a fucking break," Little Al says. "You're nothing, King. Just a worthless little soldier. I might have

een having a little fun with you, but you were never even
art of the equation."

"Yeah, well, you should have calculated better," I
ay. "Because I'm the reason Al survived."

"And I bet he's sucking your dick and kissing your
ss for that," the man's grandson says in disgust. "You've
nly been at this a few months, and he probably already
kes you better. I've been doing this my whole fucking
ife, and I'm still a measly little soldier, no better in his
yes than a rookie who grew up like a pampered prince
nd showed up barely a day over eighteen with a lollypop
n his mouth, thinking he'd take my place. You'd never
ven killed a guy, you fucking pussy."

"I never wanted your place," I say. "And I sure as
nell don't envy it now."

We stare at each other for a minute. And maybe he's
right about me, because I'm hoping Il Diavolo shows up
and puts a bullet in his brain, puts him out of his misery
so I don't have to do it.

"He wasted my talents," Little Al says at last. "I could have been something great. I could have been a legend. Instead, I was your fucking babysitter."

"Maybe he didn't trust you," I say. "Can you blame the guy?"

"I'm his fucking grandson!" Little Al throws up his hands, then howls in pain at the reminder of his broken bones. "He never respected me, never listened to me," he rants. "I had great ideas, but he passed me over every fucking time. I'm next in line, but he didn't teach me shit. I'm twenty-three years old, and I'm still doing the same fucking job I was doing when I started."

"Maybe he could tell you were a sneaky son of a bitch, and he was never going to let you take over. Al's a smart man. He probably knew you were a coward."

"I'm not a fucking coward," Little Al growls, his eyes looking feral in the pale lights reflected off the water. "If I were, I wouldn't have risked it all to get him out of the picture."

"You tried to kill your own grandfather because you idn't get a promotion?" I ask, hardly believing anyone ould be so small.

"Because I'll never get the fucking promotion I eserve," he rages. "Al's not going anywhere anytime oon. The guy's over fifty and still going strong. If no one ook him out, he'd be around another twenty years. Was I ust supposed to wait around until I'm almost fifty before take over? It's my rightful place! He had his turn. It's my urn!"

"I don't think so."

"You can't kill me," he says, his eyes going even nore wild than they already are. "I have a wife, a kid! Let ne go, King. What's it to you? Here, take my things. Bring Al my watch, tell him you killed me." He pulls off his watch and tosses it at my feet, then starts taking off anything else he can, tossing his wallet and shoes down with them.

"You know it doesn't work like that," I say, but I consider it. What would it hurt if I stripped him of everything he owns, everything that identifies him, and let him run? I could tell Uncle Al I dumped his body in the river.

I think of my sister sinking into the river. What if she didn't die that night?

But of course she did. Just like Little Al has to die tonight.

"What does it matter if you let me go?" he presses. "I was your partner, King. I did right by you. You think you'll come back a hero if you kill me, but just watch. You'll never move up. You'll be stuck at the bottom forever. He doesn't care about you. He doesn't care about anyone but himself, the selfish old bastard."

"And you did?" I ask. "That's why you thought it would be funny to send me into a death trap that you set up yourself?"

"I told you, I wasn't even thinking about you," he says. "It wasn't about you!"

"You're right," I say, cocking the gun. "It wasn't about me, but you didn't care if I died, if I left *my* wife a widow. It was all just a cruel joke to you, pushing me to in Al because you couldn't handle the fact that he saddled you with a rookie."

"Don't shoot," he says, holding up both hands. "I'm unarmed, man. You don't wanna do this. Please. I'll disappear, and no one will ever know you didn't do it."

"I'll know," I say quietly. I'll know, and I'll never sleep easy knowing he's out there, that he could show up and put another hit on me so I can't tell anyone else.

I think of Little Al telling me, "get hard or get had." I think of Eliza telling me I can do it. Of my sister, at the bottom of the ocean, sleeping in peace with her boyfriend, someone she loved enough to die for. Little Al can rest easy, too, but he's never loved anyone enough to die for them. He'll mention his wife and kid now, but he wasn't thinking about them when he risked everything. Uncle Al has shown me more kindness in our few encounters than this shithead ever did. He's the one who only cares about himself.

I care about someone else. Someone I need to get home to because she'll be waiting and worrying, wondering if tonight will be the night I don't come home.

She's been through so much, lost her brother and h
mother and her childhood. She doesn't need to lose h
husband, too. I promised her I'd never leave. I intend
keep that promise.

I'd die for her if that's what she needed. But sh
doesn't. She needs me to kill for her.

I always knew this moment was coming. I kne
before I even took the oath of omerta that I'd be her
one day. That Uncle Al would ask me to kill someon
when it wasn't in a moment of passion and instinc
someone from our own family. A cold-hearted kill. I hav
to do it or take the target's place. If I can't kill a traito
then I am a traitor. If I don't have it in me to kill a mar
then I'm a dead man myself.

Little Al made his choice. I need to make mine. T
prove I'm worthy of the Life, of Uncle Al's trust, of th
beautiful, broken wife they gave me.

For her.

I pull the trigger. Little Al drops to his knees, his eye
wide, as if he can't believe I had the balls to shoot him
He clutches his chest, his bewildered gaze finding mine

The moon behind me reflects in his eyes, and I'm grateful for what it hides.

"You—You shot me," he says in disbelief.

"You knew what you were doing," I say, my voice hard, as empty as my chest. "You chose to turn your back on family. You know this is the way it has to be."

I pull the trigger again, and he falls forward on his hands before crumpling to the dirty pavement. I'm relieved I don't have to see his eyes. But I bend and swipe a hand over his face to close them, anyway. It's the least I can do. I didn't hate Little Al. I'd rather it ended some other way. But this is how it is.

I turn and head back up the bank, leaving his body. When I reach the pillar he hid behind, just ten feet back, a figure steps out of the shadows. I nearly shoot before I register the hulking giant form of Il Diavolo.

"I stand corrected," he says. "Guess you had it in you after all."

"You were there the whole time?" I ask. "Thanks for the fucking backup."

"After your little hissy fit about the Luciani girl, didn't think you'd be able to pull this one off," he says. "You're soft, kid. In this business, there's no room for that. Eat or be eaten."

"Spare the lecture," I say. "I did my job. What was yours? Stand there and watch him kill me if that's the way the chips fell?"

"My job was to make sure *you* got the job done," he says. "And to kill him if you didn't have the balls. This was a test. Big Al wants to know what you're made of. Probably wanted to know where your loyalties lie, too. After shit like this goes down, family killing family, you have to take a hard look at everyone in your inner circle."

I'm not surprised. I knew he'd want to make sure I hadn't been tainted by Little Al's treachery. Again, that's just the way it is. I can't be offended. I get it.

All the way home, I repeat his words in my head.

He said everyone in Uncle Al's inner circle. He included me in that.

When I started this job, I wanted to be the kind of man Al Valenti approves of, hard enough to survive the life. As twisted as it is, killing his grandson is the way I proved that I am. Not just to him, but to myself. I don't know if I've become a better man, but I know I'm a stronger one. I know I'm going to be okay. In the past six months, I've gone from a boy who thought he was a man to the real thing. Eliza turned me from a cocky high school kid who thought he was all that because girls wanted to fuck him, to a real lover. And the mafia has turned me from a scared boy wondering if he could pull the trigger to a man who's taken lives in self-defense, for revenge, and as payment.

Once, I told myself I was closing the door to my old life and stepping into a new one. I didn't know how true that was. Now I do. I can never go back to my old life. I wouldn't fit. I've become what I was always meant to be. Not only a made guy but one worthy of Al's inner circle. One who does what a man has to do in this business.

What I said to Little Al is true, though. I don't want to be an heir to this empire. I want to be indispensable, though, and maybe I just proved that I am. I may not ever be a don, but maybe one day, I can be the consigliere

to one. I may have come to them without experience, bu
I've proven myself to them, proven my loyalty, my
protectiveness, my strength. After all, this is my family
now, and no one fucks with my family.

This is where I belong. And what I did tonight
shows what part I play in that family.

And best of all, there's the little family of two that
I've made with Eliza at home. That's my reason now, the
only one I need. I'll always love my brothers, I'll always
miss my sister, and protect the Valenti name, but Eliza is
what I live for. I can finally move on from the mistakes of
my past and face a future more promising than I ever
imagined. I have the kind of life I never dared to hope
for. I have a wife I love and a job that recognizes my
value, and a family that's proud of me. And I'm alive for
one more day. That's all I can ask for.

Once, I thought a family was a liability, but now I see
it for everything it offers, in all its complexity. Yes, it's a
liability, and it makes me vulnerable. It also gives me the
strength to do what I need to do while keeping me
grounded, making sure I don't lose who I am despite the

onstrous acts the job sometimes requires. When I arted working for the Valentis, I thought it was easier to el nothing than to feel pain, so that's what I would do. s true, in a way. It is easier. But sometimes it's worth it feel the pain just to feel everything else that comes ith it. After all, a man with no feeling is nothing but a onster in a suit.

Once, my sister said I'd see love differently if I felt it. ow I know she was right. If I've learned anything from ving Eliza, it's that love is hard and sometimes painful, ut it makes everything worth it. It makes even one day ith her worth risking it all. I hope Crystal got to feel that efore she died. I hope it was worth it to her.

I know it is to me. Eliza helped me see that. She elped me let go, give up control, and live in the moment, nowing that the next one is not guaranteed. This is the nly moment we're given, the only moment to tell my ife I love her, to *show* her I do. Instead of holding back nd being selfish, I'll love her with every bit of my heart, or every moment we're given, and be grateful that she oves me back. That's something worth dying for.

twenty-nine

King

After dinner each night, we clean up together. Somethin about the simple act makes the place in behind m sternum that used to fill up with cold slush so warm aches. I know that each of these moments, no matter ho sweet, is fleeting. Not only fleeting but numbered. On day, my number will be up. Until then, I enjoy eac moment, even when the sweetness hurts my teeth.

A week after she comes home, I bring her a brochur for a local school and slide it across the coffee table to her when we're having a glass of wine after dinner and cleanup.

"What's this?" she asks.

"I thought you could look at the classes they offer and maybe enroll in a few."

"You want me to go to college?" she asks, picking it up.

"If you wanted to," I say. "I just thought it might help you feel less trapped, give you some freedom, like you wanted."

"Oh, King," she says, giving me a pained smile. "I don't feel like that anymore."

"Still," I say. "If you had your own money... Even if you don't want to work, you'd have the skills to get a job if and when you want one. In case..."

"In case you're killed," she says, realization dawning on her face.

I nod. I promised to take care of her, not let her love a man with a job like mine. It's too late for that, but at least I can make sure she'll be taken care of if something happens.

I used to think leaving her a widow would be the worst thing I could do, but now I know better. Treating her like a business deal is worse. Not loving her and

showing her how much I appreciate her as my wife i
worse. Like a greedy dragon, I treated my own heart like
treasure to be hoarded and hidden away from her. Bu
she was too smart. She snuck in and stole it when I wasn'
looking. For that, I am nothing but grateful. She opened
my eyes, made me stronger, strong enough not to be
afraid to hurt again. Strong enough not to be afraid to
love.

I vowed never to love her or let her love me because
I was so afraid of hurting her. That may happen, but I
can't let that stop me from living here and now. It only
makes me treat each day with her as something sacred.
She is the treasure. Every day, I get to show her that all
over again. I'll love her hard, with everything in me, like
this day is my last. One day, it will be.

When we slide into bed one night, Eliza rolls toward
me, tangling her smooth legs with mine, rubbing my calf
with her soft toes. "Want to try again?" she asks.

"Really?" I ask, drawing back to search her face. My
cock throbs against her bare belly, only my boxers and
her underwear separating us from being skin to skin.

"Yeah," she says, pressing her soft little body up against mine. "Did you think I was done forever?"

"You cried," I remind her.

"I know," she says. "It wasn't my finest moment. But don't give up on me, okay? I'm working on it, and I was hoping you'd work on it with me."

"Of course." I didn't think she'd want to try again for a long time, and I was prepared for that. That doesn't mean I don't want to, though. She's fucking beautiful in every way, and not just physically. This is beyond frustrating. It's agonizing. It's not the waiting. I could deal with that, hard as it may be. It's not thinking of her needs, her pleasure. That can only be good for us both.

Here in the bedroom, though, I need to be the one calling the shots. It takes everything in me to give over control to her, to let her set the pace and pull the brake when she needs to, to be the one in charge, making the rules. I keep telling myself it'll make me a better lover to her later, and that's worth it. But damn if it isn't the hardest thing I've ever done.

We kiss for so long I'm dizzy with wanting her, my head spinning by the time she reaches between us, pushing down my boxers and gripping my cock in her warm little hand. I roll onto my back, pulling her on top of me so I can watch her. If I can't pound her into the mattress, at least I can watch her in all her glory as she sits astride my hips. She squiggles down the bed, pushing off the blankets and lowering her head, smiling up at me before opening her lips to take my cock. I push up into her mouth, fisting my hands in the sheet as she slides down deep, letting me feel her straining throat.

After a minute, when I'm shaking with the effort of holding back, she throws her hair back and kneels up, grinning down me as she hooks her thumbs into her panties. I can see the shape of her pussy against the thin fabric. My cock jerks against her thighs, glistening with her saliva as she draws her panties down, letting me see what I can't touch. With a groan, I take hold of her thighs and tug her up to straddle me. She sinks onto me, gasping as we make contact. Her eyes fly wide, and she tenses.

"You're safe," I remind her, massaging her thighs ntly. "I won't move a muscle until you're ready. Do ıat you need, *carina*. I'm yours."

She nods, letting out a breath and sinking down on p of me without putting me in. "Thank you," she 'eathes.

Slowly, she begins to grind against my shaft, riding e until she's as wet as I am. I love watching her move, .e sensual rolling of her hips, the sway of her tits as she >es and falls, the little frown of concentration between ∶r brows, the way she bites her plump lower lip when ıe starts getting hot. It makes it all worth it when our 'es meet and she smiles.

"Is this okay?" she asks.

"So fucking okay," I say, my voice hoarse with esire.

"I'm ready," she says.

I lift her hips, supporting her weight. "Put it in."

She swallows before reaching for my cock, guiding it ɔ her entrance. She bears down, biting her lip as I strain gainst her opening. At last, I breach her entrance, groaning at the sensation of her slick cunt gripping m

bare cock. She gasps, tensing up for a minute. I wait fo

her to adjust, trying not to move, though my cock ache

inside her as it strains against her walls. She's so tight

almost hurts. When she's ready, she moves a little deepe

panting as she goes.

I remember the last time, and how she didn't tell m

she was upset, that she'd had enough, until she'd had to

much.

I grip her hips gently, my gaze locking with her

"Talk to me, baby," I manage. "Let me in. What's goin

on in that complicated mind of yours?"

She seems to relax a little more, turning her attentio

away from her determined effort. "I'm okay," she says.

"Tell me how it feels," I say, my voice low and roug

with command. Holding back is fucking killing me, but

wouldn't change it for anything. Not when I can see ever

inch of her spectacular, sexy body being slowly impale

on my cock.

"Fucking enormous," she says, and then she gives

little laugh, and I can't help but smile, too. Not jus

ecause I'm a man, and a guy can never hear those words o many times. But because if she can laugh, maybe it'll e okay this time. Maybe she knows she's safe, that she an stop any time she wants, that I'd never push her for nore than she's ready and more than willing to give.

"Does it feel good?" I ask. I know that's not verything. Sometimes she freaks out when it feels good nore than when it doesn't.

"Yeah," she whispers. "It feels good."

"You feel good, too," I tell her. "So fucking good."

This time, she makes it until I'm all the way in again, gripped so hard inside her cunt that I want to scream. nstead, I see panic flicker in her eyes, so I sit up, vrapping my arms around her. I cradle her gently so she von't feel trapped in my embrace.

"I won't hurt you," I say, gently stroking her hair back from her temple. "It's just you and me, El. You're safe, and I love you."

She stills, not continuing but not pulling away, either. We sit there for what feels like forever while I talk her down, trying to say the right thing, do the right thing, be

507

what she needs. At last, she nods, draping her arms over my shoulders and moving a bit. I hold her hips gently, so she can pull back when she needs, and I help her move slow and gentle strokes. When she's breathing hard, loosen my grip, letting her ride me at her own pace choosing her own rhythm.

She moves faster, harder than I expected, her bare cunt gripping me like a vice as she slams down on me The sensation of her slick, hot walls around me makes me nearly explode. I stroke her tits, thumbing her nipples while she rides me. When she's ready, she throws back her head, letting her long black hair tumble down her back, and a shudder wraps around her body as she sighs That one quiet, long, breathy sigh is the most soul-satisfying sound I've ever heard.

Her walls clench around me, and I can't help but groan at how insanely hard she squeezes my cock. I watch her cum, watch her come undone, and it's the most beautiful sight I've ever seen. I want to watch her and not worry about getting mine, but I can't stop myself. The

ght of my beautiful naked wife lost in pure bliss pushes
ne over the edge.

"My turn," I growl. I slide my arm around her waist
nd flip us over, drawing back before driving my cock
eep inside her.

She cries out, but before I can worry that I've been
oo rough, she grips my shoulders, gasping out two
vords. "Take. Me."

"What?"

"Fuck me how you want," she says, her voice
oreathy and urgent. "I'm yours, King."

"You're giving yourself to me?"

"Yes," she moans. "Do what you want with me. You
own me. Now take me."

This is it, her final surrender, her admission of trust.
She's submitting to me, giving over control, giving me
what I need more than anything, what she withheld for so
long. My punishment is over. My penance is done. I've
earned her submission, earned the right to possess this
treasure and take it as my own.

I drive into her again, thrusting my cock to the hilt inside her pulsing cunt. She spreads her thighs wide, submitting to my claim eagerly this time, arching her back and raising her hips for me to go deeper. I slam into her body as hard as I can, pounding her into the mattress until she lets go again. When her cunt pulses tight around me as she finds her second release, I let myself go, too. I sink my cock into her core and grind into her as I explode with everything I've been holding back for months. She cries my name as my hot cum spurts into her.

Together, we are lost. Lost to everything but what truly matters. This moment, right here, right now, and the long-overdue pleasure we find in each other. Lost to everything but each other, two broken souls who thought they'd never find love, never deserve it.

Our bodies meld in bliss, locked together like our souls have finally fit together in perfect alignment, fusing into one love. She's made for me, and I'm made for her, filling her to her limits. I know in that moment I'm well beyond saving, that there's no hope of me ever resisting the love I thought I could deny. I love her beauty, her licateness, even her brokenness. But I also love her ength, her plotting mind, her sharp tongue. I love that e's a match for me, that she made me fall for her thout even noticing. That she challenges me and makes e grow so much it hurts. And god, I love fucking her. I ve her everything I have, not just my body but my soul, y heart, my life. She is all that matters.

We are all that matters.

This.

Us.

Forever.

epilogue

One Year Later

Eliza

"I have a surprise for you," I say, grabbing King's hand the moment he walks in the door. I pull him into the living room before he can ask.

He looks around and smiles. "It looks great," he says. "Did you clean?"

"The maid did that," I say, rolling my eyes. "Now come here. I got you something."

"You already sent me a picture today," he says, naughty gleam in his eye. Even though King can feast his eyes on me any time he wants and satisfy himself with my body instead of his hand, he likes it when I send him racy pics, so I send him a surprise text every now and then.

I hand him a small, wrapped box. "Before you open , I just want to say… Thank you. For being so patient ith me, and working with me through my therapy, and y relapses, and—Just thank you. For everything. I want ɔ say I don't deserve it, but I'm not allowed to say that nymore."

"That is correct," he says, leaning in to kiss me. And you didn't have to get me anything. But thank you."

"You taught me that," I say. "That I'm worthy of ɔve. That it's okay to accept it."

"I think you're confusing me with your therapist," he ays with a grin.

"I'm not," I say, shoving his shoulder. "She only *says* hat. You *do* it. You're the one who works with me on it. You're the one who loves me and forces me to accept it."

"Damn straight," he says. "Now, are you going to ɔropose, or can I open this?"

I laugh and shake my head. "I think you have to be narried more than a year before you can renew your vows. Open it."

"It's been a year and a half," King reminds me, but he obeys. He opens the box and stares down at the little white wand inside. I wait, not even breathing, for him to say something. I start to think this was a really stupid idea and what if he's not excited, and he doesn't consider this a gift?

At last, he raises his eyes to mine, and if I didn't know better, I'd swear they're a little shiny.

"You're pregnant?" he asks.

I nod, biting my lip to keep from squealing out loud.

"I know, it took my stubborn uterus long enough," I say. "I was beginning to think we jinxed it by saying we'd tell people we couldn't have a baby."

"Well, we have been trying awfully hard," he says with a little smile, removing the test from the box.

"You might not want to touch that," I say. "I did pee on it. In fact, now that I think about it, a symbolic gift would have been a lot more sanitary. You know, like a keepsake rattle or—"

King interrupts my rambling by leaning and kissing me hard on the mouth. I melt into him, not realizing how uch I needed him to be excited about this until he nows it. He kisses me long and deep, his tongue roughly laiming mine, his big hands wrapping around my still-tender waist. He lays me back on the couch as if I'm as elicate as the baby will be.

"So, you're happy?" I ask with a breathless little augh.

"Want me to show you how happy?" he asks, taking ny hand and pulling it to the front of his pants, so I can eel the hard ridge of his cock.

"Wow, I didn't know the thought of me getting fat and swollen was such a turn on," I say. "Or is it the hought of sealing the pact between our families that has you so hot and bothered?"

"It's the thought of what I'm about to do to you in celebration," he says, a wicked grin on his lips.

"Tell me more," I say, wrapping my legs around him. It took way too fucking long to get here, and I'm enjoying every single moment of it now that I can have sex without freaking out the majority of the time. Things were a little rocky for a while, but I've been working through them in therapy and with King, and lately, even my ovaries must have relaxed and come around to the idea. At least, that's the only explanation I can think of Lord knows we've tried—over five hundred times, if anyone's counting.

I am, but not for any creepy reasons. I feel a sense of triumph every time we cum together, as if I've earned a ribbon—#1 at Successfully Completing Intercourse. So, I started counting the victories, because my therapist said I should count small victories. I don't know if she meant literally, or if orgasms qualify as small, but I figure it doesn't hurt anyone and it makes me feel accomplished, so why the hell not?

After King and I add another tally to the number, we end up on the living room rug, staring at the ceiling.

"I guess it's time to convert the guest room into a nursery," I say.

"Maybe Bianca could help," he says. "If you're in an on-again stage of your relationship."

I grin. "She's going to be so jealous. I can't wait to ˌl her. I bet your uncle's too old to even get her ˌegnant."

King just shakes his head. "I will never understand ˌur relationship."

"So, stop trying."

"Trust me, I did that a long time ago."

I smile and lay my head on his arm. "Unless she *ˌtually* tries to get you killed, you can assume we will be ˌst frenemies for life."

"Fair enough," he says, rolling toward me and gently ˌroking his fingertips down my bare belly. "We've got a ˌt to do to prepare. Nursery, babyproofing, all the stuff, ˌames…"

"I was thinking about that," I say. "If it's a girl, how ˌˌout we name her Crystal, after your sister?"

"I'd like that," he says, his eyes going darker the way ˌey always do when he talks about her. I know he'll ˌever get over that loss, that he'll always feel the sadness, ˌut maybe this will help just a little.

"And if it's a boy," he says. "Maybe Jonathan, aft
your brother?"

"I was thinking Anthony," I say. "After all, both o
dads share that name."

"We can definitely put that on the list of options," l
says, cracking a small smile. He's bossy as hell in tl
bedroom now that he knows I need and love h
dominance as long as he's not violent, but I try to nip it i
the bud when he does it out here. I may be happy bein
his wife, but I still bristle at the thought of anyon
controlling me. But a baby name is something bi;
something we should both be on board with.

"Okay," I say, laughing. "We have nine who
months to decide. In fact, when I was on campu
yesterday, I saw someone put up a flyer about a class o
making your own baby food downtown. I thought
might go."

"What have I gotten myself into?" he groans. "Yo
want to name our daughter Crystal and make your ow
baby food? Next thing I know you'll be changing you
name to Star Child and making hemp necklaces."

I laugh and give him a shove. "And you'd love me just as much."

"Fine, you win," he says. "I would love you just as much. But I'd rather you change your name to Pussy Galore and go make me dinner, woman." He gives my ass a playful swat, and I throw a leg over his and give him my most inviting smile. I know he's kidding. He's the one who encouraged me to start taking a few classes and thinking about a nursing degree.

"You know what they say," I remind him. "A woman can be good in only one room in the house. You get to pick which one."

"Hold on, let me get a pizza," he says, reaching for his phone. "Now spread your legs and finger yourself while I'm ordering. I want to watch my cum drip out of you."

I grin and obey, loving the torment it causes him to have to talk to someone while he watches without touching. When he's done, he growls and dives for me, taking over, taking control so I can let go. I've learned how much I need his dominance, how much it turns me

on to see him step into the role he was born to play—that
of my husband, who owns my body and soul just as
own his. We were made for each other, and we find ou
perfect rhythm together, the one we taught each othe
the one that is pure magic, so perfect it created th
greatest miracle inside me.

Love.

The End.

acknowledgements

Huge thanks to all my Patrons who made this book possible through their generous support and encouragement. Special thanks to Tami, April, Anne, Ethan, Tasha, Melissa, Marisa, JG, Makayla, Becky, Jasmine, Kelly, Nikki, Doe Rae, Joyce, Michelle, Adriana, Heather, Nineette, DesiRae, Shawna, Nicole, Rowena, Terra, Emily, Tina, Kandace, Mindy, Christina, Elizabeth, Hilary, Audriana, Nikki B, Alysia, Janice, Larissa, Alex, Annalisse, Emma, Amy, Crystal, Kellie, Jennifer, Lena, Jennifer S, Margaret, Megan, & Mariam.

Printed in Great Britain
by Amazon

38138255R00300